THE STOLEN ALTARPIECE

Jack Rogan Mysteries Book 8

GABRIEL FARAGO

This book is brought to you by Bear & King Publishing.

Publishing & Marketing Consultant: Lama Jabr
Website: https://xanapublishingandmarketing.com
Sydney, Australia

Cover Design by Giovanni Banfi

First published 2023 © Gabriel Farago

ISBN: 978-0-9876283-6-7

Signup for the author's New Releases mailing list to get a free copy of *The Forgotten Painting** novella and find out where it all began ...

https://gabrielfarago.com.au/free-download-forgotten-painting/

* I'm delighted to tell you that *The Forgotten Painting* has received two major literary awards in the US. It was awarded the Gold Medal by Readers' Favorite in the Short Stories and Novellas category and was named Outstanding Novella of 2018 by the IAN Book of the Year Awards.

Also by Gabriel Farago

Letters from the Attic
The Forgotten Painting
The Kimberley Secret
The Postmaster of Treblinka
The Empress Holds the Key
The Disappearance of Anna Popov
The Hidden Genes of Professor K
Professor K: The Final Quest
The Curious Case of the Missing Head
The Lost Symphony
The Death Mask Murders

THE STOLEN ALTARPIECE

GABRIEL FARAGO

CONTENTS

DEDICATION

This book was inspired by, and is dedicated to, the people of Ukraine for their courage, bravery and resolve. Not afraid of sacrifice, hardship, even death, they are determined to fight the forces of evil, defend their freedom and win.

'True evil never dies, it just finds a new home.'

Gabriel Farago
The Stolen Altarpiece

1

ACKNOWLEDGEMENTS

Writing a book of this scope and complexity is always a challenge, especially for someone like me who insists on doing his own research and does not believe in delegating that vital task. Because this book was inspired by the extraordinary spirit and resilience of Ukraine and its people, something more than just research was required to give this demanding project the authenticity it deserved.

While it was, of course, possible to research all the necessary historical material and current affairs through the internet, one cannot get a real 'feel' for what is happening 'on the ground' right now in a country at war. Let's not forget, what is happening in Ukraine is a most brutal war, with suffering and destruction on a scale that is difficult to imagine.

To describe certain events such as a missile strike on a school, the obliteration of a block of residential apartments, the massacre of civilians in Bucha, or the bombing of a theatre in Mariupol in which hundreds of women and children perished, in a realistic way, a different approach was needed. That approach required access to eyewitness accounts. In short, I somehow had to talk to people who had actually been exposed to those war crimes and experienced the tragedies and atrocities involved firsthand. Only then would it be possible to capture the horror and pain involved, to convey those emotions to the reader in a realistic and meaningful way.

I thought long and hard about how to address this challenge and the answer was once again right there in front of me. All I had to do was turn to my dedicated readers and ask for help. And that was precisely what I did, with results that were simply astonishing.

With so many Ukrainians living in exile, many in Poland and other European countries with access to the internet – social media, in particular – the response was almost overwhelming. Once I explained that one of the main aims of writing this novel was to create awareness and understanding of Ukrainian history – especially the devastating 1932–33 Terror-Famine, the Holodomor – to help explain what was happening in Ukraine today, the information floodgates opened.

Suddenly, I had access to eyewitness accounts and stories, many of them heartbreaking, which I could draw upon to create a storyline that mirrored true events with characters that were both realistic and believable. Ukrainian refugees living all over Europe contacted me and shared their experiences in an open and honest way, which allowed me to give certain scenes a raw eyewitness quality and emotional authenticity that armchair research alone could never have achieved.

Because many of those voices wanted to remain anonymous, I cannot acknowledge them by name. However, what I can do is to thank them all for their generosity and honesty in sharing their stories on confronting subjects that were often tragic, personal and very painful.

Writing a book dealing with sensitive issues like this requires inspiration, and inspiration that has real meaning must come directly from people who have been exposed to this tragic repeat of history sweeping across Ukraine with devastating effect right now.

This book was inspired by, and is dedicated to, the people of Ukraine for their courage, bravery and resolve. Not afraid of sacrifice, hardship, even death, they are determined to fight the forces of evil, defend their freedom and win.

It is my sincere hope this book will, at least in some small way, help them to achieve that.

Preparing a book for publication, especially one as ambitious as this, requires many skills. It is a team effort. I've once again been very fortunate to have a group of talented and dedicated specialists on my team to help me deal with the many challenges thrown at us along the bumpy road to publication.

As all my books are complex projects with multi-layered storylines, I work closely with my editor, Sally Asnicar of Full Proofreading

Services, whose exceptional attention to detail and insights into the characters – old and new – and familiarity with all my books have been invaluable in bringing this bold project to fruition.

In many ways, once the manuscript has been polished and finalised and is in all respects ready for release, that is just the beginning of the next crucially important stage. Because just writing a good book is not enough; I have to get it out there, make it visible, and ensure it connects with the market and readers. This is a complex process that requires the skills of an experienced publicist.

Lama Jabr of Xana Publishing and Marketing, my publishing and marketing consultant, has been my adviser for many years. Her steady hand has patiently guided this project through the many challenges of a treacherous publishing jungle. Her insights and expertise, especially when dealing with social media and complex publishing platforms, have been invaluable and have made a huge contribution to the success of the *Jack Rogan Mysteries Series* and its worldwide popularity and appeal.

Who says we don't judge a book by its cover? In a way we all do, especially when surfing the Net for inspiration of what to read next. In my view, an engaging cover and clever design that reflect the 'spirit' of the book are essential components that give it visibility and make it stand out in a fiercely competitive market.

In Giovanni Banfi I have a talented artist who understands my work and knows how I want to present it. It is for that reason the imaginative cover designs of my books and social media banners have attracted much attention and received many compliments over the years.

Sally, Lama and Giovanni are part of my inner circle of experts who always strive for excellence and this is clearly reflected in the high quality of their work.

And finally, it would be remiss of me not to mention my wife, Joan, literary critic, fellow researcher, patient sounding board and cheerful travel companion. Without her encouragement and unwavering support, this project just wouldn't have been possible, and the many literary awards and uplifting reviews the series has received over the years belong as much to her and my team, as they belong to me.

Thank you, all, for believing in me and what I'm trying to achieve with my writing.

Slava Ukraini! Glory to Ukraine!

AUTHOR'S NOTE

I still remember most vividly the evening my aunt took me to see Goethe's play *Faust* – arguably one of the greatest works in German literature. It was a balmy summer evening in Salzburg, and the old city and stunning castle on the other side of the river were lit up like a stage. A perfect setting for a timeless play that not only made a huge impression on a fourteen-year-old boy, but also raised questions that stayed with me for years to come.

The legend of *Doctor Faustus* – a disillusioned fifteenth-century German necromancer who sold his soul to the devil in exchange for knowledge, pleasure and power – is one of those enduring legends that has inspired poets, musicians and playwrights over the ages. I always knew that one day I would incorporate this story into one of my books, and introduce Faustian characters into the storyline.

That day came on Thursday 24 February 2022, when Russian forces invaded Ukraine. I was already working on a sequel to *The Death Mask Murders* and was in the final stages of developing the characters and structure of the novel, when the extraordinary events in Ukraine changed all that. Childhood memories of that dramatic play I saw as a teenager in Salzburg came flooding back with a compelling clarity that was difficult to explain and impossible to silence.

Instead of fading away, these memories became stronger and even haunted me in my sleep, until it became clear to me this was the time to incorporate the Faustian legend into *The Jack Rogan Mysteries*. Real events had intersected imagination and provided a unique opportunity to weave fact and fiction into a seamless storyline where the reader is never quite sure where one ends and the other begins, but without losing focus or relevance.

The shocking events in Ukraine, with unspeakable brutality and atrocities that are difficult to comprehend, provided the perfect setting and subject matter to explore the dark side of human nature that is never too far away, and cannot be ignored.

But it didn't stop there. I had closely followed the controversial presidential elections in Belarus in 2020 and was fascinated by the term 'Slipper Revolution', also known as the 'Anti-Cockroach Revolution', coined by Sergei Tikhanovsky, an anti-government blogger who referred to the incumbent President Lukashenko as the cockroach.

Intrigued by these terms, I did some digging. What I found was astonishing. What Tikhanovsky had been alluding to was a popular Russian children's poem, 'Tarakanishche' – 'The Monster Cockroach' – by Korney Chukovsky (1882–1969), a famous poet, literary critic and essayist. In the 1921 poem, an overgrown, arrogant cockroach begins a reign of terror over mankind and animals through bullying and threats, only to be devoured by a sparrow.

Tikhanovsky compared Lukashenko to the monster cockroach and called for a Slipper Revolution to crush the corrupt, power-hungry insect with a slipper and bring its reign of terror to an end.

On reflection, the timeless Faustian legend and the popular children's poem – although a century apart – were an excellent literary fit for the tragic events unfolding in Ukraine, reminding us of the corrupting temptations of power and greed, and the often desperate, bloody struggle to resist these evil forces.

It therefore made perfect sense to incorporate these ideas and potent symbolism into the storyline of my next book.

A successful work of fiction is a balancing act: reality must rub shoulders with imagination in a way that is both entertaining and plausible. To this, I would like to add one more thing: in creating such a work, the author has a unique opportunity to explore historical material that is often buried deep in forgotten pages of history, or the psyche of a nation that has suffered much and is therefore not generally known. Yet it is hugely important if certain current events – however painful – are to be understood. If this is done skilfully and based on meticulous research, it is possible to create an awareness that can have profound consequences. It can bring about change and shape the future.

It is this last point that became the inspiration for this book, and it is my sincere hope that *The Stolen Altarpiece* will, at least in some small way, make a difference.

* * *

Coming home for Christmas; 24 December 1956

This will be a sad Christmas, thought the young woman, watching her son play in the snow outside. *At least he's safe.* She hadn't heard from her partner, nor did she know if he was still alive. The horror stories that had leaked out through the Red Cross spoke of summary executions, chaos, hunger and despair; the wages of defeat of a humbled nation that had dared to demand freedom, and lost.

As the little boy pushed the wooden shovel along the path at the bottom of the garden, something caught his eye: a dark shape at the gate.

Squinting through the snow falling all around him like sparkling tufts of cottonwool, he could see a man wearing an old hat and a long coat, standing motionless and silent, watching him. The boy dropped the shovel and walked slowly towards the gate. With each step came recognition, hesitant at first, but then growing stronger and more certain.

'Daddy?' whispered the boy, his eyes wide with disbelief and wonder. The man put down his little brown suitcase and took off his hat.

'Daddy!' shrieked the boy as he flew into his father's outstretched arms. It was an embrace neither of them would forget.

Of course, the little boy in the story was me. It had taken my father three weeks to walk from the smoking ruins of Budapest to my grandparents' home in Austria. Hiding in abandoned stables and chicken coops along the way, and living off the kindness of farmers prepared to risk all to help a fugitive, he finally crossed the border into Austria at night during a snowstorm. I remember his swollen

9

feet looked terrible and he was frightfully thin and very weak. But none of that mattered; he had come home for Christmas.

A couple of years later, in high school, our class was tasked to write a short story about an event that changed our lives. This was my story. The teacher entered it in a little competition run by the local paper. The story won a prize. It was my first step towards becoming a writer.

Gabriel Farago

Letters from the Attic (Bear & King Publishing, 2016)

* * *

We must never remain silent and ignore the suffering of others. Only that way can we defeat bigotry and overcome the iron grip of tyranny and evil. That was true then, and is just as true today. Freedom cannot be taken for granted. It is a treasure beyond price.

Those of you familiar with my books would have noticed that these ideas run through the storylines like a little silver thread, showing us the light in the hope that we never lose our way.

Gabriel Farago

Leura, Blue Mountains, Australia

PART I
GOLGOTHA

PROLOGUE

Safiye Sultan, the mother of Mehmed III, was the most powerful woman in the Ottoman Empire. But since her son's controversial accession to the throne a year earlier, she had lived in constant fear.

Upon the death of her husband, Murad III, she had ordered the execution of all Mehmed's nineteen brothers by strangulation, to ensure her son's accession went unchallenged. All went well until it was discovered that one brother, Osman, had escaped the deadly net of the deaf-mutes who had carried out the horrific murders during the night. While fratricidal succession was by no means uncommon, it had caused huge animosity and unrest among the mothers of the murdered boys in the harem.

The reason Safiye had lived in constant fear had nothing to do with the wrath of the women in the harem, but was due to something far more serious: her son, the sultan, was in constant danger as long as he didn't have a male heir and his brother Osman was alive. There was a simple explanation for this: if something happened to Mehmed, like an assassination, for instance, Osman would become sultan. That was the law. By having murdered all the other brothers, Safiye had unwittingly made Osman next in line to the throne after Mehmed. As long as there was no son, Mehmed wasn't safe, and that presented a huge problem for Safiye, who guarded her position at court with ruthless vigilance. Any opposition was instantly silenced and rivals banished to exile.

One of those rivals was the beautiful Fatma Hatun, Osman's mother, who had been Murad's youngest consort. Safiye was well aware that Fatma had been behind the plot to save her son and facilitate his daring escape through one of the chimneys in the palace kitchens during the night his eighteen brothers had been brutally murdered. Despite rigorous questioning, Fatma had given nothing

13

away and Osman's whereabouts remained a mystery despite extensive enquiries by agents sent into every corner of the empire to find him.

On top of all that, Fatma was very popular at court and, Safiye suspected, had secret allies and followers in the harem, which was a hotbed of intrigue at the best of times. The reason Safiye had kept Fatma at court was simple: she had hoped that somehow Fatma would lead her to Osman, but that had not eventuated. Osman had disappeared without a trace, and now it was time to make his mother disappear as well. To harm her at court was far too dangerous, and to execute or assassinate a consort of the former sultan – especially one so popular – unthinkable. Something far more subtle and imaginative was needed.

Fatma entered Safiye's palatial day chamber overlooking the magnificent Topkapi gardens where she had spent many a sunny afternoon entertaining Murad, her late husband, with her wit and conversation.

'You sent for me,' said Fatma, her voice confident, her bearing defiant and almost regal.

She is so beautiful. No wonder Murad was smitten, thought Safiye, a twinge of envy clawing at her heart because her own beauty had faded years ago. No matter, she was the Valide Sultan, and as long as her son was on the throne, Fatma was under her power.

'Do you know what date it is?' asked Safiye, watching Fatma carefully.

'I do. Murad died exactly one year ago, and you had all his sons except your own killed during the night to make sure that Mehmed became sultan.'

'All his sons except Osman.'

Fatma nodded but didn't reply, a look of contempt making her blue eyes flash like steel and her flawless, pale skin glow.

'You were brought here as a young slave girl to entertain the sultan. Never forget that!' said Safiye, reminding Fatma of the capture of her Venetian father's trading vessel by pirates en route to Beirut. Fatma, who had been on board, was taken to Alexandria by the pirates and sold on the slave market.

'You are right. I was brought here to please the sultan. I did just that and gave him a son. It seems no-one can do the same for Mehmed. As long as Osman lives and Mehmed has no male heir, he will always be looking over his shoulder, and so will you. *Never forget that.*'

Seething with anger but holding her tongue, Safiye stared at her insolent rival. No-one else in the palace would dare speak to her like this.

'My life here is over,' continued Fatma. 'My flame was extinguished when Murad died, but it lives on in Osman. I have nothing left to lose.'

'Don't be so sure,' said Safiye quietly, her voice threatening. 'You came here as a slave, and you shall leave here the same way. You will be taken to a faraway slave market and sold to whoever wants you. Should you dare to return and enter the empire, you will be instantly put to death. I never want to set eyes on you again. Now *leave!*'

'With pleasure,' said Fatma. Holding her head high, she turned around slowly and walked to the door. Just before she reached the door she stopped. 'Memories of happy times I will take with me; the rest I leave gladly behind. I will be free, even as a slave, but you will live in fear here in this golden cage. Remember, as long as Osman lives ...' With that, Fatma made a mock bow and left the chamber.

Gazanfer Aga, chief of the white eunuchs and head of the Enderûn – the Imperial Seraglio – had enjoyed a meteoric rise since Murad's death. As the facilitator of the dramatic but risky fratricide during the night Murad began his journey to paradise, he had become indispensable to Safiye. She relied on him not only to protect Mehmed, but also he and his spies were her eyes and ears in the palace, where treachery and betrayal lurked around every corner. It was therefore only natural she should turn to him to arrange Fatma's exile and return to slavery.

When she wanted to discuss something important or sensitive, Safiye met Gazanfer Aga at a fountain in the garden. This was one of the few places they couldn't be overheard in the palace, where curious eyes and ears were never far away, vicious gossip was rife and privacy almost non-existent.

Safiye sat on a stone bench next to the fountain, a silver tray of fruit on her lap, and watched Gazanfer Aga approach. She could tell by the spring in his step that he must have good news. Gazanfer Aga stopped in front of Safiye and made a bow.

'Come, sit next to me.' Safiye reached for a persimmon and handed it to her trusted ally.

'It's all arranged,' he said, sitting down. 'Fatma will be taken to a notorious market town in Uzbekistan. A dark place with a fearful reputation. One of my most loyal janissaries will be in charge.'

'Is that far enough?' said Safiye, looking anxious. 'I want her gone, banished, never to return.'

Gazanfer Aga smiled. 'Have no fear. The market town I have in mind is one of the most dangerous and remote places along the Silk Road. It's in the middle of a desert and has only one claim to fame.'

'You speak in riddles. Please explain.'

'*Slaves*. It's a market like no other, perhaps the most notorious slave market in Asia. Definitely not for the fainthearted. My janissaries have all the contacts and will go with her. It's a place of no return, I assure you. Especially for a young white woman of great beauty. Traders will pay a small fortune in that market to have something so rare and desirable to offer in their tents. She will most likely be sold on to a sultan or khan, or even a maharaja, and disappear forever. Just the mention of the market's name sends shivers of fear ...'

Mollified, Safiye nodded. 'What's it called?'

'Khiva.'

Palazzo Alberti: Venice: 3 December 2021

After purchasing the dilapidated palazzo on the Grand Canal next to the Rialto Bridge from the late pope's estate, Jack had been determined to move in as soon as possible to oversee the much-needed renovations.

The purchase had surprised everyone except Tristan, who understood Jack's needs and way of thinking. He realised that for Jack, the palazzo represented far more than a historical trophy to show off a stunning property that had once belonged to a pope and an illustrious family with a lineage reaching back centuries.

To Jack, this was an opportunity to establish a home. The first real home he had owned since his house in Sydney had been burned down by The Wizards of Oz, an outlaw bikie gang, in 2010. His precious art collection, and Australian colonial antiques he had painstakingly restored, had all gone up in flames. Since then, Jack had been homeless, drifting, and in the Palazzo Alberti he saw an opportunity to remedy that.

The fact the ancient structure had been neglected for decades and desperately needed costly repairs didn't seem to bother him. On the contrary, Jack threw himself into the task with his usual enthusiasm, much to the amusement of Countess Kuragin, who had stepped in after Lorenza's tragic death to run the Palazzo da Baggio boutique hotel close by.

The locals considered Jack a likeable if somewhat eccentric newcomer with too much money and time on his hands, who seemed to ignore the sacred siesta and worked through the entire day, and expected others to do the same. In Venice, this was bordering on sacrilege that only an ignorant foreigner would entertain.

Because Jack's needs and expectations were modest and his entire wardrobe could fit into a broom cupboard, he had been able to set up a bedroom overlooking the canal on the first floor rather quickly, and make at least one bathroom functional – most of the time. He had also established a workshop with a range of old tools for cabinet making, including woodturning, on the ground floor where the Alberti library once had pride of place.

Besides the occasional power tool to save time, Jack preferred to work with traditional hand tools, which enabled him to add character, style and authenticity to the restoration. Because he knew exactly what he wanted, Jack had sourced on eBay an array of chisels, clamps, a much-loved woodworking vice, a claw hammer, hand plane and an adjustable square.

As the room was quite large, Jack also used it as his temporary study, with a small dining table in the corner where he had some of his meals. These were usually delivered from the Palazzo da Baggio kitchen with compliments of the countess, who took pity on the hardworking bachelor who had moved out and taken up residence in a rundown ancient palazzo almost next door.

However, by far the most important feature of the room was a huge stone fireplace. It provided much-needed warmth in a damp environment without heating, where the bone-chilling cold rising from the canal waters below threatened to immobilise hands and nimble fingers attempting to reverse the relentless advance of time and neglect on precious wooden furniture that had seen better days.

To help Jack furnish the empty palazzo, Leonardo da Baggio – the late Lorenza's father who owned the Palazzo da Baggio – opened his family home storeroom and allowed Jack to take his pick of old furniture and bric-a-brac stored there over the centuries.

To Jack, who loved antiques and enjoyed nothing more than restoring them, the storeroom was an Aladdin's cave filled with beautifully decorated cassones, cedar wood credenzas and even a Renaissance-era carved walnut cabinet chair. His trained eye ignored the damage and neglect and only saw beauty and endless possibilities. A bit like ignoring the crackles in a favourite record, and listening to the music instead. He fossicked there for hours, considering the potential of various pieces of furniture, where to display them in his new home, and how to bring them to life and restore them to their former glory.

One of the first items that had caught his eye was a sixteenth-century Venetian oak writing desk wedged between broken chairs in a back corner of the crowded storeroom. To the uninitiated, it may have looked too far gone and only fit for the fireplace, but to Jack's expert eye it had huge potential.

The tooled leather on the top had rotted away a long time ago, but the counter structure with its four aligned drawers on each side of the opening and a single door and three drawers on the other side was still intact. Due to the solid oak used in its construction, the desk was in reasonable condition considering its age, including the beautiful moulded base at the bottom.

Patina, it has heaps of patina, thought Jack, and decided to make the desk his first major restoration project and the centrepiece of his future study.

Alberto Bonato entered Jack's workshop. Like his father before him, Bonato had served as caretaker for the Alberti family, and later for the pope, who inherited the palazzo from his mother. Because of his familiarity not only with the palazzo, but especially with Alberti family history, Bonato had provided Jack with valuable information that had allowed him to solve the mysteries surrounding the Postmaster of Treblinka and the questions raised by the Herzl letter.

Jack had recently published a novella about that and Bonato, now in his late sixties, had been most helpful in filling in some of the important gaps in the fascinating Alberti family saga with its mysteries and secrets. Jack and Bonato had formed a friendship during that collaboration, and when Jack bought the palazzo and asked Bonato to stay on, Bonato accepted enthusiastically because in many ways, the palazzo was his life.

'You are working late tonight,' said Bonato as he entered Jack's workshop. They often shared a nightcap together at the end of the day.

'Come in,' said Jack, 'and have a look at this.'

Bonato walked over to the desk Jack had almost pulled apart. Jack pointed to one of the drawers. 'I found a cleverly concealed compartment at the back here; look.'

'Desks and writing slopes often had such compartments. They were used to hide private letters and important documents, and valuables like gold coins and jewellery,' said Bonato.

'Correct. And it would appear this was indeed the case here,' said Jack.

'What do you mean?'

'I found a bundle of letters stashed in the back of the drawer.'

'Oh?'

'Over there on the workbench. Have a look.'

Bonato walked over to the workbench, put on his glasses and picked up one of the letters.

'Look at the date. Top right,' said Jack, unable to suppress the excitement in his voice.

'Constantinople, the twelfth of June 1605. Amazing!'

Jack walked over to the little dining table and picked up a bottle of cognac. 'Drink?'

'Better make it a big one.'

'What's particularly interesting is that all the letters are addressed to Osman da Baggio right here in Venice, and have been sent by the *same* person. Beautiful handwriting, but it's all in Italian, of course. You'll have to help me here. Reports of some kind. I recognised some of the places mentioned ...'

'Looks that way,' said Bonato. 'I've seen letters like this before in the library where I used to work. Correspondence between merchants, their agents and the captains of their ships was lively and frequent. Don't forget, Venice was one of the most important trading hubs in Renaissance Italy.'

Jack handed Bonato a drink. 'As you can see, there are quite a few letters, and they are all rather long. Some have been sent from Constantinople, others from exotic places like Bukhara and Samarkand, which couldn't have been easy at the time—'

'All along the Silk Road,' Bonato cut in. 'Merchants had excellent lines of communication and were very well organised.' He kept reading.

Jack took a sip of cognac and looked pensively at the dismantled desk in front of him. 'Perhaps, but to me the most interesting thing at the moment is the name of the sender.'

'Oh?'

'Yes. Francesco Alberti.'

Bonato looked at Jack, surprised. 'Now, that really *is* interesting. There was a Francesco Alberti who lived in this very palazzo around that time. He was one of the more colourful members of the family.'

'In what way?'

'He was more of an adventurer, an explorer if you like, than a merchant, much to the disappointment of his father and brothers who ran the family business. Claudio Alberti used to tell me stories about him when I was a boy, and jokingly referred to him as the Marco Polo of the Albertis: always away from home, always looking for adventure, often in trouble.'

'Could this be the same man, do you think?'

'Quite possibly. Surely the letters will tell us? Let's have a closer look and see what they are all about.'

As Jack watched Bonato sit down and continue reading the letter in his hand, he felt the fine hairs on the back of his neck beginning to tingle. It was a familiar premonition that rarely let him down, and usually happened when a new adventure or challenge came hurtling towards him from what he called the toolbox of destiny.

1

Palazzo da Baggio, Venice: 5 December

Countess Kuragin looked at the spectacular floral arrangement in the centre of the large dining table and smiled. The young florist who lived on a boat at the markets never disappointed, not even in winter when flowers were difficult to obtain. Everyone who was dear to the countess was seated around the table to celebrate Tristan's birthday. Even her little grandson, Billy, who had just turned nine, had been allowed to join the party and was waiting excitedly for the birthday cake to be served.

'Won't be long now,' said Anna, his mother, and gently stroked Billy's hair, aware that it was well past his bedtime.

The countess signalled to one of the waiters to dim the lights and she stood up. The mood in the room had palpably changed. The soft background music – a Vivaldi violin concerto – seemed louder as eyes adjusted to the warm candlelight radiating from the two Murano glass candelabras on the table, the flickering candles on the mantelpiece sending crazy shadows dancing up the wood-panelled walls towards the family portraits staring down from above.

'This is a very special day,' began the countess, who had comfortably slipped into the role of family matriarch and accomplished host since coming to live in the Palazzo da Baggio after Lorenza's tragic death in 2018. 'A very happy one. And on special days, we remember special people, and to me, Tristan, no person can be more special than your mother.' The countess paused, her voice quivering with emotion.

'It is only because of her that Anna is alive and here with us today. It is only because Cassandra sacrificed her life to save Anna that Billy here can sit next to his mother, and for that I will be eternally grateful. Selfless acts like that make a family, and all of us sitting around this table tonight are just that: a family. But now, it's definitely time for the birthday cake! Lights, please!'

Everybody clapped as two waitresses carried in a large silver platter with a huge chocolate cake decorated with berries and lashings of cream, and placed it on the table. Everyone cheered as Tristan blew out the twenty-two candles and cut the cake. As Tristan sat down and picked up his napkin, something rolled out and fell on the floor. Surprised, he bent down, picked up what looked like a piece of metal and looked at it, his eyes wide with disbelief as he recognised what it was. Instead of holding it up and showing it to the others, Tristan had the presence of mind to slip the strange object unnoticed into his pocket. Unable to taste the delicious cake, he tried in vain to ignore the shock caused by the unexpected find that sent a shiver of fear racing down his spine.

After everyone had enjoyed a slice of cake, Jack proposed a toast to the birthday boy, and then turned to Leonardo.

'I have something exciting to tell you,' he said.

The countess leaned across to Anna sitting next to her. 'Here we go. Jack and his stories,' she said, smiling. 'He can't help himself.'

Anna shrugged but said nothing. Instead, she sat back and looked expectantly at Jack.

Jack reached into his pocket and pulled out the bundle of letters he had found in the writing desk and put them on the table in front of him.

'As Katerina just told us, this is a special day, and on special days we remember special people. Indulge me while I begin with a story most of you already know. In your family, Leonardo, Osman is perhaps the most famous and colourful ancestor you have. He appeared out of nowhere and presented himself right here, on the doorsteps of this very palazzo, as his grandfather was dying and the family business faced ruin. Before that, Osman had survived the deadly silk cords of the death mutes, who had strangled all his half-brothers during the night his father, Murad III, died in the Topkapi Palace in 1595, to make sure that Mehmed became sultan.'

Jack pointed to one of the portraits above. 'That's Osman right there in his more mature years after he had turned the family fortunes around by opening up new trade routes in the east. After his dramatic escape from the palace, Osman became a stowaway on a trading vessel captured by pirates. Like his mother before him, he was sold into slavery in Alexandria but escaped again, and finally made his way to Venice, bringing with him a portrait of his mother, Fatma Hatun, which now hangs here in the salon. And, of course, he also brought with him the famous recipes that now decorate the walls of Lorenza's Michelin star restaurant – Osman's Kitchen – she named after him. And let's not forget one of those Ottoman recipes – Hunkar Begendi, the famous dish with medicinal properties – was prepared by Lorenza and saved the late pope's life.

'But that's not all. I now live in the Palazzo Alberti that was once owned by that very pope she saved, Pius XIII, and his family, the Albertis. Strange, how all this is interconnected, don't you think?' continued Jack, lowering his voice.

'And none of this would have been possible without Fatma Hatun, the loving mother who managed to save her son and facilitated his escape,' Jack continued. 'Just like your mother, Tristan, she was a very special person who deserves to be remembered on this special day, because she too is part of your family. But it goes further than that. Much further.'

Jack the consummate storyteller paused to let the anticipation grow and looked around the table.

'In what way?' asked Leonardo, wondering where Jack was going with this.

'History repeats itself,' said Jack, 'in remarkable ways. One could almost say that destiny was once again at play here.'

Here we go, thought the countess, smiling. *More breadcrumbs.*

'Remember how a bracelet hidden in a secretaire found in a shed on an abandoned farm in Australia started a remarkable journey that culminated in Anna's rescue?'

'How can I ever forget?' said the countess, tears in her eyes. 'The bracelet I gave to Anna. But why are you telling us all this now?'

Jack smiled, enjoying himself. 'You'll see in a moment. Leonardo kindly let me have some old furniture stored here in the palazzo, remember? Well, one of the pieces that caught my eye was a beautiful old writing desk. When I began to restore it the other day, I found something.'

Jack reached for the bundle of letters on the table in front of him and held it up. 'This here and what this represents is truly remarkable,' he said, becoming excited. 'These are letters written by Francesco Alberti to his friend Osman da Baggio. It would appear that Francesco and Osman were good friends.'

'Both belonged to prominent trading families here in Venice,' said Leonardo, who had researched the family histories and knew them intimately. 'They even jointly owned ships and warehouses in various ports in the Mediterranean and were always on the lookout for new markets in the east.'

'This all fits and makes perfect sense,' said Jack, 'when we consider what's in the letters here, and what was to come. Osman sent his friend on an important mission he couldn't undertake himself because it would have been too dangerous. He was a wanted man in the empire. Wanted, because of who he was.'

'What kind of mission?' asked Leonardo.

'Osman sent Francesco to Constantinople to find out what happened to Fatma Hatun, the mother who had saved him and he had left behind. These letters are all about that—'

'Seriously?' interrupted Leonardo, surprised.

'Oh, yes.' Jack picked up one of the letters. 'Here, listen to this. The translation is by Bonato, by the way. He has been most helpful:

'*Constantinople, 12 June 1605*

'*Good news at last. It has taken almost a week and a small fortune in bribes to finally gain access to the palace. This has only been possible because our agent here who oversees our warehouses knows the chief storewarden at the palace, who is a friend of the sergeant-at-arms, a janissary, who has the ear of the grand vizier ...*'

Jack put down the letter and looked at Leonardo. 'As you can imagine, there's a lot more in here. I haven't worked my way through all of it yet, but the letters are very detailed, and cover a period of almost two years.'

'Astonishing,' said Leonardo, shaking his head. 'I had no idea. Our family chronicles do not mention any of this.'

'Do you know if Osman found out what happened to his mother?' asked the countess.

'Yes, and no. What we do know is this: a year after Murad III died, Fatma was banished from the palace and sent into exile to be sold in a faraway slave market somewhere along the Silk Road. No doubt as punishment for saving her son. Alberti was very diligent and followed the trail. He made several trips and was gone for months at a time until he finally made his way to a place called Khiva, somewhere in the desert in Uzbekistan. That place was famous for its slave trade.'

'And?' prompted the countess.

'According to these letters, Fatma was sold into slavery in that market.'

Khiva: August 1596

The sandstorm had lasted for hours. Progress was slow, the exhausted camels and horses barely able to move. The procession looked like an apocalyptic apparition emerging from the hot desert gloom. Several beasts had died along the way.

It was almost dark when the curtain of sand parted, and the tall minarets and massive walls of Khiva came into view. The janissary riding next to Fatma pulled up his horse and, shielding his burning eyes, pushed up his turban and looked straight ahead, relieved that the long, arduous journey from Constantinople that had taken several months was finally nearing its destination.

Founded by Shem, the son of Noah, so the legend goes, the desert town of Khiva on the edge of the Karakum Desert had been a major trading post along the Silk Road for centuries and was best known for its thriving slave market. Just the mention of its name sent ripples of dread and fear along the long columns of slaves being herded to market by their Kazakh and Turkmen masters, their final destination the notorious Ichan-Qal'a, the old walled town where the slave market was held.

Early the next morning, the janissary captain in charge ordered Fatma to take a bath and put on fine clothes. In Khiva, news travelled fast. A meeting had been arranged at the East Gate of the Ichan-Qal'a with a number of prominent slave traders, who had heard about the arrival of the sultan's janissaries and were curious about the unexpected merchandise from Constantinople everyone was talking about. Rumours that one of the former sultan's concubines was to be sold raced like wildfire through the narrow, twisted alleyways and created great curiosity and interest among the traders, always on the lookout for something special they could sell on at a huge profit.

Fatma looked impressive in her fine clothes brought along from the palace especially for the occasion, her pale skin and regal bearing setting her apart from the wretched girls and women from the steppes being displayed for sale like animals in niches along the vaulted passageways leading to the East Gate.

Surrounded by four heavily armed janissaries, Fatma was taken to the market and put on display. Soon, several eager traders were expressing interest, and began to haggle a price with the captain in charge. They tried to deflate the value of the merchandise on offer because of her age, and pointed to the much younger women for sale in the niches.

An elderly Tajik trader, who could trace his ancestry back to the legendary Sogdians, stood in the shadows and watched Fatma carefully. His trained eye recognised the unique qualities of the refined woman being offered for sale. Someone like this mysterious woman from Constantinople was rarely found in the market and she was precisely what he had been looking for. By the time the haggling reached fever pitch, he made his move.

Stroking his beard, he walked slowly over to the captain and slipped a gold coin into the palm of his hand. 'Let's talk,' said the trader and pointed to a fountain by the gate. Smiling, the captain slipped the coin into his pocket and followed him to the fountain.

'When this rabble has finished, come to me and I will beat the highest price. Just by how much will depend …'

'On what?' asked the janissary.

'On my conversation with the lady. I want to talk to her first, before I make my offer.'

'Agreed.'

Trying to ignore the shouting traders, the obscene gestures and finger pointing by the gawking crowd, Fatma watched the elderly man with the white beard who had just spoken with the captain as he walked towards her.

'You have nothing to fear,' said the man, his soft voice reassuring and melodious, 'if you answer my questions truthfully. Your answers will determine your value, and the higher your value, the better your future will be.'

Resigned to her fate, Fatma nodded.

After a brief conversation, the trader established that Fatma had grown up in Venice, had been captured by pirates and had lived in the sultan's harem at the Topkapi Palace for seventeen years. He also learned that she spoke several languages – including Greek and Tajik – and was an accomplished painter, musician and storyteller. This made her the most valuable woman for sale at the market by far, but only to someone who was well connected and understood the true potential of such rare qualities. It was like finding a precious sapphire among a handful of agates.

Smiling, the trader walked over to the captain and quickly concluded the purchase, much to the dismay of the protesting traders who watched on, surprised and disappointed.

* * *

'I'm afraid that's where the story ends,' said Jack, 'because Alberti didn't make it back to Venice, but most likely something else did. Something remarkable.'

'What do you mean?' said Leonardo.

28

Jack picked up the bundle of letters and riffled through them until he found what he was searching for. 'Ah, here it is. Alberti's last letter dated October 1606, sent from somewhere along the Silk Road:

'We were attacked by bandits last night. Many in our caravan were killed. I was badly injured and have lost a lot of blood. I may not see the morning. That's why I am sending one of my most trusted men back to Venice with something precious I have secured for you. It concerns your mother, my dear friend, and may well be the only thing you will be able to remember her by. I have found the man, a wealthy Tajik trader, who bought Fatma in the Khiva market from the janissaries who had brought her all the way from Constantinople ten years ago. He remembered her well. Because she was highly prized due to her beauty and intellect, he sold her on straight away to a member of the ruling family in Samarkand. Unfortunately, he was unable, or unwilling, to tell me who that was, but he proudly showed me the payment he received for her. Because the price was so high, he was offered something far more valuable than jewels or gold. He was offered a piece of history: a famous miniature Quran in the form of an enamelled locket on a gold chain that could be worn as a necklace. It was once owned by the notorious conqueror Timur, so the legend goes. The locket is of solid gold encrusted with diamonds and rubies. When you open it like a tiny book, you find the word of the Prophet, the whole Quran inside. I have no doubt that my possession of this Quran was the reason we were attacked last night, but you will laugh when you hear how I obtained it. I gambled, and won ...'

Khiva: September 1606

It was Francesco Alberti's last night in Khiva. The caravan was due to leave the next morning to begin the long journey to Constantinople. From there Alberti would travel back to Venice by ship. The surprising breakthrough had come about in a totally unexpected way: during a game of dice.

Apart from making enquiries about Fatma's fate, the main reason for Alberti's journey along the Silk Road was to establish new trading contacts. After concluding a promising deal with a prominent merchant involving the supply of spices, Alberti had been invited to a night of gambling in the house of Aziz Kurbonov, one of the wealthiest traders in Khiva. To be invited to such a game was considered a great honour and Alberti, a passionate and experienced gambler, accepted without hesitation. It would be a fitting conclusion, he thought, to successful trade negotiations that had culminated in a lucrative contract he could take back with him to Venice.

'Did you know that dice actually originated in the Indus valley?' said Kurbonov, the host, leaning back into the comfortable cushions on the divan.

Alberti, who sat opposite, nodded. 'Apparently, the game of dice arose from the ancient use of animal knucklebones used for fortune-telling and playing games.'

'Quite so,' said another merchant, who sat on the floor covered with exquisite carpets. 'The Greeks claim that dice were invented during the siege of Troy by the legendary Palamides.'

'Stoned to death by his Achaean comrades,' said Kurbonov, 'hopefully not for having invented dice.'

'I'm not sure that's correct,' said the merchant sitting next to Alberti. 'Cubical dice like these here originated in China and were introduced to Europe by Marco Polo.'

'Be that as it may, let's begin, gentlemen,' said the host, and rolled the dice.

After an hour's gambling during which large sums of money changed hands, Kurbonov turned to Alberti. 'I hear you're making enquiries about a woman who was sent here from the Topkapi Palace in Constantinople and was sold in our markets.'

'That's correct,' said Alberti, surprised.

'Why are you interested in this? That was ten years ago.'

Alberti waved dismissively. 'It's a long story. I promised a friend ...'

'Perhaps I can help you,' continued Kurbonov, watching Alberti carefully.

'*You can?* How come?'

'I was the one who bought her.'

Stunned silence.

'You did? *Seriously?*'

'Yes. She was a former concubine of the sultan, Murad III. She was without question one of the most extraordinary women I've come across in these markets.'

'What happened to her?' asked Alberti.

'I sold her. At a huge profit.'

'To whom?'

'A prominent member of the ruling family in Samarkand, the Astrakhanids.'

'The last Genghisid descendants,' said Alberti.

'You're well informed.'

'I have been looking for the woman – her name was Fatma – for a long time. Can you be more specific?'

Kurbonov shook his head. 'All I can tell you is that she went to live in a fabulous palace in Samarkand and became quite famous.'

'*Famous?* A slave? In what way?' asked Alberti, becoming excited.

'I can't tell you more, but I can show you what someone was willing to pay for her.'

'Oh? What?'

Kurbonov reached under his shirt, pulled out a gold chain with a jewel-encrusted locket he wore around his neck and held it up. 'This.'

'It's magnificent. What is it?'

Kurbonov opened the locket and showed it to Alberti. 'It's a rare miniature Quran that was once owned by the legendary Timur.'

'Would you be willing to sell it? Name your price,' said Alberti.

'No. It's not for sale, but if you are willing to gamble …'

'I am.'

'The stakes will be very high.'

'Is that a warning?'

'No. A promise.'

'Fine by me.'

Smiling, Kurbonov picked up the dice. 'Then let's begin.'

* * *

Jack put down the letter and turned to Leonardo. 'As I said before, that's where the story ends. I think the rest of it has been lost in the mists of time because the last page here has been badly damaged.'

'Not necessarily,' said Leonardo, taking a deep breath.

'What do you mean?' asked the countess.

Slowly, Leonardo stood up, ran his fingers through his hair and walked to the door. 'Give me a moment. I won't be long.'

The countess looked at Jack. 'What do you make of this?'

'Let me answer that,' said Tristan. 'After all, we are talking about my family here, right?'

'We are,' said Jack.

Tristan pointed to Osman's portrait. 'This is by no means the end of the story. In many ways, it's just the beginning.'

'What makes you say that?' asked the countess.

'You know me. I sense ... I listen and hear.'

'Those whispers,' said the countess. She looked at Jack and raised an eyebrow.

'I can feel it too,' said Anna and closed her eyes.

Moments later, Leonardo returned, obviously excited. He walked back to his seat and for a while just stood there in the silence. Then, like a magician, he reached into his pocket and slowly pulled out a gold chain with something dangling at the end, and held it up for all to see.

The countess gasped as she stared at the exquisite little locket, which perfectly matched the description Jack had just read out, swinging slowly from side to side like a hypnotist's charm.

'I had no idea what this really was, apart from the obvious, until now,' said Leonardo. 'Handed down from generation to generation, this has been in our family for a long time. If only it could talk ...'

'Perhaps it can,' said Tristan. 'What do you think, Jack?'

Jack shrugged. 'Who knows?' he said. 'But I'm sure we'll find out. Happy birthday, Tristan!'

2

Palazzo Alberti: Venice 6 December

The fire in the salon had turned to embers and the cognac bottle on the mantelpiece was almost empty. After dinner everyone had gone into the salon to relax, have coffee and liqueurs, and discuss the astonishing events of the evening.

'Nightcap anyone?' said Leonardo. It was just after midnight.

'No, thank you,' said Jack and stood up. 'I better get going, 'Thank you for a wonderful evening, Katerina.'

'An evening we won't forget in a hurry,' said Leonardo. 'And not just because it was your birthday, Tristan. Those letters ...'

Tristan nodded, but didn't reply.

Jack looked at Tristan. 'Tired?'

'Not really.'

'Something wrong?' asked Jack, who had noticed that Tristan had been somewhat subdued since dinner.

'Could be.'

'Care to tell me about it?'

'Not here,' said Tristan, lowering his voice. 'Let me walk you home.'

'Sure. Let's go.'

'I never thought Venice could get this cold,' said Jack as soon as they stepped outside and began to walk towards the Rialto Bridge. He adjusted his scarf and turned up the collar of his jacket. 'At least it isn't far. Are you sure you want to come along?'

'Yes,' said Tristan and linked arms with Jack. As they walked down some stairs to the canal, Tristan stopped under a lamp post and pointed ahead towards the bridge shrouded in thick fog rising from the still water. 'Hardly looks real, don't you think? More like a painting by Canaletto. I feel like we're walking through a dream.'

'Venice can be like that, especially late at night after a good bottle of wine and a couple of brandies oiling the wheels of your imagination.'

Tristan reached into his pocket and searched for the shell case he had found under his napkin during dinner. 'I wish it were that simple and it would all go away in the morning.'

'What are you talking about?'

Tristan took his hand out of his pocket and held up the shell case. 'This.'

'What's that?'

Tristan handed Jack the shell case. 'See for yourself.'

'I don't understand.'

'What do you think it is?'

'A bullet, of course. Magnum, I'd say, but—'

'A normal bullet doesn't have something engraved on the shell case, does it?'

'What do you mean?'

'Have a look.'

Jack held the shell case up to the light, and paled. '*Happy Birthday?*' he whispered. 'Where did this come from?'

'It was under my napkin. At dinner.'

'*What?* Why didn't you say something?'

'And spoil the evening? Katerina and Anna would have had a fit, and Leonardo would have freaked out. And Billy ...'

'You're right.' Jack suddenly felt very cold, and it wasn't just the temperature and the damp fog that made him shiver.

'What are we to make of it?' said Jack, his mind racing. 'Inside the palazzo! That's scary. And who could possibly?'

'You can feel it too, can't you?' said Tristan.

'Feel what?'

'Evil. It's back. The nightmare in the salt mines is far from over ...'

'*Don't say that!*'

'Do you have a better explanation?'

'I have to get my mind around this, and standing here in the cold after midnight isn't the time or the place to do that.'

34

'I suppose not. Can I come and stay with you tonight?'

'Sure. If you don't mind sleeping on the couch. The *only* couch. You know the state the place is in.'

'As long as you have some blankets.'

'Blankets I have. Let's go.'

Tristan turned towards Jack. 'Before we do, I want to say something.'

'Oh?'

'Katerina told us that birthdays are special occasions.'

'They are.'

'Remember what you said to me as we stood in front of Lorenza's coffin in the palazzo just before the funeral began?'

'Of course. I thanked you.'

'For being the son you never had,' said Tristan, his voice quivering with emotion.

'That's right.'

'I just wanted you to know that those words were the most important words anyone ever said to me, apart from Lorenza telling me that she loved me.'

Jack reached for Tristan's arm and squeezed it in silent reply. 'Let's go,' he said softly, 'before the cold kills us both and I don't get to enjoy the company of the son I never had.'

After making sure Tristan was comfortable and well tucked in under the blankets, Jack went to bed, but he couldn't fall asleep. Well aware that sending a bullet to someone was a well-known Mafia threat, not to be taken lightly – and Tristan had been a Mafia target before – Jack tried to make some sense of it all, but the pieces didn't fit.

Alessandro Giordano was dead. His father, Riccardo, who had most likely ordered the hit on Tristan that had gone so spectacularly wrong and cost Lorenza her life, was in jail serving a life sentence. The historic Mafia trial in Lamezia Terme in Calabria had all but wiped out the notorious 'Ndrangheta and put most of the key players behind bars. For these reasons, Jack told himself, a Mafia threat was most unlikely, but if not the Mafia, then who had sent the bullet to Tristan? And why on his birthday?

Craving much-needed sleep after a long day, Jack tried to shut out these disturbing thoughts, but they refused to go away and kept coming back to something Tristan had said: *The nightmare in the salt mines is far from over. The evil is back! Could it be?* thought Jack, well aware that late-night speculation, alcohol fog and lack of sleep distorted everything. *Things will look different in the morning.* Feeling calmer, he took a deep breath, turned over and began to relax.

Just before Jack fell asleep, the mobile on his bedside table began to ring, the shrill ringtone drilling into his exhausted brain like an ambulance siren. Instantly awake, he reached for his phone and looked at the screen to see who was calling. It was Dupree.

'This better be good,' said Jack.

'Sorry to wake you, Jack, but I thought you would want to hear this.'

'What?'

'Lapointe just called.'

'What about?'

'Rabbi Stein has been found dead, murdered, in the Jewish cemetery in Prague.'

'*Good God!* How?'

'Lapointe said there was something strange about the way he was killed.'

'Did he say what that was?'

'No. That's all I know. It must have just happened. Lapointe called me as soon as he heard the dreadful news from Europol.'

The evil is back! was all Jack could think, feeling a sickening chill ripple through him. 'I'll try to get on an early flight.'

'Me too.'

'Do you think it's him?' said Jack.

'Must be.'

'See you in Prague.'

Jack put down the phone and switched on the lamp on the bedside table. In a strange way, he felt calmer because the missing pieces in Tristan's bullet puzzle were beginning to fall into place. *Tristan was right all along,* he thought. *The nightmare in the salt mines is far from over. True evil never dies; it just finds a new home.*

3

Old Jewish Cemetery, Prague: 6 December

Ignoring the heavy snow and freezing cold, Jack walked through the deserted cemetery gates and went straight to the Klausen Synagogue. As he remembered it, Rabbi Stein's study was on the first floor. Jack had called Dupree from the airport and arranged to meet him at the entrance.

Dupree waved when he saw Jack walking towards him. 'This is the officer in charge of the investigation,' he said and pointed to a tall man in uniform standing next to him. 'Let me introduce you. This is Major Svoboda of the Policie České republiky, who will brief us.'

'I have heard a lot about you, Mr Rogan,' said Svoboda and shook hands with Jack. 'I believe you have been here before.'

'I have. Twice, in fact. My first meeting with Rabbi Stein was in March 2017. Then I met him again only in August this year and we saw each other again in November in Jerusalem.'

'Monsieur Dupree told me. Please come, I will show you where it happened.'

As Jack followed the major up the stairs to Stein's private world he had visited before, which overlooked the cemetery, a feeling of dread came over him. He remembered Stein explaining the significance of the religious manuscripts and artefacts the Nazis had wanted to destroy as part of their sinister plan to erase all traces of the Jewish race in Europe, but couldn't because a few courageous people had fought back.

Jack gasped as he stepped into Stein's study. The entire room had been ransacked, with pages torn out of books and manuscripts, and precious artefacts smashed and broken. Drawers and filing cabinets had been emptied, their contents littering the floor.

'Rabbi Stein was sitting in his chair over there,' said Svoboda, 'facing the window, eyes open. He was looking down into the cemetery below. The wounds on his hands, and especially the fingernails, suggest he had been tortured before a deep head wound was inflicted by a blow from behind with some kind of sharp, heavy object. That's what killed him. Obviously, Forensics took everything away for analysis. The body is in the police morgue. A post-mortem is planned for later today.'

'When was this?' asked Jack.

'A security guard making his rounds heard a commotion and went into the synagogue to investigate. That was around eleven last night. He saw the light was on in the rabbi's study and went upstairs to have a look. That's when he found Stein and called the police.'

'Did he see an intruder?'

'No.'

'But the most interesting part about all this,' Dupree cut in, 'is something else ...'

'Oh? What?'

'A piece of paper had been stuffed into the rabbi's mouth. Post-mortem,' said Svoboda.

'A message? What kind of paper?' asked Jack, feeling the hairs on the back of his neck rise.

Svoboda reached into his pocket, pulled out a sheet of paper with writing on it, and handed it to Jack. 'This here. This is a copy, of course,' he said, watching Jack carefully.

'*Behold the Maharal.* How strange.' Jack shot Dupree a meaningful look, but didn't let on that the handwritten words meant something to him.

'Any ideas?' said Svoboda.

'Perhaps,' said Jack. 'May I keep this?'

'Be my guest. Needless to say, any kind of assistance would be greatly appreciated. You seem to have had some interesting dealings with the rabbi recently. I read your novella, *The Postmaster of Treblinka.* Fascinating.'

'You are well informed, Major, and full of surprises,' said Jack.

'My job.'

'A hate crime, or just a burglary?'

'Neither, I think,' said the major. 'The piece of paper in the victim's mouth seems to suggest otherwise.'

'But someone was obviously looking for something,' said Jack.

'Clearly. This is a carefully staged murder with some kind of message.'

'I agree,' said Dupree. 'Any leads?'

'We are working on it,' came the evasive reply. 'Is there anything else I can help you with?'

'Not at this stage, thank you,' said Dupree, well aware they had been dismissed and it was time to leave. Polite cooperation only went so far.

'I don't think Major Svoboda was too pleased to see us,' said Jack on their way out of the synagogue.

'His case, his patch,' said Dupree. 'No-one likes interference, especially when it has been ordered from above.'

'I suppose not.'

'The words mean something to you, don't they?'

'Come, I want to show you something,' said Jack, sidestepping the question.

'What?'

'A grave. Quite a famous one. It's just over there. The grave of Rabbi Judah Loew ben Bezalel. It's where I used to meet Stein. He insisted we meet there.'

'How odd.'

'That's what I thought at the time. But let's not forget that Stein was a historian. He lived in the past and Rabbi Loew was one of his heroes.'

'And we are going there now for a reason?'

'Yes.'

'*Behold the Maharal?*' said Dupree.

'Stein's last words. Out of his mouth – literally,' said Jack. 'And you heard that he was facing the window overlooking the cemetery when they found him. In fact, you can see the grave I'm about to show you from that window. Pretty convincing, wouldn't you say?'

'Convincing in what way?'

'Isn't it obvious? We all agree that the murder has been carefully staged, right?'

'Yes.'

'Whoever arranged Stein's body so that it faced the window with the note in his mouth is sending us to the grave of Rabbi Loew. I'm convinced of it.'

'Come on, Jack, how can you possibly know that?'

Jack smiled. 'Because Rabbi Loew was known as the Maharal.'

Stunned, Dupree shook his head. '*You* may know that, but to just about anyone else this is meaningless.'

'But this message wasn't meant for anyone else.'

'You can't be serious!'

'But I am.'

'Then, please explain.'

'Later. First, let's see if I'm right.'

'How?'

'Let's have a look and find out. Here's the grave.'

'Impressive!'

'This is perhaps the most beautiful headstone in the entire cemetery. And there are thousands of them.' Jack pointed to the lion in the centre and began to inspect the elaborate headstone by running his fingertips along the intricate Hebrew inscriptions below.

'What are you doing?'

'Looking for something.'

'Looking for what?'

'Something that doesn't belong here.'

'I don't understand.'

'You will in a moment.'

'Following your breadcrumbs of destiny again?'

'Tristan would call it that.'

Dupree shook his head.

'Ah. I knew it!' exclaimed Jack. 'Here, look at this!' Jack crouched down and pointed to the base of the centre column separating the inscriptions.

Dupree crouched down as well. 'What am I looking at?'

'This here. It's tiny. What can you see?'

'A Star of David?'

'Correct. What else?'

'A heart?'

'Exactly. And this definitely doesn't belong here. I'd say, this was recently scratched into the sandstone.'

'Seriously? What does it mean?'

'It's a signature.'

'I'm getting more confused here by the minute.'

'I will explain everything. Just bear with me.'

'What kind of signature?'

'The Star of David obviously stands for David, and the heart for Herzl, which means little heart in German. David Herzl was the Postmaster of Treblinka. But he wasn't just that. He was also known as the master forger of Warsaw—'

'You wrote about him in *The Forgotten Painting*?' interrupted Dupree.

'Precisely. I have no doubt all this is pointing us in his direction.' Jack ran his fingers through his hair and stood up. 'Why ...?'

'This feels like a treasure hunt.'

'In some ways it's just that. It's a game, but surely you can see this message is for me. I was meant to find this. I now know what the killer was looking for. I just can't work out why yet.'

'What do you think he was after?'

'David Herzl's diary. Herzl's son, Sandor Kun, donated it to the museum here. Stein kept it in his study. He showed it to me. It's all in my books.'

Amazed, Dupree shook his head.

'What does all this remind you of?' asked Jack. 'The staged murder. The carefully arranged body. The almost theatrical setting with a message?'

'The death mask murders?'

'Exactly. And what does that tell you?'

'The same person is behind this?'

'Precisely. The similarities are striking. Like you, I don't believe in coincidences. This is the work of a master manipulator who plays a long game.'

'Are you seriously suggesting Stein was murdered in this peculiar way just to send you a *message*?'

'That was part of it. The theft of the diary is obviously significant. I just can't see exactly why at the moment.'

'Come on, Jack. That's a little far-fetched, even for you.'

'Not really. This wasn't the first message ...'

'What do you mean?'

Jack reached into his pocket, took out the bullet with the Happy Birthday inscription and held it up. 'This was left under Tristan's napkin yesterday during his birthday dinner at the palazzo.'

Dupree examined the bullet. 'What's the meaning of this?'

'Not sure yet, but I *am* sure we'll find out soon. Do you know what Tristan said about all this?'

'What?'

'The nightmare in the salt mines is far from over.'

'And is that what you believe too?'

Jack pointed to the inscription on the bullet, and then the Herzl signature on the headstone. 'Do you have a better explanation?'

4

Madame Petrova's memory trees: 7 December

Jack decided to go back to Paris with Dupree and speak to Lapointe about the recent troubling events and get his take on what was happening. Detective Chief Superintendent Lapointe, a senior officer in the Paris Brigade Criminelle, had been in charge of the death mask murders case. Two young police officers involved in the case had been killed on his watch and he had made a promise to himself that he wouldn't rest until the mastermind behind the murders was brought to justice.

While the man who had killed the two police officers was dead and the other behind bars serving a life sentence, the mastermind behind it all had managed to slip through the net and was still at large.

The 'birthday bullet' and the circumstances of Rabbi Stein's curious murder strongly suggested that a new, sinister game was once again in play, and Jack wanted to hear what Lapointe had to say about it all, and what he intended to do about catching the elusive, evil genius who had evaded capture for decades, and appeared to be planning something new.

As Jack was leaving Charles de Gaulle airport with Dupree, he received a phone call from his mother.

'Where are you?' she said.

'In Paris. Just landed.'

'Good. I would like to see you. Something's happened. Something disturbing ...'

'*Disturbing*? Can you tell me what it is?'

'I would prefer to tell you in person.'

'Urgent?'

'Could be.'

'All right. I'll come over straight away.'

'Thank you.'

Since her rescue from the Cordoba drug cartel in Colombia, Rahima, Jack's mother, had lived in an exclusive retirement home – a converted chateau popular with well-heeled aristocrats and celebrities – just outside Paris.

Jack turned to Dupree, who was driving. 'Thanks for the detour.'

'No problem. It isn't really out of our way.'

'She sounded agitated, which isn't like her at all,' said Jack as they drove through the massive wrought-iron gates of the chateau Jack had visited many times.

'I'll wait in the car,' said Dupree. 'I think you should see her alone.'

'Thanks,' said Jack, appreciating Dupree's tact.

As Jack walked towards his mother's ground-floor apartment that used to belong to his great aunt, Madame Petrova, a strange feeling came over him. Stein's murder had affected him deeply, and he felt apprehensive and on edge.

'I came as soon as I could,' said Jack and kissed his mother on the cheek.

'I wouldn't have called if it wasn't …'

'I know. What happened?'

Rahima handed Jack a piece of paper folded in half. 'I found this note under my door this morning.'

Jack shivered as he read the note. '*Behold your memory tree,*' he read aloud. 'Who sent this?'

'No idea.'

'What's it about, do you think?'

'Not sure, but I'll show you what I found.'

'What do you mean?'

'After I received this, I went to visit Madame Petrova's memory trees in the park outside to have a look at mine.'

'And?'

'Come, I'll show you.'

As Jack walked along the gravel path with his mother, he remembered the first time he had visited the grove of memory trees with Madame Petrova. '*When I was invited by my friend Marguerite, who owned this chateau, to move in here,*' he heard her say, '*we made a pact. There were six of us living here at the time. We were all close friends who had known one another during the war. We agreed that whenever one of us passed away, the others would plant an oak tree right here in the grounds, in her memory.*'

'When Madame Petrova passed away,' said Jack, 'Katerina and I planted a tree for her right next to the one she had planted for you after you disappeared in Africa, presumed dead.'

'You told me. It's right next to my mother's. She died on the Coberg Mission in Australia.'

'That's correct. Well, here we are. What is it you wanted to show me?'

'Have a look at my tree.' Rahima sat down on a bench facing the grove of oak trees. Jack walked over to his mother's tree, looked at the trunk, and gasped.

5

Gatekeeper's Cottage, Kuragin chateau: 8 December

Since the fire that had destroyed his home in Montmartre and killed his son, retired French police officer Claude Dupree had lived in the Gatekeeper's Cottage next to the Kuragin chateau just outside Paris. Because the fire left him homeless, Countess Kuragin, who had known Dupree for years, had offered him the cottage and told him he could stay as long as he liked. Since then, Dupree had become a member of the extended Kuragin family, and had formed a close friendship with Jack. He had also played an important part in Jack's Russian lost symphony adventure, and the notorious death mask murders case that two years earlier had almost cost Jack his life.

'Lapointe should be here any moment,' said Dupree. 'The irrepressible Mademoiselle Darrieux has asked us to lunch. As soon as she heard you were staying here with me, I couldn't get out of it. In fact, she was really cross because we didn't come over to see her last night. You know what she's like ...'

'I understand,' said Jack, laughing.

After moving to Venice with Anna and Anna's son, Billy, the countess had handed the running of the Kuragin chateau boutique hotel over to Darrieux, who had not only risen to the task, but had excelled in ways no-one could have foreseen. A well-connected, flamboyant Paris socialite, she was well placed to attract wealthy house guests who enjoyed her sophisticated and hugely entertaining dinners and soirees. Because of its excellent location, the hotel was booked out months in advance despite the astronomical prices, and had become one of the most fashionable places to stay outside Paris.

'I don't mind. And besides, she was very helpful in the death mask murders case, and came to my rescue with Katerina in Yekaterinburg, remember? Her outrageous manner is deceptive. She's in fact very shrewd and observant, and has a good head on her shoulders. And besides, I like her.'

'I know you do. Ah, here comes Lapointe now.'

Jack smiled as Lapointe walked into the cottage, took off his coat and hat and adjusted his tie. Lapointe had always reminded him of *Maigret,* the legendary fictitious Paris detective who featured in more than seventy novels by Georges Simenon. Same quirky appearance, same mannerisms, same sharp mind.

'No doubt about you, Jack,' said Lapointe. 'It's all happening again, and with you right in the thick of it.' Lapointe reached into his pocket and pulled out his pipe and tobacco pouch. 'No wonder they call you the story magnet. So, what are these cryptic messages Dupree has mentioned? Care to tell me?'

Jack shrugged. 'Mademoiselle Darrieux has asked us to lunch. We can discuss it then.'

'She's bound to find out sooner or later. We can't keep anything from her. You know what she's like. I hope you don't mind,' said Dupree.

'*Mind?* Why should I mind? I could do with someone like her on my team. She has extraordinary instincts,' said Lapointe.

'Instincts? Is that what you call it?' said Dupree.

'Don't be too hard on her,' said Jack. 'She's a fabulous host, and I have no doubt the lunch will be memorable.'

'Everything about Darrieux is memorable,' said Dupree. 'Let's go. We'll be in trouble if we're late.'

As the trio crossed the circular driveway leading to the imposing chateau entrance, Jack pointed to Darrieux' cute little red 1980 Citroën 2CV parked between the latest Bentley and a Maserati. 'That just about sums her up, don't you think?'

'What do you mean?' said Dupree.

'A vintage classic rubbing shoulders with the toys of the mega rich. That's Darrieux, don't you think?'

'Just in time, boys,' said Darrieux, who met them in the foyer. 'Lunch is ready; come.' Dressed in a colourful – albeit a little too tight – creation by Valentino that accentuated her voluptuous Jayne

Mansfieldesque figure and generous décolleté that left little to the imagination, Darrieux looked totally at ease and at home in the sumptuous surroundings.

'What did I tell you?' whispered Dupree. 'Being late would have had serious consequences.'

'You mean she would have—?'

'Great to see you, Jack,' said Darrieux breezily. She kissed Jack on both cheeks – leaving little red lipstick smudges behind – and gave him a rib-crushing hug. 'We'll have lunch with cook in the kitchen downstairs. Your favourite place. She's dying to see you. The guests are having theirs right now in the dining room.'

'*Upstairs, Downstairs?*' teased Dupree.

'A bit like that,' said Darrieux, 'but we'll have more fun, that's for sure. And the same delicious lunch. And besides, we can talk in private and that's important; isn't that right, Chief Superintendent?'

'Absolutely, Mademoiselle,' said Lapointe, trying not to laugh, and obediently followed Darrieux down the stairs.

Jack was talking to cook, a rotund French lady with rosy cheeks, who was obviously pleased to see him. She showed him some of the food she was preparing and handed him a loaf of bread to take to the table.

Dupree turned to Lapointe sitting next to him on the bench. 'He's a popular guy down here, as you can see. Jack and women ...'

'I understand you like a chablis, Chief Superintendent?' said Darrieux and reached for a bottle on the table.

'How did you know?' asked Lapointe.

'Countess Kuragin told me,' said Darrieux, smiling. 'A good host must know the wine the guest prefers and be ready. Ah, here comes our entree. Some of cook's famous terrine. I'm sure you'll love it. Jack, please cut the bread and sit down. You talk too much!'

After lunch had finished, the table cleared and Darrieux had gone to check on her guests upstairs, Jack decided to broach the subject that had brought them all together.

He looked at Lapointe sitting opposite, reached into his pocket, took out the engraved bullet and put it on the table in front of Lapointe. 'Exhibit one,' he said. 'This was left under Tristan's napkin at his birthday dinner at the palazzo the other night.'

Lapointe picked up the bullet and held it up. 'Have you seen this?' he said to Dupree.

Dupree nodded.

'Do you know what Tristan had to say about this?' asked Jack.

Lapointe put the bullet back on the table. 'Tell me.'

'The nightmare in the salt mines is far from over.'

'And you agree?'

'Yes.'

'You obviously have more.'

'I have. It's the beginning of another game.'

'As on the notorious Darknet Bazaar gambling site; the *Death Mask Murders* game?'

'Yes. Rabbi Stein's murder was merely the next step, the next move. An important one, showing us the way.'

'Care to elaborate?' said Lapointe.

'Claude and I had a close look at the curious way Stein was murdered, especially the way his body had been arranged—'

'And then, of course, there was the piece of paper stuffed into his mouth,' cut in Dupree.

'I've seen the report.'

'But you may not know what it all *means*,' said Jack.

'And you do?'

'I believe so.'

'The writing on the piece of paper – *Behold the Maharal* – pointed us to the grave of famous sixteenth-century Rabbi Loew, who was known as the Maharal—' began Dupree.

'To cut a long story short,' interrupted Jack, who could see that Lapointe was getting impatient, 'we found something engraved on Rabbi Loew's headstone that didn't belong there. It was left there for us to find; I'm sure of it. It was a signature: the signature of David

Herzl, the master forger of Warsaw who became the famous Post-master of Treblinka after his transportation to the death camp in 1943.'

'Who became famous in Treblinka?' asked Darrieux, who had overheard the remark from the stairs.

'David Herzl,' said Jack.

'You wrote about him in your novella, *The Forgotten Painting*, as I recall,' said Darrieux.

'It's nice to have attentive readers, don't you think, Claude?'

'You tell me.'

'It is. In a way, my books have a lot to do with all this.' Jack ran his fingers through his hair. 'I would even go as far as to say that my books have been the catalyst.'

'In what way?' asked Lapointe, well aware Jack wouldn't make such an observation without good reason.

'Because unwittingly, my books contain a lot of information that could be used in certain sinister ways, I suppose. In ways I could never have anticipated, and certainly never intended.'

'By someone like O'Hara?' asked Lapointe.

'Yes. Only someone with very deep pockets and access to resources that are difficult to imagine can pull off something like this and contemplate another foray into the murky world of darknet gambling.'

'Do you really think he's behind all this?'

'I am sure of it,' said Jack. 'Everything fits and points in his direction. Matters like this don't happen in a vacuum. And I am also sure that I am the target here, just like Landru was the target in the death mask murders.'

'You can't be serious!' said Darrieux.

'But I am. I know exactly what the intruders who ransacked Stein's study and killed him in the process had been looking for.'

'What?' asked Lapointe.

'Herzl's diary. Sandor Kun, his son, left it to Stein's museum in Prague. The novella I've just released – *The Postmaster of Treblinka* –

deals with all that and provides certain detailed information, which I thought would only be of historical interest to my readers. I was obviously wrong. Someone is interested in all this for entirely different reasons that are far from historical. Those reasons are very much anchored in the present; I just cannot see at the moment exactly why. That's the real problem here.'

'But if you're right,' said Lapointe, 'we'll find out. Soon, I'd say.'

'I agree,' said Jack. 'And I would like us to be ready for that, because as long as O'Hara is out there calling the shots, as he seems to be doing again right now, we'll be in for one hell of a ride. A dangerous one.'

For a while everyone sat in silence, digesting what had just been said.

'Why do you think you are the target here?' asked Lapointe, articulating the question on everyone's mind.

'Because of what I found yesterday at my mother's retirement home.'

'Care to elaborate?'

'Once again, all the relevant information is in my books. It's about Madame Petrova's memory trees.'

'We know all about those, don't we?' said Darrieux, who as Petrova's biographer had provided Jack with a lot of background information about the unique memory trees and what they represented.

'What did you find?' asked Lapointe.

'First, a note was left under the door of my mother's apartment: *Behold your memory tree.* Weird, right?'

Lapointe nodded.

'When my mother went to investigate and had a look at her tree, she found something strange.'

'What?' asked Darrieux.

'Someone had recently carved something into the trunk of my mother's tree.'

'Carved?' said Lapointe.

'Yes. *RIP 2021*. A clear message, wouldn't you say?'

Silence.

'How are we to interpret this?' asked Lapointe.

'The way I see it,' said Jack, 'someone is targeting those closest to me. First Tristan, and then my mother. What is particularly chilling is the way this has been done. What this tells me is this: whoever is behind these threats can reach those closest to me anywhere, anytime. Simple.'

'I can see that,' said Lapointe. He perfectly understood Jack's disquiet and could see that Jack's manner was masking real concern, even a touch of fear.

'These are clear threats. Not even subtle. Right in the middle of my personal life and space. First, a bullet is left under a napkin in the palazzo dining room. *In Venice!* Then my mother's memory tree is defaced in the grounds of her exclusive retirement home right here in France. This needs resources and careful planning. It needs someone with a mind like O'Hara's, don't you think? Unique, devious, chilling. A master manipulator and puppeteer playing a long game. We've already seen firsthand what he's capable of. I have to take this seriously.'

'I suppose the uncertainty is the worst,' said Lapointe, a shrewd observation that clearly expressed what worried Jack most.

'Yes,' Jack agreed, 'but if he wanted to kill me, or those he has threatened in such imaginative ways, he could have done so easily. No, he wants more, a lot more; I just can't see what that is at the moment, but I am sure it has to do with David Herzl's diary, and the Postmaster of Treblinka.'

'Fascinating,' said Darrieux. 'Do you think this is some kind of payback for the death mask murders case? That certainly didn't end as intended and resulted in the destruction of O'Hara's secret world on the Obersalzberg. Not to mention his loss of the Inca treasure.'

'I'm sure it has,' said Jack. 'This man doesn't accept failure. Defeat of any kind isn't an option.'

'You've been clearly in O'Hara's sights before,' continued Darrieux, 'and were saved in the nick of time, mainly because of Tristan and your friends.'

'You are absolutely right,' said Jack. 'This is nothing more than the next round in a deadly game. A game where O'Hara makes the rules, calls the shots, and pulls all the strings. Just like last time. Or so he thinks.'

'So, it's on again?' said Darrieux, her face flushed with excitement.

'It would seem so,' said Jack.

'And are you ready for this?' she asked.

'Do I have a choice?'

'I suppose not,' said Dupree.

'The question is are *you* ready, my friends?' asked Jack. 'Because like it or not, I firmly believe this will involve us all.'

Lapointe nodded in agreement. 'My answer is simple. Two of my officers were killed a few metres from here. On my watch. I have told the Commissioner I will do everything in my power to bring those behind their murders to justice.'

Jack looked at Dupree. 'I already know Claude's answer. He thinks like you, Chief Superintendent. Unfinished business is not in his nature.'

Jack looked at Darrieux.

'Don't look at me like that. If you think for a moment that I'm not in, you are gravely mistaken, gentlemen. I wouldn't miss this for the world.'

'I thought you would say that, Adrienne,' said Jack, smiling. 'Any more wine?'

6

Minsk: 9 December

Ronan O'Hara was at his most dangerous when his back was against
the wall. After the destruction of his sophisticated control centre beneath the idyllic farmhouse on the Obersalzberg near Berchtesgaden
the year before, he had managed to pull off a breathtaking last-
minute escape that took authorities by surprise. By staging his death
in a spectacular helicopter crash at Lake Königssee, he was able to
escape into Belarus, where he had extensive contacts and was effectively out of reach of the European authorities pursuing him.

The dank cellar under the modest house on the outskirts of
Minsk was a far cry from his previous residence with stunning views
over the Alps. Yet, with the powerful computer, three large monitors
and a complex communications system that gave him access to
almost every corner of the globe with a click of his mouse, O'Hara
had everything he needed to rebuild his dark empire.

When the diminutive, bald man in his seventies who seemed to
hide behind thick glasses walked into the village to buy groceries, no-
one would have suspected that behind this deceptive facade was one
of the most powerful cyber-criminals, worth billions, who was on the
most-wanted list of law enforcement agencies around the globe. But
with access to virtually unlimited funds, almost anything was possible
in a country like Belarus, where corruption was rife, bribes oiled the
wheels of almost every level of government and just about everything
was for sale – at a price. This was precisely the environment O'Hara
needed to make his enterprise flourish.

A master manipulator who understood human weaknesses and
knew how to exploit them and bend people to his will, O'Hara was
once again in his element. As a man who thrived on a challenge and
needed danger like others needed air, he had been able to revive his
notorious Darknet Bazaar – also known as the DNB – which had
made him millions, and make it operational again.

55

As part of this exercise, he had also reinstated his notorious gambling empire with its ingenious computer games he had designed personally over the years. With all the necessary data safely stored in the Cloud, he had access to all the material from before, as only replaceable computer hardware had been destroyed by the explosion he had triggered himself to facilitate his escape and hide his tracks. He viewed this as a temporary setback from which he knew he would quickly recover, because precious intellectual property and all his money were safe and out of reach of the authorities.

As part of reviving his highly lucrative gambling empire on the darknet, O'Hara had contacted his major 'players' and promised them a new game to follow in the footsteps of the highly successful *Death Mask Murders* game on the DNB site that had created such excitement and a gambling frenzy around the globe for years. What O'Hara needed now was a new, imaginative game that would surpass everything he had staged before.

To satisfy the thrill-hungry gamblers always on the lookout for the next extreme gambling fix, O'Hara knew something special was needed if this comeback was to succeed. Gamblers who were prepared to wager tens of thousands of dollars on a single illegal bet, expected something big and spectacular, often involving the unthinkable and the bizarre, and O'Hara knew exactly how to cater for these appetites and create real-life scenarios using real people, with lives of entire future generations on the line.

All he needed to do now was to create such a game, and he knew exactly how he would do just that. As Jack and his friends had been, at least in part, responsible for his downfall in Bavaria, Jack would be part of his comeback, and O'Hara already had a game in mind that would deliver everything needed, and in many ways surpass the expectations of even his most demanding players. A carefully constructed outline of the game was already circulating in his head like an imaginary chess game, giving free rein to the evil and depraved creativity his games were known for. All that remained to be done was to commence implementation, which also meant the eagerly awaited gambling scenarios could begin and the wagers be placed.

O'Hara reached for the novella Jack had recently published and smiled, the excitement within making his hands tremble in a rare show of emotion. In Jack he thought he had found the perfect opponent, who had unwittingly played into his hands by providing vital information needed to construct a new computer game that ticked all the boxes. Others may not have recognised the hidden pieces of a real-life puzzle a creative mind could use in such a game, but O'Hara found these little gems hiding between the lines and knew exactly how to exploit them. His creative genius knew how to fashion them into unique cyber building blocks, where the boundary between reality and make-believe was carefully blurred so that a player was never quite sure where the real world ended, and fantasy began.

And knowing that most of these precious pieces were embedded in Jack's highly successful books and therefore available for all to see, made using them even more exciting. O'Hara put down Jack's novella, reached for the Herzl diary that his newly appointed 'field agent' – a remarkable woman with surprising talents – had recently retrieved from Rabbi Stein's study, and carefully reread a passage he had underlined.

Today I finally posted the van Eyck to Ilona's mother in Hungary. It's worth a fortune and should we ever make it out of here alive, it should give us all we would need to start a new life. And to think that it was this very painting I had been asked to copy for these barbarians, makes the thought even sweeter. It was this painting that saved me once already; perhaps it will save me again provided the Feldpost delivers it safely to Szentendre. German efficiency can be both deadly, and useful. Let's hope it's the latter this time.

Switching the paintings was Ilona's idea. That's why the original is now on its way to Hungary, and the copy on its way to Berlin. These little acts of defiance give us strength to go on and face the unimaginable atrocities being committed around us every day. I immerse myself in my art, and try to shut out the thousands of voices calling out in agony and pain to be remembered.

O'Hara put down the diary, took off his glasses and began to polish them with his handkerchief. This helped him to focus and organise his thoughts as he kept working on the next segment of the new computer game that was all about the Postmaster of Treblinka. As he put his glasses back on, the next scene in the deadly game was beginning to take shape.

I am proud to be called the Postmaster of Treblinka, O'Hara continued to read. *If I can bring just a brief moment of joy to someone by sending a letter out of here, then it was all worthwhile. That, too, was Ilona's idea. Her kindness and compassion give me something to hold onto, and tell me that humanity hasn't entirely lost its way.*

O'Hara pushed the diary aside and called up the Rabbi Stein video on his computer. It showed Stein's brutal murder in minute detail, including gruesome close-ups that O'Hara knew his gambling audience would love. The new game was off to an excellent start, and it was time to post the video online. The video included the Herzl signature clue left behind on the headstone of Rabbi Loew's grave. This would provide a thrilling wager scenario the punters would embrace, and loosen the strings of their bulging gambling purses.

O'Hara, a practical man who was acutely aware of his limitations, knew exactly what he was good at, and when he needed help. He preferred to stay in the background, anonymously if possible, and leave the fieldwork to others. This strategy had worked very well for him in the past, but had recently hit a major obstacle.

O'Hara's Mafia contacts in Italy had provided him with highly experienced and effective operatives over the years who carried out his demanding and often bizarre instructions to the letter without asking questions. The only contact between O'Hara and the operatives was the huge amounts of money paid into untraceable bank accounts buried deep in the cyber archives of secure financial institutions operating on the darknet.

O'Hara liked staying in the shadows. This had kept him safe over the years and out of reach of the many law enforcement agencies desperately trying to find him and shut him down.

With the death of Alessandro Giordano and the conviction and incarceration of his father, these arrangements had come to an abrupt end. The Mafia in Florence had been all but wiped out by Chief Prosecutor Grimaldi and the Squadra Mobile. New arrangements were therefore needed and O'Hara knew exactly who he could turn to and ask for help, because without effective agents in the field, the new game couldn't function.

The bolthole in Belarus that O'Hara had carefully prepared as insurance was the perfect location to build a new network of contacts who could deliver what he needed, and the pool of darknet gamblers gave him access to like-minded individuals with deep pockets who could be approached and explored for possible involvement. On his terms.

One of those individuals O'Hara had approached shortly after his arrival in Belarus to help him rebuild his darknet activities was Oleg Ivanov, a former KGB agent who had become one of the notorious Russian oligarchs with almost unimaginable wealth. He had made his fortune during the disintegration of the Soviet Union in the 1990s by taking advantage of Michael Gorbachev's unprecedented period of market liberalisation.

Ivanov, an addicted gambler, owned casinos around the world. Best known for his high-profile, glitzy hotels and casinos in Las Vegas, Macau and Australia, he had close connections to the underworld and was suspected of running extensive money-laundering operations that had made him a fortune. Nothing had ever been proven, but the rumours never went away and tainted his reputation. It was therefore only natural O'Hara should turn to him with a business proposition that involved extreme criminal activities, and most important of all, gambling.

Most of the time Ivanov lived on his luxurious private yacht, the *Standard*, surrounded by his mistresses and Chechen bodyguards. It was rumoured the yacht had cost over six hundred million dollars, making it one of the most expensive private superyachts in the world.

Named after Tsar Nicholas II's Imperial Russian yacht, the home port of the *Standard* was St Petersburg, and O'Hara had made contact with Ivanov there. Being one of his regular gamblers, who wagered obscene amounts, O'Hara knew that Ivanov would be receptive to what he had in mind. As the winner of several gambling scenarios, O'Hara had written him into the *Death Mask Murders* game as a character. This was highly prized by the regular punters because it gave them not only prestige in the darknet gambling fraternity, but also provided them with better odds and other advantages in the game going forward.

As expected, Ivanov was immediately interested and drawn to the idea. The proposal outlined by O'Hara appealed to a gambler like Ivanov, who was always looking for the next adrenaline hit, just as a drug addict craves the next dose of heroin.

In essence, O'Hara suggested a partnership, but on certain terms. He explained that he was rebuilding his darknet gambling activities after a raid on his Bavarian operations had temporarily interrupted his business. He hinted that by pooling contacts and resources, the darknet gambling site could reach dizzying new heights never seen before. This appealed to Ivanov, who saw himself as a gifted entrepreneur. He had never come to terms with being shunned by the establishment and was always on the lookout for opportunities to make his mark and impress his snobbish peers, who considered him a grubby little Russian upstart without class.

O'Hara sensed this and decided to use it to his advantage. While he certainly didn't need Ivanov's money, he did need his underworld contacts and he desperately needed access to potential operatives to make his comeback work. He explained that since the collapse of his Italian Mafia contacts he had been unable to source suitable field agents, as he called them, needed in connection with his unique gambling activities. He described the type of agents he had used in the past – especially the late Teodora of Spiridon 4 – and made it clear what kind of 'activities' would be involved.

Eager to impress, Ivanov indicated that he could provide exactly what O'Hara needed. A few days later he provided Irina Zarubina, to show O'Hara that he could deliver and meant business.

As it turned out, with Irina, O'Hara had everything he needed to start his new game on the darknet that he called *The Postmaster of Treblinka*, and invited his cyber punters to place their bets. O'Hara's notorious gambling site was back in business, only this time he was determined to make the game bigger and more enticing than before, and deliver thrills and temptations his punters couldn't have imagined in their wildest wager-dreams. And most important of all, he promised himself never to make the same mistakes again.

7

Travestere, Rome: 10 December

Jack got out of the taxi, turned up his collar and looked across the busy market square teeming with evening shoppers. *Some things never change*, he thought as he walked past the excited stallholders selling fresh produce straight from the farm. The lanterns and coloured lights gave the square a festive air, reminding shoppers that Christmas wasn't far away. In a city where cooking and eating was almost a religion, shopping for fresh ingredients was an important part of daily life, coming only second to sharing a homemade pasta and a bottle of Chianti with friends after church on Sunday.

Jack stopped by a stall selling flowers and bought a bunch, giving the toothless old woman his best smile while shaking his head as she tried to sell him two. *Everything looks different at night*, he thought, trying to find Francesca Bartolli's apartment building he had visited the year before.

Because there were no street numbers, he had to orientate himself in different ways. He remembered a statue of a saint not far from the entrance where Bartolli had met him and asked him to wait while she went to buy more tomatoes.

There it is, he thought, relieved, looking up at the terrace where Bartolli's mother had served a memorable lunch, and then hurried up the stairs to the first floor.

Before he could knock, the apartment door opened and Professor Bartolli, a striking woman in her late thirties wearing an apron, smiled at him. 'Just in time, come in. Dinner's almost ready. I saw you buying flowers from Signora Fratini. I'm surprised you didn't buy the entire stall. She can be very persuasive, especially when handsome strangers are involved.'

'Tell me about it,' said Jack. He handed the flowers to Bartolli and followed her inside.

'Straight from the airport?'

'Yes. Just like last time.'

'I offered to pick you up,' said Bartolli, a sparkle in her eyes.

'With your Vespa, no doubt.'

'So?'

'I'm not that brave.'

'Wimp. Mum's in the kitchen.'

'Something smells good,' said Jack, changing direction.

'Food. You are so predictable! Come. She's been cooking all afternoon and hasn't stopped talking about you.'

No-one would have guessed that the young woman adjusting her apron and tossing back her curly dark-blonde hair was one of Italy's most prominent criminal psychologists, with a fearsome reputation. Her court appearances were legendary and performances under cross-examination formidable, instilling fear in those brave enough to question her opinions and findings. Jack had worked with Bartolli on the sensational Maurice Landru case in 2018, and had consulted her more recently in connection with the Postmaster of Treblinka matter.

On that occasion, they had met in Armando al Pantheon, one of Jack's favourite Roman restaurants, but Jack had been to her apartment before, which she shared with two daughters, her mother and a dog.

'How wonderful to see you again, Jack,' said Bartolli's mother. She put down a large wooden spoon, gave Jack a hug and kissed him on both cheeks. 'I hope you are hungry.' Bartolli and her mother looked more like sisters than mother and daughter. Same striking facial features, curly dark-blonde hair and smile.

'Always,' said Jack and put the wine he had brought on the kitchen table.

'We'll eat here in the kitchen. That way we can talk while I finish dinner.'

'Fine by me. A little wine, perhaps?'

'Absolutely!'

'We'll start with a cacio e pepe.'

'Ah. Spaghetti with black pepper and grated Pecorino Romana cheese.' Jack smacked his lips and began to open the wine, a bottle of 2007 Illuminati Ilico Riserva Montepulciano d'Abruzzo he had bought because he knew that Bartolli particularly liked that wine.

'Don't mind me, guys,' said Bartolli, rolling her eyes. 'I'll set the table then, shall I?'

'Good idea,' said her mother. 'Almost ready.'

'I don't know how you do it,' whispered Bartolli as Jack handed her a glass of wine. 'You've been here only once before, yet you've got her wrapped around your little finger.'

'I have no idea what you're talking about. She loves cooking, and I like her food. Simple!'

'Oh, yes?'

'Where are the girls and the dog?' asked Jack, trying to get out of a tricky popularity contest.

'The girls are out with boyfriends, as usual. As for Paulo, he should have been back ages ago. We were just talking about that before you came.'

'You mean he should be sitting over there on his mat, looking longingly at the stove like last time.'

'Exactly. Being out this late just isn't like him.'

'Perhaps he had a better offer from one of the stallholders,' speculated Jack.

'Hardly. He's usually like clockwork.'

'Ready. Here it comes,' said Bartolli's mother and put a large bowl of steaming pasta on the table. 'Help yourselves. More cheese, anyone?'

'That was an extraordinary ceremony in Jerusalem,' said Bartolli. 'We saw it all on TV. Very moving.'

'Yes, Yad Vashem is a special place. The Postmaster of Treblinka's letter finally arrived.'

'Thanks to you,' said Bartolli's mother and filled up Jack's bowl again.

'I only had a part to play.'

'That's not how His Holiness put it,' said Bartolli.

Jack waved dismissively. 'When you hear what happened to Rabbi Stein a few days ago, you will know what I mean,' said Jack, turning serious.

'Are you going to tell us?' asked Bartolli. Jack hadn't told Bartolli about the recent disturbing events and had only indicated he wanted to talk to her urgently in connection with a serious matter.

Jack put down his spoon and wiped his mouth with a napkin. 'I wanted to wait until after dinner.'

'Come on, Jack,' said Bartolli. 'You are among friends here.'

'Rabbi Stein was murdered in the Jewish cemetery in Prague a few days ago,' said Jack quietly.

'*What?*' said Bartolli, shocked. 'Seriously?'

'Yes. I've just been to Prague.'

'Do you know why he was killed? By who? How?' demanded Bartolli, her curiosity aroused and her professional instincts on high alert.

'It's complicated. There's more to all this, I'm afraid, and it all has to do with the Postmaster of Treblinka.'

'The Yad Vashem matter?'

'Yes, and a lot more. That's what I want to talk to you about.' Jack looked at Bartolli's mother. 'I'm sorry,' he said. 'Hardly a good topic of conversation during such a splendid dinner.'

Bartolli's mother patted Jack on back of his hand. 'Don't worry. You two obviously have a lot to talk about,' she said and stood up. 'I wanted to go and look for Paulo in any case. I've been worried about him all evening. We can have dessert later. I made tiramisu.'

'How did you know?'

'Know what?'

'It's my favourite.'

'Charmer,' whispered Bartolli, rolling her eyes.

Jack reached for the bottle after the mother had left the apartment, and topped up Bartolli's glass.

'So, Yad Vashem wasn't the end of the Postmaster of Treblinka matter we discussed during your last visit?' said Bartolli.

'No. A lot has happened since then. To start with, we have a new pope. In many ways it's just the beginning. The Landru case and the death mask murders aren't over yet, either—'

'What are you talking about?' interrupted Bartolli.

Jack reached into his pocket, took out the inscribed bullet Tristan had found under his napkin in Venice on his birthday, and placed it on the table in front of Bartolli.

'What's this?' asked Bartolli.

'The opening chapter of an incredible story I'm about to tell you. A dangerous one.'

Over the next half-hour, Jack told Bartolli about Tristan's 'happy birthday bullet', Rabbi Stein's murder, and the Herzl signature chiselled into Rabbi Loew's headstone with the Maharal–Treblinka connection. Fascinated by Jack's story, Bartolli listened in silence without interrupting.

Jack took another sip of wine. 'There's more, I'm afraid,' he said, and then turned to the curious subject of Madame Petrova's memory trees, the note left under the door of his mother's apartment in the French retirement home, and what he had found carved into his mother's memory tree.

For a while Jack and Bartolli sat in silence, deep in thought.

'And you think there's a connection here?' said Bartolli.

'What do you think? You and I don't believe in coincidences like this, do we?'

Bartolli shook her head. 'What are you telling me?'

'I'm telling you that O'Hara isn't dead. We know he wasn't in the helicopter that crashed into the lake. He got away. And now he's back.'

'You think so?'

'I'm sure of it. And Dupree and Lapointe agree. I spoke with them just yesterday about all this.'

'Hm. And why exactly are you telling *me* all this now?'

'Because I want your professional opinion. I need your help here. You know the Landru case and the death mask murders better than anyone. You are one of the best profilers in Europe. I've seen you at work and I trust your instincts. You know what makes the criminal mind tick. If I'm right and O'Hara is behind all this, well, we may be looking at something similar here. Something sinister and dangerous.'

'More darknet gambling, you think?'

'Yes. That and a lot more. After all, we are talking about the same deranged mind here, and the same depraved people looking for kicks—'

'And you think that you may be the target here?'

'I do. The Landru case is far from over. I can feel it, and so can Tristan. For the first time, I've seen him worried.'

'Why do you think that is?'

'I think he can sense true evil. A psychopath like O'Hara doesn't stop. He will never concede defeat. He will try to come back stronger. Frankly speaking, I'm worried about Tristan and my mother.'

'Because they are close to you?'

'Yes. And because of that, O'Hara is using them to get to me. Surely you can see that?'

Bartolli nodded. 'Go on.'

'Just look at the "messages", because that's what they are. What do they tell you?' said Jack.

'He knows a lot about you. That's not difficult, Jack. Because of your books, you are an open book yourself. Just look at your website and your social media posts. Your readers know a lot about you. That's one of the reasons you're so popular. You don't hide. On the contrary, you're approachable and easy to reach. An internet guru like O'Hara would have no difficulty to quickly find out a lot about you just by surfing the Net. Just look at all the stuff people write about you. The TV interviews, the book launches, talkback radio. You like to talk about yourself. Need I go on?'

'I suppose you're right. You once called O'Hara a master puppeteer standing in the shadows and pulling all the strings.'

'I did. He's a ruthless manipulator who lets others take all the risks and do his dirty work. He had Landru dancing to his tune for years.'

'Do you think he could be trying to do the same to me?'

'You are not Landru,' said Bartolli, sidestepping the question. She didn't want to alarm Jack but she didn't want to play down the obvious danger, either. What Jack had told her so far made her feel uneasy. O'Hara was extremely dangerous, with no moral compass. And with the means at his disposal, he had a far reach others could only dream about, as the death mask murders had clearly demonstrated.

Bartolli could see Jack was worried. What made him vulnerable were the people close to him. If O'Hara was indeed behind everything Jack had told her, he had obviously worked that out. The way to get to Jack was through the people he loved. The bullet under Tristan's napkin was of real concern. Someone who could pull that off was capable of anything. Nowhere was safe, and Bartolli was sure that Jack could see that.

Bartolli held up her empty glass. 'I think we should have another drink and take a step back.'

'You're right,' said Jack and reached for the bottle.

'This is not the time for speculation. This is the time for cool heads. And besides, if we are right about O'Hara, I'm sure he'll show his hand soon.'

'That's what I was thinking,' said Jack, feeling relieved. 'If all this is part of a bigger picture, we'll find out soon enough what it looks like.'

As Jack was pouring more wine into Bartolli's glass, he could hear loud voices and a commotion somewhere on the staircase outside.

'That's Mum,' said Bartolli, frowning. She stood up and hurried to the front door. Jack put down the bottle and followed. Bartolli's mother stood in the doorway, tears streaming down her face. A tall man carrying something stood behind her in the shadows.

'What's wrong?' said Bartolli.

Her mother turned around and pointed to the man behind her. 'It's Paulo,' she stammered, barely able to speak.

'Oh, my God!' shouted Bartolli, staring at the man carrying Paulo in his arms.

The man, a stallholder Bartolli knew well, walked into the hallway, put the limp body on the floor and stepped aside. 'I'm sorry. That's how we found him. Look at the froth around his mouth. Poison, I'd say.'

After the man had left, Bartolli took her mother to the bathroom to calm her down. As she walked past Jack, she handed him a blanket and pointed to Paulo lying on the floor.

When Jack bent down to cover the little body with the blanket, he noticed something wrapped around the collar. A piece of paper was attached to the collar with a rubber band. *How curious*, he thought. That's when he noticed *Jack* written across the top of the paper, and gasped. He quickly took off the rubber band, unfolded the piece of paper – his hands shaking – and looked at the spidery handwriting.

Black to c5. Your move.

Meet you on the Standard *in the Port of St Petersburg on Monday 13 December, 10:00 am.*

Jack slipped the piece of paper into his pocket and covered Paulo with the blanket. Then he walked out onto the terrace and looked across to the illuminated dome of St Peters, shining like a beacon of hope in the distance. On this occasion, not even the stunning view could calm the turmoil boiling within, as Jack struggled to come to terms with what had just happened and tried to work out his next move.

8

St Petersburg: 13 December, morning

It was quite early and still dark outside, but the luxurious breakfast room in the opulent Four Seasons Lion Palace Hotel at 12 Admiralleytsy Avenue was already busy. Jack waved as Bartolli entered and looked around. She had arrived late the night before on a flight from Rome and had gone straight to bed after the long journey.

'Ah, there you are,' she said and sat down next to Jack. 'Do you know it's snowing outside?' said Bartolli.

'This is St Petersburg, and it's winter.'

'What a hotel. My room is bigger than our apartment in Rome,' said Bartolli.

'Yes, it's rather grand. Splendid location with quite a history. Echoes of Imperial Russia. It was once the Lobanov-Rostovsky Palace until it was bought by the State Treasury in 1829 for the Ministry of War of the Russian Empire. Now, it's a wonderful hotel.'

'You can say that again.'

'I stayed here with Countess Kuragin and Isis in 2017. Katerina wore jewellery fit for a tsarina and turned heads wherever she went.'

'You do get around!'

'We had a suite that occupied almost an entire floor. Dupree and Darrieux were there as well. Adrienne wore a dress none of us would forget in a hurry. She too turned heads, but for different reasons. We were here at the invitation of the Governor of St Petersburg to go to the historic premiere of Tchaikovsky's lost symphony, *Mat' Rossiya*, in the Bolshoi Zal. Now, that was an occasion. Benjamin Krakowski conducted and even played a solo on his famous Stradivarius, The Empress. Unforgettable!' said Jack.

'What an exciting life you lead, Jack.'

'That was a joyous, festive occasion. Tchaikovsky's lost symphony came home.'

'Thanks to you.'

Jack shrugged, and then turned serious. 'What we are about to do this morning may be a little different, I'm afraid. Nothing joyous or festive about that, for sure.'

'I guess not.'

Jack reached for Bartolli's hand. 'I can't tell you how much I appreciate you coming along, but before you do, I want you to be absolutely sure you know what you may be letting yourself in for. You know how dangerous this could be. After all, we're dealing with a psychopath here. Ruthless, unpredictable, perhaps even insane. Once in, there may be no turning back.'

'I know that. You don't have to worry.'

'But I do. After all, it was me who brought this mess into your life, and the lives of your family. Your mother, Paulo—'

'Hush. It's not your fault, Jack. You came to me as a friend asking for advice. Mum and I opened our home and welcomed you. No-one could have foreseen what happened that night.'

'But it did, and I feel responsible.'

'That's not rational.'

'Maybe not, but I cannot help how I feel.'

'I understand, and that's one of the reasons I've decided to come along.'

'*One* of the reasons?'

'I've given this whole, quite bizarre scenario a lot of thought since that night. I'm in this now just as deep as you are, Jack. My private world has been invaded, and I will not stand for that.'

'And your mum?'

'She feels the same way. After the shock and the sadness with Paulo, all that's left now is outrage. You know my father was a policeman. He was with the Carabinieri until he was shot and injured, and forced to retire.'

'You told me.'

'He believed, as I do, that you cannot hide from evil. You must face it and meet it head on, just as you are about to do. That's the main reason I'm here.'

'There are others?'

'Yes. This is without doubt one of the most fascinating cases I've come across in my entire career. As you rightly pointed out, the death mask murders are far from over. Until O'Hara is finally put out of business for good and brought to justice, this will not stop.'

'That's what Dupree and Lapointe said.'

'They were right, but I want to be there when it finally happens, standing next to you.'

'Okay, but don't say I didn't warn you.'

'You did. For me, there's no turning back either.'

'In that case, let's have some breakfast. To face evil on an empty stomach is never a good idea,' said Jack, smiling.

'You could be Italian, you know,' said Bartolli, grinning.

'How come?'

'With you, food always seems to come first.'

'Is that such a bad thing?'

'Not at all. It's quite endearing, actually.'

After they had finished a sumptuous breakfast, the chief concierge of the hotel approached the table.

'Forgive me for intruding, Mr Rogan,' said the concierge, 'but a hire car has just arrived to take you to your appointment. There's no rush. The driver will wait outside until you are ready to leave.' With that, the concierge made a bow and withdrew.

'What did I tell you?' said Bartolli. 'There's no turning back.'

A dense fog hovered above the harbour as the hire car approached the elaborate berth of the *Standard*. At 170 metres long, the *Standard* was one of the largest privately owned superyachts in the world. Next to the berth were facilities dedicated to the yacht's permanent crew of eighty-two, including catering, laundry, and staff accommodation.

Security was tight and the car had to stop at a boom gate blocking the way. Once Jack had identified himself, the armed guard made a phone call. After that, the gate opened, and the car proceeded to the berth.

'Are you sure this is the right place?' asked Bartolli as they approached the yacht rising out of the fog like an apparition, reminding Bartolli of a modern-day *Flying Dutchman*. 'This looks like an ocean liner, not a private yacht.'

'No doubt about it, this is it,' said Jack. 'This is the *Standard*.'

Designed by Italian studio Nauta Design and built by Lürssen – the world's leading builders of superyachts – in Bremen, Germany, the *Standard* was the epitome of opulence and style, combining elements of modern, cutting-edge yacht design with certain nostalgic features recalling a bygone age, as suggested by its name.

Jack had done some research earlier and so he knew a lot about Lürssen and the yacht. The original *Standard*, a Russian Imperial yacht, was built for Emperor Alexander III and launched in 1895. It later served the last tsar, Nicholas II and his family, until it was seized by the Bolsheviks and used in the October Revolution in 1917. After that, it was renamed several times while in naval service, and was eventually scrapped in Estonia in 1963.

Jack and Bartolli were escorted on board by two armed Chechen guards who didn't say a word, only pointed. The captain, a Russian wearing a crisp white uniform and speaking perfect English, greeted them in the saloon.

'What an exceptional vessel,' said Jack, trying to appear relaxed and nonchalant. 'Classic Lürssen design.'

'You're right, Mr Rogan,' said the captain, surprised. 'It is. The Lürssen tradition goes right back to 1895, when Friedrich Lürssen set up a shipyard in Bremen.'

'Quite so. Lürssen vessels have been famous for a long time and in many unexpected ways. Operation Jungle, for instance.'

'Oh? What's that?' asked the captain.

'Operation Jungle was a covert British MI6 operation during the 1950s. The British trained Baltic agents for assignments in the Soviet Union. Do you know how those agents reached the Soviet Union?'

The captain shook his head.

'They used a Lürssen E-boat, a fast-attack craft used by the German Kriegsmarine during World War II.'

'You don't say ...'

'Mr Rogan is absolutely right,' said a voice coming from somewhere in the back of the large saloon. 'The Soviet counter-espionage operation that later infiltrated Jungle was called *Lurssen-S*. You are very well informed, Mr Rogan.'

As Jack turned to see where the voice was coming from, he saw a woman walking slowly towards him. Dressed in a dark, double-breasted suit, white shirt and a thin black tie, the woman – in her sixties – stopped and lit a cigarette. Patently butch with short grey hair, bright red lipstick, and almost theatrical makeup accentuating her large, slanted eyes behind thick cat-eye glasses that gave her a distinctly feline look, her retro attire reminded Jack of someone who had stepped straight out of a 1920s Berlin cabaret. *Even her voice is Marlene Dietrichesque,* he thought. Nostalgic, mysterious, seductive, but with an edge of danger.

Bartolli watched the interesting woman and wondered what part she played in this staged performance. In a way, it didn't surprise her because it was all classic O'Hara: surprise, shock, unpredictability, but all part of a meticulous plan.

The woman walked over to the well-stocked bar and turned around. 'Drink anyone?'

'No thank you,' said Jack. 'A little early for me.'

The woman reached for a bottle of vodka, unscrewed the top and poured some into a glass. 'Nonsense. It clears the mind and sharpens the senses. *Na Zdorovie!*'

'You obviously know who I am,' continued Jack. 'Care to tell us who you are?'

'I am Irina.' The woman turned towards the captain standing behind her. 'Thank you, Captain, that will be all.'

The captain made a bow and withdrew. It was obvious who was in control.

Jack walked over to the bar and reached into his pocket. Then he took out the piece of paper he had found wrapped around Paulo's collar, and placed it on the bar next to Irina. 'Your invitation?'

'In a way. I had something to do with it, yes, but the invitation came from someone else. Someone you've met before.'

'The elusive Mr O'Hara, no doubt. I've spoken with him, but never actually met him and was hoping that perhaps today …'

'Is that why you came? You surprised us. I had my doubts, yet here you are. And you brought a friend.'

Jack turned around and pointed to Bartolli. 'How rude of me. Allow me to introduce—'

'I know who Professor Bartolli is.' Irina refilled her glass, walked over to Bartolli and peered at her through her thick lenses.

Bartolli held her gaze without flinching.

'After finishing school in Travestere where you grew up, a tomboy and only child roaming the markets,' continued Irina, 'you went to study law at the University of Milan. A scholarship. You excelled and became a tutor, and then a lecturer. It is said you know the criminal mind like no other. I wonder, is that true?'

'Did you ask us to come here to discuss my past, or was there something else?' said Bartolli frostily.

'I was just curious,' continued Irina, ignoring the question. 'Because your choice of husband seems to suggest otherwise. He is still in jail, no?'

Bartolli flushed and bit her lip to remain quiet.

'I see. You haven't told Mr Rogan about this, have you? No matter,' said Irina, satisfied she had exposed a raw nerve. 'You're right. We aren't here to discuss your past, Professor Bartolli. We are here to discuss the future; an interesting one as you will see in a moment. It is time for you to meet your host. And it's not the owner of this yacht – he lives in London.'

Irina took another sip of neat vodka, enjoying herself.

'You were right, Mr Rogan,' she continued. 'The invitation to come here for this meeting came from Mr O'Hara. But I must disappoint you. You will not meet him in person, but virtually. Just like last time.'

Irina walked over to a large television screen and turned it on. Moments later, an image appeared: a bundle of faded pages neatly arranged on a wooden table.

'Good morning, Mr Rogan. It's been a while,' said O'Hara, who could see everyone in the saloon, but couldn't be seen himself because the camera was trained on the table. 'A lot has happened since we first met in the dining room of the Kuragin chateau. And you were there too, Signora Bartolli. It is opportune you are joining us this morning. You will see why in a moment.'

'You have asked me to come all this way to meet you *virtually?*' said Jack with contempt. 'We could have done this anywhere. At least you could show us some courtesy and show yourself.'

'It's better this way, trust me.'

'Camera-shy, just like last time. Why here on someone else's yacht, extraordinary as it may be?'

'I wanted you to meet Irina, and familiarise yourself with the *Standard.*'

'Why?'

'Later. Do you know what this is?' asked O'Hara, ignoring the question.

A hand appeared on the screen and pointed to the pages on the table.

'No idea.'

'But you've seen this before, Mr Rogan, in Rabbi Stein's study. This is David Herzl's diary, left to the Jewish Museum in Prague by his son, Sandor Kun, who you've met before in Budapest.'

'And you are showing me this because?'

'I will tell you. Please take a seat. This may take a while. The reason I've asked you to come here this morning has to do with David Herzl, the Postmaster of Treblinka, and his diary. Please listen carefully, because any kind of misunderstanding could be very costly.'

Jack locked eyes with Bartolli and pointed to a leather chair and a settee facing the bar.

'Deep down, Mr Rogan, you are a hopeless "adventure junkie", as some of your friends call you behind your back, who is always on the lookout for the next big story. At least we have that in common.'

'You really believe that? I don't go around killing people just to create a story. Unlike you.'

'Our methods may differ, but the results are the same: excitement, power, control. Isn't that right, Signora Bartolli?'

'I don't agree.'

'Care to tell us why?'

'Not really. Some follow their own demons, regardless.'

'And you think I am one of those?'

'Yes, I do.'

'Interesting. No wonder your uncannily accurate insights into the Landru case have fascinated me for years. Pity the French police didn't find them equally useful. No matter; Mr Rogan is very fortunate indeed to have you by his side. I think you will make a formidable team. And with what I have in mind, he will need all the help he can get.'

O'Hara chuckled, clearly enjoying himself.

'You were going to tell us about the Herzl diary,' said Jack, 'and why you've asked me to come here.'

'Yes. But before I do, have you given your next move some thought?' said O'Hara, referring to his imaginary chess game.

'Sure. White to c5.'

'The Sicilian defence. Of course. I expected that. This move is the best response by far to e4, which was my first move. Most grandmasters begin with the Sicilian. After that, things usually become interesting, as you are about to find out. And far more dangerous.'

9

Peter and Paul Cathedral, St Petersburg:
13 December, afternoon

Jack and Bartolli sat in shocked silence in the back of the hire car after their unsettling virtual meeting with O'Hara on the *Standard*. They were trying to come to terms with the outrageous proposal O'Hara had put forward, and make some sense of what had occurred that morning.

'Do you think he's gone insane?' asked Jack, breaking the silence.

'He may be criminally insane, but he's actually quite coherent and has put forward his arguments – crazy as they are – in a rational and orderly way. That's what makes him so dangerous. He's actually in a position to turn monstrous ideas into reality – *his* reality – regardless of the cost and the wreckage left behind.'

'Do you think he was serious about all this?' said Jack.

'Yes, deadly.'

'What did you make of Irina? What do you think her part is in all this?'

'Now, there's a fascinating character. Eccentric, weird, but highly intelligent and competent, I'd say. As we heard, she works for Ivanov; she's in charge of security. FSB trained, for sure. After all, Ivanov is one of Palin's cronies. You don't become a billionaire in Palin's Russia and stay alive any other way.'

'And O'Hara and Ivanov have gone into business together? Do you believe this?'

'I do. In some strange way it actually makes sense. Neither Ivanov nor O'Hara live in the real world. They live in their own universe. A universe they have created. Their obscene wealth allows them to indulge in this fantasy,' said Bartolli.

'And Irina?'

'You heard what O'Hara said. She's his eyes and ears. That may be so, but I've no doubt she's much more than that. I'm sure she was behind Tristan's birthday present and your mother's strange memory tree incident. Imaginative, subtle warnings designed to intimidate. Classic FSB. It would be a mistake not to take this seriously.'

'Do you think she was the one who killed Rabbi Stein and poisoned Paulo?'

'I don't think she did that personally, but I'm sure she arranged it all. That's what people of her standing do in the murky underworld of spies, secret agents and assassins. Very effectively.'

'In other words, she has replaced Spiridon 4, Dragan and Petrinko, who used to do O'Hara's dirty work in the past,' said Jack.

'Yes. O'Hara cannot function without people like that. With the Italian Mafia connection broken, a new source had to be found. I think Ivanov has replaced the Mafia, and Irina has replaced Dragan and Petrinko and all the others.'

'He sure knows how to find them.'

'People like O'Hara always do.'

'Before we go back to the hotel, I would like to show you something,' said Jack, changing direction. 'I told the driver …'

'Oh? What do you want to show me?'

'I want to show you where this all began.'

'What are you talking about?'

'We are going to the place where I met Konstantin Vasiliev. Adrienne arranged it all. She had dealt with him before.'

'Who is Konstantin Vasiliev?'

'A Russian scholar. Without him, the lost symphony may never have been found. He helped me with the Empress Alexandra letter, and showed me the way.'

'The way to where?'

'To David Herzl.'

'The Postmaster of Treblinka again?'

'Yes. Vasiliev pointed me to Sandor Kun, David Herzl's son in Budapest. He arranged a meeting and told me to follow my breadcrumbs of destiny.'

'And did you?'

'Yes. I met Kun in Budapest, and he suggested I go and talk to Rabbi Stein in Prague about the Golem of Treblinka and David Herzl. You see? It's all connected. Rabbi Stein was killed because of the Herzl diary, and what O'Hara just told us has to do with all that. Bizarre as it is. Ah, here we are.'

'Where are we?'

'At the Peter and Paul Cathedral where it all began. Come, I'll show you one of the most remarkable places in St Petersburg. The church is inside the Peter and Paul Fortress, a star-like fortress with a violent past on the Neva River. The cathedral is the oldest in St Petersburg and has a history like no other. Almost all the Russian emperors and empresses from Peter the Great to Nicholas II are buried in the cathedral. As a depository of Russian history, it has no equal. Come.'

Jack pointed to the entrance. 'I met Vasiliev just over there. I almost walked past him because he looked like a beggar in his shabby army overcoat and threadbare ushanka hat. Yet nothing could have been further from the truth. Another lesson in how deceptive appearances can be, and to never judge a book by its cover.'

Jack opened the door and let Bartolli go in first. 'Vasiliev was a remarkable scholar with an intimate knowledge of Russian history, who had fallen on hard times. He took me on an unforgettable tour of this place, from tomb to tomb. I only hope I can remember enough to take you around.'

'I'm sure you can,' said Bartolli and looked at the rows of white marble sarcophagi, final resting places of all-powerful Russian rulers who had shaped history and dominated the lives of millions. 'Wow! This is amazing. No, overwhelming would be a better word.'

'It is. There are forty-one tombs in here. Most of them above ground. Over there is the tomb of Peter the Great, and that one there belongs to Catherine the Great, who ruled for thirty-four years. And – come over here – this is the tomb of Emperor Alexander III, who spent a lot of time on his Imperial yacht, the *Standard*. The superyacht we visited today is named after it.'

'Amazing.'

'Yes. This reminds me of the *Kapuzinergruft*, the Imperial Crypt in Vienna where all the Habsburgs are buried. Another amazing place.'

'You and your stories, Jack.'

'And there's yet another connection I want to show you. It concerns Empress Alexandra, who's buried just over there in the side chapel, the Chapel of St Catherine the Martyr, with her husband, Nicholas II, and their children.'

'I didn't expect this.'

'Neither did I at the time; come.'

Jack walked over to the chapel and stopped. 'Vasiliev and I stood right here. He insisted on telling me the amazing story about Alexandra, Felix Yusupov, Rasputin and *Mat' Rossiya*, and how a letter entrusted to a nun by the doomed tsarina the day before she was murdered found its way to my grandmother Countess Bezukhova in France twenty-seven years after it was written.'

'Amazing.'

'It is. And part of that story relates to David Herzl, the master forger we just talked about. After his deportation from Warsaw to the Nazi death camp, Herzl became the Postmaster of Treblinka.'

Jack stopped talking as a group of visitors walked past.

'It was Vasiliev who showed me David Herzl's unique signature in the top right-hand corner of Alexandra's letter,' continued Jack softly. 'A tiny Star of David and a heart; the same signature discovered by an art expert in the forged Monet in Switzerland that caused such a fuss. Of course, I had seen that signature before, five years earlier, when it was discovered that the painting was actually a forgery by David Herzl.'

'As if we didn't have enough surprises today already, now *this*?' said Bartolli.

'True, and this is where it all began. Right here on this very spot, surrounded by all this.'

Jack pointed to the rows of tombs all around them. 'Watched over by emperors and empresses long gone.'

'You're a hopeless romantic.'

Jack shrugged. 'Vasiliev paved the way to Sandor Kun, Herzl's son, in Budapest, and that was the beginning of an incredible journey that still continues today.'

'Destiny?'

'Looks that way, don't you think? So, why don't we have a closer look at what O'Hara told us while we're here? After all, it's all about David Herzl, the Postmaster of Treblinka, and his diary, isn't it?'

'What did O'Hara call you, Jack?' said Bartolli, smiling. 'A hopeless adventure junkie?'

'I can live with that.'

Jack looked pensively into the chapel – the final resting place of the last tsar and his family – as he remembered Empress Alexandra's letter and the astonishing events that had put in train.

Jack pointed to the white sarcophagus in the chapel. 'I came back here again in 2018, Easter. It was early in the morning and the cathedral was still closed to the public. The governor of St Petersburg and a small group of officials were waiting for me.'

Bartolli looked at Jack, surprised. 'What was that all about?'

'It was the final chapter in a long, tragic story. A story of friendship, devotion and love, of heartache and betrayal in which the cataclysmic forces of history swept away the last tsar and ended with the brutal murder of him and his family.'

'What was that chapter about?'

'It was about a famous Fabergé Easter egg, presented by the tsar to his wife, Empress Alexandra, in 1917 as an Easter gift and a token of his love and affection. A year or so later, they were both dead. Murdered in a cellar in Yekaterinburg by the Bolsheviks. The egg, worth millions, was found in the Amber Safe of the Ritz in Paris. It had been left behind, abandoned, by Countess Bezukhova, my grandmother, in the hotel safe. She was killed by French resistance fighters as the Germans were leaving Paris at the end of the war. The precious egg had been entrusted to her by Alexandra for safekeeping as the countess left St Petersburg just before the revolution, to join her husband in exile in France.'

'What a story, but what were you doing here?'

'I came here to honour a promise made by my grandmother a long time ago. After a complicated court case, I was declared the rightful owner of the priceless egg. As I was Countess Bezukhova's only living relative with a valid claim, ownership was awarded to me.'

'But what were you doing here?' repeated Bartolli.

'I was returning the last Imperial Russian Fabergé Easter egg to where it belonged: to Alexandra.'

'How did you do that?'

Jack pointed again to the white sarcophagus in the chapel. 'I placed it on the top of that sarcophagus over there, marking the final resting place of Empress Alexandra and her family, who are buried underneath it.'

'That's very moving,' said Bartolli, choking with emotion. 'What happened to the Fabergé egg?'

'It was taken to the Fabergé Museum right here in St Petersburg, where it joined nine others crafted by the master that were already on display. It was renamed Bezukhova in honour of a friendship that had transcended the horrors of revolutions and war, and the relentless march of time.'

'What a story!

'A lot of time may have passed, but the forces of destiny are not ruled by time alone. There are more powerful forces at play here, timeless ones. Love, devotion, loyalty, friendship and the true meaning of a promise, to name but a few.'

Bartolli reached for Jack's hand beside her and held it.

'And while we are talking about promises,' continued Jack, 'I promise that I will do everything I can to protect those I love, whatever the cost. That's why I agreed to go along with O'Hara's bizarre demands and his sinister, evil game only a deranged mind could have invented. I will bide my time, but I will defeat him in the end and win this game. That, I promise.'

'I am sure you will, Jack, but don't forget he's a cunning, devious psychopath with no moral compass, who invents the rules as he goes and will kill anyone who stands in his way – without hesitation. We've seen that in the Landru case and the death mask murders. We know what he's capable of. To defeat a man like that, you will need all the help you can get. You can't do this alone.'

'Perhaps not, but I'll certainly give it my best shot,' said Jack, grinning.

'And I promise to walk by your side while you're doing it, if you'll let me,' said Bartolli, her eyes moist.

Jack squeezed Bartolli's hand in silent reply. Then he leaned forward and kissed her tenderly on the forehead, sealing a pact that one day soon would save his life.

10

Café Gerbeaud, Budapest: 14 December

Jack was early, as usual. Trying in vain to keep out the bone-chilling cold rising from the Danube, he turned up his collar and hurried across Vorosmarty ter towards Café Gerbeaud to meet Sandor Kun. Bartolli had returned to Rome the day before, and they had arranged to meet in Venice after Jack had found out what Kun had to say about O'Hara's astonishing revelations and crazy demands.

Jack sat down at a small marble table by the window and had just ordered some coffee when Kun walked in. Looking flustered and a little disorientated, he took off his hat, scarf and heavy, old-fashioned overcoat, and sat down facing Jack.

'I came as soon as I could.'

'Thank you.'

Kun rolled his eyes. 'Budapest trains! Some things never change. I still can't believe what you told me about Rabbi Stein. Horrible! And to think that about this time two years ago we were all in Jerusalem.'

'Delivering your father's letter to Yad Vashem in the presence of the pope,' said Jack.

Kun nodded, his gaunt face looking drawn. 'The Postmaster of Treblinka's final act. The closure of a long, tragic journey.'

'Perhaps not quite.'

'Oh? What do you mean?'

'The Postmaster of Treblinka's story is far from over.'

'You can't be serious! In what way?'

'Let's have some coffee and one of those delicious desserts you introduced me to last time.'

'Rigo Jancsi?'

'Yes, that's the one. Let's order and I'll tell you. Trust me, we'll both need something to sweeten this story.'

Jack began by telling Kun about the recent sinister threats, and what he had discovered in the Jewish cemetery in Prague. He then told him about the strange encounter with Irina and the virtual meeting with O'Hara on board the *Standard* in St Petersburg.

'So, O'Hara is alive and back in business?'

'Yes, very much so. And he's after me. Unfinished business.'

'In what way?'

'A man like O'Hara doesn't accept defeat. We almost destroyed him and his evil empire on the Obersalzberg in Bavaria, but he managed to get away with most of his assets and resources intact. That makes him very dangerous. A man like O'Hara is capable of anything and never gives up, or forgets.

'And he sees you as …?'

'The one responsible? Yes. Me, and those close to me who support me.'

'I can see that, but where do I—?'

'Fit into all this?'

Kun nodded as he scraped the last morsels of the delicious dessert off his plate.

'As you'll see in a moment, the way this is all interconnected is very strange, yet classic O'Hara. Only a psychopath like O'Hara could see a connection here and come up with a demented idea, an *obsession*, like this. It's all about ego and a reality game. A bizarre internet gambling site with obscene stakes so high it's almost too difficult to imagine, and with a following of super-rich, like-minded weirdos always on the lookout for the ultimate thrill. And what is even more bizarre, it seems you and I gave him the idea for this madness in the first place.'

'What do you mean?' asked Kun, surprised.

'It was something I referred to in my novella I published recently.'

'*The Postmaster of Treblinka*?'

'Yes.'

'I saw the reviews; very impressive. Congratulations!'

'Unlike my readers and critics, O'Hara found something buried in the novella others haven't noticed.'

'What? Tell me!'

'Something about David Herzl, your father. The Postmaster of Treblinka.'

'You're speaking in riddles, Jack.'

Jack sat back, enjoying himself for the first time that morning. As a storyteller, he couldn't help but admire the unexpected twists and turns in what O'Hara had discovered and seized upon. In a way it was a stroke of genius, albeit an evil one.

'I have no doubt Rabbi Stein was murdered because of your father's diary you left to the museum in Prague.'

'Are you sure?'

'Absolutely! O'Hara actually showed it to me during our recent virtual meeting. He had it right there on the table in front of him like some kind of trophy. It had obviously been stolen from Stein's study at the cemetery, where he kept it and where his body was found.'

'This is crazy!'

'Perhaps, but don't forget who we are dealing with here. Someone who was capable of the death mask murders, spanning several decades, can easily arrange to have an old, defenceless man killed. For nothing more than a thrill.'

'I can see that, but *why*?'

'The murder was part of a carefully staged gambling scenario to feed the insatiable appetites of the gambling fraternity following O'Hara's site on the darknet. I'm sure the whole thing was recorded and posted on the Net, with hundreds of thousands wagered on various stages of the outcome. All in crypto, with untraceable bitcoins, of course.'

'Just like in the *Death Mask Murders* game?'

'Yes. However, the theft of the Herzl diary is part of something far more complicated and clever. That is part of a much bigger, more sophisticated picture with a very different agenda.'

'Paint it for me,' said Kun, frowning.

'Good choice of words, as you will see in a moment, because all this has to do with a painting. A painting your father was asked to copy by SS-Brigadefuehrer Jurgen Stoop, the SS officer who suppressed the Warsaw Ghetto Uprising in 1943 with such unspeakable brutality.'

'I told you about all that back in 2017 – right here in this cafe, actually, if I remember correctly – when you asked me about the Golem of Treblinka and we discussed the Bezukhova letter.'

'Correct. Do you remember what painting your father was asked to copy?'

'Sure. It was a van Eyck.'

'And you also told me what happened to it.'

'Yes. The copy my father made was so good that the panel Stroop had assembled to judge it couldn't tell the copy from the original. This saved my father's life. He was taken from Warsaw, where he was arrested as one of the ringleaders of the uprising, to Treblinka, and instead of being executed he was given a 'studio', all the materials he needed, and told to restore paintings the Germans looted from occupied territories. That was the job that kept him alive, and how he became the Postmaster of Treblinka. That's when he met my mother, Ilona, who was also a painter and became his assistant.'

'I remember all that, but what happened to the painting?'

'Because the copy was that good, my father kept the original, and returned the copy to the Germans. In short, he switched the paintings. It was a small act of defiance. He had outwitted the Germans through his art.'

'Obviously at great risk to himself.'

'Quite. But you took risks every day in Treblinka, deadly ones. You were always only a few steps from the gas chamber. Dancing with death.'

'The Ballroom of Death, he called it, right?' said Jack.

'You have a good memory.'

'You told me that your father sent the original van Eyck – a very valuable painting – to Ilona's mother right here in Budapest through the *Feldpost*, the postal service operated by the Wehrmacht.'

'Yes. Another act of defiance. He was making fun of the Germans and their efficiency, and using them to his advantage,' said Kun.

'Ingenious, and very courageous. And as it turns out, this is precisely what O'Hara has zeroed in on, and is using right now to make me pay.'

'I don't understand.'

'He's using me. He wants me to find out what happened to the painting. No, more than that. He wants me to *find* it. That's the challenge he has thrown my way. A deadly one I cannot refuse.'

'But if you do?'

'Those close to me will perish. That's what those threats were all about. And as we both know, O'Hara can carry out those threats with a click of his mouse.'

Kun nodded and for a while sat in silence and looked out the window.

'Is that why you're here?'

'Yes. I need your help.'

'You've decided to go along with it, then?'

'I have. For the moment. I have to buy time and wait.'

'For what?'

'The right moment to defeat O'Hara once and for all. Until that happens, no-one's safe.'

'I can see that. How can I help?'

'What can you tell me about the painting? Do you know what happened to it?'

Kun took a deep breath and looked at Jack with sad eyes.

'As you know, the painting was by Jan van Eyck, the same painter who created the famous *Ghent Altarpiece* – also known as the *Adoration of the Mystic Lamb.*'

'According to the experts, one of the most influential paintings of all time. Inspired by the divine,' said Jack.

Kun nodded. 'Quite. And one of the most frequently stolen paintings in history. The painting my father copied was a small study for part of one of the much bigger side panels of the famous altarpiece. The study was known as *Golgotha* and showed Christ's crucifixion, set in a Flemish landscape with a small church in the background.'

'You seem to know a lot about this,' interjected Jack. 'How come?'

'My mother was a painter herself, remember? She was very interested in this painting. It was precious to her, not because of its value, but because of memories. Memories of my father and Treblinka, I suppose. We often spoke about it. It was hanging above the fireplace in our living room in Szentendre for years.'

'Do you know what happened to it?'

'My mother and I left Hungary during the revolution of 1956 and went to live in Vienna with a cousin. My grandmother refused to leave and stayed behind in our home in Szentendre just outside Budapest, where I still live. Mum took the painting with her. It was the most valuable thing we owned.'

'What happened to the painting?' Jack asked again.

'Mum sold it on the black market to an art dealer in Vienna shortly after we arrived. She desperately needed money.'

'Do you have a photo?'

'No, that's just the thing. I don't think there is one. I've certainly never seen one. No-one seems to know what the painting looked like, exactly. We only know about it from various descriptions, and reputation, of course.

'I see. That's the end of it then, I suppose?'

'Not quite.'

'Oh?'

'I returned to Hungary in 1990 after communist rule came to an end and the Eastern bloc disintegrated. Slowly, Hungary became a democratic country. My mother was still alive and came with me. We went back to Szentendre. It happened a few years later. In about 1995, I think.'

'What happened?'

'An art historian who was writing a book about Jan van Eyck and the *Ghent Altarpiece* somehow tracked us down and came to visit us.

He knew a lot about *Golgotha* and wanted to find out how my mother had obtained it.'

'Fascinating. How did he find you?'

'Not sure, but he did say that during his research he had come across some art dealers my mother went to see in Vienna at the time, who remembered a Hungarian woman offering a van Eyck for sale. One of the dealers almost went through with the purchase, but got cold feet in the end because the painting was so well known and, of course, he suspected it had been stolen. He still had some paperwork with the name Kun, and Szentendre as the address.'

'Amazing. Do you remember the name of that art historian who visited you, or the name of the book?'

'No, but I do remember he sent Mum a copy later.'

'Do you think you still have it?' asked Jack.

'Could be. I'll have a look if you like.'

'Could you? You know how important this is.'

'Of course. How about we meet at the Gellert for a swim and a game of chess tomorrow? I haven't been there in ages.'

'You're on! But you'll have to let me win at least once. Not like last time ...'

'Perhaps.'

'All right, but first, how about we have another Rigo Jancsi?'

'Definitely,' said Kun, smiling at last. 'These stories need another sweetener, for sure.'

11

Gellert Thermal Baths, Budapest: 15 December

Jack got out of the taxi and looked up at the imposing Art Nouveau facade of the entrance to the famous baths that had been in use since the thirteenth century. Famous for its healing spring, the Gellert became very popular during the Turkish occupation in the sixteenth and seventeenth centuries. At that time it was known as the 'muddy bath' because sediment from the mineral spring settled on the bottom of the thermal pools, making the waters cloudy every time the bottom was disturbed.

As soon as he walked through the doors, Jack knew something was wrong. The foyer was teeming with police officers, and the entry leading to the change rooms was cordoned off. To Jack it looked like a crime scene.

A strange feeling of dread came over him as he kept looking around, searching for Kun. They had arranged to meet inside by one of the pools, as Kun wanted to arrive early before breakfast and have a swim before their meeting.

One of the uniformed attendants walked up to Jack. 'The baths are closed, I am sorry,' he said in English, guessing Jack wasn't a local.

'What happened?'

'We had an incident.'

'What kind of incident?'

'I can't say,' said the attendant, looking troubled.

'I was supposed to meet a friend here, but I cannot see him. Could he be inside the baths?'

The attendant shook his head. 'Everyone has been asked to leave. There is no-one left inside. I would suggest you leave as well, sir.'

Jack nodded and turned away. Instead of walking to the door, he walked up to one of the police officers standing at the entry to the change rooms. 'Can you please tell me who's in charge here?' he asked. 'I may have some information ...'

The officer pointed to a man in a dark suit talking to a group of uniformed officers near the entrance. Jack walked over to the man and introduced himself.

'I don't know what happened here, but I was supposed to meet a friend here this morning. I'm sure he would have arrived by now. I'm a little concerned because I cannot see him ...'

'What's your friend's name?' asked the officer.

'Sandor Kun.'

The expression on the officer's face confirmed Jack's worst fears.

'Please come with me,' said the officer and guided Jack over to the entrance to the change rooms.

'Have you known Mr Kun long?' asked the officer.

'I have known him for a number of years. Why do you ask?'

The officer stopped and looked at Jack. 'I'm afraid I have some bad news. Mr Kun was found floating in one of the pools early this morning, dead,' said the officer, watching Jack carefully.

'Foul play?' asked Jack, shocked.

'Yes, we believe he was murdered.'

12

Kremlin, Moscow: 15 December

Joseph Ilych Palin, President of the Russian Federation, sat alone at his desk in his Kremlin office. Located in the north wing of the imposing Kremlin Senate built by Catherine the Great in 1776, the modest, rectangular, oak-panelled room, without any paintings, photographs or personal effects of any kind, was a far cry from the lavish offices of other world leaders. Compared to the Oval Office, or the office of the French President in the Élysée Palace with its stunning marble fireplace and priceless antiques, it was quite ordinary and lacking in character or style, except for one thing: a famous Russian icon at the back of the office, facing the president's desk.

Anyone looking at the short, balding man approaching seventy with prominent cheekbones and heavy Slavic facial features would have walked past him in the street without giving him a second look. But looks can be deceptive. Sitting behind the desk was one of the most ruthless and powerful men on the planet, who in a career spanning more than forty years had clawed his way to the top, from KGB intelligence officer, to director of the FSB, to prime minister, and then president of Russia.

A meteoric rise like that didn't happen by chance. It required burning ambition, hunger for power and a determination to succeed at any cost, regardless of the wreckage left behind, personal or otherwise. And, of course, luck and being in the right place at the right time.

Now that he had reached the pinnacle and made constitutional changes to ensure he stayed there, it was time to focus his ambition on something lasting; something that would change the course of history and allow him to take his place next to such greats as Lenin and Stalin, who had transformed Russia and elevated it from an agrarian peasant society to a superpower.

Palin reached for a map of the Soviet Union prior to its disintegration in 1991. He always kept it on his desk and studied it often. It showed an empire of staggering size stretching ten thousand kilometres from its western borders to its coast in the Far East, with a population of three hundred million. Then, it was the largest empire in the world.

But things had changed rapidly after 1991. While still the largest country on earth, Russia had shrunk considerably and lost a lot of territory, power, prestige and influence. Fifteen former Soviet republics had gained independence. Palin ran his fingers over the map and traced the outline of Estonia, Latvia, Lithuania and Moldova, before coming to rest on Ukraine. *Russia without Ukraine is just a big country*, he thought. *With Ukraine, it is an empire!*

Then he turned to the television on his left, turned it on, and watched a recording of the recent protests and riots in Belarus after the controversial re-election of Alexander Lukashenko for a sixth term the year before.

Palin could see a stark warning in those protests. Times were changing rapidly. It was no longer possible to control the younger generation in the same way as their parents, who were used to and accepting of the yoke of the state that Palin's power depended on. Their offspring had the internet and social media to influence their ideals. Something had to be done.

The protests against Lukashenko's re-election had been loud and unprecedented, with pro-democracy activists taking to the streets and becoming very vocal.

One of these was Sergei Tikhanovsky, a popular blogger who described Lukashenko as a 'cockroach', reminding people of the popular Russian children's poem *The Monster Cockroach* in which an insect, the cockroach, came to rule over humankind by devious threats and bullying, only to be devoured by a sparrow. In Tikhanovsky's new world, Lukashenko was the cockroach to be defeated by the Slipper Revolution, which would crush the cockroach with the slipper of resistance, no longer willing to tolerate corruption and rigged elections.

Palin kept staring at the map in front of him as he did almost every day, lamenting what had been and dreaming of a place in history as the one who would restore Russia to its former glory. And to do that, he knew he had to bring lost territories back into the orbit of Mother Russia and curb the troubling influence and expansion of the West, moving steadily closer.

He had attempted to do just that throughout his presidency by way of various means, both economic and diplomatic, but had met with fierce resistance, especially from the young. The recent election protests in Belarus were a stark reminder of the ever-growing danger. Something more radical was needed, but Palin had so far hesitated to go down that path, afraid of the consequences. But time was running out, and the legacy and place in history he was craving seemed more distant and elusive than ever.

Then a soft, seductive voice whispered in his ear: *'You can do it! You are the chosen one, but first you must eliminate the one who stands in your way and can defeat you. Remember, history favours the brave.'*

Palin pushed the map aside, but the voice wouldn't go away. It became stronger and more assertive. Palin nodded; the time for action had come, however risky and dangerous it may turn out to be. Taking a deep breath, he picked up the phone on his desk and called one of his most trusted operatives in the FSB.

'Will no-one rid me of this troublesome fanatic?' he shouted into the receiver. 'It's time for action. Do it now!'

The man on the other end of the line paled. He knew exactly what that meant. The instructions he had expected, but feared, had finally arrived.

Feeling better, Palin put down the phone and sat back, not realising that his words had put in train a chain of events that would cost the lives of untold thousands, cause unimaginable misery and hardship, and transform the world order, but without restoring Russia to its former glory. What he didn't realise either was that by listening to the seductive whispers clouding his judgement, he was securing a place in history for himself that was very different from the one he had in mind.

13

Gatekeeper's Cottage, Kuragin chateau: 16 December

As soon as the taxi crossed the bridge at the entrance to the chateau grounds and approached the familiar Gatekeeper's Cottage, Jack began to relax. It had begun to snow and Jack smiled as he remembered what Countess Kuragin used to say about the old pine trees groaning under heavy snow cover. To her, they looked like bearded old men in overcoats coming home from the wars. It felt good to be back on familiar turf after a harrowing day of interrogation in Budapest, trying to make some sense of Kun's brutal murder.

Instead of going back to Venice as he had originally planned, Jack had decided to meet up with Dupree and discuss the recent turbulent events. Jack had kept Dupree informed about his St Petersburg encounter with Irina and O'Hara on the *Standard*, but had only spoken to him briefly from Budapest before boarding the plane to Paris that morning.

'You look like you need a drink,' said Dupree and reached for the whisky bottle on the kitchen table as Jack walked in and dropped his duffel bag by the door.

'Make it a big one.'

'That bad?'

'Worse than you can imagine.'

Dupree filled up two tumblers and handed one to Jack. 'Cheers.'

'This is spinning out of control,' said Jack. He took off his jacket and sat down facing Dupree. 'First Stein, now Kun. *Why?* I'm supposed to follow leads, not kill off those who help me. It doesn't make any sense!'

'Perhaps it does,' said Dupree and opened his laptop.

'What do you mean?'

'I think there are two separate explanations here. After our lunch last week, Lapointe contacted Cesaria Borroni and Grimaldi in

97

Florence and asked for their help. You know how clever their colleague Clara Samartini was in infiltrating O'Hara's encrypted *Death Mask Murders* game on his Darknet Bazaar gambling site.'

'Sure. What did they say?'

'They promised to do everything they can to help. They want O'Hara stopped and brought to justice just as much as we do, especially when we told them that you are involved and why. You have good friends everywhere, Jack. Just as well, because I have a feeling you will need all the help you can muster to get on top of this ruthless game and stay alive.'

'Thanks, Claude.' Jack pushed his empty glass towards Dupree. 'Just the encouragement I was looking for. I think I need another one.'

'You will when you see this. Well, Samartini has done it again!'

'Done what?'

Dupree called up the material Borroni had sent him earlier that day, and turned his laptop around so Jack could see the screen. 'Here, see for yourself. These two videos have recently been posted on a new encrypted gambling site.'

'Oh, my God! It's happening all over again.'

'It sure is.'

'How on earth did Samartini get this? And so quickly?'

'Grimaldi made some kind of deal with two Italian punters who were involved in gambling in the *Death Mask Murders* game on the darknet. You know how these things work. In return for a lighter sentence the punters pass on information to Grimaldi should the site become active again. It did, and they gave Samartini everything she needed to gain access to the new site. Simple and effective.'

Jack looked impressed.

The first video was a graphic close-up of Stein's brutal murder in his study above the cemetery in Prague. Jack had to look away when the camera closed in on Stein's contorted face as he lay dying on the floor in a pool of blood, the back of his head crushed to a pulp.

'This is obscene,' whispered Jack.

'Wait, it gets worse,' said Dupree and called up the second video showing Kun's murder the day before. Kun was about to get into one of the pools at the Gellert, which Jack recognised, when two large hands appeared on the screen and grabbed him around the neck from behind and expertly twisted his head violently to the right, breaking his neck and killing him instantly. The next scene showed Kun floating peacefully on his back in the empty pool, his sightless, glassy eyes staring at the vaulted ceiling.

'Only an expert assassin could have done this,' said Jack.

'Special Forces, I'd say. Mercenaries, most likely. That's what Lapointe thought as soon as he saw this. To kill someone quickly in this way takes skill and experience. It was early in the morning, and there was no-one around as yet. The killing only took seconds, but the rest must have taken careful planning and nerve.'

'And you think this answers the why?'

'Sure. It's obvious, isn't it? O'Hara's gambling site is back in business, better and stronger than before, and you are providing him with the subject matter he can turn into an exciting story and feed to the sensation-hungry punters. You should have seen the amounts being wagered on the various stages and outcome of the killing. Outrageous. Just as we saw in the *Death Mask Murders* game.'

'You said there were two explanations.'

'The second is a clear message, and a reminder. It tells you what will happen to you and, perhaps more importantly, to those you love if you step out of line. The warnings, remember?'

Jack nodded.

'We already sent a copy of this to the authorities in Budapest. Let's see what they can do with it. Very little, I suspect, but we didn't give it away for free.'

'What do you mean?'

'You know Lapointe. He's a shrewd operator.'

'Sure, but—'

'When I told him that you had arranged to meet Kun that morning to discuss an important book you needed in connection with your investigation ...'

'Yes, what of it?'

'Lapointe suggested intelligence sharing with the Hungarians. He proposed an information exchange.'

'I don't follow.'

'Lapointe wanted to know if a book had been found among Kun's belongings in his change room locker, which apparently had not been broken into. The assassin must have left in a hurry straight after the murder, or wasn't looking for anything. Disturbed, perhaps; who knows? In any case, there was no time.'

Jack looked stunned. 'And?'

'The Hungarians agreed. There was an exchange: a video for a book.'

Dupree called up an image and showed it to Jack.

'I thought you would be interested to know that a briefcase was found in the locker, and inside the briefcase was a book. This one ...'

Stunned, Jack stared at the image in front of him. It showed the cover of a book entitled *The Ghent Altarpiece. The most frequently stolen painting in history*. The author was Albert Hoffmeister.

Dupree held up the bottle of whisky and smiled. 'Another one?'

14

Winter Palace, St Petersburg: 17 December

To hold a major political demonstration in front of the Winter Palace on the Neva River in St Petersburg was a stroke of genius. It was also very brave and ambitious. The former royal residence of the Russian tsars was not only one of the most opulent and significant monuments in the country, it also housed the Hermitage Museum – famous around the world for its extraordinary art collection and visited by millions each year. As an architectural expression of wealth, power, extravagance and grandeur it had no equal.

Despite the extreme cold rising from the river and the heavy snow cover, a huge crowd had gathered to hear their hero Novotny speak. Most were familiar with the many sensational videos he had posted on his YouTube channel and social media sites, and were eagerly awaiting the big announcement about massive corruption in the Kremlin, which he had promised to expose. Not only had Novotny promised an announcement, he had also promised irrefutable proof and revelations that would rock Russia to the core.

Anatoly Novotny had been a thorn in Palin's side for years. Tall, in his early forties, well-educated – he held degrees in political science and economics from Oxford and Yale – he was a brilliant public speaker who could beguile his audience with an infectious passion that was difficult to resist. A patriot who loved his country deeply, he had made it his mission to expose the monstrous corruption that had dominated the Kremlin for years and had drained much-needed resources from a country that needed them desperately. He had skilfully used the internet to reach a huge audience and build a following in Russia and abroad that would have been the envy of many a president or business tycoon around the world.

A ripple of excitement ran through the crowd standing shoulder to shoulder in front of the Winter Palace, as Novotny's car inched its way slowly towards the makeshift podium erected in the centre of Dvortsovaya Ploshchad, the famous Palace Square.

The crowd roared as Novotny got out of the car and followed his minders to the podium, keen to begin his speech as soon as possible. As an experienced orator he knew how to work the crowd. The key was always to gauge the mood and tailor his approach. Novotny sensed urgency and expectation, and launched straight to the heart of his address and the message he wanted to get across that morning. He realised this was a watershed moment of no return that would inspire supporters, but also galvanise his enemies like never before. No stranger to danger, Novotny knew the risks and was prepared to take them and face the consequences.

The FSB agent standing near the generator powering the loud-speakers watched Novotny approach the podium. Wearing overalls with a company logo on the back, like all the other technicians near-by, he put on his gloves and waited for the right moment.

The moment came just before Novotny reached the podium. The agent walked up to the microphone and tapped it with his gloved fingertips to test the volume. Confident that no-one else would touch the mike before Novotny began, he covertly smeared deadly novichok around the handle and then quickly left the podium just as Novotny approached the microphone and held up his hands, acknowledging the rockstar welcome.

Satisfied that the first part of his assignment had been completed as planned, the agent returned to the generator. The second, even more crucial part would come at the end of Novotny's speech. The microphone would have to be removed quickly before anyone could touch it. This was critical, as even the slightest skin contact with the handle coated with the lethal nerve agent could be fatal. This had to be avoided at all costs, to make sure no evidence of the poisoning remained that could be traced and implicate the Kremlin.

After the crowd had calmed down, Novotny pointed to the Winter Palace. 'If you think this is grand, my friends, wait until you see what I have to show you. This is a story about extravagance almost impossible to imagine, and the biggest bribe in history. And it all involves your money!'

Novotny then provided a point-by-point description of an astonishing secret building project near the town of Gelendzhik on the Black Sea in Krasnodar Krai, comprising a massive estate owned by the FSB that was thirty-nine times the size of Monaco, with seventy square kilometres of land.

The crowd gasped as it heard that this estate had its own port, a church, an underground ice hockey rink, a no-fly zone, and border checkpoints, which effectively made it a private state within Russia that had cost one hundred billion roubles, a staggering amount of money impossible for most of the demonstrators to comprehend.

'And would you like to know who owns this estate?'

The crowd cheered.

'None other than our President Palin. And don't just take my word for it. I have *proof!*'

The crowd cheered again, louder.

Novotny paused to allow this to sink in. He also kept an eye on the rows of armed riot police standing in the background, fully expecting them to move in at any moment and start making arrests, but nothing happened. Encouraged, Novotny decided to continue and up the pace. He explained that the eye-watering amounts of money needed to build this project, which he called 'The New Tsar's Palace,' and the 'most audacious corruption in history,' had been siphoned off by corrupt men close to Palin from some of the biggest corporations in the country.

Novotny couldn't believe his luck: despite having made allegations of a most serious kind warranting instant arrest and prosecution, the police still hadn't moved in. Shaking his head, he decided to press on and stepped closer to the microphone.

'We have all heard about the monster cockroach in Belarus and the Slipper Revolution, and what happened to that and why.' This was a clear reference to the recent rigged elections in Belarus and the controversial re-election of Lukashenko, which had only been possible with Russia's help.

'Well, the despicable cockroach in Belarus is but a harmless, pitiful ant when compared with the arrogant, mighty cockroach here in the Kremlin, growing richer and more powerful by the day,' continued Novotny. 'But we also know what happens to mighty cockroaches when the people decide to act. They are crushed! And you, my friends, can make this happen!'

Novotny reached into his briefcase, pulled out a felt slipper and held it up.

The jubilant crowd roared.

One of Novotny's minders walked up to Novotny from behind and tapped him on the shoulder, a clear sign it was high time to leave before the peaceful demonstration turned into a riot fuelled by arrests and beatings, or worse.

Holding up the slipper with his right hand, Novotny followed his bodyguards surrounding him to the waiting car, and got in.

Even before Novotny reached the car, the FSB agent had removed the microphone from the stand, and had disappeared into the crowd.

What Novotny couldn't have known was that the police had strict instructions not to move in before Novotny had left the square. He had to be allowed to get away safely before any arrests were made and the crowd was dispersed with batons and water cannons.

Novotny was due to fly to Moscow the next morning to attend a rally in the historical Red Square, during which he would reveal the proof of his extravagant allegations. It was expected this demonstration would be attended by thousands.

During the evening, Novotny fell ill while working on his speech in his hotel room in St Petersburg. His partner found him unconscious on the floor and called the hotel doctor. After examining Novotny, the doctor indicated the symptoms suggested some kind of poisoning. Something like this had been feared, even expected, by Novotny's entourage and supporters, and his partner activated a plan that had been in place for some time. To admit Novotny to a public hospital in Russia wasn't considered safe in the circumstances. A private plane was dispatched immediately from Germany to evacuate Novotny.

The plane, with emergency medical staff on board, arrived early the next morning and Novotny – by now in a coma – was stabilised and taken to the airport. To everyone's surprise, instead of causing problems with his departure, the authorities approved the flight and Novotny was flown to Berlin and taken to the Charité University Hospital for treatment.

The FSB had kept a careful eye on Novotny after he left the demonstration at the Winter Palace and was fully aware of what was happening. To have Novotny leave Russia alive was considered a fortuitous development no-one in the FSB had expected. It was far better if he died while in the care of a German hospital, than on his way to Moscow to stage another anti-corruption demonstration. A favourable spin could then be placed on the entire affair, blaming Western propaganda for his death and the way he died.

15

Café Central, Vienna: 18 December

Jack turned into Herrengasse, the street he had been looking for, glanced at his watch, and made haste. He didn't want to be late for his meeting. Finding Albert Hoffmeister, the author of the book in Herzl's briefcase, hadn't been easy, but Jack's publishing house in New York had done a great job in tracking down the elderly art critic, who still lived in Vienna. Jack had even been given a phone number and had contacted Hoffmeister and explained his interest in the book. Instead of being cold-shouldered and fobbed off, Jack could hardly get Hoffmeister off the phone, and they agreed to meet at the historical Café Central in the afternoon.

As it turned out, Café Central was an excellent choice for several reasons. The famous cafe opened its doors in 1876 and soon became a popular meeting place for Viennese intellectuals and politicians. Leon Trotsky, Stalin and Lenin visited often, and Sigmund Freud regularly played chess on the first floor. Hitler, too, was a patron and was particularly interested in the Tarot games for which the cafe was well known. Fascinated by the occult, Hitler was drawn to séances and exotic sessions promising to explore the mystical and the unknown.

It isn't often that one is greeted by a formally dressed doorman wearing a bowler hat when entering a cafe, but that was exactly what happened when Jack approached the entrance.

'Meeting someone, sir?' asked the doorman politely as he opened to door to let Jack pass.

'Yes. Albert Hoffmeister.'

'Ah. That's him over there. One of our regulars,' said the doorman and pointed to an elderly, well-dressed gentleman sitting next to one of the striking pillars supporting the lavishly decorated, vaulted ceiling. Jack walked over to him and introduced himself.

The man, who stood up and shook his hand, reminded Jack of a portrait of Sigmund Freud he had seen in the Freud Museum in

London not that long ago. Same carefully trimmed white beard; same small, round glasses; same intense look, radiating intelligence and curiosity. The off-white shirt and limp bow tie – a little threadbare around the edges – hinted at an elderly bachelor struggling with domesticity and living by himself.

'A pleasure to meet you, Mr Rogan,' said Hoffmeister in perfect English, but with a heavy German accent. 'I must say, it isn't often someone like me – old and at the end of his journey – gets to meet someone like you, famous and in his prime. I come here most mornings to have a coffee and read the papers. On rare occasions, I have a game of chess with one of my friends; one of the few who is still alive. That's all. A mere shadow of what I once used to do and used to be. Eventually, the relentless march of time catches up with all of us.'

'Thank you for agreeing to meet with me at such short notice,' said Jack and gave Hoffmeister his best, most encouraging smile. 'But as you will see in a moment, this is both urgent and important. And I believe you, Herr Hoffmeister, are the man who can help me.'

'Intriguing. I cannot possibly imagine how, or why.'

Over an *Einspänner* – a traditional Viennese coffee with cream served in a tall glass and dusted with icing sugar – and a huge slice of Sachertorte, an Austrian culinary speciality, Jack told Hoffmeister why he had contacted him and why he was so interested in his book dealing with the *Ghent Altarpiece*, *Golgotha*, and the Herzl connection, but he didn't disclose the real reason he desperately wanted to find out what happened to the painting. He also didn't tell him about O'Hara and the threats.

'Like you, Herr Hoffmeister, I want to find out what happened to the painting, albeit perhaps for different reasons.'

Jack paused, collecting his thoughts.

'You are obviously interested in the story for academic reasons,' he continued. 'Your book makes that quite clear. You are an art historian. I, on the other hand have different interests. As you know, I'm a writer ...'

'I know. I looked you up on the Net.'

'Then you may have noticed I have just published a novella – *The Postmaster of Treblinka* – about David Herzl, Kun's father. I met Kun as part of my research. That's when he told me the story about *Golgotha* and how his father switched the paintings and substituted the copy for the original, which he later sent to Budapest through the Feldpost. A fascinating story, you must admit. As a writer, I find it irresistible.'

'I can imagine. And I suppose you are here to find out what I may know about—'

'What happened to the painting; yes.'

Sipping his coffee, Hoffmeister pointed to Jack's plate, which was almost empty. 'Who would have thought that wheat flour, apricot jam, dark chocolate, rum and almond meal could produce such a delicious creation,' he said.

Surprised, Jack looked at Hoffmeister. 'You're right,' he said. 'It's all in the know-how, not the ingredients.'

'You are absolutely correct, Mr Rogan, and the story behind the creation of this legendary dessert proves it. Often works of genius are due to inspiration and mere chance. Back in 1832, Prince Klemens von Metternich asked Franz Sacher, then just sixteen, to quickly prepare a dessert for his guest, as the court pastry chef was feeling poorly. Sacher, who loved chocolate, rose to the challenge and came up with a unique creation: a layer of cherries and apricot jam between two layers of chocolate sponge cake covered in a dark chocolate glaze; an inspired idea.'

Jack nodded, wondering where Hoffmeister was going with this.

'In a way, young Sacher was no different from painters in the fifteenth century like Jan van Eyck, who invented new materials and techniques and broke with tradition to create something extraordinary, admired through the ages. Van Eyck invented oil glazing, which replaced earlier egg tempera methods and perfected oil-on-panel painting, for which he is so famous. That's why the brilliant colours, the shades of light, and the luminous quality of his paintings have survived unchanged to this very day. The *Ghent Altarpiece* is an excellent example of this.'

'I've read all about that in your book,' said Jack, who'd had had a quick look at Hoffmeister's book – *The Ghent Altarpiece. The most frequently stolen painting in history* – online before coming to the meeting.

Hoffmeister smiled at Jack. 'Good, but I'm sure you didn't come here to discuss esoteric subjects like oil glazing on panels.'

'You're right. I didn't. I am particularly interested in *Golgotha* and your meeting with Sandor Kun and his mother in Szentendre in 1995, which you mentioned in your book.'

'You are well informed, Mr Rogan. You said on the phone that you met with Mr Kun in Budapest recently. Why didn't you ask *him* about all this?' asked Hoffmeister, frowning.

'I did, but unfortunately he died before I could fully explore this subject with him. He was murdered in Budapest three days ago,' Jack added quietly, dropping the bombshell.

'Are you serious?' whispered Hoffmeister, breaking the silence, his shocked expression a clear indication he was unaware of Kun's murder.

'Yes. I was there.'

'You were? And are you suggesting his murder could have something to do with the painting, with *Golgotha?*'

'Yes. That's why I am here, asking for your help.'

A veteran art historian, Hoffmeister was used to strange stories, even serious crimes, involving works of art. His book had made that quite clear. After Jack's shock revelation, he began to open up.

'Interesting ... But before we can talk about *Golgotha,* we must first consider the *Ghent Altarpiece* because *Golgotha* is part of it, albeit a somewhat curious part.'

'In what way?' asked Jack.

'*The Adoration of the Mystic Lamb,* as the *Ghent Altarpiece* was known at the time, has a history like no other,' said Hoffmeister, becoming animated and warming to his subject. 'It is one of the most significant and influential paintings ever conceived by an artist.'

'I understand it has been stolen more often than any other painting in history,' said Jack, who had carefully researched the subject. He knew from experience it was always prudent to have at least a basic understanding of a subject to be discussed with an expert. It was a good way to elevate the discussion to an entirely different level made possible only through mutual trust and earned respect.

'That's right. From the very moment the altarpiece was presented to the public by van Eyck in the Cathedral of Saint Bavo in Ghent in 1432, it deeply affected all who saw it.'

'In what way?'

'They saw in the painting something that became part of its fame and reputation – legend if you will – that followed it throughout its extraordinary history.'

'What did they see?'

'Divine inspiration.'

'And do you think it was because of this reputation that it was stolen so many times and involved in countless crimes?'

'Yes, I believe so. How else can we explain that during its almost six-hundred-year history it has been stolen six times and been part of thirteen major, well-documented crimes, yet on each occasion, it eventually found its way back home to the Cathedral of Saint Bavo in ways that often appear nothing short of miraculous.'

'Incredible,' said Jack, shaking his head.

'Consider this: The precious painting narrowly survived certain destruction by marauding Calvinist fanatics during the Great Icono-clasm in 1566—'

'Bent on erasing all images of God by shattering stained-glass windows and burning statues and paintings throughout the Netherlands,' said Jack.

'Correct. Do you know how the altarpiece survived these mindless acts of barbarism?'

'It was saved by pious citizens. They dismantled the altarpiece and hid the panels in the bell tower of the Cathedral.'

'I'm impressed.'

'It's in your book.' Jack shrugged modestly. 'And then the four central panels were looted by the French in 1794 and taken back to the Louvre in Paris by Napoleon's victorious army.'

'Where they remained until Napoleon was defeated at Waterloo in 1815, and the newly restored King Louis XVIII returned them to Ghent. Do you know why?' asked Hoffmeister.

'Because that city had protected him during the French Revolution and given him shelter. It was a gesture of gratitude.'

Hoffmeister nodded. 'But this reunion was short-lived. In 1816, a greedy priest stole the wing panels and sold them on the black market. For a while they disappeared and no-one knew what had happened to them until, almost miraculously, they resurfaced in a museum in Berlin—'

'Where they were on display until 1919, when they became part of the Treaty of Versailles and were eventually once again returned to Ghent,' said Jack.

'Quite so. And then came Hitler, a deranged fanatic who was obsessed with the occult and the supernatural. He was convinced the *Ghent Altarpiece* was a coded map that would show the initiated the way to certain Christian relics with supernatural powers.'

'And *Golgotha* was an important part of this, right?' said Jack, pleased by the way the conversation was finally getting closer to the subject he was interested in.

'Yes, it was. The most important one, perhaps, and that's why Hitler instructed his henchmen to locate it and bring it to Berlin. According to some sources, the altarpiece was on its way to the Vatican for safekeeping in 1943 when it was intercepted by the Nazis and hidden in an abandoned salt mine at Altaussee in Austria. This was a secret location where countless masterpieces looted by the Germans, known as *Raubkunst*, were stored—'

'And that brings us to David Herzl, the master forger of Warsaw, doesn't it?' interjected Jack.

'Yes. And do you know why?'

'For some reason we don't know, before it was hidden in the mine in Altaussee – not far from here, actually – the *Ghent Altarpiece* passed through Treblinka as part of a stolen art delivery arranged by SS-Brigadefuehrer Jurgen Stroop, who had suppressed the Warsaw Ghetto Uprising and arrested Herzl as one of the ringleaders.'

'Correct.'

'And Herzl was asked to make a copy of *Golgotha* – a small, exquisite oil painting by van Eyck attached to the back of one of the altar panels – to show the Nazis what he could do,' said Jack. 'In essence, this was a life-and-death test. If Herzl could make a copy of this stunning painting that was as good as the original, he would not be executed for his part in the Warsaw Ghetto Uprising, but instead put to work in Treblinka by SS Captain Theodor van Eupen – the commander of the Treblinka labour camp – to restore looted paintings for the Nazis before they were dispatched to Berlin.'

'Do you know what happened to the altarpiece after it was hidden in the salt mines at Altaussee?' asked Hoffmeister.

'Not really. All I know is that it was once again returned to Ghent after the war. I've just seen it displayed in its new multi-million-dollar display cage in the St Bavo cathedral.'

'Have you heard of the Monuments Men?'

'Of course,' said Jack. 'They were a group of Allied art experts trying to locate and preserve art treasures stolen by the Nazis during the war. There was even a film made about them – *The Monuments Men* – starring George Clooney, I think.'

'That's right. In May 1945, Captain Robert Posey, one of the Monuments Men, entered the salt mine and there, deep inside one of the mineshafts he found something remarkable: the *Ghent Altarpiece*. Undamaged and complete, except for one thing.'

'Something was missing?'

'Yes. *Golgotha*,' said Hoffmeister.

'The Herzl copy, you mean? We know what happened to the original.'

'Quite. Apparently, the copy was taken to Hitler and was in his bunker in Berlin right to the very end. As you know, he committed suicide with Eva Braun. Their corpses were burned just before the Russians captured the bunker and destroyed it.'

'I know,' said Jack.

'Obviously, Kun would have told you all this.'

'He did but clearly there is more, much more ...'

Lost in thought, Hoffmeister sat back and looked pensively up at the stunning ceiling. 'I've tried desperately for years to find out what happened to the original *Golgotha* after Kun's mother sold it on the black market right here in Vienna in 1957.'

'That's all in your book too,' said Jack. 'But I am intrigued by one thing that isn't.'

'What's that?'

'How did you know that Kun's mother sold the painting in Vienna in 1957, and how did you manage to trace her to Szentendre in 1995? There's nothing in your book about that, and Kun couldn't help me with this either.'

'A valid point, Herr Rogan. You are obviously a very attentive reader. I found Kun through a rumour. If a well-known painting surfaces suddenly and is offered for sale, it leaves a trace in certain circles; in this case, certain art dealers who were active at the time. As I was writing my book, I came across this rumour that van Eyck's *Golgotha* had been offered for sale in the fifties by a Hungarian woman. One dealer I interviewed remembered the painting and the woman clearly. He almost concluded the purchase, but got cold feet at the last moment. He remembered the name of the woman: Ilona Kun from Szentendre in Hungary. That's how I found Kun.'

'Quite a detective story.'

'Tracing missing or stolen art often is and, as we've just seen, the story of the *Ghent Altarpiece*, and *Golgotha* in particular, is perhaps one of the most incredible stories of them all.'

'Sure is, but unfortunately that's where the story seems to end; rather abruptly, I thought,' said Jack.

'Regrettably, yes it does, but there's a good reason for this. My investigation came to an abrupt end, as you put it.'

'How come?'

'There was ...'

'What?'

'An incident.'

'There's nothing in your book about that, either. What kind of incident?' asked Jack, reaching for his notebook.

Hoffmeister held up his right hand. 'You may have noticed I have difficulty moving my right arm and my fingers,' he said.

'I've noticed,' said Jack, wondering why this was relevant.

'Well, this is a direct result of the incident I just mentioned.'

'Oh? In what way?'

'When I asked Kun if he could remember anything at all about the sale of the painting in Vienna, he did come up with something. It may have seemed trivial at the time, but as it turned out it was in fact a breakthrough.'

'Intriguing.'

'It's more than that. It's remarkable. Kun, who was a boy of about ten or eleven at the time, remembered going to see a man in a shop with this mother about selling the painting. He couldn't remember where the shop was, or a name, but he did remember something.'

'What?'

'The man looked like a pirate. He wore a patch over one eye.'

'And this was important?'

'Yes. There were a number of shady art dealers in Vienna in the fifties, but without knowing more, I couldn't take the matter further. Then came the eye patch.'

'And this helped?'

'It did.'

'In what way?'

'There was a notorious art dealer in Vienna at the time who had a reputation for dealing in stolen paintings. He was known as – wait for it – "the Cyclops".'

'After Polyphemus, the one-eyed giant of Greek mythology?'

114

'Yes. If you wanted to sell a dodgy painting in Vienna during the fifties, you went to see the Cyclops. His real name was Erwin Strasser, a shady character.'

'And this was a helpful lead? Even after all those years?'

'It was. After I spoke to Kun, I managed to find out what happened to the Cyclops. He left Vienna in the early eighties and moved to Salzburg, where he opened an antiquarian business called Antiquariat Hephaestus in the old city—'

'After the Greek god of arts and crafts?'

'You know your Greek mythology, Herr Rogan.'

'Was he still there in 1995?'

'He was,'

'And you went to see him?'

'I did. He was a man in his late seventies by then, but he was still in business.'

'What happened?'

'Let's have another coffee and I'll tell you.'

16

Charité Hospital, Berlin: 19 December

Sasha Kovalenko sat on a bench in front of Novotny's hospital room. Oblivious to the foot traffic all around her in the busy emergency ward, Sasha had waited for hours every day for news about her partner's condition since his evacuation from St Petersburg. She only left her post in the early hours of the morning to get some sleep in a hotel nearby.

Because she had her eyes closed to shield them from the glare of the bright lights in the stark corridor smelling of disinfectant and cleaning fluids, she didn't notice the surgeon standing in front of her. The surgeon bent down and gently touched her on the shoulder.

Sasha opened her eyes and looked at him, the question on her wan face always the same. The surgeon came to see her several times a day to bring her up to date.

'Any news?' she said and sat up.

'He just came out of the coma.'

'Thank God! Can I see him?'

'Not yet. I have some news.'

'What kind of news?'

'I think I know what happened to him.'

'You do? Tell me!'

'Let's go somewhere quiet.'

'Please tell me he'll be all right,' said Sasha anxiously, feeling sick.

'Most likely, yes,' came the guarded reply.

'*Most likely?*' Sasha stood up and followed the surgeon past the security guards and down the corridor to his office.

The surgeon looked at Sasha sitting opposite. He admired the striking young woman with her long, straw-blonde hair, who had spent countless hours curled up on a bench in front of Novotny's hospital room, patiently waiting for news.

'Would you like some water? You look pale,' said the surgeon.

'No, thank you. What I need is some good news,' said Sasha, her cornflower-blue eyes wide with concern, tinged with fear. 'Have you got some for me?'

The surgeon obviously knew all about Novotny and who he was. The German papers were full of stories about his speech in St Petersburg and the explosive allegations of corruption levelled at the Kremlin. Several news teams had been camped outside the hospital since his patient's arrival and were waiting for news about Novotny's mysterious condition and prognosis.

'As you know, we have conducted extensive tests. Laboratories as far away as London and the Mayo Clinic in Minnesota were involved.'

'You told me.'

'I have no doubt the emergency evacuation saved his life. The convulsions, the breathing difficulties and the sweating were already very severe by the time I got to see him. And, of course, there was the vomiting. Another complication. Muscles were contracting involuntarily, especially around the heart and lungs. All this could easily have been fatal, quickly—'

'I was hoping for some good news,' interjected Sasha, fighting back tears. To her, this all sounded like medical speak, preparing her for distressing news.

The surgeon held up his hand. 'Please bear with me. The reason I'm telling you all this is so you understand exactly what we are dealing with here, and what to expect going forward.'

'Sorry, it's just ...'

'I understand. The toxicology reports have just come in.'

The surgeon held up a bundle of papers.

'And?'

'We believe that Anatoly has been poisoned.'

'We were afraid of that! Do we know what with?'

'Yes. Everything points to a potent nerve agent.'

'Novichok?'

'Yes. The experts seem to think so. It's the most likely candidate.'

'How could this have been administered?'

'This nerve agent can enter the body through an ultrafine powder in a number of ways. It can occur through ingestion, in other words through food or drink, or by inhalation. Perhaps the easiest way to administer it is through contact with the skin.'

'You mean by coming into contact with something that has novichok on it? Touching something?'

'Exactly. This nerve agent is incredibly powerful and we know precious little about it. It's a lethal weapon. It's that simple.'

'Then, this could have happened anywhere?'

'Theoretically, yes, but anyone else coming into contact with this poison would suffer the same consequences. It's very difficult to contain or control. Once it's out there, well ...'

'Hmm. What's the prognosis?'

'I am confident he'll pull through. He's young, healthy and I have no doubt he has an incredible will to live. A man with a mission usually has. And Anatoly strikes me as a man with a mission.'

'Not only that, he's a man of destiny, and he *believes* that, you see.'

'In situations like this, the mental state of a patient is just as important as medical treatment,' said the doctor.

'He must live, Doctor. Russia cannot afford to lose him! And neither can I,' added Sasha quietly.

'I understand. I can promise you I will do everything in my power to make sure he pulls through. He's in the best of hands here.'

'I can see that, thank you. When can I see him?'

'Later tonight, perhaps. I'll be here.'

Feeling a little better, Sasha stood up and looked at the surgeon. 'You have a special gift, you know, and it has nothing to do with medicine.'

'Oh?' said the surgeon, smiling.

'You radiate confidence and empathy. Especially empathy.'

The surgeon stood up as well and walked towards the door. 'That's one of the nicest things anyone has said to me in years,' he said and opened the door. 'You should really get some rest. I'll watch over him, promise.'

The look of gratitude Sasha gave the surgeon as she walked past was a look he wouldn't forget in a hurry.

The next morning, the German government announced that Novotny had been poisoned by a novichok nerve agent similar to the one used to poison Sergei Skripal and his daughter in England.

A short time after the announcement, a spokeswoman for Novotny's Anti-Corruption Foundation released a statement indicating that Novotny had come out of the coma and was recovering. She also stated that the Organisation for the Prohibition of Chemical Weapons, the OPCW, had examined Novotny's blood and urine samples and found traces of a cholinesterase inhibitor from the novichok group present in the samples. This was seen as unequivocal proof that Novotny had been poisoned while in Russia, most likely while attending the demonstration in St Petersburg.

17

Palazzo Alberti, Venice: 21 December

Jack ran his hands over the polished top of the huge dining table he had recently restored, enjoying the feel of the smooth, three-hundred-year-old solid oak he had brought back to life using only simple tools. Satisfied, he turned to Bonato watching him. 'What do you think?'

'Not bad. I didn't think it would ever look this good when you started.'

'Ah. You must have the eye, a vision and faith. Restoring old furniture is all about that. And so are many other things in life,' added Jack pensively.

'If you say so.'

After the surprise revelation at the end of his meeting with Hoffmeister in the historical Café Central, Jack had decided to follow the last remaining breadcrumbs that could perhaps throw some light on what had happened to *Golgotha* after Kun's mother had sold it on the black market in Vienna in 1957. He realised this was a long shot, but Jack was used to such odds and knew that even a few insignificant, shrivelled morsels had the potential to unlock the greatest of mysteries in a way one least expected. All that was needed was persistence and faith. And a little luck.

The incident in question had happened in Salzburg in 1995 after Hoffmeister had met with Kun and his mother in Szentendre.

Instead of returning to Venice as he had planned, Jack travelled directly to Salzburg alone, in an attempt to pick up the frayed threads of Hoffmeister's failed enquiry, and find out what had so abruptly stopped Hoffmeister in his tracks. What Jack had uncovered was not only surprising, but the unexpected twists of fate and connections reaching out of the past had also rocked him to the core. Moments of destiny can be confronting, and what Jack had uncovered was certainly a moment of destiny he had to come to terms with before telling anybody else about it.

After returning to Venice, Jack locked himself away in his new palazzo without talking to anybody. He didn't leave his workroom, and continued restoring the old dining table like a man possessed. His only contact was with Bonato and Tristan, who had moved into the palazzo permanently. He refused to answer calls even from Countess Kuragin to discuss what had happened, telling everybody instead he needed some time alone to digest the astonishing facts he had uncovered. In short, he needed some time to think. He had even asked Tristan to be patient and stay away for a while, which was out of character for Jack.

While everyone respected his request, there was a great deal of concern and speculation about Jack's mental state, as no-one had seen him behave in such a strange way before. Jack may have been reckless and unpredictable, even rash and impulsive occasionally, but he had never appeared irrational.

Tristan seemed to understand Jack's behaviour better than most. He accepted the fact that Jack hadn't told him anything about what was troubling him, and counselled patience. He told everybody that Jack would soon come round and tell them what had happened. He was right.

Restoring the dining table had been like a calming therapy. Working with his hands had helped Jack to put all the facts he had uncovered into perspective, and decide what to do next. The recent murders had rocked him to the core, and what had happened in Salzburg just two days earlier had almost pushed him over the edge.

Jack put down his tools and looked at Bonato. 'I think we're ready.'

'Ready for what?'

'A dinner party. Right here in my new dining room. It may be a little sparse at the moment, but we do have a table that can seat twenty, and plenty of chairs.'

'We have no kitchen. The granite bench tops you ordered haven't arrived.'

'True, not yet, but I am sure if we ask her nicely, the countess will agree to provide the food from Osman's Kitchen. I will call her and ask her to invite a few special guests. We can make a cosy fire in that fireplace over there to keep us warm, and we have plenty of excellent wine. What do you think?'

'I suppose we could arrange that. What's the occasion?'

'Christmas.'

'You want to have Christmas *here*?'

'Why not? The renovations may have taken a little longer than expected, but we are almost there—'

'Except for the kitchen.'

'True. Wasn't my top priority, I admit.'

'If Countess Kuragin agrees to supply the food, well, then we could certainly do it.'

'Good. My first Christmas in my new home. Here in Venice; incredible! The boy from the bush living in a historical palazzo once owned by a pope. Can you believe it? Outback Australia meets the magic of historical Venice. Do you know, I have never hosted Christmas before – ever!'

Bonato, like everybody else, had been worried about Jack since his return. He could sense there was some kind of deep crisis Jack had to work through, alone. He recognised all the signs because he had been there himself on several occasions in his life, and had wrestled with demons before. He was therefore well pleased about Jack's Christmas dinner party suggestion, as he saw it as a clear sign that Jack had defeated his demons, was coming out of the dark shadows, and was ready to face his friends and return to some form of normality.

'I'll call the countess and arrange it, if you like,' said Bonato. 'Just give me the guest list.'

Jack looked at him gratefully, feeling a great weight lift from his shoulders. He wasn't quite ready yet to talk to the countess and face questions.

'Would you?'

'Sure, but you have to do something for me in return.'

'What's that?'

'Have a shave. We don't want to scare your guests away now, do we? Especially not at Christmas.'

'I suppose not,' said Jack, laughing for the first time since his return.

What Bonato hadn't told Jack was that the countess and Tristan, who spent most of his time working at the Palazzo da Baggio, had called him several times a day, enquiring about Jack's wellbeing and state of mind. He was therefore sure they would be delighted to hear about Jack's Christmas plans, and do everything they could to make them work.

'Now, what about that guest list?' said Bonato. 'There isn't much time.'

'You know that my friends are my family. Now more than ever, I need them close to me, and having Christmas here would be the perfect way to do that.'

'I understand.'

Jack put his hand on the dining table and looked pensively at something in the distance only he could see. 'And besides, I have a few painful surprises in my Christmas stocking that have to be shared with friends.'

18

Charité University Hospital, Berlin: 21 December

Novotny was improving. Once the novichok poisoning diagnosis had been confirmed, removing the uncertainty and speculation about his condition, his treatment became more focused and effective. He was responding to drugs better than expected, and his strong constitution and overall good health were additional factors that made the doctors guardedly confident about a full recovery.

Sasha was allowed to visit Novotny every day, but only for short periods. They spent most of their time discussing the situation in Russia. The doctors saw this as a positive development, as they were sure that mental stimulation would speed up Novotny's progress and galvanise his determination to get better.

The main thing on Novotny's mind was not to lose the momentum of his anti-corruption campaign. Sasha had brought him articles from several newspapers, both Russian and international, about his speech in St Petersburg and the jaw-dropping allegations he had made accusing President Palin of corruption, and the proof he had promised to deliver. News about the novichok poisoning had, of course, made sensational headlines around the world, pointing the finger at the Kremlin. This had threatened to overshadow the St Petersburg revelations, and it was this very point that was causing Novotny real concern.

'I can't just lie here and do nothing,' said Novotny.

Sasha put her hand on his arm and looked at him. 'You *are* doing something. You are recovering from an attempt on your life, darling, don't forget that!'

'I know, but I promised proof, and we were going to release that proof during my speech in Moscow. Instead of that, we have *this*!'

'You must be patient and rest. That's what really matters right now.'

'I get it, but man doesn't live on bread alone.'

'A strange thing to say, but I understand what you mean.'

'I know you do. You will therefore understand that I have to do something – soon!'

'We have the proof ready to go. Why don't you release it now? Here, from your bedside. It could be very effective. A response to a cowardly poisoning gone wrong. What do you say?'

'Don't you think I've considered this over and over? I have thought of nothing else since I came out of the coma. Look at me!'

Novotny pointed to the tubes and monitoring devices attached to his arms and chest, and the life-support machine blinking ominously next to his bed. 'Do I look like a man who can threaten a corrupt regime and expose a dangerous president, a maniac, obsessed with wealth and power, who is prepared to ruin a nation to feed his dark desires?'

Sasha reached for Novotny's hand and squeezed it, a sad look in her eyes. 'All it would take is a phone call from you. The guys at the Foundation could post that sensational video we've been working on for such a long time, straight away. It would cause a worldwide sensation. You know that.'

'It would. For a while, until Palin's publicity apparatus goes on the attack. I can tell you right now exactly how that would play out. The Kremlin has already denied any involvement in the poisoning. I now know why the plane sent to bring me here to Germany was allowed to leave without any problems. That was clever. Typical FSB. They are masters of muddying the waters and creating a new narrative to suit their agenda. Now they can claim that the whole poisoning story is a CIA concoction, a plot to implicate the Kremlin and the president. I have been accused many times of being a CIA agent working for the Americans, remember?'

'True, but—'

'If we release that video now, they will claim that it is a Western fabrication without any factual foundation. Nothing more than lies designed to undermine Palin. You know what control they have over the media.'

125

Novotny became quite agitated and tried to sit up. 'No, we have to be patient and keep our powder dry, but we should release a statement right now and go on the attack.'

'How exactly?'

'By telling the media that I will return to Russia as soon as I am allowed to travel, and that I will present the promised proof *in person*. In Russia!'

'You can't be serious!' said Sasha, looking alarmed. 'You know exactly what will happen as soon as you set foot on Russian soil.'

'I do. And that would give huge credibility to my claim and validate the proof. It is one thing to release that explosive material from a safe distance. From abroad. It is something quite different to release it once I am in custody facing whatever trumped-up charges they will put me on trial for.'

'You will be convicted and go to jail. Like last time. Only for longer. That's for sure.'

'So be it!'

'You are prepared to do that?'

'I am. We have come this far. We can't stop now! This is our time, can't you see? They won't kill me in jail. That would make me a martyr and they certainly don't want that. Not after we've released the proof.'

'I can see that.'

'And don't forget we can do that from anywhere, and post the video on YouTube at the press of a button. You will stay away from Russia, of course, and keep everything going from here in Germany. The Foundation, the press conferences, the social media posts, the videos, the lot. You must stay in the background and operate in the shadows. That's where you are most effective. You mustn't forget who you are!'

'You're right.'

'They can't stop us here. The internet knows no boundaries,' continued Novotny. 'This gives us huge influence and access to people power, despite the strict censorship in Russia and the crackdown on demonstrations. That's what Palin's afraid of. Once this information is out there, there will be no stopping the momentum of change. You'll see!'

Exhausted, Novotny fell back onto his pillow just as the surgeon entered, a concerned look on his face.

'I think you better go,' he said to Sasha. 'That's enough excitement for one day. He needs rest.'

Sasha nodded and stood up.

'You do understand, don't you?' said Novotny softly.

'I do,' said Sasha, tears in her eyes, and left the room.

19

Palazzo Alberti, Venice: 24 December

Countess Kuragin was in her element. Delighted and relieved by Jack's request, she had thrown herself into the task of arranging everything at short notice as only a skilful host could. Assisted by Tristan, she had contacted all the guests Jack wanted to invite and had offered to put them up in the Palazzo da Baggio boutique hotel over Christmas. This in itself was a treat difficult to resist, as guests booked months in advance to get a room in Venice at Christmas. She also hinted at some kind of crisis involving Jack, explained the importance of the invitation, and pleaded with everyone to come to Venice and celebrate Christmas with Jack in his new home, despite the short notice.

The countess put down her phone and looked at Tristan. 'I think that's it,' she said. 'Most of them are coming, would you believe. Wouldn't miss it for the world, they said.'

'I knew they would. They are doing it for Jack,' said Tristan. 'Jana, Marcus, and Alexandra would have come as well if they could have arranged flights from Australia in time, what with all the COVID-19 complications and restrictions. Rebecca Armstrong is with Professor Stolzfus, her famous brother, celebrating Christmas in Oxford. Obviously, he can't travel. That leaves Bettany. She was the only one we couldn't contact. She's somewhere in Africa. Charity work, as usual.'

'You're right. They're all doing it for Jack. I wonder what he wants to tell us. Must be important.'

'Destiny stuff?' suggested Tristan, smiling. 'We'll find out soon enough. He asked us all to come over at four pm before the Christmas dinner, remember? You know Jack. The storyteller at work.'

'Good to see, don't you think? These last few days have been terrible. I've hardly slept a wink. I'm still very worried about him, but this invitation is a good sign.'

'Definitely. I think Jack's back. He has something important to tell us, for sure, but he's doing it his way. That's typical Jack. He has mentioned having a party to show off his new home before,' said Tristan. 'I just didn't think he would do it so soon. And certainly not at Christmas, and at such short notice. Not like him.'

'He must have his reasons.'

'Absolutely, but all this secrecy is a little baffling.'

'It is. At least he isn't hiding from us anymore,' said the countess.

'True.'

Isis and Lola flew in on Isis's private jet from London. They had given Maestro Krakowski a lift, and had also picked up Jack's mother, and Dupree and Mademoiselle Darrieux in Paris along the way. Krakowski had Christmas concert commitments on Boxing Day and could only stay for the night. He would fly back to London the next day.

Bartolli arranged for her mother and two daughters to spend Christmas with a cousin, and arrived by train from Rome in the afternoon. Countess Kuragin, Leonardo, Anna, Tristan and Billy were, of course, in Venice anyway. That concluded Jack's guest list.

Jack sent a large water taxi to the Palazzo da Baggio for the short ride along the Grand Canal to the Rialto Bridge. He wanted to make sure his guests would arrive in comfort and style.

Isis had agonised for hours about what to wear. It was bitterly cold outside and the figure-hugging Valentino pantsuit, which had been the original choice to show off her hourglass figure, was discarded at the last minute and she settled on something a little more demure by Chanel instead. When the countess offered to lend her mother's Russian fur coat and hat to keep warm, Isis was overjoyed and gratefully accepted. Used to making memorable entries, Isis waited to the last minute before joining the others on the jetty.

The countess smiled as Isis made her appearance. 'What a way to go to a party, guys, don't you agree?' said Isis, waving at the staff and house guests standing by the windows, and watching from above. Celebrity curiosity never failed to deliver.

'You look like a tsarina,' said Leonardo.

'You really think so?' said Isis, adjusting the stunning fur hat that made her look like a Don Cossack ready for battle.

'Wow!' said Darrieux, feeling rather underdressed in her eye-popping vintage Dior dress that accentuated her generous bosom. She turned towards the countess standing next to her. 'I had no idea it would be this cold. You wouldn't have another one, would you?'

'Fur coat, you mean?'

Darrieux nodded.

'Unfortunately not.'

'Bugger! She looks fabulous in it, don't you think?'

'Isis would look fabulous in a torn, oil-stained boiler suit,' said the countess, smiling.

'Don't praise her too loudly, or she'll be impossible all night,' said Lola, rolling her eyes. 'Celebrity egos!'

'Here it comes,' said Tristan, and pointed to a water taxi making a turn and pulling up at the jetty. 'Be careful. It's all very slippery and the water is ice cold.'

Standing next to Bonato on the steps of the imposing Palazzo Alberti jetty facing the canal, Jack watched the water taxi approach. Suddenly, the tension and anxiety that had almost paralysed him for days seemed to fall away, replaced by the excitement and anticipation of seeing his friends, and the joy of spending Christmas with them in his new home. He realised that with their understanding and support he could defeat his demons and find the right path. And having his mother present as well, was a special treat. They were still getting to know each other and emotionally feeling their way after almost a lifetime of separation.

The way he had felt since his return from Salzburg reminded Jack of his days as a war correspondent in Afghanistan, and the toll on his mental health that the atrocities and destruction he had witnessed had taken at the time. It had taken him several months to get over that trauma and recover, but the emotional scars were still there and could easily reopen again and bleed if triggered by certain events or in certain ways.

'Look at that,' said Isis. She pointed to the jetty and waved. 'And this is Jack's new home? Amazing!'

'Wait until you see the inside,' said Tristan. 'It's quite something.'

'Can't wait,' said Darrieux as the water taxi pulled up and Jack came down the steps to greet them.

'I know you're dying to see what this place looks like inside, and I'm dying to show you,' said Jack, after he had welcomed everybody.

'As long as it's warmer inside,' said Darrieux, shivering.

'It is. I'll show you everything except the dining room. That's for later ...'

'Christmas surprise?' ventured Isis.

'Something like that. Follow me.'

The tour of the palazzo took almost an hour. From the huge foyer, Jack took his friends up the marble stairs to the first floor and told them about the amazing history of the place. He began with the library and his study, and then showed them Anna's studio facing the Rialto Bridge.

'We chose this room because of the light,' said Anna.

'Jack has built you a studio?' said Darrieux, looking incredulous.

'Yes, he has. He even promised to put on an exhibition to promote my work. Billy and I live at the Palazzo da Baggio, but I come over here to paint. Billy will join us later for the Christmas dinner. As you can imagine, he's very excited. Uncle Jack is very popular ...'

'I can imagine. Uncle Jack is very popular with most people ...' said Darrieux.

'I love painting here, surrounded by hundreds of years of history,' continued Anna. 'It's so peaceful and inspirational, and the light is perfect. At times I feel like Canaletto, looking at the same stunning view while I work.'

'I can see that,' said Krakowski, looking down into the bustling canal below. 'I wish I had a place like this to compose and practise my violin.'

'That can be arranged,' said Jack, laughing. 'My door is always open. This place is huge, and only Tristan, Signor Bonato and I live here permanently.'

'I'm envious,' said Isis. 'You've done an outstanding job with the renovations.'

'I don't think they'll ever finish,' said Jack. 'And I really don't mind. Every time we touch something, we discover something new. Another chapter in the remarkable history of this place.'

Isis took off her fur hat. 'My art collection would look unbelievable in here.'

'That too can be arranged,' said Jack cheerfully. 'Just give me the nod and tell me when. My blank walls are waiting!'

The countess turned to Tristan standing next to her. 'Just listen to the banter,' she said quietly. 'Back to his old larrikin self again, wouldn't you say?'

'He is. I told you, he needs his friends around him. They're his lifeline and emotional energy supply. Every black dog needs some sunshine. That's what this is all about.'

'You're talking about depression here? Mental health?'

'Hm ...'

'You're talking about love, right?'

'I am.'

'A true Christmas, then?'

'I hope so.'

After bypassing the dining room, which was strictly off limits because Bonato and the catering staff borrowed from Osman's Kitchen were preparing the room for the festive Christmas Eve dinner to come, Jack's tour concluded in the large salon. 'Here we are,' said Jack. 'Adrienne, why don't you sit next to the fire and get warm.'

'I could do with a drink,' said Darrieux, admiring the tapestries and the antiques Jack had restored. 'I'm exhausted. Museum fatigue. My feet are killing me.'

'Coming up. Let's have some champagne. You've all had a long day, and this is Christmas! I thought we would celebrate Christmas the Italian way, on Christmas Eve, European style,' said Jack. 'And those of you who would like to attend midnight mass can do so. I've arranged a water taxi to take us to San Giorgio Maggiore. It should be quite an experience. The music, especially the singing, will be sublime.'

'Can't wait,' said Krakowski. 'I've always wanted to do this.'

Definitely back to his old self, the countess thought. She'd wondered when he'd tell them the real reason he'd brought everyone there and explain what had been troubling him so deeply for the last few days.

After champagne and canapés had been served and everybody was comfortably seated and beginning to relax, Jack walked over to the marble fireplace and turned around to face his guests. With all eyes on Jack, a sudden hush descended on the room, expectation rising by the second.

'I would like to begin by thanking you all for accepting my invitation at such short notice. This means a lot to me. It must have come as quite a surprise, yet here you all are, ready to spend Christmas with me here in Venice. I know this couldn't have been easy to arrange, but you did it without hesitation and without asking questions or making excuses. This is a sign of true friendship. I am humbled by your trust and generosity.'

Jack paused and looked around the room.

'As all of you would have worked out by now,' he continued, 'I didn't ask you to come here so I could show off my new home. That could have been done much easier another time. Neither have I asked you to come here specifically to spend Christmas with me. That's merely a coincidence, but a nice one, nevertheless. I have asked you to come here because I have something important to tell you that concerns all of us in this room. But most important of all, I have asked you to come here because I need your counsel and advice.'

Jack reached for his glass on the mantelpiece and took a sip of champagne. 'And your help,' he added quietly.

'You've all heard me talk often about my breadcrumbs of destiny and how Tristan can hear the whisper of angels and glimpse eternity. Well, following those breadcrumbs has recently taken me to a very dark and dangerous place ruled by true evil, which has almost overwhelmed me. That's why I had to be alone for a while, away from distractions so I could think straight, find some answers, and work my way through it all.'

Jack hesitated again and ran his fingers through his hair. It was a nervous habit that helped him focus and collect his thoughts.

'Let me explain. In essence, this is all about *Golgotha*, a mysterious fifteenth-century painting by Jan van Eyck that was copied by David Herzl – the master forger of Warsaw you are all familiar with – in Treblinka in 1943.'

'Seriously?' said Krakowski, surprised.

'It's the same man,' said Jack.

'The same man who copied Monet's *Little Sparrow in the Garden* for my father in Warsaw during the war, and then switched the paintings?' said Krakowski.

'The same painting I bought at that sensational auction in London for thirty-five million pounds,' said Isis, 'once it surfaced again?'

'Yes, but you actually bought the original,' said Jack, smiling. 'Fuchs bought the forgery.'

'We know all this from your novella *The Forgotten Painting*,' said Darrieux, bemused. Only Tristan wasn't surprised, his knowing smile the only sign he had been expecting something like this all along, and knew exactly where Jack was heading.

'That's right. I'm sure that you can see now how everything here is strangely interconnected, and why in some way we are all involved, like it or not.'

'Held together by the threads of destiny, perhaps?' teased Tristan.

'Something like that. Don't forget it was you who told me just a few days ago that the nightmare in the salt mines was far from over, remember?'

Tristan nodded.

'And it was also you who told me that we must be careful because the old evil was back. Considering what has happened recently, I should have listened to you more carefully.'

Jack looked around the room to let this sink in.

'Just consider how it all began,' he continued. 'You now all know about those sinister threats. First, Tristan and the bullet sent to him on his birthday right here in Venice, only a short while ago. A chilling message, you must admit.'

Jack pointed to Dupree. 'Then came Claude's phone call in the middle of the night telling me that Rabbi Stein had been murdered—'

'Jack and I went straight to Prague to find out what happened,' said Dupree, 'and what we found was quite astonishing. It soon became clear that Stein was killed because of one item in the museum collection.'

'Herzl's diary,' said Jack.

'How did you know that?' asked Leonardo.

'There were clues ... convincing ones.'

'But why?' asked Darrieux.

'As you will see in a moment, there's an ingenious, diabolical plan behind all this. A master manipulator is pulling all the strings and making us dance to his tune. But first, back to the warnings,' said Jack and turned towards his mother.

'The note left under your door, and the ominous message, *RIP 2021*, carved into your memory tree at your retirement home were the next warnings.'

'It was very strange and unsettling,' said Rahima. 'But most unsettling of all was how someone managed to find me in the first place. And why me?'

'Because of who you are,' said Jack. 'This is all about people close to me. And that includes everyone in this room. That's why I'm so concerned,' added Jack quietly. 'I don't want to alarm you, but with a madman like O'Hara, you're all exposed.'

Taking a deep breath, Jack pointed to Bartolli, who was watching him intently.

'Shortly after the memory tree episode came that cryptic message tucked under poor Paulo's collar. Paulo was Francesca's much-loved dog, who was poisoned while we were having dinner at her apartment in Rome. Someone was obviously watching me and knew exactly where I was and what I was doing.'

'That's scary,' said Isis.

'It is. The old evil we encountered in the dreadful death mask murders was back stronger than before,' said Jack, his eyes moist, 'and I suddenly found myself right in the middle of it all.'

Bartolli saw that Jack was becoming emotional and decided to step in.

'Following the instructions in that cryptic message, Jack and I travelled to St Petersburg,' said Bartolli, 'and finally met with O'Hara – not in person as it turned out, but virtually – on board the *Standard*, a Russian billionaire's private luxury yacht. It was during that meeting O'Hara told us about the rules – *his* rules – of this deadly game we now find ourselves embroiled in.'

'It's like stepping into a quagmire,' said Jack. 'The harder you try to get out and save yourself, the deeper you sink until you can no longer breathe or think straight. That's where I ended up a few days ago. How that came about and what I discovered along the way are the reasons I asked you to come here today. What you are about to hear will be difficult to believe and get your head around. It took me several days to come to terms with it all, but I can assure you it's all real.'

Jack went to the ice bucket, took out a freshly opened bottle of Bollinger, and went around the room filling up glasses. This gave him some time to consider how to approach the next important subject.

'Once again, this all has to do with *Golgotha*, that extraordinary van Eyck painting, and Albert Hoffmeister, the author of a book specifically dealing with the painting and its history,' continued Jack and put the bottle back into the silver bucket. 'It all happened after I met with Kun in Budapest. A few days after Kun was murdered, I travelled to Vienna and had a meeting with Hoffmeister. A fascinating man, he told me about an incident that had put a sudden stop to his investigation. It happened in Salzburg in 1995—'

'And following your breadcrumbs, as you tend to do,' interjected Tristan, 'you went to Salzburg to dig a little deeper.'

'That's right, I did. A few days ago, on the eighteenth,' said Jack, with sadness in his voice. 'Perhaps I shouldn't have. That's what has been troubling me and that's why I need your help. This is what happened ...'

20

Salzburg: Six days earlier, 18 December

Jack loved trains. After his meeting with Hoffmeister, he caught the Inter City express, which would get him into Salzburg by lunchtime. As soon as the train left the outskirts of Vienna and picked up speed, Jack settled into his comfortable seat, opened his notebook, and began to write up the notes about the meeting with Hoffmeister the day before. During the meeting, he had only written down key words, names and dates, which had to be expanded while everything was still clear in his mind. His main focus was the incident that had stopped Hoffmeister from investigating the *Golgotha* story further, despite having spent years painstakingly following the trail of that iconic painting:

Hoffmeister traces the Cyclops (real name Erwin Strasser) to Salzburg, where he is operating an antiquarian business known as Antiquariat Haephestus in the Goldgasse.

H visits the Cyclops, by now an elderly man, in his shop and talks to him about Golgotha *and the Kun sale.*

At first, the Cyclops denies knowing anything about it, but H persists and presents his arguments.

The Cyclops remains defiant. Frustrated, H threatens to go to the authorities and report the matter. Art theft is treated very seriously in Austria.

That evening, H is attacked by two men on his way back to his hotel after leaving a Gasthaus in the old city. The last thing he remembers before passing out is one of the men telling him to forget all about Golgotha, *and leave Salzburg at once if he wanted to live.*

Seriously injured by the beating, H is taken to hospital and almost dies.

He remains in hospital for several days and is eventually discharged with a permanent injury to his right arm and hand.

H leaves Salzburg and, instead of telling the authorities what he knows, decides to stop his investigation and makes no reference in his book to the Cyclops, the Kun sale, or the attack.

The Cyclops died in 1998. Antiquariat Haephestus still exists, and is run by his granddaughter, Veronika Strasser, at the same address in the Goldgasse.

After checking into his favourite Salzburg hotel, Hotel Elefant in the Sigmund-Haffner-Gasse, Jack left his backpack at reception and went to locate Antiquariat Haephestus, which was just around the corner. The narrow lane in the heart of the old city, popular with tourists, oozed charm and Mozart romance. The famous composer's birth house was close by, visited by thousands of tourists every year.

The shop was much smaller than Jack had expected. He had to duck as he entered to avoid hitting his head against the low doorframe that had greeted customers for more than three hundred years with the chime of a tiny bell attached at the top.

The first thing Jack noticed as he stepped inside was the familiar, pungent smell of leather, candle wax and varnish; smells anyone familiar with old books and restoring antiques would instantly recognise.

The small, dimly lit room was a treasure-trove of all kinds of bric-a-brac. Shelves reached from floor to ceiling along the walls, crammed with books, decorated teacups, ornate silver picture frames with sepia photographs of bearded men in bowler hats staring vacantly into space, and cheap porcelain figures once used as ornaments on mantelpieces and hall tables.

In pride of place on a small round marble table in the middle of the shop was a strange collection of wax flowers and exotic feathers under a glass dome. To Jack, the room looked more like a cabinet of Victorian curiosities than the shop of an antiquarian selling quality paintings, lithographs and etchings, as the elaborate wrought-iron sign above the entrance facing the lane suggested.

'May I help you?' said a voice from somewhere at the back of the shop. Jack turned around and almost collided with a suit of armour standing between a grandfather clock and a faded globe that had seen a little too much sun.

'I hope so,' said Jack, 'as long as the knight here doesn't challenge me to a duel.'

'It's a little crowded in here. Be careful.'

Jack looked at the tall, well-dressed woman standing next to a beautiful Edwardian oak rolltop desk, the most interesting piece in the shop as far as he was concerned.

'Veronika Strasser?' asked Jack and came closer.

'I am.'

As he approached, Jack pointed to the desk. 'Lovely piece. Late eighteenth-century, exquisite tambour—'

'Has someone referred you to me? Is that what you are looking for?' said Strasser, watching Jack but not sure what to make of him. 'It's not for sale.'

'No. I am looking for information.'

'*Information?* How curious. You would have noticed this is a shop, albeit a mere shadow of what it once was, not a library.'

'Ah, but the information I'm looking for may only be available right here, in this shop.'

The woman reached for a packet of cigarettes and lighter on the desk, and lit up. 'Intriguing. What kind of information?'

'Information about *Golgotha*, a painting by Jan van Eyck. I would like to find out what happened to it.'

If the woman was in any way surprised, she didn't show it. She calmly kept eye contact with Jack and blew some smoke in his direction.

'A van Eyck? In here? Look around you. This isn't Sothebys.'

'But it wasn't always that way.'

'I don't know what you mean.'

'Don't you? After the Cyclops left Vienna during the sixties and set up shop here in Salzburg, this establishment became well known in certain art circles; isn't that right?'

'The Cyclops? I have no idea what you are talking about. The shop may have a Greek name, but it has nothing to do with a Cyclops.'

'Perhaps not the shop itself; that's named after the god of sculptors, artisans and craftsmen, but its one-eyed owner was once known as the Cyclops in the murky underworld of art after the war ...'

'You speak in riddles.'

'Do I? The Cyclops was a nickname given to Erwin Strasser, your grandfather, and this shop was well known for selling all kinds of precious works of art that had – how shall I put this? – no credible provenance, if you know what I mean. No questions asked.'

'You claim to know a lot about this place. Who are you?'

Jack reached into his pocket, pulled out a business card and handed it to Strasser. 'My name is Jack Rogan. I'm a writer.'

'And what is your interest in all this?'

'As I mentioned before, I would like to find out what happened to van Eyck's *Golgotha*. It was once part of the famous *Ghent Altarpiece* looted by the Germans and hidden in the mines in Altaussee, not far from here. But along the way, *Golgotha* – a small oil painting attached to the back of the *Altarpiece* – was separated from its place behind one of the panels, and ended up in Treblinka. I've written a novella about this, which has just been published. You can look it up on the Net.'

'I might just do that.' She scrutinised the business card. 'So, you are a writer from Australia? Fascinating,' said Strasser and looked at Jack with renewed interest.

Jack realised if he wanted to avoid a stalemate, or worse still, a dismissal and Strasser asked him to leave, something out of the ordinary was needed to keep the conversation about *Golgotha* and the Cyclops going. It was time to turn on the charm and produce a tempting inducement.

'I noticed on the way in that you're having a closing-down sale?'

'That's right. Everything in here has been reduced and must go by the end of the month. A final Christmas fire sale, if you like. I am leaving here for good. Times have changed, Mr Rogan.'

'I can see that. I tell you what. If you come up with something useful that could help me find out what happened to the painting, I will make you an offer to buy the lot in here. Lock, stock and barrel. Literally speaking. No questions asked.'

Strasser began to laugh. 'This is crazy. You can't be serious!'

'But I am. I'm staying at the Hotel Elefant just around the corner. For one night only. If you do come up with something, we could have dinner together, say, in the Peters Stiftskeller, and have a chat. It's not far from here. What do you say?'

'Are all Australians so forward?'

'No, just the reckless ones.'

Strasser shook her head. Despite her earlier apprehension, she was beginning to like the attractive man standing in front of her, who had appeared out of nowhere and was making an outrageous proposal about a subject she hadn't thought about for years. A middle-aged woman on her own didn't get to meet many interesting men in Salzburg.

'All right, Mr Rogan. Leave it with me,' she said. 'If I do come up with something, I'll meet you at the Peters Stiftskeller. If not, you'll just have to have dinner by yourself.'

'Fair enough. I look forward to it.'

'You seem very confident.'

'Writers like me have to be. Otherwise, no stories, only writer's block. Shall we say seven?'

Strasser nodded.

'Until then,' said Jack and turned around, eager to leave before Strasser got cold feet and changed her mind. As he walked past the suit of armour, he ran his hand over the breastplate. 'I always wanted to own something like this: a knight in shining armour,' he said and left the shop.

The short walk from Hotel Elefant to the Peters Stiftskeller took less than ten minutes. The St Peter Stiftskulinarium, as the restaurant complex was known, was Jack's favourite restaurant in Salzburg. For someone like Jack, who was passionate about history and adventure, the spectacular Benedictine Abbey of St Peter founded in 803 was an irresistible attraction.

Jack made sure he arrived early. He had reserved a table in one of the cosy wood-panelled dining areas he preferred near the entrance. He had dined there many times with friends over the years after concerts in the famous Grosses Festspielhaus, the Large Festival House that was just next door. His most recent visit had been to hear Maestro Krakowski perform one of his violin concertos. Dr Rosen had flown in from Africa especially for that event and Isis had joined them from London. Jack smiled as he remembered Isis's outrageous outfit she had worn at the concert. They all had a memorable dinner in the Peters Stiftskeller after the performance to celebrate Krakowski's success, attended by the conductor and half the orchestra. After all, this was Salzburg, and Austrian hospitality and *Gemütlichkeit* were legendary. And besides, Austrians were not only tolerant of eccentrics like Isis, but actually adored them.

Soaking up the unique atmosphere of the crowded room, Jack ordered a bottle of Gumpoldskirchen Pinot Noir, a signature wine of the restaurant sourced from vineyards tended by monks reaching back hundreds of years to the days of the Benedictine wine trade in the eleventh century under the protection of Leopold VI, the Glorious. The wine therefore had a unique pedigree, difficult to emulate.

Jack had barely finished his glass of wine when Strasser walked in. Jack stood up to greet her and helped her take off her coat.

'You could at least pretend to be surprised,' said Strasser, smiling.

'But I am, pleasantly. Glass of wine?'

'Absolutely! It's been quite a day. I came directly from the shop. While I don't live far away, there was no time to go home and change. I cycle, you see. Even in winter, along the river. There's no public transport and no cars are allowed in the old city.'

'You might be hungry, then?'

'Oh, yes.'

'In that case, let's order first and talk later.'

Strasser reached for the *Speisekarte*, the elaborate menu in front of her, put on her glasses, and began to study the fare on offer.

'You must be a man of influence,' said Strasser. She closed the menu and looked at Jack, who had done the same.

'How so?'

'This place is incredibly busy all the time. People book weeks in advance and the locals hardly get near it, yet here you are with one of the best tables in the house. How come?'

'Ah. Last time I came here was with a famous composer, Benjamin Krakowski, after his concert. I used his name ...'

'Are all Australian men this resourceful?'

'Only the desperate ones. Shall we order?'

Strasser sat back and began to laugh. The ice was broken, banishing any last traces of awkwardness that may have lingered between them.

'Definitely. I'm having the duck; speciality of the house.'

'So am I,' said Jack and sat back.

'I looked you up on the Net; impressive,' said Strasser, beginning to relax.

'Glad you liked what you found.'

'I did. That's why I'm here. I also had a quick look at your novella.'

'*The Postmaster of Treblinka*?'

'Yes. The Herzl story is very moving and I now understand why you want to find out what happened to *Golgotha*.'

'You mean the reckless guy from Australia has gained some credibility?' said Jack, a sparkle in his eyes.

'Something like that.'

'Good. And do you think you can help him?'

'Perhaps. It isn't much, but you seem to be able to do a lot with very little.'

'Story of my life. Ah. Here comes that wonderful hot bread they serve as soon as you arrive. Look at this!'

'Are you always this enthusiastic about food?'

'Only when I'm starving, which my friends keep telling me seems to be most of the time. Food in outback Australia during the drought was scarce and precious. Most of the time, we barely had enough to eat.'

'Ah. Certain memories leave a big impression. They shape us and make us into who we are,' said Strasser, playing with her fork. 'What I'm about to tell you, is one such memory. You were right about my grandfather. He was known as the Cyclops in Vienna and had a certain reputation, as you correctly pointed out.'

'Go on.'

'My memories of my grandfather are nebulous and patchy, and a little confused. Childhood memories often are. Mum and I lived with him above his shop in Vienna. She was a single mother and worked in the shop with him. My grandfather was obsessed with the painting you mentioned.'

'*Golgotha?*'

'Yes. He said it was the most unique painting he had ever come across, and the most valuable. It lived in pride of place in our lounge room until we had to leave Vienna.'

'What happened?'

'My grandfather fell on hard times. We had to leave in a hurry. Gambling, debts. We came here to Salzburg and he set up shop in the Goldgasse – where we met.'

'And the painting?'

'He had to sell it. It was the only thing of value he had left. That's how he got the money to start his business here.'

Strasser looked at Jack with sad eyes. 'It almost broke him. For some reason, he loved that painting. He said there was something spiritual about it.'

'In what way?'

'As you obviously know, the painting was known as *Golgotha* because it captured the scene of Christ's crucifixion …'

'Set in a Flemish landscape with a small church in the background,' said Jack.

'Correct. But what you may not know is there was something very special about that church.'

'In what way?'

'As you can imagine, my grandfather knew a lot about art, paintings in particular, and he knew a lot about van Eyck and this work. *Golgotha* was special because it was connected to a legend.'

'What kind of legend?'

'It was rumoured the painting was a map, showing the way to a particular church in a small village near Ghent.'

'And this was important?'

'Yes, because that church was apparently associated with a big mystery, a secret reaching back to the time of Christ, known only to the initiated few.'

'Any idea what that secret was all about?'

'No, but my grandfather often spoke about it. No, more than that. He was obsessed with that secret and determined to get to the bottom of it. As you can imagine, this story made quite an impression on a young girl. That's why I remember the painting and the story so clearly.'

'Fascinating, but none of this brings us any closer.'

'To finding out what happened to the painting?'

'Exactly.'

'Not necessarily.'

'What do you mean?'

'My grandfather sold the painting to one of his regulars, a wealthy Swiss collector who had bought several paintings from him over the years without asking too many questions.'

Jack sat up, a strange sense of excitement washing over him. It was a feeling he knew well.

'Can you remember his name?' he asked quietly.

'Unfortunately, that's where the good news ends. The man had a nickname, you see. I only remember the nickname.'

'What was it?'

Jack reeled when Strasser told him the name and just stared at her, his eyes wide with astonishment.

146

'You look like you've seen a ghost,' said Strasser. 'Does this name mean anything to you?'

'Actually, I think it does.'

'You *think*?'

'Yes. It's difficult to explain, but this is too big a coincidence. And besides, I don't believe in coincidences, only destiny.'

'Does that mean I've come up with something useful, and you will make me an offer?' said Strasser, laughing, a sparkle in her eyes.

'To buy everything in your shop? Lock, stock and barrel?' said Jack.

'Don't worry, I'm only joking.'

'Yes, it does. Can you work out a price for me? I'll transfer the money to you in the morning.'

'Come on, this is silly.'

'Far from it. A deal's a deal. How much?'

'You can't be serious!'

'I am. But there's one condition.'

'What condition?'

'You have to send the knight in shining armour to my home in Venice. It's the only thing I want.'

'This is ridiculous! What about the rest?'

'Yours to do with as you please. I don't want it.'

'You are crazy!'

'Perhaps. Shall we have another bottle? I love this wine; don't you?'

21

Palazzo Alberti: Christmas Eve

'This is quite a story,' said the countess, watching Jack carefully. She knew Jack's moods very well and could see great sadness in his eyes.

'Sure is, but it has a terrible ending,' said Jack.

'In what way?'

Jack held up his hand. 'I'll tell you in a moment.'

Darrieux pointed to a suit of armour standing next to the fireplace. 'Is that it?'

'It is,' said Jack quietly. 'The knight in shining armour I mentioned. I transferred fifty thousand euros to Veronika Strasser's bank account the next morning, and she packed up the armour and sent it to me here.'

'Fifty thousand euros for *that*?' said Leonardo.

'Of course not. The payment was for information of a most extraordinary kind.'

'Care to tell us about it?'

'Later.' Jack walked over to the knight and put his hand on the helmet. 'Before the day was over and I arrived back here in Venice, Veronika Strasser was dead,' he said quietly.

Stunned silence.

'What happened?' asked Bartolli.

Jack looked at Dupree. 'I will let Claude tell you. He was the one who actually saw it first. I think it was on Sunday morning.'

'*Saw?*' said Tristan, frowning. 'Saw what?'

'Early on Sunday morning, Clara Samartini – the IT whiz kid working for the Squadra Mobile – sent Lapointe a video from Florence. It had been posted the night before. As you know, she had managed to once again infiltrate O'Hara's encrypted gambling site on the darknet, and was monitoring it. She's helping Lapointe and Europol to finally nail O'Hara and shut him down for good,' said Dupree.

'What kind of video?' asked the countess, sounding apprehensive.

'In the video, a woman wearing a fur hat and a thick overcoat could be seen cycling along a walkway close to the banks of a fast-flowing river, alone. It was almost dark and snowing, and one could just make out a stunning fortress lit up in the distance—'

'The Hohensalzburg, the massive medieval fortress dominating the skyline of Salzburg,' interjected Jack.

'As the woman approached a bridge,' continued Dupree, 'two men, also on pushbikes, came up from behind, and as they were passing the woman under the bridge, they pushed her off the embankment and into the river below. The woman and the bike disappeared in the freezing waters. The men kept going as if nothing had happened. The whole thing only lasted a few seconds, but was recorded in great detail on the video. Even with close-ups.'

'The woman was Veronika Strasser,' said Jack, 'and I am responsible for her death.'

'In what way?' asked the countess. 'You just told us you were here in Venice at the time.'

'I was, but before I left Salzburg, I sent an encrypted message to O'Hara and told him about my meeting with Strasser. Keeping him informed of my investigations is part of the strict conditions he's imposed. I did the same after I met Kun in Budapest. And you all know what happened to him. And besides, I felt sure I was being followed. Both in Vienna and in Salzburg. I should have known better ...'

Rahima put her hand on Jack's arm. 'It's not your fault,' she said quietly, trying to comfort her son, who was obviously upset. 'You are doing this to keep us all safe. You are doing it for the ones you love.'

'So much is true, but is it justifiable to endanger a life that perhaps doesn't mean all that much to you, to protect another that does?'

'Come on, Jack, that's not what happened here,' said the countess, stepping in. 'You had no idea any of this would happen. It was someone else's doing. How can you possibly hold yourself responsible?'

'Exactly,' said Rahima. 'It's not your fault, Jack. To think otherwise just isn't rational!'

'I cannot help how I feel,' said Jack. 'Early the next morning, Strasser's battered body was found washed up on rocks several kilometres downstream. This was the woman I had dinner with the night before!'

'How dreadful,' said Darrieux. 'I need another drink!'

'At first, the authorities thought it had been an accident,' continued Dupree. 'But when Lapointe sent them the video that told a different story, everything changed. Europol is now convinced the cases are connected and is looking into all three murders. This latest crime seems to have spurred them into action. Europol is finally taking Lapointe and the French police seriously.'

'At least that much has been achieved,' said Jack, feeling a little better.

'You're not only protecting us by going along with O'Hara's demands, but you're also buying time, aren't you?' said Tristan.

Jack nodded. 'Very prescient, as usual.'

'Buying time for what?' asked Leonardo.

'For the authorities, especially Europol, to get their act together and do something about O'Hara,' said Tristan. 'They've been after him for years, trying to shut down his gambling network.'

'Not easy when he's apparently hiding somewhere in Belarus,' said Dupree, 'behind a dictator's coattails. Effectively out of reach.'

'The day will come,' said Jack. 'The only question is at what cost.'

'Death and tragedy. What a Christmas!' said Krakowski, shaking his head.

'What about that information you mentioned?' asked the countess, trying to steer the conversation away from the distressing subject that threatened to overwhelm the evening.

'As I told you, it was just a nickname. A nickname for a regular customer who had done business with Strasser's grandfather over the years.'

'And this was helpful?' asked Leonardo.

'It was.'

'What nickname?' said Tristan.

Jack looked at Tristan, a wry smile creasing the corners of his mouth. 'You know, don't you?'

Tristan shrugged. 'Tell us.'

'You'll find this hard to believe,' said Jack. 'I was quite shocked when I heard it. All Strasser said was that the man who had bought the van Eyck painting was referred to by her grandfather as *der schlaue Fuchs,* which means cunning fox in German. He was Swiss, by the way, and an avid art collector who bought paintings without asking too many questions. Her grandfather regretted the sale and talked about it for years. That's why she could remember all this so clearly.'

Jack paused to let this sink in.

'Are you suggesting this was the same Fuchs who bought the Monet from my father in the Warsaw Ghetto during the war?' said Krakowski, turning pale, as ghosts from the past he had kept hidden for years unlocked the gates to his memory castle.

'Yes. It was Emil Fuchs. There's absolutely no doubt about it.'

'How can you be so sure?' asked Bartolli.

Jack made eye contact with Isis. 'Please tell them.'

'Jack rang me on Tuesday and told me the story. You will remember that Fuchs's executors sent me the forged Monet, *Little Sparrow in the Garden,* which Fuchs had left to me in his will. That was in 2014. Exactly seven years ago.'

'A remarkable gesture. I remember,' said the countess.

'It was. I still have the letter the executors sent me,' continued Isis. 'I rang them straight away in Zurich. The executor, a lawyer, was very polite and helpful. He still had all the records because Fuchs had left detailed instructions about all his paintings, which he had bequeathed to various art galleries around the world.'

'And?' prompted Darrieux.

'While there was no record of a van Eyck painting as such, there was a curious reference to one among Fuchs's papers.'

'What kind of reference?' asked Bartolli.

'Jack, why don't you take if from here?' said Isis.

'As we know, Fuchs was a meticulous record keeper. He had even kept a receipt for the Monet that the Nazis effectively stole from Benjamin's father in the Warsaw Ghetto.'

'I still have it,' said Isis. 'Fuchs left that to me as well. As I had bought the original Monet at auction, and he had left me the forgery, he must have thought the receipt somehow belonged to it. He was obviously a stickler for detail.'

'You mentioned a curious reference,' said Dupree.

'Yes, a receipt signed by Erwin Strasser on an Antiquariat Haephestus letterhead relating to the sale of a painting by Jan van Eyck called – wait for it – *Golgotha*.'

'Are you serious?' said Bartolli, looking incredulous.

'Jack's breadcrumbs,' said Tristan, shaking his head. 'I don't know how he does it.'

'They find *him*,' said Darrieux. 'Don't you know?'

'Is that it, then?' asked Krakowski. 'If it wasn't among Fuchs's paintings when he died, do we know what happened to it?'

'The executor said he would have another look through Fuchs's papers to see if he can find something that could throw some light on what happened to the van Eyck,' said Isis. 'A painting like that doesn't just disappear without a trace. Especially not when a man like Fuchs was involved, who was passionate about paintings and was such a meticulous record keeper.'

'Makes sense,' said Leonardo.

Just then, the doors opened and Bonato burst into the room with a very excited-looking Bobby, Anna's son, by his side.

'Ladies and gentlemen,' said Bonato, looking quite formal in his dark suit. 'Christmas dinner is about to be served. Please follow me.'

'My friends, let's leave all this behind for the moment,' said Jack, 'and celebrate Christmas.'

'Good idea,' said Rahima. She stood and linked arms with Jack, and together they followed Bonato down the corridor to the dining room.

The stunning dining room was lit entirely by candles, the elaborate Murano glass chandelier above the dining table Jack had only recently restored, providing most of the light, making the porcelain and the silver cutlery glow and sending shadows dancing along the walls like some crazy puppet show.

Anna made sure Bobby sat closest to the decorated, floor-to-ceiling Christmas tree. Bonato had seated Krakowski so he had a clear view of the quartet the countess had engaged as a surprise. Seated next to the Christmas tree, the quartet was playing traditional Christmas music, giving the room a festive, nostalgic air. As the host, Jack sat at the head of the table, with his mother on his right, and the countess on his left.

With a menu carefully chosen by the countess, the chefs at Osman's Kitchen had outdone themselves, eager to please not only the countess, but also Jack, who was very popular and often visited them in the kitchen to pinch a tasty morsel or two. They had come up with a Christmas dinner fit for doges and popes, served by staff borrowed from the Palazzo da Baggio and supervised by Bonato, who was thriving on the unexpected revival of Palazzo Alberti, which had been his home since childhood.

Copious quantities of splendid local wine ensured the mood in the room changed quickly from depressing news to Christmas cheer, until the animated conversation between courses almost drowned out the music.

Just before the dessert – a bombe Alaska, Jack's favourite – was served, Maestro Krakowski borrowed one of the violins and entertained his fellow guests with a spectacular rendition of 'Silent Night', with dazzling cadenzas and variations that made the musicians gasp.

After the dessert, Jack suggested everyone return to the salon for coffee and liqueurs. It was there that Jack surprised his mother with a special Christmas present: a fabulous apartment on the first floor, overlooking the Rialto Bridge. Her private domain in the palazzo whenever she wanted to visit. Deep down, Jack was hoping she would eventually come to live with him and Tristan permanently, but he realised his mother liked her independence and would most likely remain in the retirement home in France for the time being. Close to her precious memory trees.

Darrieux turned to the countess sitting next to her. 'My kind of party,' she said, enjoying her fourth glass of vintage champagne – after dinner.

The countess nodded, well pleased by the way the evening had turned out. An experienced host, she knew that every detail counted and controlling the mood of the guests was always key.

Bartolli walked up to Jack standing by the fireplace. 'Congratulations, Jack. You pulled off a memorable evening under difficult circumstances. Not easy with what's happening around us right now, but you did the right thing telling everyone about what's troubling you.'

'Do you think they can see that I'm doing all this not only to protect them, but also to buy time? The only way this will stop is if we put an end to O'Hara and his deadly games. Once and for all.'

'I think they do.'

'You think so? And for that to work, I need the law enforcement agencies to take all this seriously and become involved.'

'I'm sure they understand that too. Dupree has made that very clear. Everybody appreciates honesty. Vulnerability isn't a sign of weakness; it's a sign of humanity and strength.'

'Thanks, Francesca. A huge weight has been lifted off my shoulders tonight. I'm no longer so ...'

'Alone?'

'Yes, that's right.'

'So, what's next?'

'Not sure, but you know me, something will turn up.'

'From Fuchs's executors, perhaps?'

'Could be, but I wouldn't mind a little break from all this. Enough bodies for now, don't you think?'

'I'm not sure O'Hara would agree with you,' said Bartolli.

'I know; that's the problem here. He's a madman. A dangerous one. Are you coming to the midnight mass?'

'Wouldn't miss it for the world.'

'Good. I've arranged a water taxi.'

The Grand Canal looked magical. With many of the palazzos and bridges, and especially the churches illuminated for Christmas, the busy canal looked more like a stage than a major thoroughfare of a city. Everyone except Anna, Billy and Darrieux, who had retired to her room at Palazzo da Baggio, came along to celebrate midnight mass. Jack persuaded the water taxi owner to let him drive the boat. Isis stood next to him in the wheelhouse and watched the stunning palazzos float past.

'This is like a dream, Jack,' said Isis, enjoying the moment.

'Venice is like that.'

'I have a Christmas present for you.'

'Oh? What kind of present?'

'I spoke to Fuchs's executor just before we left.'

'Is that what you were doing in my study? On Christmas Eve?'

'Yes. He promised ...'

'And?' said Jack, excitement in his voice. 'Don't tell me he found something?'

'He has.'

'About the van Eyck?'

'Yes.'

Jack almost lost his grip as the boat turned towards the imposing Benedictine church of San Giorgio Maggiore and pulled up at the jetty.

'Did he say what it was?'

'No. He wants to do that in person. He's a lawyer, and he's Swiss ...'

'When?'

'After Boxing Day.'

'Seems my prayers have been answered even before we set foot in the church. Amazing!'

Isis put her arm around Jack. 'A few more breadcrumbs under the Christmas tree, perhaps?'

'I hope so. Dead ends could be very costly in this story.'

'With you, Jack, there are no dead ends, only challenges.'

Jack looked at Isis. 'Thank you, my friend.'

'Least I can do. Merry Christmas, Jack!'

22

Charité University Hospital, Berlin: Christmas Day

Novotny had made excellent progress and his recovery had surprised many, even the doctors. They put this down to a powerful determination to recover so he could continue his mission. Mind over disease often worked in mysterious ways that medical science couldn't explain, but that didn't make it less real.

Sasha arrived early. The doctors had stipulated no visitors before ten, but the matron in charge made an exception because it was Christmas, and admitted Sasha half an hour earlier.

'Merry Christmas, my darling,' said Sasha and kissed Novotny on the forehead, careful not to disturb the tubes and monitoring devices that still remained. 'You look so much better.'

'Merry Christmas,' said Novotny and reached for Sasha's right hand. 'And thank you.'

'What for?'

'For everything, but especially for believing in me during this difficult time.'

'We are in this together. You know that.'

'I do. That's why I know that you will understand my decision ...'

Sasha gasped and withdrew her hand. She knew what she had been so afraid of was about to become reality. While Novotny's recovery was a Christmas present, she realised it was a two-edged sword that could cut her deeply.

Novotny pointed to the iPad on the bed in front of him.

'I had another close look at our sensational video during the night. The Kremlin has every reason to be worried. This is a grenade ready to explode in Palin's face. And in politics, especially in Russia, face is everything. What we've achieved here is truly astonishing. I was looking at everything with fresh eyes. It almost doesn't seem real, yet as we both know it's all true and supported by facts. To photograph everything from the air with those drones was a stroke of genius. And it worked! You must admit, our team has done an outstanding job. It really gives a clear picture of the size of the estate, the extravagance of Palin's palace and the extent of the corruption involved. This is corruption on an industrial scale! The private harbour, the church, the ice-skating rink, the staggering opulence. And the rest. Pictures can tell the story so much better. Even the older generations will get it.'

'You're right, this will create outrage. You can only deceive people up to a point. And when that point has been reached, it takes something like this to blow the lid off this powder keg of corruption,' said Sasha, becoming animated. 'Russia has seen it all before, but perhaps not quite on this scale. By an elected president, not an autocratic ruler like the tsar!'

'You should put that in our press release.'

'Announcing your imminent return? Perhaps I will.'

'And then to have gained access to the developer's plans, and documents dealing with the cost of it all. One hundred *billion* roubles. Can you imagine? Obscene! This has to be exposed. We can't wait any longer. We must do it now! All we were missing was a title. It came to me last night.'

'It did?'

'Yes. It's so obvious. We should call the project "The New Tsar's Palace: the most audacious corruption in history". What do you think?'

'You used those words during your speech in St Petersburg.'

'Correct.'

'Excellent! Says it all, but may I make a suggestion?' said Sasha.

'Of course.'

'How about this? "The New Tsar's Palace. The Monster Cockroach and the most daring bribe in history".'

'Brilliant! You were always better with words than me. Let's do that. Many of our followers would be familiar with Chukovsky's famous fairytale poem "Tarakanishche".'

'"The Monster Cockroach"; exactly. The poem is buried deep within the Russian psyche and will certainly touch a nerve.'

'About a reign of terror through bullying and threats,' said Novotny.

'Precisely. And this title is referring to all this. In a subtle, yet most effective way without having to spell it out.'

'You're right! This was the missing link. Now we have it. Thanks to you, we are ready to go!'

'If you say so.'

'Absolutely. It's settled, then. We'll announce it straight away. The doctors told me last night that I could be discharged within days.'

'They also told you that you needed rest.'

'True, but time's a luxury we don't have.'

Sasha realised it would be futile trying to change Novotny's mind once he had decided what to do. And besides, she could see the logic in what he had in mind. She knew it was time to set personal consideration aside – however painful that may be – and consider the bigger picture and support Novotny's plan.

'So, you've made up your mind?'

'I have.'

'You're going back to Russia?'

'I must. Surely you can see that. As soon as they let me out of here, I want to deliver my Christmas present to the cockroach personally, and in public.'

'You do know what will happen as soon as you set foot on Russian soil, don't you?'

'Of course.'

'You know the likely cost, then? To you personally?'

'Of course. But since when has influencing history been free?'

Sasha nodded with sadness in her eyes. The pages of history were littered with the broken bodies of revolutionaries dreaming of change.

'I will do everything in my power to make this work for you,' she said, pushing her own reservations aside.

'I know you will, but you realise, of course, that you cannot come with me. You're needed here, outside Russia.'

'I know, and that makes it even harder.'

Novotny reached for Sasha's hand again, lifted it to his lips and kissed it. 'I love you more than I can ever put into words, and what we are about to do makes my love even stronger and draws us ever closer. But there are things that are bigger than we are.'

'Destiny?' ventured Sasha.

'Precisely.'

'Do you think we're strong enough to deal with this, or will the forces of destiny sweep us away?'

Novotny took his time before replying.

'No-one really knows what one's capable of until it's put to the test. I believe we're about to face such a test. I'm ready if you are, but I need you by my side.'

'I will be there. Whatever it takes.'

'Thank you. That's all I needed to hear. I believe that together we can do this.'

'So do I, my darling.' Sasha leaned forward and tenderly kissed Novotny on the forehead, leaving a few hot tears behind as her lips brushed against his brow.

23

Zurich: 27 December

Isis pointed to the polished brass plate above the entrance. 'This is it,' she said. 'Moser & Vogelein. We found it. Right on time.' Isis looked at Jack. 'Lola was right. One of Switzerland's oldest law firms.'

'She didn't seem too pleased when you asked her to stay with the plane at the airport and wait. I think she expected to come with us.'

Isis shrugged. 'Dupree and Darrieux understood. I don't want to overwhelm Moser. He only asked to see us: you and me. I have a feeling there may be something sensitive involved.'

'You may be right.'

'How do you feel?'

'What do you think? A little apprehensive,' said Jack.

'Understandable.'

'A lot hinges on this.'

'What's new? Moser was adamant: he said he did find something that could help, but wanted to tell us about it in person. And he did ask us to come here, to his office. Must mean something, don't you think?'

'I suppose so. He must have his reasons. Let's go in and find out what this is all about.'

The wood-panelled reception oozed understated elegance and class. Etchings of medieval Zurich lined the walls, and exquisite Persian rugs covered the polished parquetry floor, hinting at a well-heeled clientele used to luxury and privacy. Old money. Classic Swiss.

The receptionist sitting behind a large Biedermeier desk greeted them warmly. 'Dr Moser is expecting you. He won't be long. Please take a seat.'

Jack pointed to the superb floral arrangement on the desk. 'How beautiful, and in the middle of winter.'

The receptionist looked at Jack, surprised. Men rarely noticed the flowers. 'The miracle of the glasshouse.'

'Quite so.'

Jack walked over to the etchings and began to examine them, when a door next to the reception desk opened. Jack turned and looked at the tall, elderly man in an impeccable double-breasted, pinstriped suit walking towards him. 'Welcome, and a belated Merry Christmas. I am Anton Moser,' said the man and shook hands with Isis. 'And you must be Mr Rogan.' Moser extended his hand. 'I have heard a lot about you from my client, the late Emil Fuchs.'

'Nothing too terrible, I hope.'

'Not at all. He considered you – how shall I put this? – a formidable opponent.'

'Ah. The Monet affair.'

'A most fascinating case indeed. Our firm does a lot of work for art galleries and museums, and sorting out questions of title and provenance. Always a challenge. Please, come into my office. This way.'

Moser's huge office looked more like an opulent boardroom and faced the famous Bahnhofstrasse, one of Europe's most expensive and exclusive shopping strips. Moser pointed to a large conference table near the floor-to-ceiling windows.

'We have examined all the relevant Fuchs documents we have in storage that could throw some light on your enquiry. I have asked my assistant to lay them out on the table here for ease of reference.'

'Very helpful, thank you,' said Isis and walked over to the table to have a look at the neatly arranged bundles of papers.

'I have been acting for Mr Fuchs for almost forty years,' said Moser. 'And, as you know, he appointed me the executor of his will. This turned out to be a far more demanding and complicated task than I originally envisaged.'

'How come?' asked Jack.

'Because of the size and complexity of his extensive art collection. Perhaps one of the largest private art collections in Europe, if not the world. Paintings mainly, but also some exquisite bronze sculptures by Remington, and Rodin. We sent the Remington only recently to the White House. I understand it will join Remington's famous *Bronco Buster* in the Oval Office.'

'Amazing,' said Isis. 'And he had a Rodin as well?'

'Yes. That went to the Metropolitan in New York. It was valued at over twenty million US and caused quite a sensation.'

'I bet,' said Jack.

'As it turned out,' continued Moser, Mr Fuchs's collection was without doubt the most outstanding and valuable art collection I have come across. It was valued at over seven hundred million euros. A unique collection of a lifetime.'

Moser paused and looked at his visitors, obviously to make a point.

'And what was particularly remarkable, were his specific instructions about what was to happen to each piece,' he continued.

'As you know, he left his entire collection to various art galleries around the world. It has taken us several years to carry out those instructions. Some have still not been finalised. Negotiating with curators and art gallery directors can be very challenging.'

'I can imagine,' said Isis.

'Mr Fuchs's instructions were very detailed. In some cases where major works were involved, he even stipulated how and where they had to be displayed, would you believe. A little presumptuous, you may think, but when a bequest worth millions is involved, people tend to listen.'

'Amazing,' said Jack, watching Moser with interest. For someone well in his eighties, Moser was an impressive man. A shock of white hair, neatly parted in the middle, made him look younger than he was, and his aristocratic bearing radiated confidence and authority. His eyes, ice blue and clear behind gold-rimmed glasses, also belied his age as he took Isis and Jack through the maze of documents spread out on the table.

'The paintings in the Fuchs collection were remarkable, to say the least.' Moser reached for one of the files on the table. 'A Velasquez and a Goya left to the Prado, and over here a Hieronymus Bosch and a Frans Hals, both left to the Rijksmuseum in Amsterdam. When I contacted the museum director he thought at first it was all a hoax and hung up on me. Funny that, don't you think?'

'But not surprising,' said Isis.

'Fuchs understood the importance of provenance. That was the main reason he took such great care with documenting everything.'

'But surely that wasn't possible with all the paintings he acquired?' said Jack, watching Moser carefully. 'Take the Monet, for example ...'

'You are absolutely right, Mr Rogan. There were paintings in the collection that had a somewhat questionable provenance.'

Lawyer-speak for stolen, thought Jack, but didn't reply.

'Most of those acquisitions happened during the war, or shortly thereafter. Europe was in turmoil. Things happened. Desperate things. And Fuchs was very aware of it. He thought some of the acquisitions were a stain on his collection and his reputation. He tried to remedy that.'

'How exactly?' asked Jack, unable to keep the sarcasm out of his voice. 'By changing history?'

Isis shot Jack a disapproving look. Jack realised he had almost gone too far.

'By disposing of paintings that didn't have a respectable provenance; removing them from his collection.'

'Like *Golgotha?*' said Jack. 'The receipt you kindly told us about seems to suggest that this painting was bought from a dealer called Erwin Strasser. He had a gallery in Salzburg called Antiquariat Haephestus. Strasser had a nickname in certain art circles. He was known as the Cyclops and had a reputation for buying artworks that had a "questionable provenance", as you put it.'

'I completely understand where you are going with this, Mr Rogan,' said Moser calmly, 'but please understand I am not here to judge my client; I am simply carrying out his instructions.'

'Point taken. I'm not judging him either. I'm simply trying to find out what happened to a unique painting with a most intriguing history that seems to have ended up in Mr Fuchs's collection.'

'I see we understand each other. You have obviously done your research, Mr Rogan,' said Moser. 'You are correct. About Strasser, I mean. And I believe that is why there is no record as such of what happened to the painting, except for one small but important clue I will tell you about in a moment. It is the reason I asked you to come here: so I could explain it all properly and show you the relevant documents.'

'We both appreciate that,' said Isis.

'A painting like *Golgotha* deserves nothing less,' continued Moser. 'Great works of art cannot belong to just one person alone. They belong to mankind. Fuchs understood that. He used to tell me that we are only temporary custodians of other men's genius.'

'Interesting ...' said Jack, 'coming from a man who lived like a recluse in a mountain chalet surrounded by priceless art only he could see.'

'You must understand, Fuchs was a complex man with a past. I have no idea how he made his fortune. He never told me and I never asked, but the war certainly had something to do with it.'

'It sure did,' said Jack. 'Mr Krakowski could tell you certain things about Emil Fuchs that may shock you.'

'That may well be the case, Mr Rogan, but the past is the past and we should return to the present, don't you think?' came the polite rebuff.

'You're right. I'm sorry.'

'Fuchs was very methodical, disciplined and fastidious when it came to his art collection,' said Moser, moving on. 'He spent the last few years of his life in a wheelchair, and used that time to prepare his instructions in his distinctive, spidery handwriting.'

Moser reached for a bundle of papers and held it up.

'He always used a fountain pen. According to him, biros were for secretaries and clerks, not for gentlemen. That's the kind of man he was.'

Jack smiled as he remembered his own encounters with Fuchs.

'But you have, of course, met Emil Fuchs, Mr Rogan. You even interviewed him. I almost forgot. And wrote a novella about it after he died.'

'Yes, *The Forgotten Painting*. That was all about the Monet and David Herzl, the master forger of Warsaw,' said Jack.

'Fascinating,' said Moser.

'It is,' said Jack. 'And what brings us here today, once again concerns Herzl and another painting.'

'*Golgotha*,' said Moser, looking pensively out the window. 'Isis has explained the connection to me. Quite extraordinary how these matters are intertwined. One could be tempted to say, it was meant to be.'

'Threads of destiny and fate often are, as Jack here would suggest,' said Isis, smiling.

'An excellent way to put it. And what I am about to tell you, would certainly fall neatly into that category,' said Moser. '*Destiny*. It all began with an accidental meeting between two men at an auction in Paris a few years after Fuchs had bought the van Eyck. Fuchs loved auctions. He called them duels of minds and wallets, and he was a master of both when it came to bidding. He often asked me to go with him. On that occasion, the painting for sale was a rare Toulouse-Lautrec he desperately wanted. The bidding was fierce and it ended in a rare duel that Fuchs lost. That should have been the end of it, but as things turned out, it was just the beginning.'

'How intriguing,' said Jack.

'It is far more than that, Mr Rogan, as you will see in a moment.' Moser reached for a small sheet of paper on the table and held it up. 'The only reason certain pieces of this puzzle fell into place and the reason I asked you to come here is because of an obscure reference on this piece of paper. It's a note I came across accidentally because it had been filed in the wrong place. I found it when I had another look through Fuchs's records to see if I could find something about *Golgotha*. This note was written two weeks after the auction. As it turned out, the Toulouse-Lautrec did end up in Fuchs's collection after all, but how this came about is quite a story that explains what happened to the van Eyck.'

'I can't wait,' said Jack becoming excited. He took his little notebook out of his jacket pocket, slipped off the rubber band and looked expectantly at Moser. 'Please tell us.'

'I will, but first may I offer you some coffee or tea, perhaps?' Moser pointed to a lounge and leather chairs. 'Please take a seat. This may take some time.'

PART II

THE AMULET OF TIMUR

'It is better to conquer yourself than to win a thousand battles.
Then the victory is yours. It cannot be taken from you,
not by angels or by demons, heaven or hell.'
— *Buddha*

24

Deep in thought, President Palin stared vacantly into space. It had been one of the worst days of his presidency. After an exhausting meeting that had lasted several hours, the FSB officers had finally left, and Palin was now in his office with Colonel Karlov, his most trusted FSB agent and adviser. They had been friends since their days in Dresden in East Germany, before the collapse of the DDR. The threatening clouds that had been gathering for some time had unleashed a storm of epic proportions, causing unprecedented havoc that could quickly turn into a serious threat to the presidency if something drastic wasn't done.

Any hesitation to implement certain measures that Palin had previously shied away from, had quickly evaporated once Novotny had delivered the corruption proof he had promised during his speech in St Petersburg.

After his arrest at the airport, Novotny's supporters in Germany had released an explosive video on the internet, accusing Palin and the Kremlin of corruption on a scale Russia had not seen before. The timing of the release had been carefully planned because it coincided with Novotny's court appearance the day after his detention to face vague charges relating to a previous court case a first-year lawyer could easily have had thrown out of court.

Even diverting the plane from Moscow to Kaluga, one hundred and fifty kilometres southeast of Moscow, to avoid the huge crowd that had gathered at Moscow's Vnukovo International Airport to welcome their hero, had the opposite effect. Instead of dispersing, the furious, disappointed crowd regrouped in the Red Square for a well-organised demonstration supporting Novotny.

'This is a disaster!' said Palin, frowning at his friend sitting opposite.

'It's bad,' conceded Karlov, 'but we can control this, if we act now.'

'What do you suggest?'

'Arresting Novotny and putting him on trial was the first step. The most important one. The best way to kill a snake is to cut off its head.'

Palin nodded. 'And after that?'

'I know you didn't want to do this before, but mass arrests must commence immediately.'

'On what basis?'

'Your decree making Novotny's organisations in Russia illegal. You have the power to do this. This would send a clear message to Novotny's supporters. Stay away or face court and possible jail. Simple. That's the next step.'

'And then?'

'Novotny will stand trial and go to jail for a long time. That's a given. After that, we should immediately tighten censorship and send in the spin-doctors to go to work on the palace question. They can produce evidence refuting Novotny's claims and show that the palace had nothing to do with you and those close to you, but is in fact owned by one of the wealthy oligarchs.'

'All right. Let's take another look at this dreadful mess.'

Taking a deep breath, Palin turned on his TV and selected Novotny's 'fake proof video', as it was referred to by the FSB.

'If our analysts are right, this has already been viewed eighty-two million times since its release yesterday,' he said, shaking his head. 'Unheard of!'

Narrated by Novotny personally, the video was a documentary-style, step-by-step exposure of monstrous corruption within the Kremlin designed to benefit Palin and his cronies, who had appointed each other to positions of influence and power, which put them above the law and effectively made them untouchable.

Palin kept staring at the screen as one document after another exposing damaging evidence, which felt like a potential noose of public opinion around the neck of the cabal involved in the corruption, was explained by Novotny in terms that were not only compelling, but also easy to understand and follow.

'Where on earth did he get all this material from?' said Palin as evidence of huge money transfers, hidden bank accounts, bogus shareholdings and sham directorships were paraded across the screen in a never-ending litany of damning evidence involving sums of money difficult to comprehend. To make things worse, the flow of documents was interspersed with clever cartoons mocking Palin, calling him the Monster Cockroach and showing him dressed as an arrogant tsar pirouetting in front of a mirror like a vain peacock. And all the damning facts were presented by Novotny with undisguised sarcasm and contempt in his voice.

Just when Palin thought it couldn't get any worse, it did.

After explaining how the corruption had eventuated, who was involved, and how it all worked, Novotny turned to the 'Monster Cockroach's palace', as he called it, and presented the facts of a secret, colossal extravagance that had been years in the making.

Once he had explained the source of the stolen funds, he then showed how and where they had been channelled to: a project that had cost more than a hundred billion roubles, all of which, Novotny argued convincingly, had been stolen from the legitimate revenue coffers belonging to the Russian people.

Palin began to sweat and the veins on his neck began to throb as he kept watching the video, which now turned to the interior of the palace and moved from room to room, and floor to floor, showing furniture and opulence that would have made Louis XIV blush, and even quoting the cost of certain items. When the camera moved to the huge bedroom complex, the palatial marble bathrooms and walk-in wardrobes full of designer clothes, Palin couldn't watch anymore and turned off the TV, almost choking on a toxic mixture of embarrassment and rage.

The most powerful man in Russia had been humiliated by a man who had recently survived an attempt on his life by a whisker, and had returned to Russia fully aware of what would happen to him as soon as he set foot on Russian soil. It was a symbolic act of courageous defiance that earned him the respect of his followers and critics alike, and added serious credibility to his extravagant corruption claims.

'What do you make of all this?' asked Palin, barely able to speak.

'From a purely strategic point of view, returning to Russia was a brilliant move. A masterstroke. Novotny knew exactly what would happen and was ready for it. We've already seen that. His arrest has given his video credibility, and Novotny hero status among his ever-growing followers, stunned by the revelations and evidence supporting them.'

Palin nodded and looked at Karlov. At least he could count on his friend to assess the situation without distorting or embellishing the facts.

'I agree. He must have a lot of supporters in high places to have made all this possible. To obtain this material must have taken a lot of planning and many inside contacts. How else could he have put his hands on images of the interior, and copies of the actual plans and costings?'

'Absolutely,' said Karlov. 'We must definitely look into this.'

'Playing catch-up isn't going to win us this fight; something much more drastic has to be done, don't you think?'

'What do you have in mind?'

'As we both know, attack is the best form of defence.'

'It is. But to be effective it has to be swift and certain.'

'Quite so.'

'Damage control isn't enough here. We need mass arrests of Novotny's supporters, and we have to close down his organisation and make it illegal. As I see it, this is the only way.'

'I agree,' said Karlov, who was one of the most hawkish members of Palin's inner circle of advisers. 'Pussyfooting around will get us nowhere. We must come down hard! Now!'

'Let's start in the morning.'

'All you have to do is give the orders.'

'I will.'

Karlov stood up, eager to leave before Palin's anger calmed down and he changed his mind or watered down the approach.

'I'll get onto it straight away,' he said.

Satisfied, Palin looked at his friend. 'I knew I could count on you.'

'Always,' said Karlov. Making a bow, he turned and left the room.

Effectively, what Palin had just done was to declare war on his own people, and in doing so he had unwittingly lived up to his new nickname given to him by Novotny, the Monster Cockroach. Chukovsky's fairytale poem was quickly turning into reality.

25

Time Machine Studios, London: 29 December

Isis was sitting in her study on the top floor of her penthouse overlooking the Thames and looking pensively out of the window, when Lola walked in.

'She just arrived,' said Lola.

'Good. Please send her up. Where is he?'

'Still in his room.'

Isis shook her head. 'I'm worried about him.'

'Me too. He barely said anything since we left Zurich. And he hasn't eaten much, either. That tells you something.'

'Sure does,' said Isis. 'Let's see if Francesca can get through to him.'

'Let's hope so. After all, he did ask to see her.'

As soon as the lift doors opened, Isis walked over to Bartolli and embraced her. 'Thanks for coming.'

'I came as soon as I could. What's wrong?'

'Not sure. We were hoping you could find out.'

Bartolli took off her coat and sat down. 'What happened?'

'As you know, we went to see Fuchs's executor in Zurich.'

'Jack was very excited about that. He could barely wait to see him and hardly spoke of anything else over Christmas,' said Bartolli.

'I remember.'

'He was going to call me and tell me how it all went, but didn't. Instead of returning to Venice to be with his friends, he came here with you. *Why?* Abandoning his guests isn't like Jack.'

Isis shrugged.

'What happened in Zurich that was so important?'

'I think it's better if you hear it from him.'

'All right,' said Bartolli, a worried look on her face.

Bartolli knocked on Jack's door.

'Come in,' said Jack.

Bartolli opened the door and walked inside. Barefoot and wearing a baggy tracksuit that was several sizes too big, Jack sat at a desk covered with papers, his open laptop and iPad on the unmade bed behind him. Jack's hair was unkempt and he hadn't shaved. Without saying a word, Jack walked over to Bartolli and gave her a hug. It was an embrace radiating desperation and pain that Bartolli would remember for a long time.

'What's wrong, Jack?'

Jack pointed to a chair next to the desk. 'Please sit down. I need your help. And advice.'

'In what way?'

'The mind games are getting to me.'

'What kind of mind games?'

'O'Hara. I think Tristan saw it much earlier. He tried to warn me. You know what he's like. His intuition can be quite uncanny at times. I know we often joke about it, but I can tell you it's real.'

'Please explain what you mean.'

'This is all about evil, true evil. O'Hara is a genius of true evil with apocalyptic tendencies. He's the most dangerous man I've ever encountered. An antichrist with no moral compass. Anything goes.'

'Care to elaborate?'

Jack reached for his notebook and opened it. 'It's quite a story, and it's all about *Golgotha*—'

'The painting?'

'Yes.'

Bartolli smiled. Everything to do with Jack was always quite a story.

'Tell me.'

Step by step, Jack told Bartolli about the meeting with Moser.

'And then Moser mentioned destiny,' he said, 'and told us about an accidental meeting between two men at an auction.'

'What kind of auction?'

'A rare Toulouse-Lautrec painting called *The Englishman at the Moulin Rouge* was being auctioned in Paris. That happened a few years after Fuchs bought the van Eyck from Erwin Strasser in Salzburg. Fuchs was after the painting, and so was someone else. To cut a long story short, Fuchs was outmanoeuvred both financially and tactically, and lost the painting. But that wasn't the end of it. It was just the beginning.'

'In what way?'

'After the auction, Fuchs went up to the man who had just won the bidding war and introduced himself. They began to chat, and apparently got on like a house on fire. Both were avid collectors with deep pockets, and each had a huge private collection with egos to match.'

'And Moser told you all this?'

'Yes. He was there and witnessed it all. He attended the auction with Fuchs.'

Bartolli sat back in her chair and looked inquisitively at Jack, wondering where all this was going.

'Apparently, Fuchs invited the man – his name was Mohammed bin Ahmed, a wealthy sheikh from Oman – to visit him in Switzerland. He wanted to show him his collection.' Jack paused and looked out the window just as the cloak of darkness descended on the city and lights came on, illuminating the Tower Bridge and the stunning Shard in the distance, and changing the mood in the room.

'Moser forgot all about this encounter at the time,' continued Jack, 'until he visited his client at his home a few months later and noticed something curious.'

'What?'

'He saw Toulouse-Lautrec's *The Englishman at the Moulin Rouge* hanging on a wall in Fuchs's dining room.'

'How come?'

'When Moser questioned his client about that, he was evasive and didn't explain how he had obtained it. That was the end of the matter until the other day.'

'Oh?'

'When Moser went through Fuchs's records again to see if he could come up with something about *Golgotha*, he accidentally came across a brief note. Apparently, it had been filed in the wrong place.'

'What kind of note?'

Jack reached for a piece of paper on the desk and held it up.

'This here. It's very brief. It should have been filed with the Toulouse-Lautrec papers because it belonged to that painting's provenance. As we know, Fuchs was a meticulous record keeper, obsessed with provenance.'

'What does it say?'

'Only one line: *Golgotha* exchanged for *The Englishman at the Moulin Rouge,* and a date. That's all.'

'Meaning?'

'According to Moser, what it suggests is this: when the sheikh from Oman visited Fuchs in Switzerland and Fuchs showed him his collection, they came to an arrangement.'

'What kind of arrangement?'

'They exchanged paintings: van Eyck's *Golgotha* for Toulouse-Lautrec's *The Englishman at the Moulin Rouge.*'

'Why would they do that?'

Jack shrugged. 'Wealthy collectors often do such things for various reasons. No auction, no art dealers, no sales commission, no questions. And besides, according to Moser, Fuchs wanted to get rid of certain paintings in his collection that had a dubious provenance.'

'Stolen, you mean?'

'Something like that. As we know, *Golgotha* was one of them, and a lot more.'

'And the sheikh fell for that?'

'Don't forget, the van Eyck was a very rare and valuable painting. Arguably much more valuable than the Toulouse-Lautrec. To the right collector in the know, it was priceless.'

'A good deal, then?'

'It would seem so. For both parties, actually.'

'Amazing. I can see why Moser called it destiny.'

'So can I.'

'Where does this leave you, then?'

'Well, all we have to go by is this slip of paper. If this is a true reflection of what happened, then *Golgotha* found its way to Oman, and is perhaps still in that wealthy sheik's art collection. Provided it hasn't been sold, that is. This wouldn't be unusual; there's a lot of art in the Middle East. But that would have left a trace, because a famous painting like *Golgotha* would certainly have left its mark on the art market. Yet there is no mention of it anywhere. I looked, and so did Moser.'

'Unless it was exchanged on the wealthy collectors black market, where only money and egos matter, and no questions are asked,' said Bartolli.

'True. That's a possibility, and if that has happened, we'll certainly never know. The search is over. Confidentiality is key in these deals and everyone involved is tight-lipped to keep it that way.'

Bartolli reached across to Jack and put her hand on his arm. 'Is that why you are feeling a little down?' she asked quietly.

'No, that's not the reason. And it certainly isn't the reason I need your help.'

Bartolli looked at Jack, surprised. She had never seen him so vulnerable and dejected. 'Oh? Then what is?'

'O'Hara. He must have somehow found out about my meeting with Moser. I certainly didn't tell him.'

'What makes you say that?'

'Because he contacted me. We were on our way back to the airport after meeting Moser, when O'Hara called and accused me of not keeping him informed. He was furious and almost screamed at me. He said I had breached our understanding, would you believe? *Understanding?*'

'Seriously?'

'Yes. He's a madman!'

'That's incredible. Do you think he had you followed?'

'Must have.'

'But you arrived in a private plane.'

'There are ways. Hackers can get into everything. Even flight plans filed by private jets ...'

'I see. Amazing.'

'It sure is. But that's not all.'

'What do you mean?'

'O'Hara gave me an ultimatum.'

'Seriously? What kind of ultimatum?'

'Find *Golgotha* by the end of the year, or else. That's two days away, for Christ's sake!'

'What do you think that means?'

'Isn't it obvious? He's threatening me, turning the screws. I think he needs more action for his gambling site.'

Jack turned away and stared out of the window. 'And then he said the most chilling thing ...'

'What chilling thing?'

'*Behold the memory trees,*' Jack whispered without turning around.

Oh, my God, thought Bartolli. She reached for Jack's hand and held it. Suddenly, everything began to make sense.

'Your mother?'

'Yes. And coming from someone like O'Hara, I must take this seriously. Look what happened to Stein, Kun and Strasser.'

'I understand.'

'I know you do. That's why I asked you to come. We have to talk about how to deal with this. I feel trapped, helpless. A new approach is needed. You know the criminal mind better than anyone.'

'What about Dupree and Lapointe?'

'All the right intentions, but they are thinking within the square. Lapointe is doing everything he can and has brought Europol on board, but these wheels turn slowly.'

'And the Squadra Mobile in Florence?'

'Samartini is doing an outstanding job in hacking into O'Hara's gambling site, but that too has its limitations. We know he's hiding somewhere in Belarus. The signals she traced made that clear, but unfortunately she's been unable to pinpoint the exact location. She needs more information before she can do that. But that's only part of the problem.'

'What do you mean?' asked Bartolli.

'Effectively, Belarus is out of European law enforcement reach. As long as O'Hara doesn't run out of money, he's safe there. Lukashenko, Europe's last dictator, will make sure of it.'

Jack turned around at last. 'We need a new approach. We must think *outside* the square.'

'Have you spoken to Tristan?'

'Yes, of course. He didn't seem concerned.'

'How come?'

'He said he was sure something would turn up soon. Can you believe this?'

'With Tristan, I can. Maybe that's where our new approach will come from.'

'Maybe. But in the meantime, I need something a little more tangible to give me peace of mind. I spoke to Katerina about the threat. She's taking it seriously. I suggested she speak to Grimaldi in Florence. He told her to hire a live-in security guard for the time being. He even suggested someone.'

'It has come to this?'

'For the time being, yes. Mum is staying at the Palazzo da Baggio. She's safer there than back in the retirement home in France, on her own.'

'I can see that.'

'But this can't go on; surely you can see that too?'

'Yes, of course not.'

Jack let go of Bartolli's hand. 'There is one thing ...'

'What do you mean?'

'Lola's come up with something unexpected. She remembered something ...'

'Remembered? What?'

'An invitation.'

'What kind of invitation?'

'A New Year's Eve party. Right here in London.'

'A party? And this is relevant? I don't follow.'

'As you can imagine, Isis gets lots of invitations to many exclusive social events. Most of them are politely declined, but this one could be different. That's the other reason I asked you to come.'

'I still don't follow.'

'It's not the party as such, which will no doubt be quite something. It's at an exclusive townhouse in Chelsea that's owned by a billionaire. What is of interest here is *who* the invitation's from.'

'Tell me.'

'A sheik from Oman called Khalid bin Ahmed.'

Jack paused to let this sink in.

'Are you suggesting there's a connection—'

'Between the man who exchanged his Toulouse-Lautrec for Fuchs's *Golgotha*? Yes, there is. Sheik Khalid bin Ahmed is his son, and you and I have been invited to his New Year's Eve party. Lola arranged the invitation and Isis is, of course, coming along as well. After all, she's the star attraction here, and the only reason we've been invited. Interested?'

26

Unter den Linden, Berlin: 30 December

Feeling drained and exhausted, Sasha went back to her flat on Unter den Linden near the State Opera House. It was only a short walk from the rented offices that served as the HQ-in-exile of Novotny's organisation. The takeaway meal in the paper bag had gone cold a long time ago, and she no longer felt hungry, only tired and, she had to admit, somewhat dejected. While she had supported Novotny's return to Russia because it made sense, the brutal crackdown on his supporters had surprised all, and she began to have second thoughts about her partner's strategy and judgement.

After the release of the sensational corruption proof video viewed by millions, the mass arrests and incarceration of thousands had taken the momentum out of Novotny's campaign, replacing outrage with fear – an old and tested FSB strategy of suppression and misinformation.

However, the video, with its overwhelming evidence and inflammatory rhetoric of endemic corruption involving the president and his inner circle had not only been hugely embarrassing to Palin, but had also severely damaged his reputation and standing in Russia. From that point of view, Novotny's strategy had been a spectacular success, but it had come at a big cost not only to him personally, but also to his organisation both in Russia and abroad. In short, Novotny and his movement were quickly becoming a victim of their own success. When you wound the bear, prepare to be mauled.

Sasha had barely left the office since Novotny's departure and had carefully followed his arrest at the airport and what followed as various news channels reported the sensational events live. But the initial euphoria caused by the release of the video and the hundreds of thousands of posts on social media voicing outrage and demanding change were soon replaced by chilling silence as the

Kremlin came out fighting, cracking down on the internet and making demonstrations and access to social media not only difficult, but also illegal.

Deep down, Sasha suspected that Novotny had counted on a somewhat different reception in Russia, and had not anticipated Palin's reaction correctly. Underestimating an opponent is a classic mistake that can quickly result in disaster despite the merits of the cause, or the moral high ground that might suggest otherwise. When people find their own little world under threat, voices quickly fall silent and withdraw, seeking the safety of the familiar and comfort of the status quo. And that seemed to be happening all over Russia since Novotny's arrest.

The smartest thing Novotny had done was to keep his organisation functioning and operational outside Russia. And by placing Sasha in charge, he had someone at the helm he could not only rely on, but also trust with his life. Sasha was as committed to the cause as Novotny, and she was respected for that by all who knew her.

Unshaken in her belief that Novotny and his ideas would triumph in the end, Sasha had vowed to continue the fight whatever the cost. Yet, when one considered her background and privileged upbringing, this was surprising to say the least.

While she didn't try to hide the identity of her high-profile, albeit notorious father, she didn't use it to open doors either. She preferred to stay discreetly in the background and be herself. Since the very public divorce of her parents ten years earlier, Sasha had drifted away from her father and taken her mother's name – Kovalenko – a classic Ukrainian surname. After the divorce, her mother returned to Kyiv, where she had grown up and still had relatives, and Sasha visited her there regularly. Her father lived in London, and despite their differences he doted on her. She was his only child.

Sasha made some tea, had a hot bath, and then went to bed. She had just turned out the light on the bedside table and was drifting towards much-needed sleep, when her iPhone rang. Instantly awake, she reached across and answered it. It was Henry Blackstone, her father's lawyer, whom she had known almost all her life, telling her that her father had had a stroke and had been admitted to a London hospital.

'How bad is it?' she asked.

'Difficult to say. He's in the best of care. The doctors are doing everything they can,' said Blackstone.

Must be really bad, thought Sasha, reading between the platitudes.

'You must come to London at once. You have his power of attorney. You are needed here urgently. You know what your father's like. So much is going on …'

'I understand. I'll be on the first available flight.'

'Come to the hospital and we'll go and see him together. I am so sorry, Sasha.'

Taking a deep breath, Sasha turned on the light and put on her dressing gown. Then she went into the kitchen to make some more tea.

How quickly life can change, she thought. With the love of her life in a Russian jail facing an uncertain future, and her father in a hospital in London facing the same, she suddenly felt terribly alone, unaware of just how much her own life had changed in an instant.

27

South Kensington, London: 31 December

Having barely slept at all, Sasha went from the airport straight to the hospital. Her father's lawyer – a man in his late sixties – was already waiting for her in the elegant lobby of the private clinic, one of London's finest.

'I came as soon as I could,' she said. 'How is he?'

'Still in ICU, I'm afraid. He had a haemorrhagic stroke.'

'Good God! What's the prognosis?'

'I will let the doctor explain that, but it's not good, I'm afraid.'

'Where did it happen?'

'At home. After a swim in his indoor pool. The housekeeper found him just in time. Otherwise ...'

'Can I see him?'

'Yes. It's all arranged. Come.'

Seeing her father – a big, powerfully built man – connected to all kinds of tubes and monitoring devices brought tears to Sasha's eyes. To see a man who had always been larger than life reduced to a slave of machines to keep him alive was both profoundly sad and humiliating.

Their differences and many arguments they'd had over the years evaporated. What remained was a stark reminder of the fragility of life, and the relentless passage of time.

Composing herself, Sasha turned away. There was no point in staring at her motionless father any longer, only to be reminded of a situation she had no control over. Reality was calling with far more urgent business.

After a brief consultation with the doctor in charge, who delivered a very sobering prognosis, Sasha turned to Blackstone.

'What now?'

'We have to talk. Urgently.'

'All right. Let's do it here.'

'Fine by me.'

Blackstone found a private corner in the lobby and they sat down.

'You heard what the doctor said,' he began.

'I did.'

'This is a serious situation that requires honesty and courage. We must face reality. Head on.'

'Agreed.'

'It's unlikely your father will recover from this and regain his faculties. There is serious and permanent brain damage.'

Sasha nodded with tears in her eyes.

'Let me explain the legal consequences.'

'Please do.'

The lawyer opened his briefcase and placed a bundle of papers on the table in front of him.

'As things stand, you are the sole heir of your father's empire. You are his only child, but as he is still alive, it is premature to consider that right now. What is far more important is the fact you have power of attorney. In short, at the moment, you are the one who can, indeed must, make all the decisions needed for the day-to-day running of his affairs. And that includes his treatment and associated matters, like life support ...'

'I understand.'

'What you may not fully appreciate is the sheer size and complexity of his business interests. Your father is a billionaire, several times over, with investments all over the world.'

'What's your point?'

'This is a huge job, and there are urgent matters that require your immediate attention.'

'I'm a fast learner.'

Blackstone smiled. 'I know you are. Your father has been a very astute man. He surrounded himself with the best brains and advisers in the business and, most importantly, he was always prepared to listen—'

'You speak of him if he were already dead,' interrupted Sasha, steel in her voice.

'I'm sorry, but legally and practically, well ...'

'I understand.'

'What I'm trying to say is there's help available and there are competent, loyal professionals you can turn to who will show you the way.'

'Will you be one of them?'

'If you want me to be, yes, of course.'

'You've been with my father for as long as I can remember. He's always referred to you as the man he could trust with his life. You've been his adviser and close friend for a long time. I would like to be able to rely on you in the same way.'

'You can.'

'You know of my involvement with Andrei Novotny and his organisation, don't you? It's been the main reason my father and I have ... grown apart.'

'I know. Your father and I have often spoken about this and have followed Novotny's recent return to Russia and his arrest with great interest. I have seen the corruption video, and so has your father. Extraordinary! It really shocked him. I think he was beginning to see things in a different way ...'

'The reason I mention this is that since Andrei's arrest, I am running his organisation. This will not change. No, it *cannot* change. It's his life's work, and quickly becoming mine too. Therefore, whatever I have to do in connection with my father's affairs will have to fit around that.'

'Understood. That shouldn't be a problem, but may I make a suggestion?'

'Please do.'

'To make this work, you should move here, to London.'

'I thought that too.'

'Why don't you move into your father's house?'

'I think I'll do that and gradually move Andrei's organisation over here. We often spoke about it. We always thought that London would be the perfect place for that.'

'Excellent, but for now there are a number of matters that require your urgent attention and there are documents to sign. I have your power of attorney right here ...'

'Let's do it.'

Blackstone looked at Sasha and smiled. 'You're definitely your father's daughter,' he said and reached for a bundle of papers on the table in front of him. 'These have to be signed before the end of the year. And that's almost upon us. I'll tell you what they are.'

28

Chelsea, London: New Year's Eve

Boris, Isis's bodyguard-cum-chauffeur, drove the Bentley slowly towards the brightly lit townhouse at the end of the exclusive, tree-lined street. Lola sat in the front, and Isis in the back with Jack and Bartolli. Lola turned around and winked at Isis. 'Time to make an entrance,' she said, 'and impress your fans.'

'Don't be silly,' said Isis and adjusted her hair. 'Fans? Here? Hardly. This is a Middle Eastern billionaire's mansion, not a concert venue, and we are here to impress the host, not fans.'

'Then why did you insist on squeezing yourself into your spectacular Aztec-inspired bodysuit you wore at the Mexico City concerts?' teased Lola.

'Ah. The costume I was wearing at the time Jack called me a "dead girl walking", you mean?'

'Come on, you had just recovered from a serious brain operation,' said Jack. 'And besides, your *Dead Girl Walking* album was a mega hit. It was a compliment.'

Isis sighed. 'My God, that was ten years ago! Can you believe it, guys? I'm turning into an old chook. The reason I wore this tonight is to show you all that I can still dress for a party.'

'You sure know how to do that, no doubt about it,' said Lola, smiling. What she hadn't told Isis was that she had spoken to a few of her contacts at the tabloids, hinting that Isis would be attending a New Year's Eve party in Chelsea, and gave them the address. She was therefore certain that news crews would be waiting at the venue, and so would some fans because of a social media post Lola had released earlier that day, which had gone viral. Isis the megastar still attracted huge attention and made news wherever she went.

'Look at that crowd,' said Isis as the Bentley pulled up. 'Quite a party.' A security guard walked up to the car and opened the back door. As soon as Isis got out of the car she was recognised, and the waiting crowd erupted and began to chant: 'Isis, Isis, Isis!'

Jack put his hand on Lola's shoulder. 'You arranged this, didn't you?'

'Aha. If we arrive making the right impression, we are bound to be received accordingly, don't you think?' said Lola, grinning. 'Don't forget, we're here on a mission and not just to drink a rich man's champagne. We could have done that at home. And besides, just look at her.'

Isis was posing for photos in front of the house and throwing kisses at her adoring fans, who were being held back by security guards. Looking stunning in her tight-fitting bodysuit inspired by the elaborate ceremonial cloaks worn by Aztec priests, Isis walked slowly up the stairs to the entrance, aware that all eyes, and cameras, were on her.

Following the contours of her athletic body, the feathers and glass beads shimmered like precious stones, accentuating her short hair and prominent facial features with her trademark, almost theatrical makeup.

Jasmina stood next to her father at the top of the stairs and watched Isis come closer. '*Is this really her?*'

'Yes, it is,' said Sheik Khalid bin Ahmed, beaming. His New Year's Eve party was surpassing all expectations, and was quickly turning into the social event he had always dreamed about. Money alone was not enough. Recognition was everything, especially in London, and having one of the most famous entertainers on the globe as his guest would propel him up the society ladder and into the social limelight he had craved so desperately for years.

'Welcome to my humble home,' said Sheik Khalid, making a bow. 'You honour me with your illustrious presence.'

'The honour is all mine,' said Isis, surprised by the effusive welcome, albeit Sheik Khalid's heavy accent making it quite difficult to understand what he was saying. 'Thank you for your kind invitation. Allow me to present my PA, Lola Rodriguez, and my dear friends Jack Rogan and Professor Bartolli.'

'Ah, Mr Rogan the famous author,' said Sheik Khalid. 'I so enjoy your books and so does my daughter, Jasmina. It is a pleasure to meet you.'

Sheik Khalid introduced his wide-eyed, almost speechless daughter first to Isis, then to Jack, and then proudly led the way into the house.

Isis caused quite a stir as she walked into the crowded room bustling with politicians, celebrities and guests from all walks of life. Used to the limelight, she revelled in the attention and mixed with ease with London's social elite. She graciously posed for photos with elderly lords and their frightfully thin wives, and joked with cabinet ministers, eager to be photographed standing next to a megastar, to impress their constituents.

'What do you think, Jack?' said Lola. She reached for a glass of champagne on the tray of a passing waiter and handed it to Bartolli.

'I'd say we're off to a good start,' said Jack, also grabbing a glass each for himself and Lola. 'I think we should split up. Isis will talk to Sheik Khalid as arranged, and Francesca and I will try to talk to Jasmina and see how we go. Daughters have influence with their fathers. Especially this one, I'd say.'

'And I will just stand here and get "pissed", is that it?' said Lola, rolling her eyes.

'No. You will keep an eye on Isis and make sure she doesn't dominate the party and get out of hand, right? Well, not entirely anyway.'

'Why do I get all the good jobs?'

Jack bent down and kissed Lola on the cheek. 'Because you're the only one who can do it. Let's be thankful Adrienne isn't here as well. Otherwise, the two of them, well … Thanks for arranging this. It was a masterstroke.'

'You think so?'

'Absolutely. I have good vibes about this evening.'

'I hope you're right,' said Bartolli. She turned towards Jack and they touched glasses. 'Salute! The old year is almost over. I wonder what the new one will bring.'

'So do I, but let's get through this one first. I'll have to tell O'Hara something encouraging before midnight, remember?'

'I know, but remember what Tristan said.'

'Something will turn up?'

'Exactly.'

'We'll find out soon enough, but I can promise you one thing.'

'What's that?' asked Lola.

'It won't be boring, guys. Cheers!'

'He can see another book in all this, you know,' said Lola softly.

'Doesn't he always? That's Jack, I'm afraid. At least he seems to have left his demons behind and is coming out of his dark days ...' said Bartolli.

'Looks that way. Let's hope the demons don't get their claws into him again and drag him into a dark night.'

'We won't let that happen, right? That's what friends are for.'

'True. Look, he's already chatting with Jasmina over there. No doubt about our Jack and women! Better go and join him and make sure he stays on track.'

'Good idea. And you keep an eye on Isis.'

Lola sighed. 'Won't be easy, but I'll give it my best. It's difficult to stop her once she gets going. Like all entertainers, she craves the limelight. Artistic oxygen. Cheers.'

A few minutes before midnight, Isis walked up to Jack and took him aside.

'We're in,' she said, her face flushed with excitement.

'What do you mean?'

'Tell you later. I have to get ready.'

'Ready for what?'

'You'll see in a moment. It's what got us over the line. You can tell O'Hara you're getting close. That should keep him off your back for a while. Look, it's almost midnight. Must dash.'

Waving at the curious crowd watching her, Isis walked over to the band, had a word with the guitarist, and then joined Sheikh Khalid on stage.

Jack looked at his watch. It was three minutes to midnight. Then he quickly pulled his phone out of his pocket and sent an encrypted message to O'Hara.

'What did she tell you?' asked Bartolli, linking arms with Jack.

Jack was about to reply when his phone began to vibrate. Jack looked at the screen and paled. *He knows exactly where I am and what I'm doing,* he thought, a cold shiver racing down his spine. *Scary!*

Just then, Sheikh Khalid reached for the microphone. 'Ladies and gentlemen,' he said, 'please count with me: five, four, three, two, one ... Happy New Year!'

'Happy New Year, Jack,' said Bartolli and kissed Jack on the cheek. 'What did you tell O'Hara?'

'Enough for now, I hope.'

'He replied?'

'He did. Just now.' Jack showed Bartolli the screen on his phone: *You are cutting it fine. Enjoy the party!*

'Wow!' said Bartolli, shaking her head. 'Someone must be watching us.'

'That's what I thought.'

'Ah, here you are,' said Lola, pushing through the excited crowd. She pointed to the stage. 'Watch this!'

'Ladies and Gentlemen,' said Sheikh Khalid, 'I have a surprise for you. We will begin the new year in the best way possible: with a song. Not just any song, but a famous one.'

Moments later the lights went out, plunging the room into darkness. Then the drummer began the stirring solo introduction to 'Resurrection', one of Isis's signature songs that had been a worldwide hit. As the throbbing base joined in and the guitars screamed into life, a roar could be heard coming from outside as the crowd partying in the street recognised the tune and began to cheer.

When the lights came back on, Isis stood on the stage, alone. Looking like an Aztec goddess, she began to sing. Surprised by the unexpected treat to hear one of the icons of the music world usher in the new year, the room erupted in spontaneous applause.

Sheikh Khalid watched his excited guests begin to dance and smiled, secure in the knowledge he had just taken his rightful place among the London social elite, with a New Year's Eve party no-one would forget in a hurry. While he didn't quite understand how he had managed to pull this off, he did realise he owed it all to Isis.

29

Time Machine Studios, London: 1 January 2022

Despite having slept only a few hours, Jack felt remarkably refreshed. For the first time in days, he no longer felt helpless and lost. He couldn't quite explain the sudden mood change, but realised the unexpected events at the New Year's Eve party had something to do with it. Somehow, everything pointed to Sheikh Khalid and Isis. Despite rigorous questioning by both Lola and Jack on their way home after the party, Isis had been uncharacteristically tight-lipped about what had transpired between her and Khalid. All she said was she'd had a brief but productive conversation with the sheikh and would reveal all once certain matters had been resolved. This was classic Isis, who loved the theatrical and dramatic and was taking a leaf out of Jack's own storytelling book.

Feeling terribly thirsty, Jack put on his tracksuit and went to see if anybody was up yet. It was just after eight. As he passed Bartolli's room, he noticed the door was open, but Bartolli was nowhere to be seen. *Up already?* he thought, and went to the kitchen to make some coffee only to find Bartolli had beaten him to it.

'How are you feeling?' said Bartolli and handed Jack a mug of coffee.

'Surprisingly well, and I don't really know why. Nothing's changed, yet.'

'Perhaps it has and we just don't know yet how, or why.'

'Could be. It all comes down to what Isis and Khalid talked about last night. All Isis told me just before midnight was that we were getting close. Whatever that means. Cryptic words. That's all we have to go by at the moment. And that's what I told O'Hara to keep him off my back, at least for the moment. I suppose you haven't seen Isis or Lola?'

'Yes, I have. They've been up for hours.'

'Where are they?'

'I'll show you; come.'

Jack and Bartolli caught the lift to the top floor and stepped out onto the large terrace overlooking the Thames. It was a sparkling but chilly morning, with fog hovering above the river like cottonwool.

'There they are,' said Bartolli and held the door open for Jack. 'Watch.'

Isis and Lola were doing their morning stretching exercises. This was a rigorous routine before combat began.

Lola attacked first with a lightning kick from behind that would have floored a less experienced opponent. But not Isis. She sensed it coming and deftly side-stepped the kick and at the same time took hold of Lola's ankle, her grip vice-like.

'I've seen this routine before,' said Jack, sipping his coffee. 'In Mexico. Ten years ago, when I first met Isis. She's just as good as she was then. Remarkable.'

The bout continued for a few more minutes with some impressive manoeuvres and contortions that seemed almost impossible, until Isis pinned Lola to the ground and Lola held up her hand in surrender.

Isis wiped her face with a towel and walked over to Jack and Bartolli.

'Remind you of something?' she said.

'Sure. The morning I met Señora Gonzales at her stunning home in Mexico City, full of Aztec ruins and ghosts from the past. You were only eating fruit, and were preparing for your concert performance.'

'Good memory. Yes, that was the morning you met Mamina, my grandmother.'

'And that was the beginning of a journey that changed everything,' said Lola.

'Sure was. You'd just flown halfway around the world in a private jet to invite me to accompany you to Mexico to meet Isis, without any explanation, and I was crazy enough to accept and come along.'

'Any regrets?'

'Certainly not. It was the start of an adventure none of us could have anticipated at the time.'

'And none of us would forget,' said Lola.

'True,' said Jack. 'It was a classic example of how following the breadcrumbs of destiny can change your life in a way you wouldn't have thought possible, or expected in your wildest dreams.'

'Is that what happened?' asked Bartolli.

'It sure did, in more ways than I can explain just now.'

'Have you considered that what happened last night could be the beginning of something similar?' said Isis, winking at Jack.

'Seriously?' said Jack. 'Going by what you've told us so far, it's difficult to imagine just how.'

'Then let me enlighten you,' said Isis. 'Let's go inside. It's freezing out here, especially as Lola seems to have thrown in the towel.'

'I have done no such thing. That was merely round one. You got lucky with your scissor hold.'

Isis waved dismissively. 'Nonsense. You surrendered and everyone here saw it. Isn't that right, guys?'

'I'm keeping out of this,' said Bartolli.

'Very wise,' said Jack. 'You don't want to mess with these girls, I tell you. They're dangerous!'

Inside Isis's study next to the terrace it was warm and cosy, and the fog above the Thames had lifted, the river sparkling with the promise of a new day and the beginning of a new year. The maid was serving fresh vegetable juice – carrot, celery and ginger – and Isis was settling into one of the comfortable chairs facing the floor-to-ceiling windows.

Isis's study was a fascinating place. The epitome of industrial chic, the huge, glass-domed study was Isis's favourite place in the spectacular three-storey apartment on top of the Time Machine Studios. It was her private world, full of curios and memorabilia assembled during a lifetime of performing. Filled with her most treasured possessions, guitars of all shapes and sizes were displayed on the walls above rows of gold records, framed posters and celebrity photographs. Around the room spectacular costumes adorned mannequins in glass display cases. Next to the piano was a life-sized wax figure of a much-younger Isis wearing a sparkling bikini, which looked better than the one at Madame Tussauds. It reminded Isis of her first mega concert in South America, which broke the one-hundred-thousand-spectator record in Buenos Aires. There was even a stuffed condor – a mascot from one of her South American concerts – suspended above the grand piano like a bird of prey hunting stray notes.

'Is that it?' asked Bartolli. She pointed to a painting on an easel that faced a large desk covered in leather-bound photo albums and photos in silver frames of Isis posing with adoring celebrities from around the world.

'Yes, that's it,' said Jack. 'Monet's *Little Sparrow in the Garden.*'

Bartolli walked over to the painting and had a close look at it. 'It's magnificent.'

'Sure is,' said Isis. She pointed to another painting hanging on the wall behind it. 'And so is this one, albeit for different reasons. It's Herzl's famous forgery that caused Fuchs so much heartache.'

Bartolli turned towards the painting. 'And that famous Herzl signature is somewhere hidden in it?'

'Sure is. I'll show you,' said Jack. He walked over to the painting and pointed to a tiny Star of David and a little heart below a stone by the pond. 'Right here.'

'And Herzl's legacy lives on,' said Isis, enjoying herself, 'in unexpected ways. I just had a phone call from Sheikh Khalid.'

Everyone turned around and looked at Isis.

'This early on New Year's Day?

'Sure.'

'How come?'

'Because Muscat in Oman is three hours ahead of London time.'

'And this is relevant because?' asked Bartolli.

'Khalid wanted to talk to his father first, before giving me an answer.'

'An *answer?*' said Jack, frowning.

'Just before midnight, I managed to corner Khalid and have a private word. It wasn't easy, I can tell you. You saw how excited he was to meet us.'

'You especially,' said Lola.

'Yes, I suppose so. Last night was all about face and social standing, and showcasing wealth and influence. We knew that and I played that card.'

'How exactly?' asked Jack.

'I explained to Khalid that accepting his invitation had an ulterior motive ...'

'What kind of ulterior motive?' asked Jack, frowning.

'I told him that I wanted to meet him, but for specific reasons that had nothing to do with his party. I referred to the legendary art collection assembled by his father, which he keeps in his palace in Muscat. I mentioned several well-known paintings rumoured to be in that collection. My own interest in art is well known, and so is my collection. The Monet over there is a good example. That auction caused quite a sensation in art circles a few years ago. I'm sure Khalid would have been well aware of that.'

'And the depth of your pockets, no doubt,' said Lola.

'No match for his own, I'm sure,' retorted Isis.

Jack looked expectantly at Isis.

'I asked Khalid if it would perhaps be possible to meet his father and view his famous collection,' continued Isis, turning serious. 'Coming from a collector like myself, such a request sounded very plausible.'

'Let's not forget, this is the man who exchanged the Toulouse-Lautrec for *Golgotha*,' said Jack.

'If our interpretation of the note found in Fuchs's records is correct,' interjected Bartolli. 'There are lots of assumptions here.'

'Sure. If Khalid was in any way surprised by this,' continued Isis, 'he certainly didn't show it. Let's keep in mind we're dealing with a shrewd businessman here, always looking for angles to advance his own interests. He said there could be a way.'

'Really?' said Jack.

'Apparently, his father's eightieth birthday is coming up. He's planning a big party in Muscat as a special celebration and is currently looking for an artist with international standing to entertain his guests. Someone like Elton John, or Rod Stewart ...'

Lola grinned. She knew exactly where Isis was heading.

'He indicated that if I were to agree to perform at the party, which, incidentally, is in less than two weeks, he was sure he could arrange a private audience with his father, and a viewing of his art collection.'

'Amazing!' said Bartolli, shaking her head.

'He also said he would have to talk to his father first about all this to get his approval. No doubt, his father still calls the shots in this family.'

'And to get him over the line, you arranged to sing a couple of songs at the party last night, just to show him what kind of impact that would have, especially as far as his guests were concerned?' said Lola.

'Exactly!'

'This is bloody brilliant!' said Jack.

'You mean coming from someone not only with a stunning figure, but brains as well?' teased Isis, looking coy.

'Something like that. Is that why you told me that we were getting close?'

'Yes. Khalid is a social climber. We could all see that. He was using us to make an impression, and I was happy to let him do that; simple. Vanity and ego did the rest. I knew he wouldn't be able to resist the offer. Speaking to his father was only a formality. He did that, and true to his word he called me this morning.'

'And?' said Jack.

'We have all been invited to Muscat to attend the birthday party of the year, and view the family art collection. If *Golgotha* is among the collection, we are bound to find out. What do you think, guys?'

'And on top of all that, you will, of course, be performing,' said Lola, smiling, 'to a huge, international audience, right?'

Isis sighed. 'Well, someone has to do the heavy lifting here. And besides, it's for a good cause: *ours!* And the appearance fee I negotiated isn't bad either: two million.'

'Dollars?' asked Lola.

'No, pounds!'

30

Minsk: 2 January

The winter in Belarus was particularly severe that year. Temperatures had plummeted to levels not seen in decades and icy winds from the north drove temperatures down even further, adding a wind-chill factor that made going outside almost impossible.

Inside his well-heated underground 'control centre', as he liked to call the cellar under the modest house he now called home on the outskirts of Minsk, O'Hara was oblivious to all this. Surrounded by the latest state-of-the art computer equipment including a powerful, military-strength server a police department would have been happy to own, O'Hara had everything he needed. This was his world, and in this world he was in control. He felt like the captain of a spaceship obeying his every command and taking him wherever he wanted to go, with lightning speed at the click of his mouse.

In the past, emperors would send armies and generals into battle to defeat their enemies and conquer new lands, but O'Hara had something much more powerful and effective at his disposal: the internet. Few understood the awesome reach and almost infinite possibilities of the darknet like O'Hara, who used it to run his Darknet Bazaar and obscene gambling empire almost singlehandedly, just by sitting in front of his computer.

Yet despite all that, he did need some contact with the outside world to make it all work. He knew this was his weak spot and where he felt most vulnerable because he had to depend on others. So far, Irina had done an outstanding job in carrying out his instructions. In certain ways, she was even better than Spiridon 4, and Ivanov had been more reliable and easier to deal with than the Italian Mafia. Yet, for some reason he couldn't explain, O'Hara felt uneasy about the arrangement. In some ways, dealing with the Mafia had been a lot simpler as it involved only money. The relationship with Ivanov was much more complicated because O'Hara was dealing with a gambler, and gamblers were slaves of their obsession, always looking for the next adrenaline rush and excitement fix while on the hunt for that elusive big win. As for Irina, she only did what Ivanov told her to do. She seemed totally loyal, but was not beholden to him. O'Hara had therefore no control over her whatsoever. It was like dealing with an emotionless but efficient robot under the control of someone else.

And then there was Jack.

While Jack's book and the Herzl connection had given O'Hara the perfect opening and subject matter for his next darknet gambling project, just like Landru's paper on the Llanganates treasure had been the key to the exceptional success of the *Death Mask Murders* game, Jack was a far more complex personality, and therefore more difficult to predict and control than Landru had ever been.

Landru had been ruled by fear and greed. Fear of having his homosexuality exposed, which in the conservative academic circles he moved in would have destroyed him and his career. And greed to finance a lifestyle to which he had become accustomed and allowed him to indulge his homosexuality and cover it up. Fear and greed were therefore interrelated and highly effective tools O'Hara had used for years to control Landru.

Jack, on the other hand, was a totally new challenge. Jack was doing O'Hara's bidding for entirely different reasons. He was motivated by love for those close to him. He would do anything to protect the people he cared about. While O'Hara had instinctively recognised this and was effectively using it to bend Jack to his will, he also realised it had serious limitations and was full of hidden dangers, because love could make someone like Jack do things that were totally unpredictable and therefore almost impossible to anticipate and control. For O'Hara, the most formidable adversary was an incorruptible man, because such a man was above temptation and capable of sacrificing himself for what he believed in – and that could have devastating consequences.

And on top of all that there was another complication.

O'Hara realised that choosing Jack as his next adversary was entirely motivated by personal considerations. This, as he knew well, was fraught with danger because personal motivations cloud judgement. Jack and his friends had almost obliterated his entire darknet empire in Bavaria. O'Hara couldn't just walk away from something like that, yet he was astute and objective enough to realise this presented a serious threat to his enterprise. Not because it made Jack a superior adversary, but because it made O'Hara a weaker one, captive to his own feelings and desires for retribution and revenge. Dangerous bedfellows at the best of times, never to be underestimated.

O'Hara had given Jack's latest message a lot of thought: *We are getting close.* What exactly could that mean? he wondered. Was it simply something Jack told him as a last-minute response to the ultimatum, or was there more to it? O'Hara had embedded a sophisticated tracking app in Jack's phone the first time Jack had contacted him on the encrypted phone number he had been given. O'Hara could therefore track Jack's every move provided his phone was switched on, which it was, of course, most of the time. That took care of Jack's movements, but didn't explain the reasons behind them.

Everything had made sense until the surprise invitation to Sheikh Khalid's New Year's Eve party. That had come out of left field, and O'Hara couldn't quite work out its relevance or possible connection to the search for *Golgotha.* And when he couldn't work out something, O'Hara became nervous.

So far, most of Jack's moves had been logical, even predictable, and had made perfect sense. Others had not only been surprising, but also inspirational, showing initiative and imagination that were unexpected and quite ingenious. While O'Hara had welcomed these developments and had used them in his gambling scenarios to great effect, they also told him never to underestimate Jack and his friends.

O'Hara tried to dismiss his concerns, but his unease wouldn't go away. In fact, it was becoming stronger. Perhaps the answer was right there in front of him and he just couldn't see it, or hadn't looked hard enough? Or perhaps he had missed something altogether? The only way to find out was to review the facts, and the best way to do that was to go back to the beginning.

But what exactly had been the beginning? O'Hara asked himself. Had it been the intriguing clues buried in Jack's novella *The Postmaster of Treblinka* or something else? Or was it payback for a humiliating defeat that had almost wiped out his empire and could have cost him his life? If so, he had to tread carefully, because Jack had almost defeated him once already, and someone who had been able to do that, could do so again. Whatever the odds.

It took O'Hara several hours to review all the material he had assembled in his search for *Golgotha* so far. The painting Herzl had sent through the German Feldpost from Treblinka to Hungary had become an obsession that made living in humiliating exile in Minsk bearable.

O'Hara studied Herzl's diary stolen from Rabbi Stein's study after his murder, line by line, and reviewed all the reports received from Jack since their virtual meeting on the *Standard* in St Petersburg on 13 December. He carefully followed the trail Jack had uncovered, paying particular attention to the book found in Kun's locker at the Gellert, Jack's meeting with Veronika Strasser in Salzburg, and the surprising Emil Fuchs connection Jack had discovered.

After that, everything had come to a sudden standstill over Christmas until Jack's surprise visit to Zurich to meet with a Swiss lawyer. Jack hadn't explained why this was relevant, and that had been the start of O'Hara's unease. What was Jack hiding? He wondered. What was he not telling him? And why?

Deep in thought, O'Hara closed Herzl's diary and stared at it. *We are getting close* was the last cryptic message from Jack he had received a few minutes before midnight on New Year's Eve. He was certainly cutting it fine, he thought. Was he playing games, or was he really getting close?

O'Hara concluded that putting Jack under more pressure could be counterproductive and jeopardise the entire project. If Jack was indeed making progress, it made sense to wait and see where he was heading.

Irina had made the *Standard* her command centre. This was a clever choice because the ship could be positioned wherever it was needed, to provide valuable backup and resources other operatives could only dream about. Soon after the virtual meeting with Jack and Bartolli in St Petersburg, the *Standard* sailed to Venice and Irina monitored Jack's movements from there. She had two of her most trusted Chechen agents on board, who could be deployed at a moment's notice and sent into the field.

O'Hara looked at the chessboard on his screen. It showed the latest positions of the pieces in the game he had been playing with Jack since the beginning. It was definitely time for another move, he thought. Feeling calmer, he reached for his phone and sent Jack an encrypted message:

You are getting close? How? It's your move. Time's up. You don't want to lose this game, do you?

Moments later came Jack's reply:

I have reason to believe Golgotha *is in Oman. I am attending a sheik's birthday party on the 15th in Muscat and will investigate further. The day of reckoning is coming closer.*

Jack concluded his message as he always did, with his next move on the chessboard. This time it was *Be5*.

Ah, this explains a lot, thought O'Hara. Suddenly, the pieces of the frustrating puzzle seemed to be falling into place. Smiling, O'Hara called Irina.

'He's going to Oman. I suggest you sail to Muscat now. Can you be there by the fourteenth?

'Yes, we can. It should take us no more than ten days to get there.'

'Excellent. Please leave now.'

'Will do.'

O'Hara entered Jack's latest move on the electronic chessboard in front of him, and considered its strategic implications. *Not bad*, he thought. *Gutsy and original.* If *Golgotha* was indeed somewhere in Oman, then it was definitely time to prepare for the endgame. As every experienced chess player knows, the endgame is the most critical – and most difficult – part of the contest.

Oman opened many interesting possibilities and O'Hara was determined not to lose this game. This time he would make sure Jack didn't slip through the net and get away. *The day of reckoning is coming closer,* thought O'Hara. What a strange thing to say. He would show Jack a day of reckoning he would remember for the rest of his days!

While O'Hara was still smarting from his unexpected defeat on the Obersalzberg in Bavaria, he had no intention of killing Jack. O'Hara's humiliation demanded something far more sinister and dramatic he could also use to great effect in his complex darknet gambling scenarios. Exotic locations and unexpected twists in the story and the action were very popular with the punters, and loosened the gambling purse strings.

It was therefore definitely time to turn up the heat and deliver a level of excitement his punters hadn't experienced before. Extreme brutality, violence and blood were the perfect vehicles to ignite gambling passion. An exotic country like Oman, with its colourful history and a penal code based on Islamic sharia law, which listed several crimes punishable by death and still amputated the hand of a thief, was the perfect setting for a betting frenzy. And as every casino knows, ultimately, the house always wins.

However, what O'Hara had missed altogether was a subtle shift in the power play between himself and Jack. By having made so much surprising progress in such a short time, Jack had turned the tables. Suddenly, O'Hara had more to lose by threatening him and putting those close to him in jeopardy than by letting him do things his way. By following his instincts, Jack was slowly gaining the upper hand. The puppet was turning into the puppet master, and beginning to pull the strings in this deadly game.

31

Kremlin, Moscow: 4 January

The FSB agents had presented their daily reports and were anxious to leave. Being in the president's office was always a tense situation. Anything could happen. Palin's moods and outbursts were legendary and could be triggered at any time and for no obvious reason. On certain occasions these outbursts turned into tirades that could last for hours and cost careers, or worse. The only one who was able to control him when that happened was Colonel Karlov, but even he was subdued that afternoon because the news about the growing unrest in the country wasn't good.

Palin appeared unusually calm and controlled. He thanked everybody and asked them to leave.

'What do you think?' asked Palin as soon as he was alone with his friend. He opened one of the drawers in his desk, pulled out a bottle of vodka and two shot glasses, and filled them up.

'We've done everything we can ...'

'That's not what I asked.'

'We have arrested hundreds of Novotny supporters and introduced new laws. This has put an end to the demonstrations, for now.'

'What do you mean *for now*?' demanded Palin.

'They haven't gone away, Joseph. All this has done is drive them underground.'

'They will calm down and forget all about this.'

'I doubt it. That video was incredibly—'

'You don't have to remind me,' interrupted Palin. 'I know.'

'And there's more coming. Just this morning, they released another one with more damaging information.'

'And we can't put a stop to this?'

'Our control of the internet only goes so far. All this material comes out of Germany.'

'I see. What about Novotny?'

'As you know, he's been arrested and is awaiting trial. A custodial sentence is guaranteed. He will be out of action for quite some time; solitary confinement in a high-security prison. He won't be able to communicate with anyone, not even a mouse.'

'Good. The harder we come down on him, the better.'

'But that makes his cause even stronger, and his supporters more determined,' said Karlov, well aware this was the real issue troubling Palin.

'What else can we do?'

'The most damaging thing by far is the palace issue. You could try to distance yourself from it and say it doesn't belong to you, but to one of the oligarchs, and that the whole story is a Western propaganda concoction. I'm sure we could find someone to step forward and hold up his hand.'

'Let's do that. Will it work?'

'Up to a point. But the younger generation will not buy it. They will see through all this. Novotny is their hero, come what may.'

'Are you suggesting this will get worse? Even without Novotny?'

'I believe it will. This has a momentum of its own now. Difficult to stop.'

'I see. What about closer to home?'

'What do you mean?'

'You know exactly what I mean. Corridor whispers, right here.'

Karlov had been afraid of this question. He reached for his vodka and gulped it down, the welcome burning sensation making him feel better. 'There's some unease about all this,' he said after a while.

'Where exactly?'

Karlov took his time before replying. 'All around you,' he said, choosing his words carefully. He certainly didn't want to name names.

'Why do you think that is?'

'Fear. They've seen what almost happened to Lukashenko in Belarus.'

'The cockroach and the Slipper Revolution?'

'Exactly. You can silence a voice, but not an idea. You can crush a body, but not the soul.'

'And they think something similar could happen here? Is that it?'

'This is a big country,' said Karlov, sidestepping the question. 'You cannot seal off a hundred and forty million people from the outside world and control their thinking.'

'What are you suggesting? We need something *stronger*?'

'*Stronger?* What do you mean?' said Karlov, looking worried. He didn't like the direction the conversation was taking.

'Leave it with me. Another?' said Palin, holding up the vodka bottle.

'No, thank you.' Karlov picked up his files and stood up. 'You know where to find me.'

'Sure. Thank you. You're the only one I can trust to tell it as it is.'

'Not easy at times.'

'I know. Promise me that you will never change.'

'Only if you promise never to shoot the messenger.'

Palin began to laugh. He held up his vodka glass and looked at his friend. 'Never,' he said. *'Na Zdorovie!'*

As soon as Karlov had closed the door behind him, Palin stood up and began to pace back and forth in front of his desk. He always did this when he was wrestling with a difficult question. His friend had just confirmed his worst fears.

You can silence a voice, but not an idea. You can crush a body, but not the soul, thought Palin, feeling a ripple of fear.

What few outside his most inner circle knew about Palin was his obsession with the occult, especially the work of Helena Blavatsky, a nineteenth-century Russian esotericist, and that many of his decisions were based on astrology and the ideas of Éliphas Lévi, a French occultist also active in the eighteen-hundreds. One of those ideas was that the uneducated 'masses' were unable to emancipate themselves and establish a meaningful order; they needed instruction.

Deep down, Palin saw himself as the 'chosen one' who was destined to provide those instructions and make Russia great again. He also believed in the Tarot and astrology and, just like Hitler, never made a major decision without first consulting the cards and horoscopes.

The people he looked up to for guidance and inspiration were the great conquerors and generals of the past like Alexander the Great, Attila, Genghis Khan, Timur and Napoleon, but the general he admired most was Count Suvorov, arguably Russia's greatest general, who had never lost a battle under his command and advanced the interests of Russia like no other.

Palin returned to his desk, opened the bottom drawer and took out a copy of Suvorov's famous military manual, *The Science of Victory,* and began to read several passages he had underlined. As he read the familiar text he began to calm down. The best way to silence an idea, he told himself, was to replace it with another one that had more appeal and could be used to control the 'masses'.

Smiling, Palin closed Suvorov's manual and reached for the map of the Soviet Union prior to its disintegration in 1991, which he always kept on his desk. Slowly, he ran his fingers over the map and traced the outline of Estonia, Latvia, Lithuania and Moldova, before coming to rest on Ukraine. *Russia without Ukraine is just a big country; with Ukraine, it is an empire. That's it!* thought Palin and reached for the vodka bottle.

Feeling relaxed at last because he now knew exactly what he had to do, Palin walked to the back of his office and looked at the famous icon facing his desk he had recently had installed in his office. According to legend, the icon had spiritual powers that had protected Russian military commanders like Pozharsky and Kutuzov, and had shown them the way to victory.

Lost in thought, Palin stared at the Virgin Mary. Then he lifted his glass in silent salute, dreaming of glory. In his arrogance, what he didn't notice was that the Mother of God was crying, not because she was mourning her son, but because of where Russia was heading.

32

Palazzo Alberti, Venice: 5 January

Jack was seated at his desk overlooking the Grand Canal, when his mother walked in. 'You're up early,' she said and went over to the window.

'So are you.'

'I'm helping Katerina and Tristan in the restaurant. I'm really enjoying it. She's incredibly busy, especially at breakfast. The place is booked out.'

'That's great.'

'What a view,' said Rahima, watching the *vaporetti* packed with morning commuters drifting out of the morning fog hovering just above the water.

'Timeless. History in motion.'

'How was your trip?'

'Eventful.'

After returning from London late the night before, exhausted, Jack had gone straight to bed.

'Are you making progress?'

'Yes, I believe so.'

Jack closed his laptop and joined his mother by the window.

'This is like a dream, you know,' said Rahima and linked arms with the son she hadn't seen in more than fifty years. 'My life in Colombia – especially the way it ended – seems like some distant nightmare. I lost the son I knew I had, and found the one I thought I had lost ...'

Jack reached for his mother's hand and stroked it. 'Tristan would explain it this way: he would say we are but instruments of fate, being moved around on the chessboard of life by forces beyond our control.'

'That's very poetic for this early in the morning,' said Rahima, smiling, 'but a little too fatalistic for me. How long do you think I should stay here?'

'That depends on what I find out when I get to meet Mohammed bin Ahmed in Oman.'

'You are going to *Oman*?'

'Yes. Next week, actually. Isis has been invited by one of the prominent families to perform at a sheik's birthday celebration event in Muscat.'

'How exciting. Who is this sheikh? Has he something to do with your search?'

'Yes, he has.'

'In what way?'

'Let's sit down and I'll tell you.'

Sitting on a mahogany chaise longue he had recently restored, Jack told his mother about the meeting with Moser in Zurich. He showed her a copy of the note suggesting that van Eyck's *Golgotha* had been exchanged by Fuchs for a Toulouse-Lautrec owned by a wealthy sheikh from Oman. He explained how an invitation to an exclusive London New Year's Eve party had resulted in an invitation to a birthday celebration party in Muscat to meet Sheikh Mohammed bin Ahmed, and view his famous art collection.

'I think Tristan is absolutely right,' said Rahima, shaking her head.

'When he calls us instruments of fate?'

'Yes. Do you have a better explanation for all this?'

'Breadcrumbs?' said Jack, smiling. 'I was just looking into the background of the bin Ahmed clan when you came in. I must say, the history of that family reads like a page out of "Ali Baba and the Forty Thieves".'

'*Arabian Nights*. How romantic!'

'"Open Sesame!" Let's hear it,' said Tristan, who had overheard the remark as he walked into the room.

'See? Right on cue,' said Jack, shaking his head. 'I don't know how he does it, but somehow he always seems to appear at the right moment.'

Jack looked at Tristan. 'Sit down; you may as well hear this now.'

'Something about a bin Ahmed tribe?'

'Yes.'

'And this is relevant because?'

'You are coming with me to Oman next week to meet a sheikh.'

'Great. I do need a break from my restaurant duties. Playing the cheerful host, setting tables and shaking hands can become a little tedious after a while. And besides, Katerina is very tough.'

'I bet.'

'So, where are we going, and why?'

'We're flying to Muscat with Isis and The Time Machine.'

'She's giving a concert?' said Tristan, becoming excited.

'Something like that, but the real purpose of our visit is to meet the sheik, who, if we are right, exchanged a French impressionist painting for *Golgotha*.'

'See? I told you something would turn up,' said Tristan casually and sat down.

'Muscat truly has a most colourful history, mainly because of its location on the Arabian Sea in the Gulf of Oman, close to the Strait of Hormuz. A most strategic location, especially as far as trade is concerned. A wealthy port between the east and the west. Apart from various indigenous tribes, Muscat was ruled by the Persians, the Portuguese and the Ottoman Empire, and each left its mark. Not surprisingly, the history of the Ahmed tribe is all about trade and slaves. Mainly slaves.'

'*Slaves?*' said Rahima. 'How awful.'

'The tribe made a fortune out of the slave trade. The Ahmed clan came out of the desert during the eighteenth century and supported the Al Bu Sa'id dynasty, which has ruled Oman ever since. The clan came to prominence when the capital was moved from Muscat to the notorious Stone Town, an ancient quarter of Zanzibar, in 1840.

That's when they made their real fortune. For centuries, Zanzibar was the most prominent slave market in East Africa. The Portuguese started it in the sixteenth century, and Stone Town was one of the last slave markets in the world until it was closed down by the British in 1873.'

'You've certainly done your homework,' said Rahima.

'It's always good to know who you are dealing with, don't you think?'

'Absolutely.'

'Especially as I want to get to know Sheikh Mohammed bin Ahmed. He was the one who modernised the family business after the war and diversified mainly into oil and gas, and construction. Very astute.'

'Built with money earned from slavery, I imagine,' said Rahima. 'Human misery for profit.'

'No doubt. He became a billionaire with investments all over the world and an art collection to match. Apparently, even now at eighty, he rules the family and the business with an iron fist from his palace in Muscat.'

'Sounds like a fascinating man,' said Rahima.

'He's certainly that. And from what I've heard, a ruthless one.'

'Most powerful men usually are,' said Rahima, remembering her time in Colombia.

'Tell me about this birthday celebration,' said Tristan.

'It's the sheik's eightieth birthday party, arranged by his son when we met in London. The concert will be held in front of one of the historical forts in Muscat built by the Portuguese. A grand building. Isis is very excited about it. This will give her the dramatic setting a flamboyant entertainer like her dreams about. She hasn't stopped talking about it and is planning her big entrance.'

'I can imagine,' said Tristan. 'Remember the concert in Mexico?'

'Who could forget it? She's designed a stunning set of costumes and has already had rehearsals with The Time Machine. She brought the band together again just for this occasion. She's on fire, I tell you.'

'Wow! Should be quite something.'

'Sure will. After all, we want to impress the sheikh. The costumes are incredible. I saw the designs just before I left – on paper only, I may add. All based on *One Thousand and One Nights*. Isis will appear as Scheherazade and tell stories through her songs.'

'What a wonderful idea,' said Rahima. 'To enchant the sultan and postpone her execution in the morning, I suppose?'

'You know the story?'

'Of course.'

'What story?' asked Tristan.

'You don't know the story of Scheherazade, the ultimate storyteller who invented the cliffhanger?'

Tristan shook his head.

'It's about a powerful king ruling over India and China who discovers his wife has been unfaithful. Shocked and humiliated, he has her killed.'

'Understandable. A jealous king is not to be messed with,' said Tristan.

'Disillusioned, the king decides all women are the same and begins to marry virgins. He executes each one the morning after the wedding night to make sure she cannot dishonour him.'

'An extreme solution, but an effective one,' joked Tristan.

'This goes on for some time until there are no more virgins left in the kingdom. Then the daughter of the Vizier, who had been in charge of procuring virgins for the marital bed, offers herself as the next bride. On their wedding night, she begins to tell her new husband a tale, but as soon as she finishes one, she begins another. Fascinated by the stories, the king wants to know how each one ends, and postpones his new wife's execution each morning.'

'A true page-turner,' said Tristan, 'or should we call it fate-turner?'

'Absolutely. This goes on for a thousand and one nights.'

'How does the story end?'

'Versions differ, but in the end the king pardons his wife and she is not executed,' said Jack.

'She's rewarded for a series of cliffhangers?'

'It would seem so.'

'The power of storytelling never ceases to amaze,' said Tristan.

'What do you know about his art collection?' asked Rahima, changing the subject.

'It's one of the most extensive private collections in the Middle East. The sheikh's been a keen collector for decades. He owns some extraordinary paintings. Rembrandt, Picasso, Rubens, Carvaggio, even Botticelli are said to be among his collection, but no-one is quite sure, because he's a very private person. In addition to that, there are rumours about the way he has acquired certain paintings ... no questions asked, if you know what I mean. A typical trader. Anything goes as long as there's a profit or advantage at the end of the deal.'

'And you think *Golgotha* is among them?' asked Tristan.

'I hope so. It's the only credible lead we have.'

'Is that what you told O'Hara?'

'I did, but I didn't tell him how, or why.'

'And he accepted that?'

'I gave him no choice.'

Tristan nodded. 'Clever. You did exactly what Scheherazade did in the story.'

'What do you mean?'

'Can't you see? O'Hara wants to find out how this story ends. He isn't going to do anything to jeopardise this as long as you give him cliffhangers.'

'I didn't see it that way, but I think you may be absolutely right,' said Jack.

'I agree with Tristan. You're keeping us safe with your stories, the only difference being they are anchored in real life,' said Rahima. 'And should you actually find *Golgotha*, well ... I believe you will hold all the cards with the biggest story of them all.'

'I hope you're right.'

'See? I told you something would turn up,' said Tristan. 'And when your life depends on a story, what better way than to have it told by a storyteller extraordinaire, right?'

'I couldn't agree more,' said Rahima, smiling. 'I think our lives are in safe hands.'

33

Blackstone Chambers, Temple, London: 10 January

Sasha and Blackstone were watching Novotny's sentencing on TV in his office. Located in the heart of London's legal district, it was just around the corner from the Temple Church.

Sasha gasped when the sentence was handed down. 'Five years,' she whispered, tears welling in her tired eyes, 'for a minor breach of stupid bail conditions! Can you believe this?'

Blackstone stood up, walked over to Sasha and put his hand on her shoulder. 'It's Russia, I'm afraid, not the Old Bailey. What this tells us is they are really afraid of Anatoly.'

'His corruption exposure, you mean? The video?'

'Yes. As we know, it's been viewed many millions of times. I can't imagine what impact that must have had in Russia. The Kremlin is obviously worried. Palin's reputation has been severely damaged. And when you do that, you must expect a reaction. I'm afraid this is it. He's coming out fighting.'

'We certainly didn't expect this. Anatoly was counting on something quite different.'

'I can see that, but he must have known that going back to Russia was a risky move.'

Sasha looked at Blackstone with teary eyes. 'They'll take him to a high-security prison. We may never see him again, you know.'

'We don't know that.'

'My God, five years is a long time. I think Anatoly has underestimated Palin and his grip on Russia and its institutions. Things have progressed much faster and much further than we thought. What we didn't see was that the dictatorship we were afraid of has already arrived!'

Sasha wiped away a few tears and looked at Blackstone. 'It's all up to me now.'

'What do you mean?'

'As you know, I'm running Anatoly's Anti-Corruption Foundation. I'm his insurance policy. That's why he didn't want me to come with him. He keeps me in the background. And it's why the video was released from a safe place like Germany, and that's why we operate his Foundation from outside Russia.'

'Smart move,' said Blackstone. 'What's your plan now?'

'I'm moving the entire organisation over here to London. After that, we'll carry on with our agenda. That's what Anatoly told us to do in case he was sent to jail in Russia. Release more damaging material and carry on the fight.'

'What fight?'

'To expose Palin for what he is, and ultimately remove him from office and liberate Russia from the grip of corruption and oppression.'

'You do realise what that means?'

'I do.'

'And are you ready for this?'

'I believe I am.'

'And you believe you can do this from the *outside*, so to speak? From right here in the UK?'

'Yes. Anatoly has thought of that too. He has built an extensive network of supporters in Russia we can trust and call upon to do things from the *inside*. Many of his supporters come from within the Russian Orthodox Church. There are monks and priests—'

'But the Russian Orthodox Church is supporting Palin,' interjected Blackstone. 'He has the backing of the Patriarch.'

'True, the church leaders are supporting the president. The Orthodox leadership has effectively become an arm of the state, but that has caused huge division and unrest within the Church. This can be exploited and ultimately bring about change. Anatoly saw that too, and thought it was our best chance to overthrow Palin. The Church has huge grassroots influence and support among the people. If we supply the damaging information, especially the *proof of corruption* from the outside, those disgruntled priests will spread the word and do the work from the inside. And Anatoly's incarceration for a trumped-up charge will add credibility to his claims and further validate the evidence he has presented.'

'That's quite a plan, Sasha,' said Blackstone, 'but a dangerous one. And you think you can head the organisation and carry it out?'

'Yes, I believe so.'

'Don't think for a moment you are safe here and beyond the reach of Palin's henchmen in the FSB.'

'I'm not that naive, but we have a huge amount of damaging propaganda ammunition we can release going forward, to keep the momentum going. Anatoly has prepared a number of videos with explosive material. More proof.'

Blackstone shook his head. 'I hope you realise that ultimately, there is only one way to remove a man like Palin, don't you? History is full of examples ...'

'You mean kill him?'

Blackstone shrugged.

'Let's take it one step at a time. Russia has faced dangers like this before and has survived.'

'But at what cost?'

'Change like this is never free.'

'And are you prepared to pay the price should it come to that?'

'Anatoly is already doing that right now. You've seen what happened.'

'I realise that, but I am talking about *you*.'

'I know. Do you believe in destiny, Henry?' said Sasha, changing direction.

'I'm a lawyer. I believe in facts, not speculation.'

'I believe in destiny. Just look at what's happened. Right now.'

'You're talking about your father?'

'Yes, I am. As we both know, he's unlikely to recover. That makes me his sole heir. Effectively, I now have total control of his empire. That makes me a very rich and, dare I say, powerful woman, right?'

'Yes, without doubt it does.'

'And I am determined to use that power to carry on Anatoly's work and bring about that change in Russia, whatever the cost, but I can't do this alone.'

'At least you're realistic about that.'

Sasha looked at Blackstone. 'Just consider the timing. Why did it all happen right now?'

'You mean your father's stroke?'

'Yes. Coincidence? Hardly. I say it was meant to be. I *believe*, you see, and so does Anatoly. With my father's billions behind me, I can do a lot, don't you agree? I can make a difference!'

'You can, if you use it wisely.'

'I need help.'

'Yes, you do.'

'Will you be the one to help me?'

'Sasha ...'

'It's a simple question and we have little time. You said yourself, there's so much to do to keep Dad's business affairs going.'

'Yes, but you're talking about merging your Anti-Corruption Foundation plans with your father's affairs, and making the Foundation your priority.'

'Exactly.'

'I want to think about this, Sasha.'

'All right, but please don't take too long. Things are moving very quickly.'

'I understand. I'll give you my answer in the morning.'

34

On the way to Oman: 14 January

The trip to the airport in the water taxi had been wet and miserable. Dark clouds hovered above Venice and it had begun to drizzle. Bartolli had arrived from Rome by train the day before and, despite the inclement morning, she was looking forward to what promised to be an interesting journey.

Jack stood next to Tristan and Bartolli near the departure gates on the first floor of the Marco Polo Airport terminal and watched *Pegasus* – Isis's private jet – make a turn and then line up for landing beneath the clouds.

'Here she comes,' said Jack and pointed to the sleek jet looking like a gracious bird as it touched down. The colourful Time Machine logo on the fuselage looked striking and clearly set the plane apart from the other private aircraft as it taxied towards its designated spot.

Bartolli linked arms with Jack. 'This is fabulous, Jack. Thanks for asking me along. This is definitely a first for me.'

'We're in this together. And besides, you promised to walk by my side and keep an eye on me, remember?' said Jack.

'You don't have to worry. I always keep my promises.'

'Things could get rough, you know. We're stepping into a different world here. Muscat isn't London.'

'He's right, you know,' said Tristan.

'Are you trying to scare me?' said Bartolli.

'No. Just a friendly warning. People have disappeared without a trace in Oman, and if O'Hara were to plan something sinister, it would be the perfect place. Effectively out of reach of the law as we know it,' said Jack.

'My daughters were most envious when they heard I was getting picked up in Venice by a rock star and hitching a ride on a private jet on our way to Oman,' said Bartolli, changing the subject. 'They even came to the train station with me yesterday to say goodbye. Another first.'

'You're in for a treat. The jet is quite something, and Lola is a hell of a pilot. She loves flying.'

'You can say that again,' said Tristan. 'Remember when we made our getaway out of Mogadishu?'

'Let's hope we don't have to resort to anything quite like that again,' said Jack, laughing. 'We made it by a whisker. Look, here comes Lola.'

'Ready?' said Lola, looking very crisp in her dark navy pilot's uniform. 'You checked in, as I told you to?'

'Yes, Captain, we did!' said Jack.

'That was quick. How did you get through all the red tape so fast?'

'It's not what you know, but who; right, Tristan? We've been here many times before. The authorities know us. And besides, Isis is very popular in Italy. Autographs for airport staff go a long way. They've allowed everyone to stay on board provided we leave straight away.'

'Perfect,' said Lola. 'Let's go, guys.'

'Isis is very excited about this trip,' said Lola, as they walked towards *Pegasus* waiting on the wet tarmac. 'She's hardly slept a wink in days. For heaven's sake, praise her outfit! She's been agonising for hours over what to wear.'

'Sure,' said Jack, smiling. 'We all know what performing means to her, and this is promising to be big.'

'I think you're right. From what we've been told so far, the preparations for this event are huge. They even flew in a whole orchestra from London and a planeload of flowers from Amsterdam. The Time Machine guys are already in Muscat, rehearsing with the orchestra.'

Isis was waiting for them at the top of the airstair built into the jet. Wearing a stunning blue-embroidered African abaya kaftan and matching hijab, a headscarf that covered Isis's head and neck but left the face exposed, she looked like an Arabian princess welcoming her guests.

'Wow!' said Jack. 'Is it allowed to kiss someone wearing a hijab in public?'

'In Italy, for sure. I don't know about Oman,' said Isis, turning her cheek towards Jack. 'Better make hay while the sun shines. Great to see you, guys. Come in. We'll be on our way as soon as we're cleared for take-off.'

'When did you leave London?' asked Jack, strapping himself into a seat next to Bartolli.

'About three hours ago,' said Isis. 'Short flight, but it's a long one from here to Muscat.'

'How long?' asked Tristan.

'About ten hours. But don't you worry, we have plenty of provisions on board.'

'I bet,' said Jack. 'Stunning outfit, by the way.'

'You think so?' said Isis, adjusting her hijab. 'Wasn't easy to find something that complies with the dress code in a Muslim country and still looks reasonable.'

'Very exotic. Suits you, especially the hijab.'

'I'll take it all off in a moment and put on my tracksuit. I don't want to look like a crumpled mess when we arrive.'

Jack gave Bartolli a conspiratorial nudge with his elbow and smiled. 'Certainly not! Imagine what they would make of that. A star always has to look the part.'

'Exactly.'

'All right, guys. I hope you're all strapped in. We are about to take off,' said Lola though the loudspeakers from the cockpit. 'Enjoy the ride. Here we go.'

Jack always enjoyed the moment of take-off, because that was the time the awesome power of the jet was most apparent. After a steep climb, the aircraft levelled out and the engine noise became a hum as the clouds parted and bright sunlight filled the cabin.

'She's all yours, guys,' said Lola and got out of her seat as the other pilot and co-pilot took over. 'I'll come back later to give you a break.'

'Definitely time for refreshments,' said Lola as she stepped into the spacious cabin behind the cockpit. 'Champagne anyone?'

'Why not?' said Jack and stretched out his legs. 'It's going to be a long flight.'

Lola walked to the galley at the back, took a bottle of vintage champagne out of the fridge and began to open it. 'We went shopping yesterday at Harrods after Isis picked up her costumes from her tailor.'

'Costumes?' asked Jack. 'What kind of costumes?'

'Custom made for the occasion. Absolutely stunning. There was this—'

'*Stop it!*' said Isis. 'We agreed. It's a surprise.'

'Oops,' said Lola and began to fill up the champagne flutes. 'Sorry. Isis got mobbed by some Japanese tourists who recognised her at the seafood counter at Harrods,' continued Lola, changing the subject. 'It took two security guards to control the crowd in the food hall.'

'The price of fame,' said Jack, trying hard not to laugh.

Lola handed Isis a glass of champagne. 'You didn't help. You kept autographing food parcels on the way out. Thank God Boris was waiting with the car at the exit, or we would still be there.'

'At least we managed to buy some nice stuff for the flight,' said Isis, sipping her champagne and taking the rebuke in her stride.

'Do we have any idea about the arrangements when we arrive?' asked Bartolli.

'We do,' said Isis. 'There's an event coordinator – Ali something – who's in charge. He spoke to Lola several times. He'll meet us at the airport. Even our accommodation has been arranged. Suites at the Intercontinental, I believe. Arab hospitality. Not bad.'

'That's right. All taken care of. This party will cost a fortune,' said Lola, pouring herself a mineral water.

'What about the concert?' asked Jack.

'That will be held outdoors after the banquet in the palace,' said Isis, 'in front of a Portuguese fort guarding the entrance to the harbour. Should look stunning all lit up at night. I've seen pictures. And there will be fireworks at the end.'

'No glass coffin entrance, I suppose, like in Mexico?' teased Jack. 'And no mock bullfight like we had in Colombia?'

'Certainly not! That would be highly inappropriate for a birthday celebration for a sheikh. I've arranged something much better.'

'Can you tell us?' asked Bartolli.

'Sure,' said Isis, glad to have been asked. 'Because the square facing the fort where the concert will be held is right on the harbour, I will arrive by boat, on a traditional dhow in full sail.'

'How original,' said Bartolli. 'Sounds like a fairytale.'

'Funny you should say that. All my performances have themes based on where I'm performing. I've chosen something time-honoured and steeped in history that everyone will recognise. This allows me to wear traditional costumes that will not offend.'

'No diamond-studded bikinis that leave little to the imagination, I presume?' teased Jack. 'Or figure-hugging bodysuits with feathers?'

'Definitely not! This is more about harem pants, colourful turbans and flowing robes.'

'Nothing to show off your stunning figure? What a pity!' teased Jack, enjoying the banter.

'Just as well. I'm much too fat for all that.'

'We saw that the other day in London, didn't we, Francesca? Judo on the roof terrace, remember?'

'Taekwondo,' corrected Lola.

'All I remember is a figure a supermodel would kill for,' replied Bartolli.

'I wish,' said Isis, and held up her empty glass. 'I'm getting old.'

'Seriously, my friends, we mustn't forget why we're really here,' said Jack. 'This is all about finding *Golgotha*, not just a great party.'

'Of course,' said Isis. 'Leave it all to me, and remember who got you the invitation in the first place. After the performance we'll have the sheikhs eating out of our hands, trust me. If the painting is in Mohammed bin Ahmed's collection, we'll find it. Cheers!'

'I hope you're right,' said Jack, turning serious. 'I've done some research ...'

'What kind of research?' asked Bartolli.

'I wanted to find out more about Mohammed bin Ahmed and his art collection.'

'And did you?' asked Isis.

'Yes, quite a lot, in fact. He's building a stunning museum right now. Next to his palace. There was even a design competition a few years ago. Leading architects from around the world entered. The winner was a young architect from Granada. Apparently, his design was inspired by the Alhambra.'

'Interesting,' said Isis. 'Good choice. As an expression of Moorish and Andalusian culture the Alhambra has no equal. And besides, it's one of the best examples of Islamic architecture.'

'No doubt that's why this was the winning entry, because this museum will focus on Islamic art.'

'I thought bin Ahmed's art collection was all about European art?' said Lola.

'It is that too, but according to my sources, bin Ahmed changed direction twenty or so years ago. He shifted his focus and began to collect Islamic art in a big way. He spent millions buying up pieces whenever something significant came on the market. Still does. He also began to sell part of his Western art collection. The museum will be his legacy, and it's all about Islamic art. He's now one of the biggest collectors of Islamic art in the Middle East.'

'Fascinating,' said Bartolli.

'It certainly is, because it gives us a little insight into the man's thinking.'

'And that could have a bearing on how we deal with *Golgotha*, should we find it in the collection?' said Tristan.

'Very perceptive of you, as usual. Absolutely. We must have a plan.'

'We do,' said Isis. 'You've been instructed by O'Hara to find the painting, and if you do, you have done your part.'

'If only it were that simple. Do you really think O'Hara will be satisfied with that and just go away? I think not. He's after my head; of that, I'm sure. I have to defeat him once and for all. That's what is really at stake here. He and I are playing some crazy chess game right now, and he seems to be winning. Every time I report something, he makes a move on our imaginary chessboard and I have to respond. It's madness!'

'Classic psychopathic behaviour,' interjected Bartolli. 'How do you intend to defeat him, once and for all?'

'As I see it, the best way to do this would be to hand him over to the French authorities. Lapointe and Dupree would do the rest. He would go on trial for murder and go to jail for life.'

'But he's in Belarus, out of reach,' said Isis.

'I know that, but if we could somehow lure him ...'

'Perhaps I should just make the dear sheikh an offer and buy the painting?' speculated Isis.

'What makes you think he would consider selling it?' asked Jack. 'This man doesn't need money. And besides, it wouldn't solve my problem with O'Hara.'

'You obviously have something in mind,' said Tristan, smiling.

'You know me too well. I have an idea, but it's early days. Let's see how all this unfolds first, and take it from there.'

'Good suggestion,' said Isis and stood up. 'I'm exhausted. I'll go and lie down for a while. A little beauty sleep is in order here. I've been on the hop for days; hardly slept at all, and my voice needs a rest too. Arriving hoarse and with bags under the eyes wouldn't be a good look.'

'Certainly not,' said Lola, grinning. 'I'll make up your bed. You still haven't figured out how it works.'

'What would I do without you?' said Isis and blew Lola a kiss. 'I'm glad you like my abaya, guys. You should get some rest too. Something tells me that we'll be on the go as soon as we arrive.'

35

After Novotny's devastating sentencing to five years in jail that had surprised many, followed by the brutal crackdown on his supporters, making demonstrations in Russia not only illegal but also virtually impossible, Sasha threw herself into the running of Anatoly's Anti-Corruption Foundation with renewed vigour. This helped take her mind off the fact that she was unlikely to see Anatoly for years, and quite possibly never again.

Sasha had moved into her father's mansion on the outskirts of London and made it the headquarters of the Foundation. Step by step, she was moving all the key staff from Berlin to London and using her father's money, which was now effectively under her control, to bankroll it all. This had provided a welcome boost to the organisation's meagre resources, and was breathing new life into the corruption-exposure campaign being waged through the internet from outside Russia.

Determined not to allow Anatoly's arrest and unjustified incarceration to be forgotten, Sasha had authorised the release of several damaging follow-up videos Novotny had prepared in advance for just such an eventuality. It was as if he had actually foreseen his fate, and was ready to use it to advance his cause.

Blackstone had given Sasha his answer, as promised: He told her that he would support her in any way he could and help her not only to run her father's business affairs, but would assist in running the Foundation as well. He understood that Sasha was unable and unwilling to separate the two and she was determined to manage both, difficult as that may turn out to be. To make this work, Blackstone was spending most of his time with Sasha and took over the day-to-day management of her father's business while briefing her at the same time and bringing her up to speed. This allowed Sasha to devote most of her time to the Foundation.

Sasha sat in her father's study overlooking the manicured grounds of Hartley Hall, an Edwardian mansion just outside London. Blackstone had just given her a pile of papers to sign, while at the same time doing his best to explain what they were all about.

'It will take a while to get my head around all this,' said Sasha. 'I had no idea Dad had such a huge property portfolio and such extensive interests in casinos and gambling generally.'

'He made a fortune out of gambling, especially in the US and Macau. It's been a huge money-spinner for him.'

Sasha's eyes flashed with anger. '*Gambling!*' she said. 'That was what drove my parents apart and why my mother wanted a divorce. She couldn't take it anymore. Let's not pretend. We both know Dad is a compulsive gambler, albeit a lucky one so it seems, looking at all this.'

'True, he's always been prepared to take huge risks, especially when others get cold feet, and has always been willing to entertain projects others won't touch. Most of the time it's paid off, sometimes spectacularly so.'

'You've spent hours inducting me into Dad's business affairs; allow me to tell you a little about Anatoly and the Foundation, and what we are trying to achieve and why. I think it's important you understand what this is all about and what's at stake here.'

'Agreed,' said Blackstone. He sat back, took off his glasses and looked expectantly at Sasha.

Sasha held up a bundle of papers. 'This is a draft of Anatoly's manifesto. He started work on this quite some time ago. Looking at it now, it reads almost like a prophecy, a glimpse into the future, albeit a dark one. It sends chills up my spine just to read it. Scary stuff!'

'What do you mean?'

'Well, Anatoly begins by analysing Palin's illegal annexation of Crimea in 2014 and the complacency and inaction by the West. He calls it "complicity through silence". At the time, Crimea was part of Ukraine, but Catherine the Great had incorporated the strategically located Crimea into the Russian Empire in 1783 after having defeated the Ottomans. Since then, Crimea had a complicated history, but in 1954 it was transferred to the Ukrainian SSR and effectively remained part of Ukraine until it was forcefully annexed by Russia in 2014. However, most countries still recognise Crimea as part of Ukraine. Anatoly argues this forceful annexation by Russia marks the beginning of dangerous, imperialist ambitions by Palin, who has never accepted the disintegration of the Soviet Union after the Cold War and is determined to "make Russia great again" by regaining what's been lost.'

'You really think so?' asked Blackstone. 'In this day and age? In present-day Europe?'

'Yes. That's the really scary thing about all this. Anatoly suggests that human nature is very predictable and history repeats itself. All we have to do is open the history book and have a close look at the pages. All the answers are there.'

'An interesting idea.'

'It's more than that,' continued Sasha. 'Anatoly is convinced Palin has his eyes on the entire Ukraine, not just Luhansk and Donetsk in the Donbas region, but the lot, and this will inevitably result in war.'

'*Seriously?* That's a bit of a long bow, don't you think?'

'No, I don't. All the signs are there, and we are already closer to all this than we may think. According to Anatoly, the question is when, and to what extent this conflict will involve the rest of Europe. He also notes that sooner or later a dictator like Palin needs a war to assert his authority, justify his actions, and muddy the political waters to hide his real ambitions. Anatoly is convinced we're getting very close to this point right now.'

'How close? What are we talking about here? Months, years?'

'No, *weeks!*'

'Come on ...'

'Anatoly acknowledges that his own *actions* – especially the recent corruption revelations – may actually be accelerating this process.'

'Fascinating. If that is so, what does Anatoly hope to achieve through the Foundation?'

'That's a very good question, which to me has only one answer: removing Palin, the dictator, from power, and liberating the country from the grip of a corrupt elite bleeding the country dry.'

'What does this mean, exactly? An *assassination*?'

Sasha shrugged. 'All I know is there are many in Russia right now who feel the same way, and many of them are in the Russian Orthodox Church or associated with it. Deep down, Russia is a deeply religious country and the power and influence of the Church, especially in the country, is huge. Religion is embedded in the Russian psyche. They are terrified about the direction Russia is heading right now, and are determined to do something about it. Whatever it takes.'

Sasha looked pensively out the window.

'Look at the Foundation as a match, igniting forces within Russia from the outside,' she continued. 'This is a powder keg, Henry. Once you light this fuse, there's no way of stopping it.'

'I was completely unaware of all this,' said Blackstone, looking incredulous.

'You're not alone. Most of Europe is in your shoes and will have a rude awakening once all this begins to unfold in earnest.'

'And then what? Let's say Palin and his cronies are removed. What happens then?'

'Free elections, independently monitored and supervised, giving Russia an opportunity to decide its own fate for the first time since Gorbachev opened the window of freedom with *perestroika*, and allowed Russia to dream ... Sadly, the dream didn't become a reality because then came Yeltsin and the rise of the oligarchs with all the monstrous corruption that Anatoly is exposing right now. This is all still a direct result of those times.'

'A little too speculative, perhaps?'

'I don't think so. I would call it inevitable. Once you let the freedom genie out of the bottle there's no way of putting it back, as Palin will find out. The only question is at what cost and who will pay, because the price is bound to be high. The wheels of history are relentless and have crushed many.'

'And Anatoly? What are his dreams?'

'He hasn't told me everything, but for now he's content to be playing a part in bringing about change. After that, who knows? Provided he's still alive, of course. He knows the risks.'

'And is he trying to stay away from the crushing wheels of history, do you think?'

Sasha shook her head. 'I doubt it. That's just not like him. He's actually oiling them.'

Blackstone stood up, walked over to Sasha and put his hand on her shoulder.

'Then let's make sure that he never runs out of oil,' he said.

'Thank you, Henry. I was hoping you would say something like that.'

36

Muscat: 15 January

Feeling refreshed after the long flight the day before, Isis, Jack and Tristan were waiting for Ali Khan, the events coordinator, in the hotel foyer as arranged. It was just after nine am and already quite warm.

'Sun feels good,' said Isis, adjusting her hijab.

'A nice change after freezing winter weather in Venice,' said Jack. 'Should be an interesting day. O'Hara already called me. He wanted to know what's going on.'

'What did you tell him?'

'I told him to be patient and wait for my report. He didn't sound happy.'

'Hardly surprising,' said Tristan. 'But you're now in control; you can see that, surely.'

'Pity I don't quite feel that way. It's difficult to imagine that *Golgotha* should have ended up here, in this place.'

Tristan pointed to two black limousines pulling up at the entrance. 'Here he comes, I'd say.'

A tall man got out of the front car and walked over to Isis, smiling. Wearing a white *dishdasha*, an ankle-length collarless robe and a *kuma*, a traditional rounded cap decorated with colourful embroidery, Khan looked almost regal.

'Allow me to compliment you on your splendid attire,' he said and made a bow.

Isis, who was wearing the blue African abaya kaftan and matching hijab she had worn on arrival in Venice the day before, looked pleased.

'You think it's appropriate?' she said. 'We weren't quite sure ... local traditions ...'

'Absolutely! Sheik Khalid will be delighted. You have obviously gone to a lot of trouble to learn about our customs. He will feel honoured.'

'No trouble at all,' replied Isis. 'The least I could do to repay his generous hospitality.'

'I hope you found your accommodation to your liking?' continued Khan breezily and turned towards Jack.

'We certainly did, thank you,' said Jack. 'Excellent hotel.'

'I hope the ladies didn't mind,' continued Khan, holding up his hands and spreading his fingers apologetically. 'Local customs, especially at the palace ...'

'No problem. They understood,' lied Isis, who'd had to placate an incensed Lola and offended Bartolli after Khan had told them – ever so politely – that the invitation to meet Sheikh Mohammed and view his art collection was for Isis, Jack and Tristan only.

'Sheik Khalid will meet us at the palace and introduce you to his father. The palace isn't far; just a short drive. Please, come.'

Khalid welcomed them at the imposing entrance of the Al Ahmed Palace, an elegant gold and blue structure with wooden balconies and lots of marble. As an example of modern Islamic architecture it was impressive, without being flamboyant or gaudy, like many of the other palaces and residences owned by billionaires in the Middle East, and incorporated many traditional Islamic features reaching back to a glorious past.

Khalid was beaming. To have been able to persuade an internationally acclaimed artist like Isis to come to Oman and perform at his father's birthday celebrations was considered a great coup, word of which had spread through Oman and neighbouring emirates like wildfire. It was viewed with admiration and envy by other prominent families in the area, always trying to outdo one another.

For Khalid, who even now in his fifties still lived in his father's shadow, such a coup represented a huge achievement and welcome boost to his ego and reputation that he was eager to capitalise on.

Any kind of praise coming from his father was rare, and Khalid was determined to make his father's birthday celebrations a huge success many would talk about for years to come. Isis and the spectacular concert planned for later that evening were a major part of this.

Instead of holding the concert in the palace grounds, it had been decided to hold it after the banquet in a public place in front of the historical Al Jalali Fort, built by the Portuguese to protect the harbour of Old Muscat. This would not only entertain fellow citizens eager to hear Isis perform in public rather than behind closed palace doors, but would also make them part of the birthday celebrations honouring his father. It was a shrewd move that Khalid knew would please his father, as face, respect and standing in the community had always been the things he had valued above all else.

The public birthday concert had been the main reason Khalid's father had agreed to let Isis and her friends view his art collection, which was usually strictly off limits to all but a select few.

After a formal welcome at the entrance flanked by two massive Portuguese cannons that had once defended the harbour, Khalid introduced Isis, Jack and Tristan to Professor Doncaster, a retired British art historian. As the private curator of Sheikh Mohammed's art collection for more than three decades, Doncaster knew the collection like no other, and would be their guide. A meeting with Sheikh Mohammed was scheduled for later, after the tour. This too had been carefully planned, as Sheikh Mohammed wanted to show off his collection to his guests before meeting them, well aware that a Goya, Rubens or Titian could only enhance the prestige and standing of a man who actually owned them.

'The collection is located in the basement,' said Doncaster, leading the way down a wide set of marble stairs. 'Because of the extreme temperatures and humidity here, the area is climate controlled, but very soon the entire collection will be moved to a new art gallery presently under construction next door. You may have seen it on your way here?'

'We did,' said Jack. 'A stunning piece of architecture; very imposing.'

'It reminds me of the Alhambra,' said Isis.

'I'm glad you like it,' said Khalid. 'It's a project close to my father's heart. The design is the result of an international competition and has in fact been inspired by the Alhambra.'

During the next hour, Doncaster guided them through Sheikh Mohammed's breathtaking art collection located in a maze of underground corridors. A subterranean art gallery housing the collective genius of many, assembled over decades by the vision and determination of one.

'As you can see, the collection traces the history of European painting from the Middle Ages to the present. There are more than two hundred paintings down here covering various periods from the German Renaissance, to impressionism, to Russian constructivism.'

'This reminds me of the Thyssen-Bornemisza National Museum in Madrid,' said Jack as he admired works by Durer, Rubens and Frans Hals.

'You're absolutely right, Mr Rogan,' said Doncaster. 'We've tried to arrange the paintings in a similar, chronological order, divided into specific periods. An art stroll through the ages.'

'Impressive,' said Isis and pointed to a Picasso hanging between a Kandinsky and a Dalí.

'We also have a number of avant-garde works,' said Doncaster, who was obviously pleased the visitors seemed to know a lot about art and were genuinely interested. 'Fauvism, expressionism and surrealism are all represented.'

Isis stopped in front of a painting by Jan van Eyck. 'Ah, a van Eyck,' she said. 'Magnificent. Is this the only van Eyck in the collection?'

'Yes. Why do you ask?' said Doncaster.

'I thought there were more.'

'What makes you say that?' asked Doncaster, surprised.

'I thought Jan van Eyck's *Golgotha* was part of the collection,' said Isis casually.

Silence.

Here we go, thought Jack and squeezed Tristan's arm.

Doncaster shot Khalid a meaningful look, but didn't reply.

'You better ask my father about that,' said Khalid, stepping in. 'He keeps several paintings in his private rooms. For his eyes only, so to speak.'

'I understand,' said Isis, smiling. 'I do the same. I keep certain paintings I am particularly fond of close to me. *Little Sparrow in the Garden,* a Monet I bought a few years ago, is a good example. The auction caused quite a fuss at the time because the painting had such an interesting provenance. You may have heard about it?'

'Yes, I remember,' said Doncaster. 'It had to do with the war. The painting was stolen by the Nazis and found its way back to its rightful owner, who was actually present at the auction, if I'm right?'

'Yes, Maestro Krakowski. You have an excellent memory, Professor. Mr Rogan has written a novella about this – *The Forgotten Painting.* It was a huge success. Actually, the reason I was asking about *Golgotha* also has to do with the war years. There's in fact a fascinating connection between the two paintings Mr Rogan is looking into right now. Research; isn't that right, Jack?' said Isis, grinning at Jack.

'It is,' said Jack, his mind racing. He hadn't expected the sudden turn in the conversation. It was always a fine line between revealing too much, or too little.

'Perhaps we should continue this conversation once we've spoken to Sheikh Mohammed?' suggested Tristan, coming to Jack's aid. 'All this may not even be relevant if the painting isn't here, right?'

'Excellent suggestion,' said Khalid, sounding relieved. 'Please follow me. I know my father is looking forward to meeting you.'

Even at eighty, Sheikh Mohammed bin Ahmed was an impressive man. His almost biblical face with the trimmed white beard and piercing eyes of a zealot, made Jack imagine him catching the attention of someone like Michelangelo, for sure. Perhaps in a busy town square or market, or in quiet contemplation in church, he would have been tempted to incorporate the man's image into the ceiling design of the Sistine Chapel, or one of the seven square panels as a prophet like Jonah, Ezekiel, or Zachariah, looking down from above to spread the word of God.

Speaking perfect English, albeit with the distinctive, sing-song accent of a multilingual, well-educated Arab, Sheikh Mohammed greeted them warmly and offered refreshments. In Isis, he immediately recognised a fellow collector, and was eager to hear what she thought of his art collection.

After some friendly chit-chat about various pieces in the collection, Sheikh Mohammed came straight to the point that intrigued him most.

'My son tells me that you seem to think Jan van Eyck's *Golgotha* is in my collection. What makes you say that?'

Isis had been expecting this question. She reached into her pocket, pulled out a piece of paper folded in half and handed it to Sheikh Mohammed. It was a copy of the note Moser had discovered among Fuchs's records dealing with the *Golgotha*–Toulouse-Lautrec exchange. 'This was recently discovered accidentally by his executor among the late Emil Fuchs's papers,' said Isis, watching Sheikh Mohammed carefully.

For a while there was complete silence in the room as Sheikh Mohammed studied the note. Then he folded it in half again and handed it back to Isis. 'May I ask why you are so interested in this?' said Sheikh Mohammed softly.

'It's all part of a literary journey of discovery,' said Isis.

'How intriguing. Can you tell me more?'

'Ah. Mr Rogan here can do this much better than I. After all, it's really his journey. Jack, would you mind?'

Taking his time, Jack the storyteller recounted the *Golgotha* saga and explained the Herzl connection. He spoke of the Postmaster of Treblinka involvement, and how the painting ended up in Budapest and was later sold to Erwin Strasser in Vienna before it ended up in

Salzburg. He didn't mention the Rabbi Stein challenge, nor did he refer to O'Hara and the murders, or the bizarre game he was playing.

'What an extraordinary story, Mr Rogan, but then again, you are no stranger to extraordinary stories, especially when lost treasures are involved. Isn't that so?'

Jack looked surprised.

'You found Kazanskaya Bogomater, the Russian holy icon, and returned it to the Alexander Nevsky Cathedral in Yekaterinburg. You also located Tchaikovsky's lost symphony and presented it to the Russian people in St Petersburg. And then, more recently, you delivered a lost letter with precious Holocaust records to Yad Vashem in Jerusalem, to honour a promise made a long time ago. Impressive, I must say.'

'You are full of surprises, Sheikh Mohammed. Yes, somehow these wonderful stories seem to find me, and have become the subject matter of my books.'

'Surely, it's not quite as simple as that,' said Sheikh Mohammed. 'Just like me, you are a believer in destiny, are you not?'

'He sure is that,' commented Isis. 'And doggedly follows his breadcrumbs wherever he goes.'

'I see,' said Sheikh Mohammed, stroking his beard. 'And those breadcrumbs have brought you here. Is that the case, Mr Rogan?'

Jack nodded.

'But he doesn't do these things alone,' said Isis. 'He has help.'

'Help? In what way?'

Isis pointed to Tristan. 'This young man can hear the whisper of angels and glimpse eternity.'

'Is that so?' said Sheikh Mohammed and looked pensively out of the window towards the distant mountains shimmering in the morning sun like beacons beckoning from another world. 'And what are those angels whispering about *Golgotha*, I wonder?' he said softly.

Tristan closed his eyes and took his time before replying. 'I can hear many voices, because *Golgotha* has such a long history and harbours secrets that have mystified many over the ages.'

Sheikh Mohammed turned around and looked at Tristan. 'And are these voices telling you that the painting may be here?'

'Yes, that's exactly what they are telling me.'

'All right. Let's see if you are right, shall we?' Sheikh Mohammed walked over to Doncaster and said something to him in Arabic. Doncaster listened intently, made a bow, and left the room.

'We certainly have a big day ahead,' said Khalid, anxious to steer the conversation back to what mattered most to him: the impending birthday celebrations.

'You will, of course, join us for the banquet?' said Sheikh Mohammed. 'It will be held right here in the great hall.'

'We would be honoured,' said Isis, making a bow.

'It will be a feast,' said Khalid. 'Traditional food and music. And then the celebrations will conclude with the concert by the harbour for all to enjoy, followed by fireworks.'

'Sounds fabulous. I will have to join my musicians soon,' said Isis. 'Final rehearsal! Mr Khan has been most helpful and seems to have arranged everything perfectly.'

'Excellent,' said Khalid, hoping to conclude the audience as soon as possible. He didn't like the way his father had taken over completely.

Just then the door opened and Doncaster entered, carrying something under his arm. It was obviously a painting. Without saying a word, he walked over to Sheikh Mohammed, placed the small painting on the table in front of him and stepped back.

'Please come over here,' said Sheikh Mohammed and pointed to the painting on the table. 'Destiny at work? What do you think?'

37

O'Hara put down the phone and looked at Herzl's diary on the desk in front of him. *Is this how it's going to end?* he thought. He was trying to come to terms with the full implications of what Jack had just told him. So, he'd found the painting. And so quickly! Remarkable.

Jack's detailed report about his meeting with Sheikh Mohammed in his palace had taken O'Hara by surprise. While he had found the trail Jack had been following fascinating, he certainly hadn't quite expected such spectacular results. Deep down he had even suspected Jack had been bluffing, just to buy time.

Golgotha in a sheik's private collection in Oman. *Unbelievable!* thought O'Hara and entered Jack's latest move on the chessboard on his computer screen. *Ah. The Bishop Sacrifice. Big mistake. Gotcha!* The endgame was unfolding better, and faster, than he could have hoped. It was now time to plan the final moves and the all-important climax: Jack's annihilation.

The endgame O'Hara had in mind for Jack was ingenious, combining cruelty and irony he would be able to savour for a long time to come. For O'Hara, causing death by a thousand cuts was far more satisfying than one brutal, crushing blow. Turning defeat into triumph was the ultimate victory. It was the appropriate payback for an enormous humiliation, and proof of his superior intellect. A classic psychopathic vindication and the best way to repair a killer's bruised ego.

Having positioned the *Standard* in Muscat ahead of Jack's arrival had been a masterstroke. It allowed O'Hara to plan his next move in unexpected ways. By having Irina and her agents right there where it was all happening gave O'Hara options he couldn't have imagined before. Options he could now incorporate into his darknet betting game to great effect, and give his sensation-hungry cyber punters a

245

betting scenario that was bound to put a small fortune on the gaming table and further line his bulging pockets.

The plan he had in mind was both risky and daring, but if Irina's agents were as good as she claimed, it was certainly achievable. All O'Hara had to do was convince Irina this was so, and get her to agree to implement it.

The biggest hurdle O'Hara could see was time. For his plan to work, it had to be carried out right away, that very evening. There were no second chances because a certain chain of events had to fit together perfectly for the plan to succeed. And to find it was Jack himself who had given O'Hara the idea in the first place added an irresistible touch that sent a wave of excitement rippling through O'Hara. It wasn't often a condemned man showed the hangman a better way to tie the knot.

O'Hara sat back in his chair and went over the steps one more time to make sure nothing had been missed. Satisfied, he picked up his phone and called Irina.

38

The banquet, Muscat: 15 January

'So, women are allowed to attend a banquet celebrating a sheikh's birthday, but not an audience to view his art collection,' said Bartolli as the car pulled up in front of the Ahmed Palace.

'Not my rules,' said Jack and opened the car door. 'Should be an interesting evening. Let's go inside before they change the rules.'

Khan greeted them at the entrance. 'I have seated you at a smaller table for ten guests with a journalist from Abu Dhabi, and an actress from Mumbai who is very popular here in Muscat. Other guests at your table are Professor Doncaster and friends of the sheikh's family from London. I am sure you will enjoy their company. Please follow me.'

'Wow! Look at those flowers,' said Lola as they entered the great hall and were shown to their table. 'And those carpets!' Garlands of flowers and colourful lights and lanterns attached to the vaulted ceiling, and exquisite carpets covering the marble floor, made the hall look like a tent of a desert prince. Most of the guests had already arrived, and a local band was playing traditional music in the background, the *oud* and the *nay* conjuring up nostalgic images of Bedouins sitting around a campfire telling tales of high adventure and distant lands.

'I thought Isis would meet us here,' said Jack.

'She will join you later,' said Khan. 'The rehearsal is taking a little longer than expected. Some last-minute changes ...'

'I bet,' said Lola and turned towards Jack standing next to her. 'She likes arriving late, but she'll time it to perfection,' she said, lowering her voice. 'You know she's a master when it comes to making a memorable entrance. And besides, I know what she'll be wearing.'

'Nothing too outrageous, I hope. This looks like a very conservative crowd to me.'

'I wouldn't call it outrageous. Flamboyant, yes. Original, absolutely.'

'Thanks for the warning.'

'Here we are,' said Khan. 'Let me introduce you.'

The Indian actress sitting next to Jack seemed to know a lot about him, and so did the journalist from Abu Dhabi. Khan had obviously briefed them earlier. Doncaster looked introspective and subdued and Bartolli's attempts to make polite conversation seemed to fall on deaf ears. Formal dinners were clearly not his forte, as he seemed uncomfortable and on edge.

A ripple of excitement washed across the room when Khalid and his father entered with Isis by their side. Lola put her hand on Jack's arm. 'Here she comes. I told you; watch,' said Lola softly.

Wearing a traditional turquoise Omaniya dress consisting of a female dishdasha, *sarwal* and a beautifully embroidered headpiece, the *waqaya*, which made her look like a desert queen, Isis looked stunning.

Sheikh Mohammed and his son each wore traditional white dishdasha and a precious *khanjar*, an Omani dagger with a wide, curved blade and a handle of giraffe horn, attached to a silver belt. The dagger was a symbol of prestige and virility, and was always worn with pride. Everyone stood up as Sheikh Mohammed approached their table and escorted Isis to her seat.

A hire car, a black Rolls Royce, pulled up near the *Standard* where it was moored next to several other superyachts. Two bearded men wearing white dishdashas and traditional Kumas walked down the gangplank and got into the back of the car. The drive from the harbour to the Ahmed Palace only took a few minutes.

As soon as the car pulled up at the entrance and stopped, the uniformed driver got out, walked up to one of the security guards standing at the entrance and spoke to him briefly. The guard nodded and then hurried into the palace.

The security guard walked up to Doncaster sitting at Jack's table. 'Someone at the entrance would like to see you, sir,' he said, 'and deliver a present personally. Looks important.'

Doncaster excused himself, stood up and followed the security guard out of the hall.

The guard pointed to the driver standing next to the Rolls Royce. 'He's the one who asked for you.'

Doncaster walked over to the man. 'You wanted to see me?' he said.

Without saying a word, the driver opened a rear passenger door.

A bearded man – one of Irina's Chechen agents – got out and made a bow. Another man got out on the other side.

'Good evening, Professor Doncaster,' said the first man. He walked to the back of the car and opened the boot. 'We have a present for Sheikh Mohammed.'

Looking puzzled, Doncaster followed him to the back and looked into the boot. As he was bending forward, the man, now standing behind him, pressed something hard against his back.

'In case you're wondering, this isn't my finger, but the nozzle of a Mini Uzi, a machine gun that can fire nine hundred and fifty rounds a minute. My friend standing next to me has one too. We could kill everyone out here within seconds. If you want to avoid a bloodbath, I urge you to stay calm and do exactly as I tell you. Do we understand each other?'

Doncaster nodded.

'Good. Now, reach into the boot and take out the parcel.'

Doncaster did as he was told and took out a flat, rectangular parcel wrapped in gold paper with a red ribbon around it.

'Excellent,' said the man. 'This is a present; a painting for Sheikh Mohammed that we will now take inside. You will explain this to the security guards over there and take us into the building. Clear? We have no invitations and will not stay. We only want to deliver the present. The lives of everyone out here, including your own, are in your hands. Clear?'

Doncaster nodded again.

'Good. Once inside, you will take us downstairs into the vault where the art collection is kept; understood?'

'Yes.'

'All right. Let's go. And please be convincing.'

Isis was on a high. The rehearsal had gone better than expected, and the setting for the concert was without doubt one of the most exotic and spectacular she had ever encountered. It was an ageing rock star's dream and Isis was determined to savour every moment of it. Khalid had made sure that major international and local TV networks were all represented and had good vantage points to transmit a performance that would not only be a fitting tribute to his father, but would also showcase Muscat and Oman and, by implication, enhance the standing and prestige of his family.

Every smallest detail of the evening had been carefully planned and rehearsed to make sure nothing went wrong. After the banquet, the guests would be taken to the harbour in designated buses, to view the concert and then the fireworks that would conclude the festivities. With no expense spared, and a small army of dedicated staff to take care of every detail, Khalid was confident the evening would be a triumph, with Isis, the international star performer, the jewel in the festive crown.

Doncaster swept confidently past the security guards at the entrance and then walked down the stairs to the gallery entrance in the basement. As someone in authority who lived in the palace, no-one challenged him or the two men walking alongside him.

Doncaster stopped in front of the steel doors leading into the gallery. 'What now?' he asked.

'We go inside, of course,' said one of Irina's agents, looking around to make sure they had not been followed. 'Punch in the code — *now!*'

Doncaster punched in the required numbers on the keypad that activated the security door. The door clicked open and the three men quickly went inside.

The second agent, who had been recording everything with a small video camera concealed in the folds of his dishdasha, took his time. First, he took a close-up of Doncaster holding the parcel, and then began taking close-ups of the rows of paintings lining the walls of the corridor.

'Now take us to *Golgotha*,' said the agent with the gun. 'We know the painting is down here. So, no tricks. Understood?'

After countless courses of delicious Omani dishes, including huge platters of *shuwa*, an Omani delicacy consisting of grilled meat, mainly lamb and goat, and *majboos*, a popular rice dish served on special occasions, Khalid made a short speech paying tribute to his father. After that, Khan took over and explained how the rest of the evening would unfold, the excitement and anticipation in the room rising by the second.

Isis had left earlier to get ready and had made a spectacular exit. Khan, who acted as the MC, told the guests that very soon they would see Isis again, only this time not as a dinner guest, but as a megastar.

'Whereto from here?' asked Bartolli as they made their way to the waiting buses outside.

'To the concert, of course,' said Jack.

'That's not what I meant ...'

'Ah. You're asking about *Golgotha*.'

Bartolli nodded. 'Now that you know the painting is here, what are you going to do about it?'

'I have another meeting with Sheikh Mohammed tomorrow,' said Jack.

'Oh? What about?'

'Jack has a plan,' said Tristan, who had overheard the remark.

'What plan?' asked Lola.

'Tell them, Jack,' prompted Tristan. 'This is as good a time as any.'

'Doncaster let something slip yesterday after Mohammed showed us the painting. I think it was deliberate.'

'Let what slip?' asked Bartolli.

'He indicated there are a number of similar paintings in the collection, kept in a separate vault in the gallery because they don't fit into the "spirit" of the collection. He also said Sheikh Mohammed had decided to divest himself of those paintings.'

'Similar in what way?' said Lola.

'I'm sure he was referring to *Golgotha's* questionable provenance. He knows, of course, that we know the painting had obviously been stolen by the Germans during the war and that it had once been part of the famous *Ghent Altarpiece*, which is a national treasure that belongs to Belgium,' said Jack.

'The altarpiece has recently been placed on display in a thirty-five-million-dollar display case in the Sacrament Chapel in the Cathedral of Saint Bravo in Ghent,' said Tristan.

'What are you getting at?'

'What I think Doncaster was telling us was this,' said Jack. 'To have in his collection a famous painting like *Golgotha*, which has obviously been stolen, is not only an embarrassment to Sheikh Mohammed, but it's also a liability. He cannot sell the painting without having to explain how he got it. The sheikh also knows I've written a book about Herzl and am following the trail of the painting, which has brought us right here, to his doorstep. He's aware of the Fuchs note referring to the Toulouse-Lautrec exchange and that it is therefore only a matter of time—'

'Before the present whereabouts of the painting becomes public knowledge, leading to all kinds of questions and speculation?' said Bartolli.

'Which a man in his position wants to avoid, right?' said Lola. 'Because it would be a stain on his reputation. Remember, face is everything around here ...'

'Exactly. But the really telling thing was a question Sheikh Mohammed asked just before we left,' said Tristan.

'What question?' said Bartolli.

'He asked me what I would do if the painting were in *my* collection,' said Jack.

'What did you say?' asked Lola.

'I told him that I would return it to where it belonged. Reunite it with the *Ghent Altarpiece* and make history.'

'Just as you returned the holy icon to Russia?'

'Kazanskaya Bogomater? Yes. Just like that.'

'And are you suggesting he might be receptive to such an arrangement?' said Bartolli.

'Good question. Perhaps under certain circumstances. I think he liked the idea. Why would he have otherwise shown us the painting and admitted to having it in his collection? He must have a plan. It's the only explanation I could come up with. He's a shrewd man, used to being in control.'

'What kind of circumstances? What kind of plan?' said Lola.

'Not sure, but I'm working on it,' came Jack's evasive reply. 'Here's our bus now, guys. Let's go and enjoy the show. Judging by what Isis has told us during dinner, it should be quite something,' said Jack, and got on the bus.

During the commotion outside, nobody paid any attention to the two men wearing white dishdashas walking calmly towards a waiting Rolls Royce. Only Tristan could feel a twinge of unease as the man carrying a parcel wrapped in gold paper walked past him, handed the parcel to the driver, and then got into the car.

39

The concert, Muscat Harbour: 15 January

Irina stood on the upper deck of the *Standard*, which gave her an uninterrupted view of the concert venue and the Al Jalali Fort lit up like a stage behind it. Once a prison but now a private museum, the Portuguese fortification had protected Old Muscat for centuries and had a long and bloody history.

It should all be done by now, she thought and looked at her watch again. O'Hara had called several times already, desperate for news he could incorporate into his darknet gambling scenario, which was reaching a betting climax.

Initially, Irina had had second thoughts about O'Hara's crazy plan and its obvious risks, but in the end she relented because the daring idea appealed to her as it reminded her of assignments she had successfully tackled in her younger years at the KGB. In some ways she wasn't so different from an ageing rock star like Isis looking forward to a performance that would once again propel her into the limelight.

The invited guests had taken their seats in the cordoned-off area with rows of portable, tiered seating reserved for VIPs, but the huge crowd lining the harbour foreshores was getting restless and noisy while waiting behind barricades for the concert to begin. Free public concerts featuring a megastar like Isis were rare in Muscat, and eager spectators had arrived hours earlier to secure a place with a good view.

At ten o'clock sharp, the concert venue was plunged into darkness except for a spotlight illuminating the empty stage near the water's edge, a clear signal the performance was about to begin. The conductor had taken up his position facing the orchestra in front of the stage. He raised his baton as coloured lights came on, flooding the symphony orchestra with light as the first bars of Rimsky-

Korsakov's stirring *Scheherazade* echoed through the loudspeakers and enthusiastic applause erupted from all sides. A few moments later, Khan walked up to the microphone on the stage and held up his hand. The music continued, but softer, and almost melted into the background as Khan began to speak.

'A long time ago, a sailor called Sinbad set out on a long journey from Baghdad to explore the world. Along the way he had many adventures and supernatural encounters. On one occasion he landed on an island after a storm, only to find that the island was the back of a huge sleeping whale with palm trees growing on top.'

Khan paused as the sublime music became louder, conjuring up images of sea monsters, bloody battles and danger, only to fade away again after a while.

Bartolli turned to Jack sitting next to her. 'Magic, don't you think?'

'Sure is. I wonder how Isis is going to fit into all this.'

'You'll find out in a moment,' said Tristan. '*Watch.*'

'According to stories still being told in the desert, Sinbad sailed past these very shores on a vessel very similar to this one,' continued Khan. He turned to his right and pointed to the harbour as a beam of light raced across the dark water and came to rest on the slanted triangular sails of a traditional dhow sailing towards him. The music became louder as the vessel approached and tied up at a wooden wharf near the stage.

As Khan held up his hand again, the music stopped and the lights went out, plunging the stage and the orchestra into darkness, the sudden silence causing tension and anticipation, and making the illuminated vessel appear almost ghostlike and surreal.

Suddenly, the mesmerising beat of a drum came floating out of the darkness like the heartbeat of a giant. As the drumbeat became louder and more urgent, a figure appeared on the deck of the dhow. Dressed in baggy, wide-legged red trousers, a loose embroidered shirt and an emerald-green turban, the figure jumped onto the wharf and pointed towards the fort. Projected by laser lights, a floating Persian carpet appeared like magic and moved slowly along the walls of the fort before coming to rest on one of its ramparts. Then a beam of blue light illuminated first a drummer, then two guitarists standing on top of the ramparts, their long grey hair moving gently in the evening breeze.

'Ladies and gentlemen,' said Khan, his voice booming out of the darkness through the speakers, 'Isis and The Time Machine!'

The crowd erupted in cheers and applause as the guitars screamed into life, playing the introduction of 'Resurrection', one of Isis's biggest hits. As the orchestra joined in, the carpet moved on, descended from the ramparts and, hovering just above the ground, began to float towards the lonely figure standing on the wharf. Isis stepped onto the carpet at her feet and, appearing to float, started walking towards the stage, the clever illusion adding to the drama as Isis began to sing.

'*Wow!*' said Jack. 'What an entrance. I think this is even better than Mexico. Amazing what you can to with laser lights these days.'

'She certainly hasn't lost her touch. What do you make of those guys playing on top of the ramparts?' said Lola.

'The original Time Machine? Incredible! They must be well into their sixties. A magic carpet ride in more ways than one. Just look at that crowd,' said Jack, clapping enthusiastically. 'She has them eating out of her hands.'

Irina heard footsteps on the deck behind her and turned around. 'All done?' she said to her Chechen agents walking towards her.

'Without a hitch,' said one of the agents. 'The concert was the perfect distraction, especially at the hotel. Everyone was preoccupied. We were invisible and had no trouble getting in.'

'Everything recorded?'

'Of course.'

'Excellent. Did you upload the video?'

'Yes. It's ready to go.'

'I'll have a look at it later before we send it to O'Hara.' Irina pointed to a bottle of vodka on the table in front of her. 'But first, let's have a drink. We leave as soon as the concert's over. After that, all that's left is a phone call to the local police. I hope Mr Rogan is enjoying the concert and his last few hours of freedom.'

'And perhaps one last use of his right hand? What do you think?' said one of the agents, laughing.

'In a crazy country like this with its brutal medieval practices? You never know,' said Irina.

One of the agents handed Irina a tumbler of vodka. She turned towards the illuminated stage and raised her glass just as Isis launched into 'Dead Girl Walking', another of her mega hits. *How appropriate,* thought Irina and smiled. 'To Jack Rogan, a dead man walking,' she said. *'Na Zdorovie!'*

40

Muscat: 16 January

At first, Jack tried to ignore the loud banging on his door, but it wouldn't stop. It became louder and more urgent. Jack looked at his watch. It was just after six am. Still half asleep, he put on his bathrobe, walked to the door and opened it. Three uniformed police officers stood outside. 'Mr Rogan?' said one of them and held up a piece of paper.

'Yes.'

'We have a warrant to search your room. Please step aside.'

It took the officers only a few minutes to find a painting wrapped in gold paper hidden behind an ironing board in the back of the wardrobe.

'Mr Rogan,' said one of the officers, 'you are under arrest.'

Being an early riser, Isis heard the commotion in the corridor and stepped outside to investigate. 'What's going on?' she said and walked over to Jack's room, which was next to her suite.

'Please, go back to your room,' said an officer standing in front of the open door.

'I will do no such thing,' said Isis and looked inside. 'Jack! What's going on?'

'No idea,' replied Jack. 'They just found *Golgotha* hidden in my wardrobe. I'm under arrest. This is no magic carpet ride, but a setup. I can see O'Hara's fingers all over this. Better call Khan and see what this is all about,' said Jack as he walked past Isis with two police officers by his side. 'And call Dupree. This could be serious,' he added, before he disappeared down the corridor.

It took Isis over an hour on the phone to track down Khan.

'The police received an anonymous tip-off early this morning, by satellite phone,' said Khan, obviously feeling uncomfortable about the situation.

'What kind of tip-off?' demanded Isis.

'All I know is that the police turned up at the Al Ahmed Palace early this morning, looking for Professor Doncaster. They found him tied up in the art vault in the basement. Barely alive because he could hardly breathe. His mouth had been covered with duct tape. After that, the police searched Mr Rogan's hotel room and found *Golgotha,* the van Eyck painting, hidden in his wardrobe. He's in the police station right now being questioned.'

'You don't seriously think Mr Rogan had anything to do with this clumsy nonsense?' said Isis.

'I don't know what to think at the moment. The entire palace is in turmoil. Sheikh Khalid is beside himself. A major scandal is threatening to overshadow the festivities. If the press—'

'Unless we resolve this matter right now,' interjected Isis.

'How? This is now in the hands of the police.'

'There could be a way.'

'Seriously?'

'Yes, but we have to move quickly before this spins out of control.'

'Agreed. You have something in mind?'

'Yes.'

'What?'

'Exposing those who are behind all this and are trying to frame Jack. It won't be easy, but I'm working on it. I would like to meet with Sheikh Khalid, urgently. Can you arrange it?'

'I'll do my best.'

Isis put down the phone and looked at Lola, who was glued to her laptop. 'What did Dupree have to say?'

'He has spoken to Lapointe and is talking to the Squadra Mobile in Florence right now. Apparently, Samartini has been monitoring O'Hara's darknet site round the clock and is making some progress. There has been a great deal of gambling activity through the night. She indicated she may have something that could help us.'

'I hope so because we may need all the help we can get. Theft is taken very seriously around here; sharia law. Do you know what the punishment is for theft?'

'Tell me.'

'They cut off your right hand.'

What?' said Lola as her mobile began to ring. She closed her laptop and answered her phone. It was Dupree. 'Are you serious?' she said. 'That's amazing! How? Doesn't matter, I suppose, just send it through.'

Lola put down her phone and looked at Isis.

'Well?' said Isis.

'Should be coming through in a moment.'

'What?'

'Something that could save Jack's right hand, and perhaps his neck as well.'

O'Hara's control centre, Minsk

Elated, O'Hara monitored the numbers on his screen and smiled. The betting had gone through the roof since he had posted the Muscat video Irina had sent through earlier. Her agents had done an outstanding job and recorded everything. Despite the obvious risks, everything had gone off without a hitch and in many ways had actually surpassed expectations. Once O'Hara had embellished the story with his own action-cartoons providing an intriguing blend of fact and fiction that introduced possibilities for various outcomes the punters could bet on, an exciting, lucrative climax was all but guaranteed.

And to know that Jack had been arrested and would no doubt be facing serious charges based on solid evidence difficult to refute, added a great sense of satisfaction O'Hara was determined to enjoy to the fullest. The endgame was in its final stages; his adversary's defeat was imminent. The slate of humiliation and defeat had been almost wiped clean.

* * *

'Thank you for seeing us, Sheikh Khalid,' said Isis. She made a bow that was almost a little theatrical, and walked towards Khalid waiting with Khan in the palace foyer. Isis had only asked Tristan to come along to the meeting as Lola and Bartolli were busy on the phone talking to Dupree and Lapointe and various officers at Europol. And besides, women weren't included in Oman in the same way as in non-Muslim countries.

'Allow me to congratulate you on a most memorable performance last night,' began Khalid. 'It was enthralling. My father and I are indebted to you, and so is the whole of Muscat.'

A good icebreaker under difficult circumstances, thought Isis, who had approached the meeting with understandable trepidation.

'Thank you. Even more reason why this dreadful business has to be resolved quickly before it overtakes us, and casts a dark shadow over celebrations that should be remembered with affection for years to come.'

'My thoughts entirely,' said Khalid. 'Please, this way.'

'How is Professor Doncaster?' asked Isis as she followed Khan into the opulent reception room on the ground floor where the meeting with Sheikh Mohammed had taken place the day before.

'Resting. He will be fine once the shock wears off.'

'That's good to know. Allow me to begin with a reassurance.'

'What kind of reassurance?' asked Khalid, frowning.

'None of us – and that, of course, includes Mr Rogan – had anything to do with what happened last night and are as eager and determined as you obviously are, to get to the bottom of this woeful affair as quickly as possible, before this regrettable incident causes irreparable harm,' said Isis, choosing her words carefully, well aware of the circuitous way Arabs approached delicate subjects.

'That is precisely what we are hoping to achieve as well, but with the police involved it may not be that easy. Fortunately, our family, and my father in particular, are held in the highest regard here, and we have excellent relations with the police. It is for that reason the Chief of Police has agreed to join us. He should be arriving any minute.'

'That is very fortuitous,' said Isis, 'because I have something to show you that may have a significant bearing on all this and answer many questions.'

'Oh? Can you elaborate?'

'It would be better if we could wait for the Chief of Police.'

'As you wish.' Khalid looked at Tristan. 'Destiny, perhaps?'

'Could be,' said Tristan.

'Very well. Some tea while we wait?'

'Yes, please.'

The Chief of Police, a young man sporting an impressive moustache and wearing a crisp uniform, arrived moments later. If he was surprised to see Isis standing next to Khalid, he was too polite to show it. 'Wonderful performance; congratulations,' he said, and shook hands with Isis and Tristan. 'To combine a rock concert with themes from *One Thousand and One Nights* was inspirational. East meets West; very clever. And to position the drummer and the guitarists on top of the ramparts of the old fort was genius.'

'Thank you,' said Isis, flattered by the compliment.

'And then to have that costume change in the middle of the concert and reappear as Scheherazade, the storyteller, with the lead guitarist standing behind you, was amazing. Telling stories to each other. You with your voice, and he with the guitar; brilliant! The crowd loved it!'

Khalid was beaming, soaking up the effusive praise. The concert he had arranged to honour his father had obviously been a huge success.

'I have asked Isis to join us because she has some information that could throw further light on this unfortunate matter,' said Khalid.

'Oh? In what way?'

'Perhaps before I answer that, could you tell us where your investigations are up to,' said Isis, 'and what you have been able to find out so far about this curious case? It could have a bearing on what I'm about to show you and make it more meaningful and relevant. It may even provide some of the missing pieces in this baffling puzzle.'

'Very well. This is what we know: No doubt you are aware of the anonymous tip-off we received early this morning.'

'We have already discussed all that,' said Khalid.

'And, of course, you know what was found in Mr Rogan's room,' continued the Chief of Police, undeterred, 'which led to his arrest?'

'Yes, of course; the painting,' said Isis. 'I was there.'

'But what you may not know, is what the driver of the hire car that was involved just told us.'

'What hire car?' asked Khalid.

'The hire car used by the two men who assaulted Professor Doncaster, broke into the vault in the basement here, and stole the painting later found hidden in Mr Rogan's room.'

'What did he tell you?' asked Isis.

'He picked up two men from one of the luxury yachts in the harbour and brought them here. The yacht was the *Standard*, a famous vessel. It left the harbour just after midnight and is now in international waters.'

'The *Standard* was here?' asked Isis, stunned.

'You know this vessel?' said the Police Chief, watching Isis carefully.

'I know of it. I have never actually seen it or been on it. It's owned by a Russian billionaire. The *Standard*'s home port is St Petersburg.'

'We know. Mr Rogan already told us.'

'I don't understand,' said Khalid. 'This is all very confusing. What's the relevance of all this?'

'It may sound confusing, but it's highly relevant, as you will see in a moment.' Isis opened her handbag and took out an iPad. 'My PA received this a short while ago from Chief Superintendent Lapointe of the Paris police. It's a video on the darknet that was intercepted by the Squadra Mobile in Florence this morning as part of an ongoing investigation by Europol and the French police into a series of shocking murders, and illegal gambling.'

The Chief of Police looked puzzled. 'May I see it?'

'Of course.' Isis clicked on the video and positioned the iPad on the table in front of her so that everyone could see the screen. It was a visual, step-by-step account of what happened after Irina's two agents left the *Standard*. It showed how they gained access into the palace and what happened inside Sheikh Mohammed's art vault, and how they managed to leave with the painting without being challenged. The video continued in Jack's hotel room and showed where, and how, the stolen painting had been hidden. The final scene showed the two men getting out of the hire car and boarding the *Standard*, and concluded with a view of the spectacular fireworks over the harbour.

After a long silence, the Chief of Police turned to Isis. 'Could you please explain to us what all this means?'

'Isn't it obvious? It tells us what happened last night.'

'It may show us what *happened*, but doesn't explain what it all *means*. It shows us the how, but doesn't tell us about the why. Can you help us with that?'

'It's complicated. I think it would be better if you were to hear this from an official channel like Europol. Chief Superintendent Lapointe will call you shortly and explain it all. He knows us all very well and can vouch for Mr Rogan.'

'Very well. May I have a copy of this video?'

'Of course. I'll send it to you now.'

Khalid turned towards Tristan, sitting quietly by himself. 'You don't seem surprised by any of this.'

'I'm used to Jack's breadcrumbs.'

'And the whisper of angels?'

'That too.'

'Ah ...'

41

Irina sat in the opulent saloon of the *Standard* and looked pensively out to sea. Apart from the bartender, the room was empty because there were no guests on board and the ship was operating with a skeleton crew. She was trying to come to terms with the disturbing news she had just received from her source in Muscat. Outside it was already very hot, but inside it was pleasantly cool and the tinted windows kept out the glare bouncing off the still waters of the Gulf of Oman. Irina reached for the vodka bottle and poured herself another drink.

'How could things have gone so spectacularly wrong?' she asked herself aloud. As a former senior KGB agent, she knew that meticulous planning and reliable inside information were the cornerstones of a successful mission, however risky or daring. Arriving in Muscat two days before the start of the festivities had given her enough time to gather sufficient intelligence to plan her move, and in Ali Khan, the events coordinator, she had found the perfect source for inside information.

The arrival of the *Standard,* one of the biggest and most luxurious private superyachts in the world, radiated influence and almost obscene wealth, and attracted attention wherever she went. Khan had therefore enthusiastically embraced an invitation to come aboard, because he sensed that an important visitor wanted to make contact, which was by no means unusual.

An excellent judge of character, it hadn't taken Irina long to find Khan's weak spot: money. Like so many officials in the Middle East used to a widespread baksheesh culture, Khan was open to bribes, and when the information he had been asked to provide appeared almost trivial, he willingly walked into the trap and accepted the huge amount Irina had offered for certain information.

All Irina told Khan was that an important visitor was on board who wanted to keep his identity confidential for the time being, as he wanted to surprise Sheikh Mohammed at the appropriate time. To make this possible, she had to know what was planned, and when. A line of communication was established and it all went from there. By the time Irina's agents had broken into the art vault at the palace on the night of the banquet and stolen the painting, it was too late. Khan was implicated and compromised with nowhere to go. After that, he had to do Irina's bidding to save himself. That was how she had found out about Isis's meeting with Khalid and the Commissioner of Police earlier that day.

How the video she had sent to O'Hara had found its way to Isis, effectively exonerating Jack, was still a mystery, with devastating consequences that had placed the entire operation in jeopardy. Not used to failure or conceding defeat, Irina regrouped and immediately went on the attack to salvage whatever she could before it was too late. And to be able to do that, she had to know exactly what was happening. With the video in the hands of the Paris Police and Europol, she realised O'Hara's darknet operation, and by implication Ivanov's involvement, were at risk and somehow had to be protected.

Irina knew she had to come up with a plan and a plausible explanation for what had occurred, and distance herself from an embarrassing situation that could easily ruin her.

Putting herself into Sheikh Mohammed's shoes, she realised he would desperately want to avoid a public scandal, especially with a high-profile international star like Isis involved. Jack's release was therefore only a matter of time. The stolen painting had already been returned and Doncaster set free, unharmed. Isis and her entourage were no longer implicated. How Jack and his friends had managed to turn the tables so quickly and extricate themselves from a potentially serious situation that could easily have resulted in jail time, or worse, was astonishing. O'Hara's plan to frame Jack had gone completely off the rails, with devastating consequences on the darknet gambling site. This not only required an explanation, but something also had to be offered in return to placate an understandably furious O'Hara.

While Irina didn't quite know what that would involve, she knew from experience that something would turn up. It always did. All that was needed was patience and nerves of steel, and Irina had ample quantities of both, and in Khan she had the necessary eyes and ears on the ground to keep her ahead of the game. Feeling better, Irina drained her glass, reached for her satellite phone and called O'Hara. It was time to tell him the bad news.

42

Al Ahmed Palace: 17 January

Jack sat up when his cell door creaked open and looked at the Commissioner of Police standing in front of him in his crisp uniform. It was early in the morning, and Jack felt stiff and tired after an uncomfortable night spent in jail.

'An early morning execution?' said Jack, rubbing his sleepy eyes.

'Far from it, Mr Rogan. You are free to go.'

'Seriously?'

'Yes. All charges have been dropped. Your friends are waiting outside and will explain everything. Follow me.'

Bartolli and Lola burst out laughing when Jack appeared at the jail entrance, rubbing his eyes after he had been discharged. Wearing the bathrobe he had been arrested in the day before, Jack looked like a vagrant who had spent the night in a cell to sober up after a day on the booze.

'A little underdressed for the occasion, but it'll do,' said Lola. 'Better get in the car before someone recognises you and takes a picture.'

'How are you?' said Isis, who was waiting in the hire car. 'Never a dull moment with you around.'

'I've been better. How did you manage this?'

'It's a long story,' said Bartolli.

'I bet. I would kill for a shower and breakfast. I'm starving! You can't imagine the muck they give you to eat here in jail.'

Tristan looked at Bartolli and winked. 'Nothing wrong with this guy; what do you think?'

Bartolli nodded.

'You'll just have time for a shower before—'

'Before what?' said Jack.

'We are due at the palace.'

'You mean we haven't totally fallen out of favour and disgraced ourselves?'

'Not at all. Quite the contrary,' said Isis breezily. 'We are, in fact, flavour of the month. After that concert, we can do no wrong; isn't that right, Lola?'

'Absolutely! You were amazing,' said Lola, rolling her eyes.

'We'll wait for you at the pool,' said Isis as the car pulled up at the hotel and the uniformed concierge opened the car door. If he was surprised when Jack got out of the car in his bathrobe, he was careful not to show it. Neither did the staff at reception when Jack asked for his room key and then confidently walked to the lifts, ignoring the curious looks of the guests going to breakfast.

Back in his room, Jack found several encrypted messages from O'Hara on his phone. It was obvious from the content that O'Hara had inside information about Jack's situation and movements and was changing his tactics. During a long, hot shower, Jack considered his next move.

Isis, Jack and Tristan were welcomed at the palace entrance by Khalid and Khan, who escorted them to the reception room on the ground floor to meet Sheikh Mohammed.

After some pleasantries, during which no mention was made of Jack's arrest or his night spent in jail, Sheikh Mohammed thanked them for coming and then introduced the subject of real interest.

'Last time we met, Mr Rogan, I asked you a question about *Golgotha*. Do you remember what it was?'

'Of course. You asked me what I would do with the painting if it were in my collection.'

'Correct.'

'I was intrigued by your answer and have given it a lot of thought, especially in light of recent events.'

Sheikh Mohammed turned to Tristan sitting next to Jack. 'Do you remember Mr Rogan's answer?'

'Of course. He said he would return the painting to where it belonged,' said Tristan.

'Because Mr Rogan always follows his breadcrumbs of destiny? Would that be the reason?'

'Yes. *Golgotha* is an extraordinary painting surrounded by many voices,' said Tristan.

'And can you hear those voices?'

'Yes, I can.'

'Because you can hear the whisper of angels?'

'Yes.'

Sheikh Mohammed looked at his son. 'Would you, please?'

Khalid nodded, stood up and left the room. He returned moments later with *Golgotha* and placed it on an empty chair next to his father.

'Can you perhaps hear what the voices are saying about the painting right now?' continued Sheikh Mohammed.

Tristan closed his eyes and sat in silence for a while. 'The painting hides a great secret that has been waiting for centuries to be discovered, but only when the time is right,' said Tristan without opening his eyes. 'The time has come for *Golgotha* to give up its secrets.'

'I see,' said Sheikh Mohammed, stroking his beard.

'I too have given this subject a lot of thought,' said Jack, 'especially in light of recent events ...'

'You have?' said Sheikh Mohammed. 'In what way?'

'Spending a night in jail accused of a theft I didn't commit can focus the mind in illuminating ways, especially as *Golgotha* was at the very centre of my contemplation. Enforced solitude can reward us with clarity that otherwise would be buried in the trivialities and distractions of ordinary life.'

'Quite so,' said Khalid. 'Your point?'

'I believe destiny is once again at play here,' said Jack softly.

'In what way?' asked Sheikh Mohammed.

'Destiny has recently guided me to an extraordinary artefact that has been waiting for a long time to be discovered.'

'Oh? What kind of artefact?'

'Just as van Eyck's *Golgotha* and the *Ghent Altarpiece* are anchored in Christianity and have special religious and historical significance, the artefact I just mentioned has a similar significance to Islam.'

'I am intrigued, Mr Rogan,' said Sheikh Mohammed, his curiosity aroused. 'Care to elaborate?'

Here it comes, thought Jack. Taking a deep breath, he looked first at Tristan, then at Sheikh Mohammed. 'As I understand it, much has been written about this artefact, and Islamic scholars have been searching for it for centuries.'

'What are we talking about here?' asked Khalid, unable to hide his impatience, only to see his father shoot him a disapproving look.

'Please go on, Mr Rogan,' said Sheikh Mohammed calmly.

'I am talking about the Amulet of Timur.'

After a moment's silence Sheikh Mohammed asked, 'Are you suggesting you know something about this amulet that the scholars don't?'

'I do. I believe I've found it and know where it is.'

'Are you serious?' said Khalid, breaking the stunned silence.

'I am. And just like *Golgotha* should be returned to where it belongs, I believe an Islamic treasure like the Amulet of Timur belongs in a museum, to be preserved for posterity and displayed for all to see,' said Jack, inching closer to what he had in mind. 'You're building just such a museum right now; isn't that correct?'

'I am, but for that to be possible, just knowing where the amulet is may not be enough. One would have to have access to it, yes?'

'Quite so. I do have access, or more accurately, Tristan here does, because the amulet is owned by his late wife's family, the da Baggios of Venice.'

Silence again as everyone digested the surprising news.

'How can you be sure this artefact we are talking about is in fact the Amulet of Timur?' asked Sheik Mohammed at last.

'Because of its history; its provenance, if you like. I believe we have all the necessary information and proof to support this and persuade even the most sceptical scholar. It's all part of well-documented da Baggio family history. And then, of course, there's the amulet itself.'

'Do you know what this amulet looks like? Have you actually seen it?' probed Sheikh Mohammed.

'Yes, I have, and so has Tristan. Quite recently, in fact. On his birthday on five December, the day it was discovered, or to put it more accurately, *re*discovered.' Jack reached for his iPhone. 'Here, I can show you,' he said casually.

Jack selected a photo of the amulet taken during Tristan's birthday dinner and showed it to Sheikh Mohammed and his son. Both men gasped as they looked at the exquisite jewel-encrusted locket dangling from a gold chain.

'You are obviously telling us this for a reason, Mr Rogan,' said Sheikh Mohammed, watching Jack carefully.

'I am. Certain sacred objects or works of art are beyond price and the concept of ownership as we know it, because they belong to humankind. Like the *Ghent Altarpiece*, for instance.'

'Or Kazanskaya Bogomater?' said Sheikh Mohammed.

'Exactly. And for that reason they cannot be owned or sold, and trying to do so would not only be immoral and wrong, but also futile.'

'I agree. So, what are you suggesting?'

Jack smiled, because this was the question he had been waiting for. 'I have a proposal.'

'What kind of proposal?' asked Sheikh Mohammed, frowning.

'An exchange. As we know, *Golgotha* has been part of an exchange once before,' said Jack, referring to the Fuchs matter.

'It has.'

'So, why not again? *Golgotha* for the Amulet of Timur? It makes perfect sense.'

Lost in thought, Sheikh Mohammed stroked his beard in silence, contemplating what had been suggested.

'Would you be prepared to have the amulet authenticated by an expert?' he asked at last. 'There is a famous man who knows Islamic art and history like no other. A descendant of Tippu Tip.'

'The notorious Afro-Omani slave trader who used to work for the sultans of Zanzibar in the nineteenth century?'

'You are full of surprises, Mr Rogan. Your breadcrumbs must be hiding in unexpected corners of history.'

'And should that expert authenticate the amulet, would you be prepared to entertain such an exchange?' said Jack, ignoring the comment.

'I may, but under one condition.'

'What condition?'

'That my involvement never becomes public. It must not be referred to in your books or anywhere else.'

'Agreed.'

'And the authentication?'

'No problem. Where do we find this expert?'

'In Doha. He's quite elderly and does not travel. We would have to see him there. Would that cause a problem?'

Jack looked at Isis, the question on his face obvious.

'No problem. I always wanted to see the famous Islamic museum,' said Isis.

'Very good, but I would have to make some phone calls first to arrange it all … Venice ...'

'Understandable.'

Sheikh Mohammed turned to Tristan. 'Just like last time, you don't seem to be surprised by any of this?' he said, shaking his head.

'Just like last time, Sheikh Mohammed, my answer is the same: I'm used to Jack's breadcrumbs.'

'And the whisper of angels too, I suppose,' said Sheikh Mohammed.

'Yes, that too.'

O'Hara's control centre, Minsk

O'Hara kept staring at the message that had just come in from Irina. *More bad news?* he thought. *Surely not!* O'Hara was still reeling from the unexpected twist of Jack's sudden release from jail, all charges

273

dropped. The endgame had taken an unexpected turn for the worse. This guy had nine lives! And then there was Jack's masterful chess move after he had been released from jail. It had put O'Hara in check, and on the back foot. He realised he could now easily lose the game.

Khan had dutifully reported details of the meeting at the palace earlier that day, and Irina had immediately informed O'Hara of what had been discussed. It was this information O'Hara was looking at on his screen.

Ingenious, he thought, trying to make sense of the discussion between Jack and Sheikh Mohammed, and understand Jack's proposal regarding *Golgotha.* He was attempting to get his hands on the painting. *Brilliant!* Instead of being annoyed or angry, O'Hara immediately decided to use this unexpected development to his advantage by incorporating it into the computer game, his grudging admiration for Jack growing by the second. O'Hara liked nothing more than a challenging opponent worthy of his intellect, and unexpected setbacks were all part of the game, making the ultimate victory even sweeter.

After O'Hara had designed several new gambling scenarios that elevated the darknet game to new, almost dizzying heights, he watched the numbers on the screen as the bets kept flooding in. His mind racing, he was already working out a new endgame to defeat Jack once and for all. Only this time, he intended to remain in control and not leave it up to others to deliver the coup de grâce.

In order to savour the moment and hone his strategy, O'Hara decided to give Jack a free hand for the time being, and just keep an eye on where he was heading with this mysterious proposal involving Sheikh Mohammed. All O'Hara knew was that something significant was planned in Doha. No doubt Irina's contacts would find out in due course what that was all about. The *Standard* was already on her way via the Persian Gulf to Doha and was due to arrive there the next day.

For a man who preferred to stay in the shadows and wield his power through others by pulling the strings from a distance, this was an ideal setup. In Ivanov, O'Hara thought he had found the perfect business partner: a man with extensive underworld contacts, unlimited means and, most important of all, hopelessly addicted to gambling. And if that wasn't enough, Ivanov was giving him a free hand and had placed someone like Irina and the *Standard* at his disposal to carry out his instructions, however difficult or risky, no questions asked.

In some ways, this was almost too good to be true, and if something was too good to be true, O'Hara became nervous. What was making him feel uneasy was the fact Ivanov had stayed in the background without asking any questions or making contact. Of course, there was the money and Ivanov's accountants in London, but that was strictly business; administration, nothing personal. For O'Hara and Ivanov, this venture had never been just about money.

At first, there had been some enthusiastic gambling by Ivanov on the darknet, but even that had stopped, and every time O'Hara had tried to get in touch with him, he had been referred to Irina. O'Hara sensed something wasn't right, but he couldn't quite work out what it was. And that made him *very* nervous because it had all the hallmarks of hidden danger.

43

Hamad International Airport was busy, as usual. With flights to more than ninety countries, Qatar Airways reached every inhabited continent on the globe. Flights from Buenos Aires, Montreal and Venice had just landed.

Tristan pointed to the arrivals information screen. 'They're right on time. Not bad after such a long flight.'

Bartolli turned to Jack. 'I meant to ask you earlier; how did you manage to persuade Leonardo—?'

'To drop everything and bring the da Baggio family heirloom we just discovered here to Doha?'

Bartolli nodded.

'I didn't. Tristan did.'

'How?'

'Why don't you ask him?'

Tristan, who had overheard the question, looked at Bartolli. 'Jack told Leonardo about our meeting with Sheikh Mohammed the other day, and explained what he had in mind and why.'

'The exchange, you mean?'

'Yes. Understandably, Leonardo was quite taken aback, and said he wanted to think about it. That's when I stepped in.'

'What do you mean?'

'I rang him later that day and told him that we had little time, and really no choice but to go along with it all.'

'And he accepted this? Just like that?'

'No, not at first. It wasn't until I told him about the voices and what I heard.'

'*Heard?* What do you mean?'

'Tristan's whispers,' said Jack, cutting in. 'You know what he's like. He can sense things.'

'Yes, but—'

'I told Leonardo it made no sense to keep an Islamic treasure like the Amulet of Timur locked up in a safe in the palazzo. It belongs in a museum.'

'If it's genuine,' said Bartolli.

'True. That's what we are here to find out,' said Jack. He looked at his watch. 'In about two hours. We're cutting it fine.'

'What really got Leonardo over the line,' continued Tristan, lowering his voice, 'was this: I told him that Jack was doing this to keep us all safe, and that *Golgotha* could actually do that because destiny was at play here. All we had to do was keep an open mind and listen. I reminded Leonardo of Kazanskaya Bogomater ...'

'The Russian icon Jack returned to where it belonged? And that did it?'

'Not quite,' replied Tristan. 'It's when I told him that we should do this for Lorenza that he came round. Evil forces destroyed her life, and we have to make sure that those forces are stopped once and for all. That's when he agreed. I also spoke to Katerina. She understood at once and said she would talk to him and come along. You know they are very close.'

Tristan pointed to the arrivals gate. 'Look. Here they are.'

Isis had chosen the Mandarin Oriental in Msheireb Downtown Doha for its close proximity to the Museum of Islamic Art. When Lola made the reservation and explained who Isis was and that she and her guests would be arriving by private jet, the hotel management jumped into action. Not only were hotel limousines waiting for them at the airport, a luxurious Bahara View Suite with private dining room had also been reserved for Isis, and junior suites for her guests.

The drive from the hotel to the breathtaking museum took only a few minutes. Located on an island near Dhow Harbour at the end of a long corniche surrounded by parks, the stunning building looked like a glass-and-steel sentinel guarding the soul of Islam.

'Wow! Look at that,' said Bartolli as the car approached the museum that beckoned like a sparkling white bastion floating on water.

'Quite something, isn't it?' said Jack. 'It's the brainchild of a genius, architect I.M. Pei, who travelled for six months through the Islamic world to study Muslim architecture, looking for inspiration for the project. And if that wasn't enough, he immersed himself in Islamic history and literature to find the ideas and meanings behind specific designs.'

'Not bad for a ninety-year-old,' said Isis. 'Apparently, the ablution fountain of the ancient Mosque of Ibn Tulun in Cairo was the inspiration for what you see over there.'

'Unbelievable,' said Leonardo, finding it difficult to suppress his building excitement as they approached the museum at the end of the corniche. Understandably, he was approaching the meeting with trepidation, as he was still trying to come to terms with the surprising proposal Jack had dropped out of the blue with such a sense of urgency it left little time for contemplation. Yet, everyone close to Leonardo, especially Tristan and Countess Kuragin, seemed to support the idea without hesitation.

Khan was waiting for them at the imposing entrance behind the fountain.

'Sheikh Khalid has arranged a private meeting room. Please follow me,' said Khan, and made a bow.

The large meeting room on the first floor overlooked the sparkling harbour framed by the Doha city skyline in the distance. Khalid greeted them warmly and pointed to his father sitting by the panoramic windows next to a frail-looking old man with an impressively long white beard.

'Thank you all for coming,' said Sheikh Mohammed after introductions had been made. 'I sense this is a momentous occasion. And so does my dear friend here.' Sheikh Mohammed put his hand on his friend's arm. 'This is Dr Haji Abdalla. He's almost ninety. We have known each other for more than seventy years. We both grew

278

up in Zanzibar. I became a merchant and followed in my father's footsteps, and he became a scholar, one of the most respected Islamic historians of our time. No-one knows more about Islamic art and history than this man, and that is why I have asked you to come here to meet him.'

So far, Abdalla hadn't said a word. He sat motionless next to Sheikh Mohammed but seemed to be watching everyone with interest. He looked frail in his white dishdasha, but behind thick glasses his eyes radiated intelligence as they darted from one person to the other before coming to rest on Tristan sitting opposite.

'My friend tells me you can hear the whisper of angels and glimpse eternity,' said Abdalla, sounding remarkably strong. Slowly, he lifted his right arm and pointed a shaking finger at Tristan. 'Is that so?'

'Yes, I can. And so could my mother. She too had the gift, as did her mother before her.'

Abdalla nodded. 'Islamic artists through the ages have claimed to be able to do the same, and have tried to express what they experienced through their art.'

'I believe those are the voices I can hear when I encounter certain objects of historical significance. They speak to me.'

'And is that what happened when you first set eyes on *Golgotha*?'

'Yes, it was.'

'And could you hear voices when you first came across what's thought to be the Amulet of Timur we have come here to examine?'

'Yes, I could.'

'And what did those voices tell you?'

Tristan took his time before replying. 'I could hear the sounds of battle, drums beating, horses snorting, hundreds of hoofs pounding the ground like approaching thunder, and the cries of men dying in agony. I could feel jubilation and fear, exhilaration, death and despair.'

Abdalla closed his eyes and nodded.

Mesmerised, Bartolli watched the old man with interest as he seemed to enter a secret world of his own.

'Before we begin,' said Abdalla, his eyes still closed, 'let me tell you a few things about Timur that you should know. Timur was known as the "sword of Islam". On the battlefield he was a brilliant, undefeated commander and tactician of Mongol and Turkic descent. As one of the last nomadic conquerors of the fourteenth century, he saw himself as Genghis Khan's heir and as such, used his military might to restore the Mongol Empire of Genghis Khan. He almost succeeded. He defeated the Khans of the Golden Horde, the Delhi Sultanate of India, the Mamluks of Egypt and the Knights Hospitaller at the Siege of Smyrna.'

At last Abdalla opened his eyes. 'To put these conquests into context, Timur's armies were feared throughout Africa, Asia and Europe, and military scholars have estimated his campaigns killed over seventeen million people. This amounted to approximately five per cent of the world's population at the time. Much has been written about Timur and I have studied many texts that deal with this intriguing man, who was not only an outstanding military leader, but also a patron of the arts. According to legend, he owed his prowess on the battlefield to a sacred amulet he always wore around his neck to remind him that he was a servant of Islam. It was a jewel-encrusted gold locket with a precious miniature Quran inside that became known as the "Amulet of Timur".'

Abdalla paused to let this sink in. Countess Kuragin reached for Leonardo's hand and squeezed it. He squeezed hers in silent reply as he realised he had made the right decision.

'Timur died in 1405 and was buried in Samarkand,' continued Abdalla. 'Rumours have circulated since his death that his famous amulet wasn't buried with him. There are many stories about what happened to it, but as far as we know, it has never been found. Scholars have been searching for it ever since. I am sure you can now appreciate just how important our meeting here is. Should the artefact we are about to examine turn out to be the Amulet of Timur, we would be making history today, here, right now. And that moment would be the crowning achievement of my entire career. No, my entire life.'

Realising the right moment had arrived, Sheikh Mohammed turned towards Leonardo. 'I understand that you have brought the amulet with you?'

'Yes, I have.' All eyes were on Leonardo as he unbuttoned the top of his shirt, the room deathly silent. Slowly, he reached under his shirt and first pulled out a gold chain, and then a pendant that was attached to it. As he slipped the chain over his head and placed it carefully on the glass table in front of Abdalla, a shaft of sunlight lit up the exquisite pendant, making the jewels sparkle and come alive like an echo from a distant, violent past.

Abdalla gasped, and Sheikh Mohammed leaned forward to see better. Khalid got up and came closer. Khan followed and craned his neck trying to make sure he didn't miss anything.

Abdalla looked at Tristan. 'Can you hear something?' he asked softly.

'Yes, I can. I hear the sounds of battle, drums beating, horses snorting, hundreds of hoofs pounding the ground like approaching thunder, and the cries of men dying in agony. I can feel jubilation and fear, exhilaration, death and despair,' said Tristan, repeating exactly what he had said before.

'So can I,' said Abdulla. He leaned forward, his hands shaking, and picked up the locket. Then he reached for a magnifying glass on the table and examined the polished back of the locket.

'It's here,' he whispered and with the tip of his trembling finger he traced the outline of the *Khatim* symbol, an eight-pointed star engraved on the back of the locket. 'The Black Star, the seal of the Prophet Muhammad.'

Overcome by emotion, Abdalla put the locket on the table and turned towards Sheikh Mohammed. 'I'm too afraid to open it. Could you?'

Sheikh Mohammed nodded, picked up the locket and looked at Leonardo watching him. 'May I?'

Leonardo nodded.

Sheikh Mohammed opened the locket and handed it to his friend.

Using his magnifying glass, Abdalla peered at the tiny Quran inside. 'It's written in Kūfic. That fits, and so does the text I can see. According to legend, the miniature Quran inside Timur's locket dates back to the Abbasid Caliphate and was most likely created during the Abbasid Golden Age in the ninth century. It appears to be in excellent condition, bearing in mind what it must have witnessed.'

Abdalla put the locket back on the table. 'May I ask how you obtained this?'

'It's been in my family, the da Baggios, for generations, but we only found out recently what it was, and how it came into my family's possession. It's all about a letter sent from the Silk Road a long time ago.'

Leonardo reached into his pocket, pulled out some sheets of paper and handed it to Jack. 'This is a copy of it here. Jack will be able to tell the story much better than I, because he's the one who found the letter. Jack, could you?'

'Sure,' said Jack, the storyteller in him welcoming the opportunity. 'It all began with a desperate mother trying to save her son after Murad III, Sultan of the Ottoman Empire, died in 1595.'

Jack then told the story of the horrendous fratricide and how Osman managed to escape from the Topkapi Palace, helped by his mother. He explained how Osman made it to his family home in Venice and how, ten years later, he sent his friend, Francesco Alberti, to Istanbul to find out what happened to his mother. Warming to the fascinating subject, Jack read out passages from the letter to illustrate the story and explained what Alberti had discovered about the fate of Osman's mother.

'She was taken to Khiva in Uzbekistan by the sultan's janissaries and put up for sale in the notorious slave market in the desert. This was punishment for helping her son escape. Because of her beauty, refined manners, intellect and background, she attracted great attention among the slave traders and was eventually sold to a Tajik trader, who saw in her an opportunity to make a huge profit—'

'What has all this to do with the amulet?' interrupted Khalid, unable to control his impatience.

Sheikh Mohammed held up his hand and shot his son a disapproving look. 'Please, let Mr Rogan continue. I'm sure he will tell us.'

'Because she was exactly what he had been looking for. It wasn't often a former concubine of the mighty Ottoman sultan was offered for sale. She was taken to Samarkand and sold to a prominent family. And now comes the really interesting bit, as far as the amulet is concerned.'

Jack looked at Abdalla and paused to let the tension grow.

'Because she was so special and unique, the trader drove a hard bargain and asked a small fortune for her. After much haggling, he was eventually offered something more valuable than jewels or gold to seal the deal. He was offered a piece of history: the Amulet of Timur.' Jack held up the letter. 'It's all in here.'

'But this doesn't tell us how the amulet ended up in the da Baggio family,' said Sheikh Mohammed.

'But the letter here does,' continued Jack. 'Francesco Alberti won the amulet in a dice game played against the Tajik trader who had sold the beautiful, refined slave in Samarkand. Alberti didn't make it back to Venice – he died along the way – but he sent the amulet, along with this letter, back to his friend Osman.'

'An extraordinary story, for sure,' said Sheikh Mohammed. 'But is it enough?'

'To establish authenticity?' said Abdalla, looking at his friend. 'Actually, it is.'

'*It is?*' said Sheikh Mohammed, surprised. 'Why do you say that?'

'Because of what the documented history of the Amulet of Timur tells us, that's why,' said Abdalla.

'Can you tell us more?' said Khalid.

'I can. I told you before that there are many stories about what happened to the amulet after Timur died in 1405. As you know, Timur was the founder of the Timurid Empire and the Timurid Dynasty, which at its peak ruled over much of Central Asia, including modern-day India, Syria, Pakistan and Turkey. After Timur's death, Samarkand became the capital of a huge empire.'

Abdalla took off his glasses and began to polish them with his sleeve.

'After the fall of the empire in the sixteenth century,' he continued, 'Timur's great-great-great grandson Babur founded the Mughal Empire and became the first Mughal Emperor, who ruled most of the Indian subcontinent. Scholars who have investigated this over the years agree the amulet remained in Samarkand as a treasured heirloom of descendants of Ulugh Beg, Timur's grandson, who wore the amulet around his neck during his reign. After that, the amulet seems to have disappeared from the pages of history until it resurfaced again for the last time, in an unexpected way.'

Abdalla put his glasses back on and looked at Tristan. 'Are those voices telling you what happened?'

'Yes. The amulet was used to buy a slave in Samarkand.'

'Correct.' Abdalla took a deep breath because he realised the next question was critical. 'Can someone please tell me what Osman's mother was called?'

'Fatma Hatun,' said Leonardo. 'Unfortunately, we don't know what happened to her after she was sold.'

'But I do,' said Abdulla, tears in his eyes because he had just received the final proof he had been looking for: The locket on the table in front of him was without doubt the long-lost Amulet of Timur, which had just drifted out of the mists of time and reappeared in a most surprising way.

'*You do?*' said Jack, stunned and feeling a little dizzy, because he could sense another great story was imminent. 'Can you tell us?'

'I can, because two halves of a wonderful story have just been joined to form a single page in history that has been missing for a long time, but is, thanks to you, missing no more.'

44

Porto Arabia, Doha: 20 January

Jack was putting on his joggers when Tristan walked up to him carrying a mug of coffee. Jack and Tristan were sharing a suite next to Isis's stunning Bahara View Suite on the top floor of the hotel. It was just after sunrise.

'Going for a run?' asked Tristan and handed Jack the coffee.

'You're up early.'

'Couldn't sleep. Not after what happened yesterday,' said Tristan.

'It's all a little overwhelming,' said Jack. 'I need some air. Let's go for a run before it gets too hot. I want to see the Pearl Monument. Coming?'

'Sure.'

Jack didn't notice the car following them as they were jogging along the corniche, approaching the entrance to Dhow Harbour.

'There it is,' said Jack, pointing ahead.

'Impressive.'

The Pearl Monument, a giant oyster shell fountain commemorating Doha's pearling past, looked cool and inviting. Because it was still quite early, the popular spot, usually crowded with tourists taking photos, was almost deserted and only a few morning joggers ran past. Jack sat down on the sea wall facing the harbour and wiped the sweat off his face with his handkerchief.

'That was an amazing meeting. How do you feel about what Abdalla told us? Surprised?'

'I certainly didn't see it coming.'

'That's quite something, coming from you. You should have seen Leonardo's face when Abdalla spoke about Fatma Hatun and what happened to her. You must admit, it's quite a story.'

'She was certainly the catalyst here; the *proof* that made it all possible. And the letter you found has filled in all the gaps in this fascinating saga. Amazing.'

'At least now we have some idea of what happened to her.'

'Looks that way, but it all sounds more like a fairytale out of *One Thousand and One Nights* than fact, don't you think?' said Tristan.

'The passage of time can distort reality, but there's always a kernel of truth in these stories if you know where to look.'

'True. Let's have a closer look at what Abdalla told us. Perhaps we can find that kernel? What do you think?' said Tristan.

'All right. Let's do that. To begin with, let's put what Abdalla told us into context,' said Jack. 'There's no doubt he's a serious scholar with extensive knowledge of Islamic history.'

'Agreed.'

'We know from Alberti's letter that Osman's mother was sold into slavery by the sultan's janissaries in the Khiva markets in 1606 and ended up with a Tajik trader, who onsold her to a prominent family in Samarkand, one of the Astrakhanids, the last of the Genghisid descendants,' said Jack. 'We also know the Amulet of Timur was the payment. After that, the story becomes really interesting.'

'Sure does. First question: Why would someone hand over something as precious as that amulet in exchange for a slave?'

'Abdalla explained that. Remember what he told us?' said Jack.

'Sure. He said the head of one of those ruling families – a direct descendant of the famous Ulugh Beg in Samarkand – was looking for a slave with certain qualities to care for his invalid father. Apparently, as soon as he set eyes on Fatma, he fell under her spell. Why? Because she reminded him of his late mother. So uncanny was the resemblance, he was convinced she was a reincarnation of his mother and had reappeared to comfort his ailing father, who was almost blind and needed a cultured companion mainly for conversation, reading and storytelling.'

'Plausible.'

'Plausible or not, Fatma ended up living in luxury in a palace as a respected and much-loved member of the household.'

'A fairytale ending, if we can believe all that.'

'Well, according to Abdalla, who seems to be familiar with the relevant historical texts dealing with this story, Fatma survived the old man she was looking after by almost two decades, and was buried next to him in a mausoleum in Samarkand. That's how highly thought of she was. And on top of all that, the mausoleum is close to Gūr-e Amīr, the famous Mausoleum of Timur. That too tells you something, especially about the family, don't you think?' said Tristan.

'It does, but does it really matter? Surely, what really matters here is the successful exchange.'

'You mean a Christian treasure for a Muslim one? *Golgotha* for the Amulet of Timur?'

'Precisely. That's what you wanted to achieve, and you did. I'm just not sure exactly why,' said Tristan.

'Still working on it, but in the end that's what really matters here,' said Jack.

'I would have thought so. The rest, while captivating, may be true, or perhaps not quite. So what?'

'But what if the grave's still there?'

'That would certainly strongly support the story. Perhaps one day we'll go and have a look?' said Tristan.

'I'd like that. It would be a fitting conclusion to this fascinating story and add another exciting chapter to the da Baggio family history. Let's go back and have some breakfast. I'm starving.'

Before Jack could stand up, two men came jogging along, stopped, and sat down next to Jack and Tristan.

'Good morning, gentlemen,' said one of the men. Jack looked at him, recognition dawning.

'If you do exactly as we tell you, no-one gets hurt,' said the other man.

'Ah, the painting thieves from Muscat,' said Jack. He had recognised the men from O'Hara's video. 'If you're planning to break into my room again, there's no need. I can give you the key right now, but the painting isn't there.'

'We're not interested in the painting,' said the man sitting next to Jack. 'There's someone who wants to meet you.'

'I see. This is an invitation?'

'Something like that. Do you see that car over there?'

Jack nodded.

'We'll walk over there now, and you will get into the back; clear?'

'Fine by me. It's already too hot for jogging anyway, don't you think, Tristan?'

'Definitely,' said Tristan casually and stood up. 'Let's go.'

The drive from the Pearl Monument to Porto Arabia took less than twenty minutes.

'I thought so,' said Jack and pointed ahead. 'There, the *Standard*.'

'That's a private yacht?' said Tristan.

'Sure is. One of the largest and most luxurious in the world.'

The biggest and most striking vessel in Porto Arabia by far, the *Standard* looked stunning with the morning sun accentuating its elegant lines and dwarfing all the other superyachts moored close by.

Irina was waiting for them in the saloon. Dressed in khaki shorts, desert boots, and a long-sleeved, matching shirt buttoned up at the top, she looked more like a butch Afrikaans prison guard than a former senior KGB agent who could eliminate people with a click of her fingers.

'Ah, the young man with the sixth sense,' said Irina as she watched Tristan and Jack coming towards her. 'Drink?'

'Glass of water would be great,' said Jack casually.

'Apologies for the abrupt invitation, but as you will see in a moment, there were good reasons for that.'

'There always are,' said Jack. 'Like framing me for a robbery I didn't commit?'

Irina waved dismissively. 'No longer relevant; all in the past.'

'Until Mr O'Hara comes up with some crazy new plan, I suppose.'

'That's very unlikely. He's no longer involved.'

'What do you mean?' asked Jack, frowning.

Irina shrugged.

'Irina is right,' said a voice coming from somewhere at the back of the large saloon. 'He's no longer pulling the strings around here; I am.'

Jack spun around and looked at a striking young woman with long, straw-blonde hair walking towards him. *I've seen her before,* thought Jack. *Quite recently. On TV.*

'I am Sasha Kovalenko,' said the woman, extending her hand. 'It's nice to meet you, Mr Rogan. I've heard a lot about you.'

As soon as Jack heard the name, the penny dropped.

'The Novotny affair. The poisoning, the sensational videos, The New Tsar's Palace, the trial ... You are—'

'Anatoly Novotny's partner. Very good, Mr Rogan. Then you will also know I'm running Anatoly's Anti-Corruption Foundation from abroad. While he's in jail that is,' said Sasha, with sadness in her voice.

Jack looked stunned. 'I don't understand. What are you doing here?' he asked, shaking his head.

Sasha turned to Tristan. 'Any ideas, Mr Te Papatahi? After all, they tell me that you can hear the whisper of angels ...'

'You're much more than you've just told us,' said Tristan, choosing his words carefully. 'You're ... related to Oleg Ivanov, who owns all this.'

'Excellent! There must be something to this rumour about you. I'm Oleg Ivanov's daughter. The *late* Oleg Ivanov. Sadly, my father passed away two days ago. Heart attack. I'm his only child and heir. For certain personal reasons, I'm using Kovalenko, my mother's name. I know this is a lot to take in. May I offer you some tea? Please take a seat.'

'That would be nice,' said Jack softly, trying to digest the staggering implications of what he had just heard.

Tristan turned to Jack as they were taking their seats. 'I told you something would turn up, didn't I?' he said calmly and sat down.

'You and your bloody whispers,' said Jack and sat down next to him.

'Obviously, I owe you an explanation,' began Sasha. 'As you would be aware, my father was an addicted gambler. I have no doubt that was the reason for his – let's call it *arrangement* – with O'Hara and the darknet gambling site. I only found out about it recently. My father's gambling was the reason my parents separated and our family fell apart. I want nothing to do with gambling. I have already given instructions to stop all contact with O'Hara.'

'Are you aware of what has happened since your father and O'Hara entered into this "arrangement" as you call it?' Jack pointed to Irina sitting at the bar. 'Why don't you ask Irina here about our meeting in St Petersburg on this very ship not that long ago. Three brutal murders, and the rest ...'

'I may be my father's daughter, but that doesn't mean I share his ideas or values. I don't. I'm not like him, Mr Rogan, and I am not responsible for his actions,' came the frosty retort.

'Point taken,' said Jack.

'Unfortunately, I cannot change the past, but I can do something about the future.'

'Fair enough. And you brought us here just to tell us this?'

'No. There's more, a lot more. I only arrived here last night from London. Things are moving very fast and I was hoping to bring someone with me who could explain what this is all about much better than I, but there have been certain complications—'

'This has to do with *Golgotha*, doesn't it?' said Tristan.

Sasha looked at him, surprised. She wondered how he could possibly know this. 'Yes, it has.'

'Care to explain?' said Jack.

'To exchange the amulet for the van Eyck, as you've done yesterday, was brilliant.'

'You mean exchange a Muslim treasure for a Christian one?' said Jack.

'Yes. This now opens many doors—'

'Because the painting hides a great secret?' said Tristan, cutting in.

Right again, thought Sasha. This guy was amazing!

'You're no stranger to secrets and lost Russian treasures, Mr Rogan. You're also a man of destiny who follows his – how did he put it? – *breadcrumbs,* right?'

'Who's the *he*?' asked Jack.

'The man I was hoping to bring with me to meet you. A man you have dealt with before and would trust implicitly because he's already been part of your destiny. A man who would be able to explain all this.'

'Explain what exactly?'

'Why we need your help. Why *Russia* needs your help.'

'I don't know what you mean. Is this perhaps something to do with your Foundation?'

'In some way, it is.'

'You have to give me more.'

'I'm afraid I can't. Not right now.'

'So, whereto from here?' asked Jack, frowning.

'I have a favour to ask,' said Sasha softly, changing direction.

'What favour?'

'I understand that you're planning to return home later today. So am I. I must get back to London urgently. In fact, my jet is parked almost next to the Time Machine jet at the airport, ready to depart.'

'You know my movements better than I do,' said Jack, shaking his head. 'What favour?'

'To come to my home in London and meet the man I couldn't bring with me, and listen to what he has to say. That's all I ask. He will be there by tomorrow.'

'And why should I do that?'

Sasha looked at Tristan. 'Why don't you tell your friend, Mr Te Papatahi?' she said. 'I'm sure you know why.'

It was Tristan's turn to look surprised because someone had managed to peep into his soul. 'Because destiny demands it?' he said quietly.

'Exactly. And I have something I can offer you in return.'

'You can?' said Jack.

'Yes. I have broken off all contact with O'Hara. The arrangements he had with my father have been terminated. Irina has told me all about you and O'Hara and, of course, the search for *Golgotha*. She also told me about the threats, your past history, the deadly games.

As of now, the threats and the hold he had over you are no more, because O'Hara is alone and isolated. A virtual prisoner in Belarus. And alone, he's powerless.'

'But Irina and her agents?'

Sasha held up her hand. 'I have known Irina almost all my life. Her unconditional loyalty to my late father and my family has endured for decades and is beyond question. Now, this same loyalty has been transferred to me. Isn't that right, Irina?'

'Absolutely!' said Irina.

'Irina acts only on instructions from me. She can be trusted implicitly. Without Irina, O'Hara is impotent. At least for now. He can't leave Belarus.'

'Why should I trust you?'

'Because you are the chosen one,' came the cryptic reply.

Jack looked at Sasha, thunderstruck. *My God, it can't be!* he thought as he remembered the only other person in his life who had called him that.

'Did the man you want me to meet tell you that?' asked Jack, his head spinning.

'Yes. That's what he calls you, and that's why he wants to meet you, because *Golgotha* has the answers ...'

'More riddles,' said Jack and looked at Tristan. 'What do you think?'

'I told you something would turn up. Looks like we are safe for now. I believe you are actually winning this game. No harm in listening.'

For a while, Jack watched Sasha watching him, her blue eyes like deep pools drawing him towards her. For an instant, Jack saw a vulnerable young woman behind the facade of confidence and power, pleading for his help. As Sasha looked away and the moment passed, Jack felt a familiar wave of excitement.

'Day after tomorrow?' said Jack and stood up to leave.

'Perfect. Thank you. I 'll be in touch.'

'You know where to find me?'

'Oh, yes. I know where to find you.'

45

Hartley Hall, London: 22 January

'Not bad,' said Jack, as Boris manoeuvred the Bentley through the security gates and drove slowly up the circular driveway leading to Ivanov's Edwardian mansion. They had returned from Doha after a long flight the day before, and spent the night at the Time Machine Studios.

'So, that's how Russian billionaires live in exile,' said Bartolli. 'I wonder who this mystery man is she wants us to meet.'

'Jack knows,' said Tristan. 'Don't you, Jack?'

'Just a hunch.'

'Come on, it's more than that, admit it. I saw your face when she called you "the chosen one".'

Jack turned to Bartolli sitting next to him in the back. 'There's nowhere to hide from this guy,' he said. 'Isn't it annoying?'

'So you *do* know?'

Jack shrugged. 'I may know the who, but I don't know the why. But I'm sure we're about to find out. Here we are.'

Sasha greeted them in the foyer and thanked them for coming. 'He arrived early this morning,' she said, 'just in time. Have you brought it with you?'

'Yes.' Jack pointed to Tristan, who was carrying a leather case under his arm.

'This way, please ...'

Jack saw the tall man standing motionless near the windows like a statue, and gasped.

Tristan turned to Bartolli standing next to him. 'Watch,' he said softly.

'Abbot Serapion? *You? Here?* How is this possible?' said Jack.

'Is it any stranger than last time we met in Yekaterinburg?' said Serapion, smiling. 'Destiny and fate brought us together then. Destiny and fate seem to be doing so again.'

Seeing Serapion standing there conjured up images of a meeting five years earlier in dramatic circumstances. At the time, Jack had been searching for Kazanskaya Bogomater, a famous lost Russian icon. The meeting had been arranged by Rabbi Stein and had profound consequences, impossible to forget. Jack could still hear the eerie chanting of the monks he had met that day in a hidden underground chamber below a deserted church.

'That's what Rabbi Stein would have said,' Jack replied.

Bartolli watched the fascinating man with his long white beard walk over to Jack and embrace him. In his black cassock and conical fur hat, he looked like a Russian saint about to bless the faithful.

'How true. I spoke to him after your meeting in Prague in November, and again just a few days before he was murdered,' said Serapion, sadness in his voice.

Jack was desperately trying to make sense of the unexpected encounter. 'Is that what this is all about?'

'It is in a way, but it's more complicated than that. This is all about David Herzl – the Postmaster of Treblinka – and his diary. I read your novella. We all did ...'

'That diary again,' said Jack, shaking his head. 'My novella seems to have caused quite a stir in unexpected places.'

'Your books always do. Just as Empress Alexandra's letter to her friend Countess Bezukhova showed you the way to Kazanskaya Bogomater, we believe the Herzl diary will show you the way to something even more precious and important. Especially when we consider the times we live in, and the dangers Russia is facing.'

'*We* believe?' said Jack. 'Who's we?'

'The Seeker and the Guardians.'

'They are involved too?'

'They are, because this is all about Russia.'

This is becoming more bizarre by the second, Jack thought. 'Show me the way to what exactly? *Golgotha?*'

'The painting is certainly part of it, but there is so much more at stake here, as you will find out in a moment.'

Jack turned to Sasha, watching him intently. 'Can you please explain to us what your involvement is in all this? I must be missing something because so far, there are just too many gaps in this perplexing puzzle.'

'Sure,' said Sasha and stepped forward.

Henry Blackstone, Sasha's lawyer, held up his hand. 'Before you do, Sasha, I have to ask your friends here something. Something important that concerns not only you, but also many others.'

'All right. What is it?'

'A promise.' Blackstone turned to face Jack. 'Before Sasha tells you the background and meaning of all this, I have to ask you to promise to keep everything you hear about this absolutely confidential. It is imperative none of this information gets out and falls into the wrong hands. As you will see in a moment, lives depend on it, and that could easily include your own.'

Surprised, Jack looked at Serapion. 'Is that true?'

'Yes, it is, in more ways than you can possibly imagine. None of what you're about to hear must get out.'

Jack looked at Bartolli and Tristan. 'Any problems?'

'No,' said Bartolli.

'Fine by me,' said Tristan.

'You have your answer,' said Jack.

'Have you brought it with you?' asked Sasha, repeating her earlier question.

'Yes. Tristan, could you please?'

Tristan walked over to a small table by the window and placed the leather case he had brought with him on top.

Jack looked at Serapion and pointed to the case. 'Please open it.'

Sasha watched as Serapion opened the case, took out the small painting and placed it carefully on the table, his shaking hands the only sign of the turmoil boiling within.

For a long moment there was complete silence in the room as everyone stared at the exquisite little painting, radiating mystery and whispering of secrets reaching out of the past.

'If it is this painting that has brought you here, then there must be a lot more to it than I know,' said Jack, breaking the silence at last. 'Obviously Sandor Kun didn't tell me everything.'

'There is. The Herzl story is only one chapter in the painting's long history. But the mystery surrounding it goes back much further and deeper ...'

'Is that what cost Stein his life?'

'Most likely, yes. There are forces at play here that are difficult to comprehend. It's all about an ancient struggle. Good and evil. Darkness and light. It's all reflected in the painting. The tranquil setting is deceptive. Just look at those colours, and the three men suffering on the cross.'

'And do you know what that mystery is all about?' asked Jack.

'I do, and it was that mystery that inspired van Eyck to paint *Golgotha* in the first place.'

'All I know,' said Jack, 'is that according to legend, this painting is some kind of map showing the way to a particular church connected to a secret known only to the initiated few. But, of course, that was a long time ago. Van Eyck unveiled *Golgotha* in 1432.'

Serapion looked at Jack, surprised. 'You know a lot more about this than I thought. But then again, I shouldn't be surprised. After all, you are the chosen one ...'

Tristan put his hand on Bartolli's arm. 'See? I told you so,' he whispered.

'You are correct,' continued Serapion. 'The small church here in the background, with its distinctive belltower, holds the key to this mystery.'

'What mystery?'

'You correctly referred to a legend. According to that legend, a famous relic – a piece of the Life-Giving Cross of the Lord with a nail embedded in it – was kept for centuries in a small church in a village near Ghent. The identity of the village and the church has been lost long ago, but was obviously known to van Eyck at the time he painted *Golgotha* because this painting had a certain reputation.'

'What kind of reputation?'

'It was rumoured that the painting was a map showing the way to the church and, by implication, the holy relic. That's why van Eyck decided to set the crucifixion in a Dutch landscape with that particular church in the background. This provided a link between the event, the crucifixion, and the famous relic, a piece of the cross, kept in that church.'

'Is that why the Nazis were so interested in the *Ghent Altarpiece*?'

'Yes. Hitler was obsessed with the occult. The relic was supposed to have mystical powers, just like Kazanskaya Bogomater. The Nazis were after these artefacts for the same reason.'

Jack nodded.

'Do you know what happened to Kazanskaya Bogomater only recently?' asked Serapion.

'As far as I know, the holy icon is in the Alexander Nevsky Cathedral in Yekaterinburg, where it belongs. We returned it there in May 2017. You were there.'

'Then you don't know what happened to it?'

'Tell me.'

'It was removed a short while ago by order of none other than President Palin, and taken to the Kremlin by the FSB. According to my sources, Palin is keeping it in his is office.'

'Seriously? Why?'

'Why do you think? Like Hitler before him, Palin, too, is obsessed with the occult. Megalomaniacs often are. They are superstitious, insecure and rule by fear, and fear rules them. That is their main weakness. They turn to the occult for reassurance and for answers. And that's where the *Golgotha* mystery comes into play ...'

Sasha listened to the exchange with interest, well aware of the enormity of the occasion. She realised better than anyone else in the room what was at stake, and was waiting for the right moment to step in.

'What I'm about to tell you is directly related to what Abbot Serapion has just told us,' said Sasha.

'What, the holy icon taken from the cathedral?' asked Jack.

'There are many threads to this story reaching out of the past. They are intersecting right now in ways no-one could have imagined. That is the reason Abbot Serapion is standing before you, and why I have asked you to come here this morning and listen to what he has to say, and hear what I have to tell you. I believe this is a moment of destiny with far-reaching consequences none of us could have foreseen – especially you, Mr Rogan – yet here we all are.' Sasha paused and ran her fingers through her beautiful hair.

'Very soon, you will have a decision to make,' she continued. 'You can either walk away right now and forget about everything you've been told, or you can join us. But please remember once you do, there will be no turning back. The dangers and challenges will be considerable and the outcome uncertain, but you will become instruments of destiny that could shape the future, not only of Russia, but also of humankind.'

Jack was impressed. No wonder Novotny had entrusted her with running his Foundation. She was an inspirational speaker. *Let's hope what she has in mind is equally impressive*, he thought.

46

Isis was pacing impatiently up and down on the roof terrace of her penthouse. Still annoyed about not having been included in the meeting, she was nevertheless anxious to hear about the outcome of that intriguing 'kidnap-invitation' as Jack called it, on board the *Standard* in Doha, which had all the hallmarks of a new chapter in the fascinating *Golgotha* saga.

Looking down, Isis saw the Bentley turn into the underground garage. *At last*, she thought.

'How did it go?' asked Lola, meeting them at the lift. 'She's been fretting all morning.'

'I bet. Where is she?' asked Jack, still on a high from the extraordinary meeting with Sasha and Serapion. He wanted to share the experience with Isis as soon as possible, to get a fresh perspective on what had been discussed and, more importantly perhaps, what had been proposed.

'Upstairs, in the study,' said Lola.

'Perfect.'

'Drink anyone?' said Isis as soon as Jack walked in, followed by Tristan and Bartolli.

Jack turned to Tristan. 'Put *Golgotha* next to *Little Sparrow in the Garden* over there,' he said. 'Most appropriate, wouldn't you say?'

'Herzl's creations meet again?' said Bartolli, enjoying herself.

'Reunited at last,' said Jack. 'What a journey!'

'Reaching out to us from the past,' said Tristan as he placed the small painting on an empty easel next to Monet's *Little Sparrow in the Garden*.

'So, who was this mystery man?' asked Isis and opened a bottle of champagne.

'You'll never guess,' said Jack. 'Abbott Serapion.'

Isis almost dropped the bottle. '*What?* Are you serious? This doesn't make sense!'

'Difficult to believe, but in a strange way it does.'

'It's a lot to get your head around, but Jack's right,' said Tristan. 'And once again, we are standing at the crossroads.'

'In what way?'

'Decision time,' said Bartolli, looking across to the Tower Bridge and Henry III's Bloody Tower, whispering of assassinations, treachery and beheadings.

'We've been there before,' said Jack. 'And the best way to face moments like this is to go back to the very beginning.' Jack slipped the rubber band off his notebook and opened it. 'Make yourselves comfortable, guys, because this is quite a story.'

Isis smiled and handed Jack a glass of champagne. 'Storytellers need sustenance.'

'Sure do; cheers!' said Jack. 'As we know, it's all about that painting over there.' He pointed to van Eyck's *Golgotha* on the easel next to Monet's *Little Sparrow in the Garden*. 'And David Herzl, the Postmaster of Treblinka.'

'Or more precisely, what you wrote about all this in your novella,' interjected Tristan.

'Correct. Because O'Hara's twisted mind saw certain connections in my novella – *The Postmaster of Treblinka* – and used that information in ways no sane person could have imagined, to make it the subject of a deadly, bizarre game that has affected us all.'

'We first heard about it on board the *Standard* the day we met Irina in St Petersburg in December,' said Bartolli. 'That was the day of our virtual meeting with O'Hara. The day he outlined the terms of the deadly game that has brought us here.'

'Sasha was right when she said there are many threads to this story reaching out of the past,' said Jack. 'She was also right when she said these threads are intersecting right now in ways no-one could have imagined, and in order to understand what these threads are all about, we have to go back to the very beginning.'

Jack stood up, walked over to one of the easels by the window and pointed to *Little Sparrow in the Garden*, the original painting Monet had presented to Benjamin Krakowski's father in his garden in Giverny in 1920.

'This is the painting that started it all. Following the clues in Brother Francis's diary, Tristan and I located the original Monet in 2012, hidden during the war in a sarcophagus in the Imperial Crypt in Vienna.'

'And that led to the controversial forgery allegations after I bought the painting Maestro Krakowski had put up for auction here in London in 2014,' said Isis.

'The sensational Emil Fuchs affair,' said Lola.

'That's right. But what we didn't know at the time was that Herzl had copied another famous painting later, just before his deportation to Treblinka in 1943.' Jack pointed to *Golgotha*. 'This one.'

'While restoring stolen paintings for the Nazis in Treblinka, he became the Postmaster of Treblinka,' said Bartolli, 'and sent the original van Eyck to Budapest through the Nazi Feldpost.'

'Correct. This is one of the main threads in this remarkable story,' continued Jack. 'The next thread is Herzl's diary, which was left to his son, Sandor Kun, who gave it to the Jewish Museum in Prague.'

'And then came your meeting with Avigdor Stein in Prague in 2019,' said Tristan.

Jack nodded. 'When I gave that fateful Empress Alexandra letter we found in Madame Petrova's music box to Stein for the museum, he appeared very moved because that letter had been at the very centre of the Kazanskaya Bogomater discovery in the pope's study—'

'And the return of *Mat' Rossiya*, Tchaikovsky's Lost Symphony, to Russia,' said Tristan.

'Quite so. And that's when he mentioned another intriguing letter and quietly threw me another challenge.'

'Involving Herzl, the Postmaster of Treblinka, knowing full well you wouldn't be able to resist,' said Tristan.

Jack shrugged. 'Which ended at Yad Vashem in the Hall of Names in Jerusalem three months later,' said Jack, 'when we finally delivered that long-lost letter with the precious Treblinka records—'

'In the presence of the new pope,' said Lola.

'Exactly. And this is the very subject matter O'Hara used for his bizarre darknet gambling challenge, which was all about locating van Eyck's lost *Golgotha*,' said Jack. 'And with your help we managed to find it in Muscat. Here it is.' Jack pointed to the painting. 'The next thread in this story is perhaps the most important one.'

'How come?' asked Isis.

'Because of what happened this morning.' Jack walked over to the painting and pointed to the church in the background. 'It's all about this church and its secrets.'

'What secrets?' asked Isis.

'This painting isn't just about the crucifixion. It's much more than that. It's a riddle pointing to arguably one of the most important Christian relics brought back from the Crusades: a piece of the Life-Giving Cross of the Lord with a nail embedded in it.'

'And that's where Abbot Serapion and Sasha enter and become the next thread in this remarkable story,' said Tristan.

'A little perplexing, you must admit. Please explain it for us,' said Isis, shaking her head.

Jack looked at Isis. 'Remember the Seeker and the Guardians?'

'Yekaterinburg. Of course. They helped you find Kazanskaya Bogomater, the holy icon you returned to the Alexander Nevsky Cathedral. I was there, remember?'

'Correct, but what we didn't know until today was that they've also been looking for van Eyck's *Golgotha*. Why? Because according to legend it is a map showing the way to that important relic I just mentioned. In fact, that relic has a name – *Dextera Dei*, the right hand of God, because according to that legend, the nail embedded in a small fragment of the original cross is the very nail that had been driven through the palm of Christ's right hand.'

'A wonderful story, but how is this relevant now? How is it connected?' said Isis.

'This brings us again back to my novella, *The Postmaster of Treblinka*, which Serapion and the Guardians have read. They knew, just like O'Hara obviously did, that *Golgotha* held the key to finding the relic.'

'Because it was a coded map, so to speak?' asked Isis.

'Precisely.'

'And this was important?'

'Yes.'

'Why?'

'Because of the relic's great spiritual powers. The right hand of God can defeat evil,' said Jack softly. 'And this brings me to the final thread in this extraordinary story. It's directly related to an imminent catastrophe looming in Russia right now. We had to promise not to disclose any of this to anyone. What I'm about to tell you must under no circumstances leave this room, understood?'

'Sure,' said Isis. 'We're used to secrets; right, guys?'

Lola nodded.

'As we know, Sasha is running Novotny's Foundation from right here in London. In fact, the Ivanov mansion where we've just been is the new headquarters of the organisation. Novotny and the Foundation have only one aim: to expose the outrageous corruption in the Kremlin, overthrow Palin and liberate Russia from his corrupt regime. The Foundation is very well connected in Russia and has many supporters, especially in the Russian Orthodox Church. That's where Serapion and the Guardians enter the story. They have been Novotny supporters for years and have joined forces with Novotny and the Foundation to overthrow Palin.'

'All right, but what about that imminent catastrophe you mentioned?' Isis asked.

'Novotny's sensational video that exposed Palin's appalling corruption has been viewed by millions. This has had a much greater impact in Russia than expected. There's a huge groundswell of outrage in the country, which has been exacerbated by Novotny's recent arrest, conviction and shameful imprisonment on trumped-up charges. The Kremlin is, of course, acutely aware of this, and according to Serapion's sources close to the president, Palin feels threatened because mass arrests of demonstrators, internet censorship and new draconian laws have been unable to suppress the movement, which is getting stronger by the day. And a cornered Palin is about as dangerous as it gets.'

'What does all that mean? How is this relevant to that painting over there?' demanded Isis.

Jack held up his hand. 'Please bear with me. What does a dictator like Palin, a megalomaniac, do when his back's against the wall and he and his regime are under threat from within?'

'Go to war,' said Tristan softly.

'*Exactly!*' said Jack.

'You can't be serious,' said Isis.

'I am. Deadly. As I mentioned before, Serapion and the Church have reliable sources inside the Kremlin, close to the president. What I'm about to tell you must not leave this room because if it did, it could put us all in great danger.' Jack turned over a page in his notebook and looked around the room to let the tension grow.

'Come on, Jack, *tell us*,' prompted Lola.

'Palin has decided to invade Ukraine. He's dreaming of returning Russia to its former glory, and that means territorial expansion. He's prepared to go to war to achieve this. Large-scale mobilisation will begin shortly. It will start with exercises near the border with Ukraine in preparation for a full-scale invasion.'

'How reliable is this information?' asked Isis.

'Very. There's no reason to doubt the accuracy of this.'

'When?'

'Imminent. Within weeks; perhaps days.'

'Jesus! And the West knows nothing of this?'

'I'm sure there's a lot of intelligence and speculation out there, but also confusion and uncertainty. And most important of all, I'm sure no-one wants to believe this. Why? Because no-one knows what can be done about it if it happens. Don't forget, Russia has one of the biggest nuclear arsenals in the world and the whole of Europe depends on Russia for most of its energy supplies. Without Russian gas, the lights go out, industry comes to a standstill and the population begins to freeze. If someone like Palin is prepared to go to war and use all this, well ...'

Isis shook her head. 'I don't understand. Where do we fit in here? What has geopolitics to do with an old legend, a mystery surrounding a lost painting, and a Christian relic with mystical powers?'

'I asked the same question,' replied Jack.

'And?'

'Serapion and Sasha were conspicuously evasive about this. All they said was that certain plans involving the relic to achieve the ultimate goal of the Foundation – removing Palin – were still being worked out, and for our own safety it would therefore be best for all of us if we could stay away from that question for the time being.'

'That's nonsense, surely,' said Isis. 'And I still don't understand the connection between Sasha, Serapion and *Golgotha*. Do you?'

'Not completely, except for this: Novotny and the Foundation have close ties to the Church in Russia. They appear to have joined forces to overthrow Palin, and *Golgotha* and the relic seem to be playing an important part in this. Don't forget, Russia is a deeply religious country. Spiritual matters are hugely important. We've seen that with Kazanskaya Bogomater.'

Jack ran his fingers through his hair. 'Serapion wants to meet me tomorrow, alone. He insisted we meet in Ghent in the Cathedral of St Bavo. In front of the altarpiece.'

'A strange request. Did he say why?' asked Bartolli.

'To introduce me to someone,' said Jack, lowering his voice. 'Someone important who could show us the way.'

'*See?* I told you something would turn up,' said Tristan. 'We all worry too much. Just do what you always do.'

'What's that?' asked Jack.

'Follow your breadcrumbs. What else?'

'Good idea, because as I see things at the moment,' said Isis, 'we are intentionally being kept in the dark.'

'Not so sure. I trust Serapion, and he was adamant. How did he put it, Francesca?'

'He said it's imperative the relic be found because it has the power to defeat evil. As war in Ukraine is about to erupt, this is highly relevant – and urgent,' said Bartolli.

'He also said if we want to help resolve this looming crisis and avoid a global catastrophe, we have to find the relic – *fast*,' said Tristan softly.

'All right, guys. Let's see where this takes us, but for now, whereto from here?' asked Isis.

'Decision time, I suppose,' said Jack. 'I promised to give Sasha our answer tomorrow, but before you give me yours, there's one more thing we must take into consideration.'

'What?' asked Isis.

'My conditions.'

'*Conditions?* What kind of conditions?'

'Sasha and the Novotny Foundation may have an agenda of their own, but so do I.'

'Agenda? What do you mean?'

'Let's not forget O'Hara in all this,' said Jack. 'He may have suffered a major setback with Sasha terminating all Ivanov arrangements, but he certainly hasn't gone away. The danger may have retreated for now, but O'Hara is a cunning and resourceful foe. I'm sure he'll be back sooner or later. Until he's defeated once and for all, none of us are safe.'

'Agreed. So, what's on your mind?'

'I'm still working on it. I would like to talk to Serapion first, to find out exactly where he and the Guardians fit into all this.'

'I understand,' said Bartolli. She stood up, walked over to Jack and put her hand on his shoulder. 'Back in the Peter and Paul Cathedral in St Petersburg, right in front of Empress Alexandra's final resting place, you promised to do everything you could to protect those you love, whatever the cost. You said you would bide your time, go along with O'Hara's bizarre demands for now, but you would defeat him in the end.'

'And you said I couldn't do this all by myself, and promised to walk by my side.'

'I did, and I'm doing so right now, Jack,' said Bartolli. 'No questions asked.'

Slowly, Isis walked over to Jack and put her hand on top of Bartolli's. 'You will never walk alone in this; right, guys?'

'Never,' said Tristan.

'Are we all agreed, then?' asked Jack, almost overcome with emotion.

'Looks that way,' said Isis.

'Don't leave me out,' said Lola.

'No way!' said Isis. 'After all, someone has to fly that bloody plane!'

'There wouldn't be another book in this perhaps, would there?' teased Bartolli, a sparkle in her eyes.

'What do you think?' said Jack, closing his notebook.

47

Minsk: 22 January

O'Hara could deal with setbacks, but not with losing. The phone call from Irina two days earlier terminating their arrangements because Ivanov had died suddenly of a heart attack, had come as a shock that had taken O'Hara completely by surprise. An unusual situation for a micro-manager and meticulous planner used to being in control. O'Hara's precarious situation in Belarus and dependence on Irina and her agents made this setback even more serious and dramatic.

And just when he thought things couldn't get worse, they did. A few hours after Irina's bombshell phone call, a sinister logo had appeared on O'Hara's darknet gambling site. It was the round ENFAST logo with a snarling black wolf's head surrounded by eight yellow stars, which had instilled fear in criminals on the run since its establishment in 2013. ENFAST – European Network of Fugitive Active Search Teams – represents a network of highly trained police officers charged with tracing and arresting criminals on international most-wanted lists. Effectively, a special taskforce to hunt down villains on the run.

And if this wasn't enough, the text below the logo delivered an even more chilling blow: *We are watching and we know who you are, and where to find you. We have you in our sights. There's nowhere to hide!*

Not surprisingly, this represented the death knell and total collapse of O'Hara's darknet gambling site as all the punters ran for cover, tried to hide their tracks and terminated all contact and involvement with the site. Effectively, this had put O'Hara out of business and shut down his notorious gambling empire, a situation from which a comeback was difficult to imagine.

However, having dealt with setbacks before, O'Hara had a fallback position and a backup plan to save himself from complete defeat and humiliation. To see his gambling site collapse was one thing; to be defeated by Jack in a contest he had instigated was something quite different. One only concerned money, which O'Hara had in abundance. The other was far more precious and personal. This was all about pride, identity and ego, the very essence of what made O'Hara tick. Someone like O'Hara, who believed in his superior intellect and thrived on being in control and calling the shots, had to prevail in the end, or face annihilation and oblivion. There was no room for error, middle ground, or compromise on this emotional pride-and-ego tightrope. It was all or nothing.

The disturbing ENFAST logo on his screen told O'Hara that his darknet site had been infiltrated and compromised. It was therefore only a matter of time before his location could be traced unless he took steps to change his server and encryption protocol immediately. An expert like O'Hara could do this quickly and efficiently, because he had the required know-how at his fingertips to make it work. With a few clicks of his mouse, O'Hara had disappeared from the darknet without a trace, and could reinvent himself and safely re-enter the cyber world as a new man from a different country without internet history baggage to betray him. The name of the game was to keep one step ahead of the authorities pursuing him, and O'Hara was a master of this cyber cat-and-mouse game, which seemed to energise him like a raging bull charging the matador in the arena, ready for the kill.

Feeling better in the safety of the new, anonymous cyber haven he had created for himself, O'Hara could now turn to the subject that was foremost on his mind: defeating Jack. While losing Irina and the Ivanov connection, which had worked so well, was a serious blow, it wasn't fatal because O'Hara had a backup plan.

O'Hara's Mafia contacts had all but been destroyed by Italy's largest Mafia trial in Lamezia Terme in Calabria the year before. The feared 'Ndrangheta had been virtually wiped out, with most of its key players now in jail. And that included Riccardo Giordano, who had provided O'Hara with operatives like Spiridon 4 for years. The unprecedented success of this mega trial, which had involved more than nine hundred witnesses and three hundred and fifty high-profile accused, had only been possible because of one astonishing phenomenon: *"Vedo, Sento, Parlo"*, "I see, I hear, I speak", a powerful movement by Mafia women who'd had enough and gave evidence against their husbands, lovers and family members, to stop the violence and bloodshed that had dominated their lives for generations. The code of silence that had protected the perpetrators was finally broken, providing the prosecutors with evidence to secure convictions on a scale never seen before.

O'Hara, a cautious, far-sighted man who valued his contacts and always kept his channels of communication open, had kept in touch with Riccardo Giordano, the head of an infamous Mafia family from Florence, now serving a life sentence in the notorious Pagliarelli Prison in Palermo.

Through contacts on the darknet, O'Hara had found a prison guard open to bribes working in the maximum-security prison, with its fearsome reputation. This had allowed O'Hara to make contact with Giordano in jail and establish a line of communication, which he now activated to try to replace Irina.

O'Hara looked at the latest encrypted message he had received from the prison guard in Palermo and smiled. Consumed by hatred of his wife, Giuseppina, who had given evidence against him and a number of his associates, Giordano had only one thing on his mind: *revenge.* He was planning to have his wife, who lived in a safe house somewhere in Calabria, killed, and was prepared to do whatever it took to achieve this.

Because most of his assets had been confiscated or frozen and were therefore out of reach, Giordano desperately needed money to finance a hit on his wife. O'Hara had the money, and Giordano had the underworld contacts to replace Irina. This resulted in a partnership of mutual need that O'Hara liked and understood, because it was uncomplicated and could be trusted.

In return for a name and a phone number, O'Hara transferred the agreed amount into a nominated, untraceable bank account. Operation 'Behold the Memory Trees', a gamble O'Hara was hoping would turn his fortunes around, had begun.

48

St Bavo Cathedral, Ghent: 23 January

The train trip from London to Ghent via the Eurotunnel had taken just under three hours. It was still early when Jack entered the almost empty cathedral and looked for the Sacrament Chapel, where the newly restored *Ghent Altarpiece* was now displayed in a six-metre-tall, pneumatically controlled, bulletproof glass cage that had cost millions.

To see the famous altarpiece for the first time was an experience impossible to forget. Illuminated by subtle lighting from above that accentuated the brilliant colours of the painting, Jack remembered his recent conversation with Hoffmeister in Vienna. So, this was the most frequently stolen painting in history, thought Jack, which was almost destroyed by marauding Calvinists during the Great Iconoclasm in 1566.

'Magnificent, isn't it?' Jack heard a soft voice say from behind. As Jack turned around, he saw Serapion coming towards him, but didn't notice the tall man standing in the shadows, watching.

'It sure is. It's difficult to imagine that it's had such a turbulent history.'

'You are right.' Serapion pointed to the four main central panels. 'The French removed these and took them back to the Louvre in Paris.'

'Where they remained until Napoleon's defeat at Waterloo and Louis XVIII returned them here to Ghent, the city that had given him protection during the French Revolution.'

'Very good. Yet, only one year later, a greedy priest stole the wing panels and sold them. They ended up on display in a Berlin museum until the Treaty of Versailles in 1919, which facilitated their return to Ghent.'

'And then came Hitler,' said a voice out of the gloom.

Jack watched a tall man melt out of the shadows and walk slowly towards him, his beard and wavy white hair making him look like one of the saints in the panels above, providing a momentary link between the past and the present.

'Allow me to introduce Bishop Peeters,' said Serapion.

Peeters extended his hand. 'I've heard a lot about you, Mr Rogan. Welcome to St Bavo.'

'And with Hitler, things become really interesting,' said Jack, shaking hands with the bishop. 'Because it brings us right up to the time of David Herzl and *Golgotha*.'

'Correct,' said Peeters. 'And the circle is almost closing, perhaps bringing *Golgotha* back home? What do you think, Mr Rogan? Someone like you who believes in destiny would understand that, right?'

'Mr Rogan knows all about destiny. The return of Kazanskaya Bogomater, the famous icon, to Yekaterinburg, has demonstrated this in a most dramatic way,' said Serapion.

'It certainly did that, and could something similar perhaps be repeated right here?' said Peeters, watching Jack carefully.

'Quite possibly, but that's not my decision to make.'

'I understand. Abbot Serapion has explained the extraordinary circumstances of the painting's recent discovery in Oman.'

'It's quite a story, but not surprising, taking the history of *Golgotha* into account.' Jack pointed to the altarpiece in front of him. 'Or the history of this masterpiece here.'

'And history doesn't stand still,' Serapion cut in. 'It evolves and continues.'

'Quite. As I understand it, Mr Rogan, what brings you here are the clues buried in *Golgotha*. The clues pointing to *Dextera Dei*?'

'That's correct. I am sure Abbot Serapion would have explained why.'

Peeters nodded.

'Mr Rogan is following his breadcrumbs of destiny,' said Serapion, smiling, 'and was hoping you could perhaps add a few more to show him the way.'

'I understand. I may have some information that could be of interest here.'

Peeters turned towards Jack. 'Abbot Serapion has shown me a recent photograph of *Golgotha*. That by itself was quite historic, because to the best of my knowledge, no reliable image of *Golgotha* has survived.'

'Are you suggesting no-one knew what *Golgotha* actually looks like?' asked Jack, surprised.

'Exactly. We only have *descriptions* of the painting. Only words, but nothing specific. In short, no actual representation of it.'

'While the significance of the church in the painting has been known for a long time, without actually seeing it, it was impossible to identify it. Until now,' said Serapion, watching Jack carefully.

'Are you saying the church in the painting has been identified?' said Jack, unable to suppress his excitement.

'Yes,' said Peeters. 'I have already followed this up with historians here at the Ghent University—'

'And?' interjected Jack.

'That's where the good news ends, I'm afraid.'

'Why?'

'Because unfortunately, the church – which stood in a village not far from here – was destroyed by fire during the Great Iconoclasm in 1566.'

'Oh. Does this mean the holy relic was destroyed at the same time?'

'Not necessarily,' said Serapion, taking pity on Jack, who appeared crestfallen.

'How come?'

'There is a scholar, a Carmelite monk living in a monastery here in Ghent,' said Peeters, 'who has made it his life's work to find *Dextera Dei*, arguably one of the most important relics in Christendom.'

'And this is significant?' said Jack.

'It is,' continued Peeters. 'Because when I showed him the photograph of *Golgotha,* he fell to his knees and cried tears of joy.'

'Why would he have done that?'

'Because according to him, this was the missing clue in the long search for the holy relic,' said Serapion.

'Incredible! So, whereto from here?'

'I have arranged for you to meet Brother Frederick. He lives in the Karmelietenklooster not far from here. He's quite elderly ...'

Serapion walked over to Peeters and gave him a stern look. 'Before we do, we should discuss the proposal you have in mind. Only fair, don't you think?'

'Yes, we should.'

'What kind of proposal?' said Jack, frowning.

'A proposal someone like you, Mr Rogan, would understand perfectly,' Peeters replied calmly. 'Ah, here come the tourists. Let's go over to the monastery and I'll tell you what I have in mind. Please follow me.'

49

On the back way to London: 23 January

As soon as the train left the station and headed towards the outskirts of Ghent, Jack began to unwind. He found train travel not only relaxing, but also an excellent way to reflect on both the journey and the destination. And there was certainly a lot to reflect upon after a day full of unexpected surprises.

Jack opened his notebook and began to go over the entries he had quickly jotted down during the meeting with Brother Frederick earlier that day, which had changed everything.

Transported by the comforting, gentle swaying of the carriage that acted like a rocking cradle watched over by a doting mother, Jack closed his eyes. He could see the elderly Brother Frederick sitting in the library of the Karmelietenklooster, and hear him talk about a legend handed down through generations of Carmelites. The legend told the extraordinary story of how a holy relic – *Dextera Dei* – had entered Europe at the end of the Third Crusade. It was a story of heroism and defeat, of bloody battles and cruelty, of hardship and humiliating imprisonment, but also of a remarkable friendship between a king and a minstrel, united through song.

The year was 1192 and Richard the Lionheart was on a perilous journey home from the Holy Land after the Second Crusade. He had just been captured outside Vienna by Duke Leopold, whom he had grievously insulted during the crusade.

Dürnstein Castle, Austria: February 1193

After a long and bloody campaign that had lasted several years, but had failed to achieve the capture of Jerusalem and defeat the forces of Saladin, Richard the Lionheart had encountered an almost fatal obstacle on his way home: a storm. Shipwrecked at Aquileia near

Venice, and disguised as a Templar knight, Richard was compelled to take the longer and far more dangerous land route home.

Just before Christmas of 1192, he was recognised and captured outside Vienna by Leopold's men, and taken to Dürnstein Castle overlooking the Danube. A sad and humiliating situation for the famous crusader.

The winter was particularly harsh that year. Heavy snow covered the steep hills leading down to the Danube below the castle and large chunks of ice floated down the river, threatening to crush anything foolish enough to get in their way.

It was perishingly cold in the cell high up in the tower. The small fire had almost gone out and the little warmth that remained was not enough to make the dank cell comfortable. A bleak place for a king and hero crusader who had occupied Sicily to sort out his sister Joanna's inheritance, conquered Cyprus and made it into a Christian stronghold, played an important role in the Siege of Acre, and almost captured Jerusalem, inflicting heavy losses on the forces of Saladin.

Richard sat on the stone floor in front of the fireplace. Wrapping a bearskin, which also served as his bedding, around his shoulders, he contemplated his unfortunate situation. Asking for guidance, he reached for the holy relic that he wore around his neck – a small piece of the holy cross with part of a nail embedded in it – raised it to his lips and began to pray. Feeling calmer, he looked through the small, barred opening and watched the snowflakes drift past like frozen messengers of hope.

No stranger to hardship and setbacks, Richard had been in difficult situations before and had never let adversity get the better of him. Once during the Siege of Acre, too weak to walk due to a serious illness wracking his emaciated body, he had picked off defenders on the ramparts with his crossbow while being carried along on a stretcher below the fortified walls.

When action wasn't an option to keep sane and focused, Richard turned to music; he liked to sing and even composed his own ballads. Richard had been working for days on a new song – *Ja Nus Hons*

Pris' – 'No Man Who Is Imprisoned', a melancholic poem that dealt with his harsh incarceration, reflecting feelings of loneliness, betrayal and abandonment, but also of hope and love. It was a song that would reverberate for centuries and inspire troubadours and songwriters well into the future; in many ways it even outlived Richard's considerable fame and legacy.

After hearing rumours of Richard's capture and imprisonment in an Austrian castle, the French troubadour Blondel travelled from castle to castle looking for his friend, the king. When he reached Dürnstein he met a soldier in a tavern who told him that a king was being held in the castle above the village.

The next morning, Blondel went up to the castle. As he approached one of its forbidding towers, he could hear singing coming from somewhere above. It was a song he recognised, a song only he and his friend the king knew. Standing below the tower, Blondel replied by singing the next verse. When Richard heard this, he was overjoyed. He knew that his friend had found him and the holy relic had answered his prayers. Over the next hour, the king and his trusty troubadour conversed by singing to each other.

Richard asked his friend to do two things for him:

First, he asked him to memorise the new song, *Ja Nus Hons Pris'*, which he had just composed about his predicament, and recite it to his half-sister – Marie of France, Countess of Champagne – who was not only a powerful regent, but also a well-known patron of literature, and ask for her help to free him.

Then Richard did something brave and inspirational: he took off the precious relic he wore around his neck, threw it out of the window into the snow below, and asked Blondel to take it to his friend and fellow crusader – the grandmaster of the Knights Templar residing in Poitiers – as proof he was alive and being held in Dürnstein by Leopold. Richard knew his friend would immediately marshal his supporters as soon as he saw the holy relic – a rare treasure he had presented to Richard before the Battle of Jaffa, the final battle of the Third Crusade – and do everything in his power to free him.

As the holy relic fell into the pristine snow below, *Dextera Dei* had arrived in Europe and was on its way to help the faithful defeat evil.

* * *

As the speeding Eurostar entered the Chunnel, Jack opened his eyes. Refreshed, he jotted down a few more points he'd remembered and then, just before the train pulled into St Pancras International in London, he called Sasha and gave her his answer as promised.

50

Mercato di Porta Nolana, Naples: 24 January

It was just after sunrise when Fabio Falcone's phone rang. He was toiling in the notorious Mercato di Porta Nolana seafood market near the medieval city gates in Naples, where casual work was available without too many questions being asked. Surprised, Falcone answered the call. Since leaving his remote underground sanctuary high up in the hills above Catanzaro in Calabria two months earlier, and then hiding on a fishing boat owned by a friend, he had hardly received any calls because few knew his encrypted number. Being a wanted man on the run, he had to be careful and vigilant.

Falcone, a short, powerfully built man in his forties, was one of the few high-profile members of the 'Ndrangheta, the notorious organised crime syndicate in Calabria, who had escaped the deadly net of the Lamezia Terme trials in 2021. A loyal foot soldier and hit man working for the Giordano family, he and his brother had carried out several daring assassinations over the years. Because the targets of these assassinations had been witnesses, prosecutors, and even a judge, the Falcones had been at the top of the most-wanted list in Calabria for years.

Forensically speaking, the spectacular success of the Lamezia Terme trials, which resulted in many convictions of previously untouchable *capos* protected by the code of silence that had ruled family lives for generations, was largely due to one thing: OMERTA, an encrypted messaging app developed by law enforcement agencies and covertly distributed by the FBI among the criminal underworld via informants with links to the Mafia.

So successful was this operation, which allowed police around the world to monitor conversations among senior crime figures, that it was described by Europol as the 'biggest law enforcement operation against encrypted communication' ever. This ingenious sting, made public in June 2021, involved eight thousand police officers, resulted in countless arrests in more than sixteen countries, and the confiscation of tonnes of drugs and millions of dollars of proceeds of crime.

But this operation also had a dark side. It turned wives against husbands and brothers, lovers against lovers, and mothers against sons, destroying families and causing unimaginable pain. Women were murdered as they left church on Sundays, or were found dead in public squares where they'd been shopping, or killed while working in the fields. Others were living in secret locations under witness protection, which didn't adequately protect them all the time and often resulted in brutal murders, even on their way to court to give evidence. Blood was running in the streets. Calabria was at war.

At the time, Falcone and his younger brother had been working for Riccardo Giordano – a feared Calabrian Mafia boss and head of a powerful crime family in Florence – when an assassination attempt on Nicola Donizetti, the lead prosecutor in the trials, had gone spectacularly wrong. Donizetti, her bodyguard and Falcone's brother were both shot at the airport. Donizetti survived and went on to conduct the trials, but the bodyguard and Falcone's brother didn't. Fabio had managed a getaway and had been on the run and in hiding ever since.

'Who is this?' asked Falcone.

'My name is unimportant, but what I'm about to tell you is. So, listen carefully. Riccardo Giordano gave me your number.'

'Go on.'

'I have a job for you.'

'What kind of job?'

'Later. First things first.'

'I'm listening.'

'One hundred thousand dollars has been deposited into a bank account in your name. The money is yours, no questions asked. Another two hundred thousand is waiting once the job has been completed ...'

Falcone reached into his pocket, retrieved a cigarette and lighter, and lit up. 'And?'

'Do you have a pen?'

'Sure ...'

'Then write this down.'

Falcone turned to a nearby counter, grabbed a pen and scrap of paper and jotted down access details to a secure, untraceable bank account.

'Now listen carefully. We will not meet, and you will never find out who I am. Clear so far?'

'Fine by me.'

'Good. We understand each other. I want you to make your way to Venice and call this number when you arrive. You will receive further instructions then. Understood?'

'Perfectly.'

'Good. I await your call.'

Falcone slipped the phone into his pocket, took off his apron and, without saying a word to the surprised workers gutting fish next to him, walked out of the noisy hall.

Smiling, O'Hara took a deep breath and put down his phone. Feeling in control for the first time in days, he contemplated his next move on his imaginary chessboard.

51

Gatekeeper's Cottage, Kuragin chateau: 24 January

Dupree was sitting in front of the fireplace, reading, when Jack walked in. It was quite late and the fire had almost gone out. Jack dropped his duffel bag by the door, took off his snow-covered overcoat, and walked over to the fire to warm his hands.

Dupree pointed to a bottle of Scotch on the small table next to his armchair. 'Drink?'

'Sure.'

'You look terrible.'

Jack took the glass Dupree handed him and flopped down in an armchair opposite. He'd spent the night in London at Isis's apartment, but had barely slept. Despite Isis's protests, he flew back to Paris the next morning. He wanted to see Dupree, a voice of reason who could help put things in perspective. He also desperately needed rest.

'It's been hectic. Wait till you hear what I've got to tell you.'

Dupree smiled. This was classic Jack. 'Hardly surprising. You've been halfway around the world. Where are Bartolli and Tristan?'

'Francesca's gone back to Rome to make sure her daughters haven't completely gone off the rails, and Tristan has returned to Venice. He said he needed some time to think and sort out what's been happening.' Jack ran his fingers through his hair. 'He also said something else I found a little disturbing.'

'What?'

'You know what he's like. He often speaks in riddles.'

'Try me,' said Dupree, pouring whisky into two tumblers and handing one to Jack.

'He said he felt uneasy about something and wanted to be there when it happened,'

'Strange. Did he say what that was all about?'

Jack shrugged. 'No, he didn't. I think he just needs a little time out, that's all.'

'Understandable. And I suppose you've come here to do the same?'

'Something like that. You've always been an excellent listener and sounding board, Claude. A clear head in the fog of confusion. I, too, need to reflect a little, take a step back and put everything into perspective. Things are moving at lightning speed and there's a lot at stake here.'

'With you there always is.'

Jack shrugged. 'Information overload. The sad lot of a story magnet. Cheers!'

'Ah. Is that what it is?'

'It's a little more complicated than that, I suppose.'

'Do you want to talk about this now, or in the morning?'

Jack reached into his pocket and pulled out his notebook. 'Now. If I don't put some order into all this, I won't be able to sleep anyway.' Jack pointed to his head. 'The mind can be a strange place.'

'Tell me about it. I also have things to tell you. About Lapointe, Borroni and Samartini in Florence. They haven't been idle, either.'

'Good.' Jack opened his notebook. 'Let's begin.'

Dupree reached for the bottle and poured a little more Scotch into Jack's tumbler.

'You already know all about Sheikh Mohammed and how we located *Golgotha* in Muscat,' began Jack.

'And you told me about Leonardo's visit to Doha and the exchange.'

'*Golgotha* for the Amulet of Timur?'

'I must say, that was clever. Exchanging a Muslim treasure for a Christian one; brilliant!'

'It seemed obvious and the only way forward in the circumstances.'

'Is that what Tristan thought?'

'No, Tristan *knew*. He was the only one who wasn't surprised by all this. And do you know what he had to say once we concluded the exchange arrangement?'

'Tell me.'

'He said finding *Golgotha* was just the beginning, not the end.'

'Intriguing.'

'At the time I had no idea what he meant by that, but now I do. He was right, as usual.'

'An extraordinary young man with a special gift.'

'He's that, for sure.'

'Was it because *Golgotha* is much more than just a painting by a famous artist?'

'Yes, that's exactly what this is all about. *Golgotha* has all the answers here.'

'Because it is a map, showing the way?'

'Yes. This is all about *Dextera Dei*, the holy relic that has mysteriously disappeared. And now there are a number of interested parties who desperately want to find it, albeit for different reasons.'

'And you are one of them?'

'I am. I think the best way to look at this and make some sense of it all is to examine the motives of each of those interested parties. And who those parties are is remarkable in itself; perhaps the biggest surprise in all this.'

'Go on.'

'Well, first there's Sasha Kovalenko, the daughter of a billionaire Russian oligarch. She burst onto the scene in Doha in a way that changed everything. And if that wasn't surprising enough, she brought Abbot Serapion with her.'

'An intriguing connection, I must admit.'

'Absolutely. I had no idea at the time why, or how, they were connected.'

'But now you do?'

'Yes. The link here is Palin and what's happening in Russia right now. Serapion has joined forces with the Novotny Foundation to overthrow Palin and liberate Russia. That's where Sasha Kovalenko and the Novotny Foundation step into the picture. Novotny is in jail in Russia, and Sasha is now running the Foundation from London.'

'What about Serapion?'

'That's a little more complicated. His motives are clear enough and are effectively the same as those of the Foundation, but his methods ... well, they seem a little far-fetched.'

'Even for you? Tell me.'

'Serapion arranged to meet me in Ghent. In front of van Eyck's famous altarpiece. He insisted. It was obviously quite deliberate; he had a plan. He introduced me to Bishop Peeters, who in turn introduced me to a Carmelite monk, Brother Frederick. And that's when things really became interesting.'

'How come?'

'Because in a strange way, the various intriguing pieces began to fall into place. It all comes back to finding *Dextera Dei*, the holy relic that has the power to defeat evil, and apparently has already done so in the past. On several occasions.'

'Come on, Jack, this sounds more and more like one of your books. Thriller fiction.'

'True, but as we both know, fact can often sound stranger than fiction.'

'Also true.'

'Let's take a step back. For some reason or other, everyone here is after that relic.'

'Looks that way.'

'Yes. There are three parties involved here: Sasha Kovalenko. She wants to overthrow Palin, free Novotny and liberate Russia. Serapion wants the same. He appears to have connections close to Palin,' said Jack, 'and he has a plan to achieve all this.'

'Did Serapion say more about ...?'

'No. He said it was better if I didn't know.'

'Very convenient.'

'Perhaps.'

'And the third party?'

'Bishop Peeters and Brother Frederick. They both want the same.'

'What's that?'

'The return of *Golgotha* to where it belongs: the *Ghent Altarpiece*.'

'Of all the motives you have outlined so far, this is the one that makes sense. You said there are three parties, when in fact there are four.'

'What do you mean?'

'What about you? Where do you fit into all this?'

'A fair question. I made a deal with Sasha Kovalenko, and another with Bishop Peeters.'

'*A deal?* What kind of deal?'

'We haven't spoken about O'Hara in all of this, yet he's right in the middle of it and certainly hasn't gone away,' said Jack, sidestepping the question. 'He's the real threat here, certainly as far as I'm concerned.'

'Sure, but where does he fit into this puzzle?'

'He's a serious danger to me and those I hold dear, and until he's silenced once and for all, this will continue. Don't forget the recent threats. I believe they're as real now as they were then. O'Hara hasn't gone away. He's just become more dangerous.'

'I understand, but what has a stolen painting and a lost relic to do with all this?'

'Another fair question. I'll tell you. It all comes back to *Dextera Dei*, the holy relic with the power to defeat evil, and the two deals I mentioned before.'

'In what way?'

'Both Kovalenko and Serapion are after the relic for the same reason, and they are both convinced I can help them find it.'

'Can you?'

'I believe so, and so does Tristan.'

'How? By following your famous breadcrumbs?'

'You're mocking me.'

'Far from it. I've seen them at work too often not to take this seriously. But *here*?'

'Yes. I believe I can find the relic. I can *sense* it, and so does Tristan. And the relic will help us defeat O'Hara once and for all. That's what's in this for me. For *us*.'

'And how are you planning to achieve all this?'

'By giving Kovalenko and Serapion what they are after, in return for their help to nail O'Hara.'

Dupree looked at Jack, nonplussed. 'Seriously?'

'Yes.'

'How?'

'As we've already seen, Kovalenko has the means and the connections in Belarus to get to O'Hara.'

'Irina and her agents?'

'Exactly. I've made a deal with Kovalenko. If I deliver the relic to her and Serapion, she has agreed to help us nail O'Hara in Belarus.'

'How? We don't even know where he is. Belarus is a big place.'

'Something will turn up, you'll see.'

'You sound like Tristan.'

'Perhaps. But he's been right before – often.'

'And your deal with Peeters and the monk?' asked Dupree. 'What's that about?'

'I'm convinced they can help me find the relic. Brother Frederick is an expert on *Golgotha* and the relic. He's already given me some helpful information and clues that could show me the way.'

'This sounds very much like your quest to find Kazanskaya Bogomater.'

'There are similarities.'

'You're enjoying this, aren't you?'

'Yes, I don't deny it, but there are serious matters at stake here.'

'There always are. That's why these quests of yours are so riveting. You're playing the big game here, with the big boys.'

'Some truth in that.'

'What kind of deal have you made with Peeters?'

'Isn't it obvious? He's after *Golgotha*. He wants the painting returned to the altarpiece where it belongs.'

'And Leonardo is okay with this? After all, *Golgotha* belongs to him. At least for now.'

'He's on board, provided we can silence O'Hara once and for all, and remove the threat.'

'Something for everyone, then.'

'Correct. And don't forget that includes you and Lapointe.'

'Oh? In what way?'

'Surely, bringing O'Hara to justice and making him pay for the murders, especially the brutal murders of the two police officers killed right in front of that door over there, must mean something.'

'It does, of course, but is that how you want to defeat O'Hara? Hand him over to Lapointe?'

'Yes.'

'How?'

'Something will turn up,' said Jack, a cheeky little smile creasing the corners of his mouth.

'You can be so infuriating! The Tristan solution again.'

'Worked before.'

'So, let me get this straight,' said Dupree. 'You are after the relic because it could help you nail O'Hara. In order to achieve this, you need Sasha's help, and Sasha has promised to help you in return for the relic. Sasha and Serapion both want the relic for the same reason: to remove Palin and liberate Russia from his dictatorship, but exactly how they plan to achieve this and what role the relic is to play in this, is still somewhat of a mystery. How am I doing so far?' said Dupree.

'Very well. You're spot on. And I need the help of Bishop Peeters and Brother Frederick to find the relic. If it really exists, that is,' added Jack.

'Do you know how crazy this sounds?'

Jack shrugged. 'I've been involved in worse. And besides, I cannot see another way forward just now.'

'To defeat O'Hara?'

'Yes.'

'Don't you think this is perhaps a little too personal?'

'It *is* personal. O'Hara made it so. But I believe we must remove him once and for all, or we'll live forever under his spell and doing his bidding. He's evil, I mean *really* evil, and is obsessed with turning an earlier defeat into some kind of victory. Until that happens, he will not leave us alone.'

'I agree with you on that.'

Jack closed his notebook. 'This is really good, Claude, thank you. A brief chat with you is cathartic. Everything is already a lot clearer.'

'I'm glad you think so, because my looking glass is still a little foggy.'

'It may look a little clearer in the morning.'

'Perhaps.'

'I'm going to hit the sack. I'm buggered,' said Jack and stood up.

'An Aussie goodnight?'

'Something like that.'

Jack preferred to stay in the modest cottage with Dupree. Since the chateau was once again being used for luxury guest accommodation under the watchful eye of Mademoiselle Darrieux, who had taken the Kuragin boutique hotel to an entirely new level of popularity, he no longer felt comfortable or at home in the sumptuous surroundings now frequented by celebrities. In some way, Darrieux' soirees and dinners had even surpassed the legendary evenings previously hosted by Countess Kuragin, attracting well-heeled guests from all over Europe.

For the next several days, Jack bunkered down at the cottage. He got up uncharacteristically late, spent the day reading, ate meals with Dupree, and then retired early. Glad of his company but realising Jack was exhausted, Dupree mostly left him alone.

31 January

Feeling relaxed at last, Jack lay in bed, but for some reason sleep wouldn't come. Not entirely awake but not asleep either, Jack's mind began to wander and he found himself with Brother Frederick in the Karmelietenklooster library in Ghent. He could hear him tell the remarkable story of *Dextera Dei*, and what happened to it after Richard the Lionheart asked his friend, Blondel, the travelling troubadour, to take it to the grand master of the Templars in Poitiers.

'After Blondel delivered the holy relic to the grand master and Richard had been finally set free after a staggering ransom had been paid for his release,' said Father Frederick, '*Dextera Dei* became a treasured badge of office handed from grand master to grand master until it reached Jacques de Molay, the last grand master of the Knights Templar. Jacques de Molay's terrible death and his famous curse are well documented, but what happened to the holy relic is less clear, and this has troubled scholars like me for centuries. Until now ...'

52

Île aux Javiaux on the Seine, Paris: 11 March 1314

Finally, the day of execution had arrived. After a long trial and years of incarceration and delays, countless interrogations and complex political intrigue, King Phillip the Fair of France would finally have his way. Jacques de Molay, last grand master of the Templars, would be publicly executed. The power, influence and fabulous wealth of the Templars that had been a thorn in the king's side for years, because of a mountain of debt he owed the Templars he could never hope to repay, had been broken. With fanciful charges of heresy, mass arrests and executions across Europe, the carefully orchestrated campaign to wipe out the Templars, authorised by the king and reluctantly sanctioned by a weak pope, was reaching its tragic climax. What had begun with mass arrests of Templars across Europe on Friday 13 October 1307 – the original Black Friday – would go down in history as one of the most brutal and infamous crusades against a religious order of devout Christian knights, who had sworn an oath of poverty, chastity and obedience to protect travellers to the Holy Land.

Before leaving jail to face his executioners, Jacques de Molay was granted a last wish: a final meeting with his confessor and long-time friend, a humble priest at Notre Dame.

The priest was shocked when he was finally admitted into the condemned man's cell he had not been allowed to visit for months. Years of barbaric imprisonment had taken their toll. The once all-powerful grand master of the Templars was a mere shadow of himself. Dirty, dressed in rags, with sores covering his legs and bare feet, he could barely stand, his emaciated body too weak to carry out even the most basic tasks. One thing, however, hadn't changed: the look in the prisoner's eyes radiating courage, defiance and resolve, reflecting the inner strength of a man who may have been defeated, but was not broken.

Without saying a word and ignoring the filth and stench, the priest walked over to his friend and embraced him.

'So, the day has finally arrived,' said de Molay, his voice calm and strong for a man about to face a most horrible death.

'So it would seem,' said the priest, tears in his eyes. 'Do you want me to hear your confession?'

'No, I made peace with God a long time ago. My conscience is clear, but I do have a request, my friend.'

'Oh? What kind of request?' said the priest, his curiosity aroused. It wasn't what he had expected.

'You know about the holy relic, don't you?'

'*Dextera Dei?* Yes, of course. It has been in your Order since the Third Crusade, handed down from grand master to grand master.'

'It has indeed.'

De Molay reached under the filthy rags hanging from his bony shoulders and pulled out the little relic he wore around his neck. 'I may not have been able to save much, least of all myself, but I have managed to save this.'

The priest stared at the relic in astonishment and wonder, surprise and disbelief on his face. 'All these years, in here, you had it on you?'

'Yes. I suppose that's a miracle in itself, but here it is. It would be a sin to let something so precious burn at the stake, consumed by flames like I will be shortly, don't you think?'

'Yes, it would be that.'

'Well, with your help that will not happen.' De Molay slipped the leather thong over his head and handed the relic to the priest. 'Now, please listen carefully, there isn't much time. This is what I would like you to do ...'

Just before sunset, de Molay was taken to the Île aux Javiaux on the Seine. As he walked slowly to the hastily erected pyre, the last grand master of the Templars smiled, secure in the knowledge that in the end justice would prevail, because the holy relic was in safe hands and would carry on its fight against evil for centuries to come.

As the flames began to devour the flesh, first on his feet and then up his legs, causing excruciating pain that would have made a lesser man cry out in agony and go mad, de Molay collected his thoughts, and with a strong, clear voice called out a chilling curse: 'I appeal from this heinous judgement to the living and true God, who is in Heaven, that within a year and a day' – De Molay began to choke and almost lost consciousness as the flames raced up his body, but instead of giving in to the pain and escaping to the sanctuary of oblivion, he marshalled the last of his remaining strength, looked towards heaven and continued – 'you, Clement, and you, Phillip, be obliged to answer for your crimes in God's presence.'

Moments later, the flames engulfed de Molay's head, igniting his long beard and hair and making him look like a living halo of an avenging angel, a sight that terrified all who witnessed the spectacle.

Within a month of de Molay's execution, Pope Clement V was dead, and before a year had passed, Phillip the Fair died of a stroke while on a hunting trip. This marked the rapid decline of the Capetian kings of France. Three of Phillip's sons and one grandson all died within a few years, and by 1328, fourteen years after de Molay's death, the House of Capet was no more. De Molay's curse had become reality.

53

Palazzo Alberti, Venice: 1 February, 3:00 am

A light sleeper, Rahima opened her eyes, a feeling of unease and apprehension washing over her and making her heart beat faster. *Bad dream*, she thought and turned her head towards the window facing the Grand Canal. A narrow shaft of moonlight reached into the room like an accusing finger pointing to a strange shadow in the room. The moonbeam crossed the foot of the bed and, becoming fainter, ran along the polished floorboards before coming to a sudden stop in front of an armchair facing the bed.

Rahima was about to reach for a glass of water on her bedside table when something caught her eye: a dark shape that wasn't part of the chair. *There's someone in here*, she thought, trying hard not to move. *Stay calm!* Years of living in Colombia in the fortified headquarters of a notorious drug cartel surrounded by armed guards had taught Rahima how to deal with the unexpected. Lying perfectly still, she kept staring at the dark shape, trying to make sense of it by willing it to reveal itself.

Falcone had noticed Rahima move. Sitting in the armchair in the dark, he had a clear view of the bed near the window. Rahima's open eyes reflecting the moonlight reaching through the window told him that she was looking in his direction.

'You're awake; good,' he said, his voice sounding distant and strange. 'Don't make any noise. Just listen to what I have to say. Clear so far?'

Rahima nodded ever so slightly.

'Good. We understand each other.' Falcone reached into his pocket and took out a torch.

Without saying a word, Rahima kept staring in Falcone's direction. Moments later, a shaft of light illuminated something frightening as Falcone turned on his torch.

Rahima gasped, but desperately tried not to panic. Dressed all in black, the man sitting in the chair was wearing the distinctive white mask of a plague doctor, usually worn during the Carnival of Venice. The mask covered his entire face and was the reason the voice sounded muffled and otherworldly. Looking like some strange, exotic bird with a huge hollow, curved beak and large round eye holes covered with glass, the creature radiated danger, conjuring up images of death and disease that had wiped out entire cities. A black tricorne hat and cape completed the costume, giving him a theatrical, stage-like air.

A dangerous man, thought Rahima, trying to stay calm as she recognised all the familiar signs of someone used to being in control and obeyed. *Obviously not a burglar. I wonder what he wants.*

Pleased by Rahima's controlled reaction, Falcone relaxed. Things were going better than expected. A hysterical woman would have been the last thing he needed.

'Who are you? What do you want?' asked Rahima.

'Who I am is irrelevant,' said Falcone. 'Just think of me as *Il Medico della Peste*. The only thing that counts here is how well you follow my instructions.'

'What instructions?'

'Well, to begin with, turn on your bedside lamp.'

Rahima did as she was told.

'Now, get out of bed and get dressed. Put on something warm. It's cold outside.'

'We are going somewhere?' asked Rahima, her mind racing, desperately searching for answers.

'We are. If you do exactly as I tell you, no harm will come to you. If not ...' Falcone didn't complete the sentence, the threat in his voice sufficient.

Rahima realised the only way to deal with the situation was to do exactly what the man wanted. Any kind of resistance would not only be futile, but could even aggravate her predicament. It took her only a few minutes to get dressed. After putting on her shoes she reached for her phone on the bedside table.

'Leave it!' barked Falcone. 'Where you're going, you won't need it, nor anything else, for that matter. Now, walk over to the door and open it.'

Rahima walked over to the door without making eye contact with the strange creature as she walked past.

Falcone stood up and held up his torch. 'We'll now walk down the stairs and go to the back door facing the canal, understood?'

Rahima nodded, followed the cone of light coming from Falcone's torch from behind and began to walk slowly down the stairs.

Before leaving the room, Falcone pulled a piece of paper – a handwritten note – out of his pocket and placed it on Rahima's pillow. O'Hara's instructions had been quite specific.

Bonato lay in his bed, awake and listening. A strange noise coming from the back of the building where the tradesmen stored their tools and materials had woken him earlier, but now all was silent. *Rats again*, he thought and was about to turn over and go back to sleep, when he saw a flickering light shining through the partially open door of his room. He knew it wouldn't be Tristan because he was staying the night at Palazzo da Baggio, and apart from Rahima sleeping upstairs, the building was empty.

An intruder! thought Bonato. He jumped out of bed and turned on the light. As he stepped into the hallway to investigate, he saw Rahima standing at the bottom of the stairs with a strange creature standing behind her. The creature was pointing a gun at him.

'What's going on?' demanded Bonato, feeling cold and vulnerable in his pyjamas. Rahima shook her head, and Falcone put the index finger of his left hand against the beak, the gesture obvious. Bonato stopped in his tracks and stared at the frightening apparition.

'Go back to bed, old man. *Now!*' commanded Falcone. 'It's either that, or you can lie there with your head blown off; your choice.'

Shaking, Bonato walked back into his room and got into bed.

'Now count to three hundred. Loud, so I can hear you. If you stop, I'll be back. Understood?'

'Yes,' said Bonato.

'Now start counting.'

'One, two, three, four ...'

'*Louder!*'

Falcone turned towards Rahima and pointed with his gun to the back door. 'We're going outside onto the pontoon facing the canal. There's a boat there. Get into it quickly. *Move!*'

Outside it was bitterly cold and foggy. Rahima almost slipped on the wet boards as she tried to climb awkwardly into the boat. Falcone jumped on board after her, his black cape flapping like wings of a bat, and said something to the man at the wheel.

Rahima could still hear Bonato counting through the open door before a powerful engine roared into life, the boat pulled away from the pontoon, accelerated and disappeared into the night.

O'Hara put down his phone and smiled. *Done!* he thought, feeling energised and back in control. *Dear Jack's in for one hell of a surprise in the morning. Let's see how he deals with this.* Then O'Hara reached for the keyboard in front of him and transferred two hundred thousand euros into Falcone's bank account he had set up earlier.

O'Hara had to admit the unique solution Falcone had come up with for Rahima's detention was simply brilliant, and definitely deserved a bonus. O'Hara transferred an additional fifty thousand into the account and called it *Book in the Library Bonus*. He realised Falcone would know exactly what that meant because of the explanation he had provided for the ingenious arrangements. 'There's no better place to hide a book than in a library,' Falcone had argued. It was the kind of solution that instantly appealed to O'Hara because it was daring, impressive in its simplicity and effective. In short, it ticked all the boxes perfectly and added a satisfying touch of irony to the entire exercise.

The chess game that had almost been lost had not only been turned around, but the black knight was also back on the attack.

* * *

At first, Jack tried to ignore the intrusion into his restless sleep, but the stubborn ringtone of his mobile on the bedside table wouldn't stop. As images of de Molay's dramatic execution faded away, Jack opened his eyes, reluctantly reached for the phone and answered it. It was Countess Kuragin.

'Jack, something terrible has happened!'

Jack sat up, instantly awake, a wave of fear washing over him. 'What?' he asked.

'I just had a call from Bonato—'

'What about?' Jack interrupted impatiently.

'Your mother has been abducted.'

'What do you mean, abducted?'

'A man broke into the palazzo during the night and took her away at gunpoint.'

'What are you saying?' Jack almost shouted.

'That's not all. The man left something behind. A note on her pillow.'

'A note? What does it say?'

'Behold the memory trees.'

'Jesus!'

PART III
DEXTERA DEI

'Sit at my right hand
Until I make your enemies
Your footstool'
— *Hebrews 1:13*

54

Gorky Park, Moscow: 1 February

Serapion walked out of the Park Kultury Metro station and turned up the collar of his heavy overcoat. It was bitterly cold and had begun to snow again. Watching out for speeding cars, he crossed the busy road and hurried to the entrance of Gorky Park near the Moskva River. As he approached the imposing main gate he could see Karlov waiting for him under the colonnade, as arranged.

Named after writer and political activist Maxim Gorky, the park had become famous through the 1983 American film *Gorky Park*, based on a mystery thriller written by Martin Cruz Smith. The popular park had a colourful history, starting out as a Moscow rubbish dump before the First All-Russian Agricultural and Handicraft Industries Exhibition in 1923 led to the creation of a Central Park of Culture and Leisure, Russia's first park of its kind. The popular park had since undergone several significant transformations, elevating the park and its attractions to an international level that could compete with leading parks around the world.

'Thanks for coming at such short notice,' said Karlov, stamping his feet to keep warm, and shook hands with Serapion. 'Let's walk.'

The expression on Karlov's face told Serapion all he had to know: something was wrong – very wrong. A man of Karlov's standing wouldn't have arranged an urgent meeting, with all its risks attached, without good reason.

Karlov and Serapion had met in Gorky Park before. The reason was as obvious as it was simple: they couldn't be overheard. While the FSB was well aware of the connection between Karlov – one of Palin's closest advisers and confidants – and Serapion, the enigmatic abbot from Yekaterinburg, it had no idea of the true nature of their relationship and collaboration. That was a closely guarded secret only known to the two men and, if discovered, it would certainly have cost them their lives.

Karlov and Serapion had first met the year before at Yekaterin-burg. Karlov had approached the abbot with a special request from high up in the Kremlin. The sensitive matter involved Kazanskaya Bogomater, the famous Russian icon that had finally been returned to the Alexander Nevsky Cathedral in 2017 with great pomp and cere-mony, attended by the pope himself and high-ranking Russian dignitaries and church leaders, including Patriarch Nicodemus, Pri-mate of the Russian Orthodox Church.

Because the request had come directly from the president, it was more of an order. Serapion realised at once, of course, that refusal was out of the question. Because he and Karlov had got on very well from the beginning, Serapion decided to dig a little deeper to find out what had motivated the strange request in the first place.

That's when Karlov told him about Palin's obsession with the occult and why he was so interested in the icon and its legendary spiritual powers. Karlov realised he was taking a considerable risk in telling Serapion about this, but instincts honed by many years in the FSB told him that in Serapion he had found a like-minded spirit he could trust. As it turned out, he had been right.

The two men formed an instant friendship and a strong bond as they recognised they shared the same love of their homeland and despised any form of tyranny and oppression of its people. Encour-aged by Karlov's comments, Serapion disclosed that he not only supported Novotny and his ideas, but also that he and many senior members of the Church secretly collaborated with Novotny and his Foundation.

Normally, telling a high-ranking FSB officer something like that would have resulted in certain arrest and robust interrogation followed by a trial, even for a member of the Church. However, by then Serapion felt confident enough to share this with Karlov because both men had taken considerable risks in disclosing confidential information, which showed mutual trust and commitment to shared principles and ideas.

During the months that followed, one particular event stood out: Serapion's personal delivery of the holy icon to the Kremlin, which resulted in an audience with Palin arranged by Karlov. From then, Serapion and Karlov became even closer and shared more confidences and ideas, until an alliance was forged that had only one aim: to overthrow Palin and liberate Russia from a corrupt megalomaniac who was leading the country towards certain disaster. And that was when a unique and daring plan was hammered out that resembled thriller fiction rather than reality. The plan was ingenious because it attempted to turn a man's strange obsession against himself in a creative way: by using a rare weakness in an otherwise brutal and ruthless man as a weapon of self-destruction.

The risks were considerable, but so were the rewards. Karlov and Serapion realised this. With so much at stake, both were prepared to put their lives on the line as one small mistake would easily mean certain death. Because of his influential position close to the president, Karlov had many enemies lurking in the shadows, waiting for an opportunity to strike. It was a deadly cat-and-mouse game in the Kremlin corridors of power, where insignificant bureaucrats became overnight billionaires just because they were in the right place at the right time, supporting the right man, and were prepared to do almost anything to stay there and defend their corrupt place in the sun.

This meant Palin was surrounded by 'yes men' eager to please their leader by telling him what he wanted to hear in return for favours and promotion. This included generals, high-level diplomats and economic advisers. Suspicious by nature, Palin sensed this and turned to Karlov for advice. This gave Karlov a unique opportunity to influence policy and gain advance notice of what Palin had in mind and wanted to achieve.

However, because facts and reality were often distorted by the time they reached the president, Palin was seriously out of touch with what was actually happening. This created a dangerous environment that had a momentum of its own, like a snowball rolling down the hill becoming an unstoppable avalanche as it races towards the valley below.

Patient and perceptive, Karlov used this to his advantage to keep his adversaries in check and disguise his own plans until the time was right and his plans could turn into an unstoppable avalanche of their own. It was a delicate balancing act that required constant vigilance, and it was that vigilance that had triggered the urgent meeting with Serapion in Gorky Park.

'Things are happening much faster than we thought,' said Karlov.

'What do you mean?'

'Remember we discussed the military exercises between Russia and Belarus?'

'Sure.'

'Manoeuvres are taking place right now near Belarus's western border with Poland and Lithuania and also to the south, close to the border with Ukraine.'

'I know. NATO is on high alert and fears an invasion of Ukraine.'

'And with good reason.'

'What are you telling me?' asked Serapion, frowning. 'Surely not …'

'Palin has just ordered tens of thousands of troops to take up positions near the Ukraine border, and having troops in Belarus brings Russian forces much closer to Kyiv, which is just ninety kilometres from the border with Belarus. Well within reach of long-range, multiple-launch rocket systems.'

'He wouldn't dare.'

'That's what I thought, until yesterday.'

'But only a week ago the deputy foreign minister denied there were plans to invade Ukraine.'

'All lies and deception.'

'Seriously?'

'Yes. Palin talks about denazification of Ukraine and the threat of imminent genocide of the Russian population living there.'

'This is absurd!'

'Absurd or not, he's preparing the way for war.'

'And the generals are going along with this?'

'Many of them are war hawks. They're encouraging Palin and grossly exaggerating the capabilities of the Russian forces. At the same time, they're dismissing Ukraine's military capacity and will to put up resistance and fight.'

'Dangerous. What happened yesterday?'

'Palin made a decision.'

'To invade Ukraine?'

'Yes.'

'When?'

'He's waiting until the Beijing Winter Olympics are finished. The closing ceremony is on 20 February. The invasion will happen shortly after that. That way, no rain will fall on the president's parade.'

'Palin made a deal with the president?'

'Let's call it an understanding.'

Serapion shook his head in disbelief. 'Ukraine will fight. There will be massive resistance, and NATO – no, the entire West – will support Ukraine and stand behind its people; you'll see. And there will be serious opposition to this in Russia too. Novotny and his Foundation will see to that.'

'I agree. It's so obvious but Palin doesn't see it, or doesn't want to. He believes the Russian troops will be welcomed as liberators.'

'Really?'

'He does. That's what the generals are telling him. It will all be over in three days, they say. Reality is on a collision course with fiction here.'

'That's crazy.'

'I agree. Tank crews are to be issued with dress uniforms for a victory parade in Kyiv, would you believe, and provisions for only three days.'

'*Madness!* They should be issuing them with body bags.'

'You're right. This makes our plans even more urgent; you can see that, can't you?'

'About finding *Dextera Dei*, the holy relic?'

'Yes. Can you tell me how that's going?'

'I can, but you still haven't told me how an ancient relic, however significant, fits into all this and can make a difference. We're talking about war here, not some esoteric spiritual matter.'

'I know. It's better we leave it that way,' said Karlov, who had been expecting the question but was not prepared to answer it. 'You have to trust me with that.'

Not satisfied with the answer, Serapion decided to press on. 'Are you seriously suggesting that *Dextera Dei* can somehow influence events here?'

'I am.'

'Divine intervention?' came the tongue-in-cheek question.

'You could look at it that way, but with a little secular help,' said Karlov, smiling for the first time that morning.

'Ah, you're speaking in riddles.'

'I can't tell you more right now. In many ways I've already said too much. I can only repeat what I've told you before: *Dextera Dei* is key here. I have prepared the way with Palin. He *believes*, you see.'

'And that will make a difference?'

'Yes, I think so if handled correctly, because there's only one way to deal with someone like Palin. Ultimately, there is only one way to stop a deranged megalomaniac with so much power ...'

Karlov looked across to the large ice rink teeming with skaters of all ages. 'Power that includes access to one of the largest nuclear arsenals in the world,' he added quietly.

Serapion turned and frowned at Karlov as he realised what Karlov was talking about.

'Armageddon?'

Karlov nodded.

'Stopping ... or removing?' asked Serapion.

'One and the same thing.'

'I see.'

'Have you been able to persuade Jack Rogan to come on board?' asked Karlov, changing the subject.

'As a matter of fact, I have. If anyone can do this, he can. After all, he was the one who found Kazanskaya Bogomater and returned it to where it belongs. And now he's found *Golgotha*.'

'Excellent.'

'I often see Palin standing in front of Kazanskaya Bogomater in his office,' said Karlov, changing the subject again.

'Doing what?'

'Dreaming of his place in history.' Karlov sighed. 'We speak of nothing else lately, and that worries me more than all the other things.'

'Why?'

'Because it's a sign of an unhinged mind, capable of anything.'

'And how are you planning to influence such a mind?' asked Serapion.

'Ah. That's where *Dextera Dei* comes into play. I've told him a lot about the holy relic, its history and its spiritual power. I told him the Germans were after *Golgotha* for the same reason: trying to find the relic.'

Serapion looked at Karlov in surprise. For the first time he could see where this was heading, even if he didn't quite understand how *Dextera Dei* could stop or remove Palin.

Karlov glanced at his watch. 'I have to get back. Please do everything you can to find that relic and keep me informed. I've put the idea into Palin's head that the success of his Ukraine venture depends on it. With the right hand of God on his side, well ...' Karlov shot Serapion a meaningful look. 'The fear of failure can be very powerful. Especially in a man like Palin.'

'I understand.' Serapion realised pressing Karlov further was pointless, but in a subtle way Karlov had provided sufficient hints to show where this was heading and why.

'As you can see, time is of the essence here,' continued Karlov. 'This is a race against one man's insanity and burning ambition. Once war starts, it has a momentum of its own. War is unpredictable. It's like stepping into the unknown, and for a man like Palin it's a point of no return. For him, losing is unthinkable and he will do whatever it takes to claim victory, and that could be very costly indeed. Not just for Russia and Ukraine, but for the entire world. Surely you can see that. Think of the nuclear arsenal.'

'Oh, I do.'

Karlov stopped at the colonnade and put his hand on Serapion's arm. 'We are instruments of destiny here, you and I, my friend. We cannot afford to fail.'

Serapion smiled as he remembered Jack saying something similar just before he handed over Kazanskaya Bogomater in the Alexander Nevsky Cathedral. 'No, we can't.'

Without saying another word, Karlov turned, adjusted his scarf and hurried towards the black Aurus Senat waiting for him with his security detail to take him back to the Kremlin.

55

Palazzo Alberti, Venice: 1 February

Jack stepped off the water taxi and knocked on the massive wooden door that faced the canal, which had welcomed visitors for centuries. Moments later a very pale-looking Bonato opened the door and, without saying a word, embraced him.

Jack had caught the first available flight from Paris to Venice, and with Dupree's words – *You'll get through this, just keep a cool head* – still ringing in his ears, followed Bonato inside.

Countess Kuragin, Tristan, and Cesaria Borroni, who had arrived earlier by train from Florence, were waiting in Jack's study. 'The nightmare I've been afraid of has become reality. What on earth happened?' said Jack. He took off his coat and sat down by the fireplace next to Cesaria.

'It's surprisingly simple,' said Cesaria, 'when you have a close look. Someone broke in through the temporary back door used by the tradesmen next to the pontoon. It was properly secured, but some kind of bolt cutter was used to cut through the chain and the lock was broken. Would have taken only a couple of minutes. Expert job.'

'When was that?'

'According to Bonato, around three am.'

'And then?'

The countess looked at Bonato standing by the door. 'Why don't you take it from here? After all, you saw most of it.'

In a few sentences, Bonato described his surreal encounter with the plague doctor.

'... When I heard a boat take off, I stopped counting and went outside to investigate. Nothing. I then called the countess and told her what happened.'

'And I called you and then Cesaria,' said the countess. 'She notified the local police here. They arrived an hour or so later.'

Jack ran his fingers through his hair and looked at Cesaria. 'Thank you for coming so promptly. I can't tell you what this means to me.'

'What are friends for? As soon as Grimaldi heard about this, he went straight to work.'

Cesaria held up the note left on Rahima's pillow. 'This was all he needed.'

'What do you mean?' asked Jack, frowning.

'This note is the crucial link that clearly points to O'Hara. And O'Hara is now firmly on the Europol radar with top priority.'

'At least that's something, I guess.'

'It is. In more ways than you can imagine. Thanks to Samartini, who managed to once again infiltrate O'Hara's DNB gambling site, ENFAST is now involved and has effectively closed down the site. The scared punters are running for cover.'

'When did that happen?'

'Just over a week ago.'

'That's marvellous. Congratulations.'

'And because O'Hara has recently lost his Oleg Ivanov connection, he's becoming increasingly isolated in Belarus.'

'Dupree told you?'

'We speak almost every day. Thanks to Lapointe and his dogged persistence, there is now a dedicated international law enforcement network hunting O'Hara. It's only a matter of time.'

Jack pointed to the note. 'Then how do we explain this? A professional, brazen abduction in the middle of the night? This isn't the action of an isolated man in Belarus losing his grip. On the contrary, this is the response of a dangerous, resourceful man – perhaps under pressure – but certainly not beaten.'

'True, but thanks to Bonato, we may have an important lead here,' said Cesaria.

'What kind of lead?'

'While the man's disguise gave nothing away, his voice did.'

'In what way?'

Cesaria pointed to Bonato. 'Tell us.'

'The man spoke with the distinctive accent of someone who comes from the south. Calabria, to be precise. I've worked with men from that area and recognised it straight away,' said Bonato. 'It's like a signature.'

'And what does that tell us?' said Cesaria.

'Mafia?' ventured Jack.

'Precisely. O'Hara is turning to his old contacts for help. Unfortunately for him, most of them are either dead or in jail. That narrows things down considerably. He must be really desperate.'

'And this could be helpful?'

'Definitely. Grimaldi certainly thinks so. He's confident that if we are patient and play our cards right here, we'll get to O'Hara.'

'*How?*'

'Through you.'

'What on earth do you mean?' snapped Jack, looking incredulous. 'My mother has just been abducted right here in my home, and I should be patient and play my cards right in the hope to get her back, preferably alive; is that it?'

Tristan walked over to Jack, put his hand on his shoulder and looked him in the eyes. 'Please listen to what Cesaria has to say,' he said quietly. 'It makes good sense, as you will see.'

'She told you already?'

'She did. Just before you arrived. Everyone is doing their utmost to help here. You will have to do the same and be part of the team. Never easy, I know, especially for someone like you.'

Feeling calmer, Jack looked at Cesaria. 'Sorry, it's just ...'

'No need to apologise, Jack. Just listen,' said Cesaria.

'All right. Let's hear it.'

56

Kraków, Poland: 2 February, morning

The short flight from Venice to Kraków took less than an hour and a half.

'Almost there,' said Jack and turned towards Tristan sitting next to him. He reached for Tristan's hand and squeezed it. 'Thanks.'

'What for?'

'For being the voice of reason.'

'What brought this on?' asked Tristan.

'I'm sure you know.'

'Persuading you to leave the investigation to Cesaria and the authorities, and focus instead on staying in contact with O'Hara?'

'To do his bidding again, you mean?'

'Yes, for now. Since his gambling site has effectively been closed down, you're the only point of contact left that will give Samartini a chance to locate him.'

'That's why I agreed to all this.'

'Nothing to do with finding the holy relic, then?' teased Tristan and raised an eyebrow.

'Am I that transparent? Of course I want to find *Dextera Dei*, after all we've been through. Everything here is somehow interconnected.'

'Why do you think Serapion wants to meet us in Kraków so urgently?'

'We'll find out soon enough. All he said was that he has received some vital information from Bishop Peeters in Ghent. Apparently, Brother Frederick has made some progress.'

'Ah, the Carmelite monk. Another smart move.'

'What do you mean?'

'Leaving the scholarly detective work to the experts.'

'You're right. We could never compete with that.'

'You found *Golgotha*. That was the breakthrough. You achieved in a couple of weeks what scholars have been trying to uncover for ages. That's your forte, Jack.'

'Right again.'

'I know you're terribly worried about Rahima; we all are.'

'What do you think? I'm sick with worry.'

'And the best thing you can do for her is what you do best.'

'And what's that?'

'Follow your breadcrumbs. The answer here is patience, keeping a cool head and biding your time.'

'*Not* my forte.'

'Necessity is a good teacher. Buckle up, we're about to land.'

Because there was little traffic, the taxi ride from John Paul II International Airport Kraków–Balice to Wawel Cathedral in Stare Miasto, Kraków's old town, took less than half an hour. Jack had called Serapion from the airport, and the abbot was already waiting for them at the entrance to the cathedral where a newly ordained Karol Wojtyla, later to become Pope John Paul II, had celebrated his first mass in the Wawel Crypt.

Serapion waved as Jack and Tristan crossed the square and walked towards the cathedral. 'I am very sorry about your mother,' said Serapion. 'Looks like we both have serious issues, yet you answered my call.'

'Always,' said Jack. 'There's no doubt O'Hara is behind the abduction, and until he's stopped once and for all, this isn't over. As you know, that's why I'm here.'

'I understand.' Serapion turned towards Tristan. 'And to have someone like you stand next to him will be a great help, especially when you hear what I have to tell you.'

'Thank you, Abbot,' said Tristan, taking a bow.

'As you will see in a moment, there are good reasons for meeting here.'

'I don't doubt it,' said Jack.

'We are following the trail of *Dextera Dei*?' asked Tristan.

'We are indeed. All thanks to *Golgotha* and the church in the painting. Let's go inside. I want to show you something. Please follow me.'

It was impossible not to be impressed by the grandeur inside the spectacular cathedral that housed the soul of a nation. A national treasure that had seen the coronation of Polish kings for centuries was also the place where most of the Polish royalty had been buried, together with Poland's greatest national heroes, poets, four saints and many bishops.

Serapion seemed to know the cathedral well and led the way down into the crypt, where Polish kings had been laid to rest since the fourteenth century. As a depository of Polish history it had no equal.

'Here we are,' said Serapion and pointed to a large black sarcophagus with a wreath and wilted flowers on top. 'This is the tomb of Jan III Sobieski, arguably one of Poland's greatest kings. He died in 1696.'

'King of Poland and Grand Duke of Lithuania who defeated the Turks in the famous Battle of Vienna in … 1683?' said Jack.

Serapion looked impressed. 'Very good. He defeated the Grand Vizier Kara Mustapha and earned the gratitude of Europe for stopping the Ottoman advance. The Ottomans called him "Lion of Lechistan" and the pope called him the Saviour of Western Christendom. And in many ways he was just that. Had the Ottomans taken Vienna, there may have been no way to stop them.'

'Fascinating,' said Jack. 'But I'm sure you didn't bring us here just for a history lesson.'

'Of course not, but the history of all this is certainly relevant and important. It will put what I am about to tell you into its proper context. And as you will see in a moment, it's quite a story.'

Tristan squeezed Jack's arm, and Jack gave him a gentle shove in silent reply, the storyteller in him on high alert.

'The reason I brought you here is this: According to Brother Frederick, who knows this subject like no other, *Golgotha* pointed the way to a small church in the village of Grotenberge near Ghent. This was the missing link that had eluded him for so long, and now seems to have opened many doors and possibilities. The pieces of this baffling historical puzzle seem to be finally falling into place.'

'I can sense a *but* coming up,' said Jack.

'You're right. Unfortunately, there is. While Brother Frederick has been able to clearly identify the church in van Eyck's painting by its distinctive bell tower, that's where the good news ends.'

'Because it no longer exists?' said Tristan.

'Perceptive, as usual. Correct. The church was razed by marauding Calvinists during the Beeldenstorm, the Great Iconoclasm that spread like madness through Flanders in 1566. Not only did the fanatics destroy paintings and statues, they even burned down the church itself. Perhaps by accident; who knows?'

'Does this mean the holy relic – if it was in fact kept there – was also destroyed?' asked Jack.

'It seems not. Brother Frederick has some amazing contacts in unexpected places. He has been able to track down some old village records that specifically mention the fire.'

'And?' prompted Jack.

'To cut a long story short, there's a reference to a village priest who heard about the approach of the Calvinist mob. Apparently, he was able to hastily collect certain church treasures and leave the village before the mob arrived and began their rampage.'

'Is that it?' said Jack.

'No. There's more. A precious holy relic – the church's greatest treasure – is specifically mentioned.'

'Amazing. Do we know what happened to it?'

'The priest came here to Kraków and brought the relic with him. Apparently, he was welcomed here and given sanctuary because of it.'

'How extraordinary,' said Jack, shaking his head. 'And Brother Frederick has been able to find all this out in such a short time?'

'Looks that way.'

'Do we know if that holy relic was in fact *Dextera Dei*, given by the last grand master of the Templars to his confessor for safekeeping just before he was burned at the stake?' asked Tristan.

'You will be able to judge that for yourself when you hear what else I have to tell you.'

Jack pointed to the sarcophagus. 'There's obviously a connection here, otherwise you wouldn't have brought us to this place, right?'

'There is. Once Brother Frederick realised *Dextera Dei* may have ended up here in Kraków, he immediately followed up another lead, a legend circulating here in Poland that could shed more light on this whole saga.'

'He has been busy,' said Jack.

'He's waited a lifetime for this breakthrough,' said Serapion. 'And it seems he's about to be rewarded for his diligence.'

'What legend?' asked Tristan.

'Just before going to fight the Ottomans at Vienna, King Jan III Sobieski was given something precious by the Archbishop of Kraków, right here in this very cathedral.'

'A blessing?' ventured Tristan, smiling.

'That too, of course, but more than that. Something not only to protect him, but also to help him defeat the invaders threatening Christendom. Something that had the power to fight evil, and triumph.'

'What was he given?' said Jack.

'A holy relic that had been kept right here in the cathedral.'

Jack had the familiar feeling as the fine hairs on the back of his neck stood up. 'Do we know what it was?' he asked quietly.

'Not exactly. We do know it was called *Zbawiciel*, which means Saviour in Polish. We also know that the king wore it around his neck during the battle.'

'Astonishing!' said Tristan. 'Do we know what happened to it?'

'Unfortunately, Brother Frederick wasn't able to take this further at this stage. He ran out of contacts.'

'Is that it, then?' said Jack.

'No, it isn't. He may have run out of contacts, but I haven't.'

'What do you mean?' asked Jack.

'I've taken a leaf out of your book.'

'Oh? In what way?'

'I'm following my own breadcrumbs.'

'*You are?* Can you tell us more?'

'The archbishop here is a good friend of mine. We've known each other a long time. When I approached him with this fascinating conundrum, he was able to help.'

'How?'

'He introduced me to someone special.'

'Special?'

'A former Carmelite nun who had to leave the order because she was too worldly for a life of prayer and contemplation. A brilliant historian in her youth, she joined the order after a great personal tragedy, only to find out years later she wasn't suited for monastic life because her passion for history was too strong. She left the order and wrote a book that is quite famous here in Poland. It's all about Jan III Sobieski and the Polish–Ottoman Wars, especially the Battle of Vienna.'

'And this could help us?' said Jack.

'I believe so.'

'You've already spoken to her, haven't you?' said Tristan.

'Yes, I have.'

'And?'

'I think it would be best if you could meet her in person and hear firsthand what she has to say. That way, nothing can get lost. Intriguing woman by the way, with a special aura. A little eccentric perhaps, but otherwise ...'

'That important?'

'Could be. She's quite elderly, but speaks good English.'

'So, where can we meet her?' asked Jack.

'The archbishop has kindly arranged a meeting.'

'When?'

'Today.'

'She's coming *here*?'

'No. While this would have been an excellent choice for a meeting, right here in front of the king's grave, there's another place that is even more appropriate and meaningful as far as our enquiries are concerned. That's why we're meeting her there.'

'What kind of place?' asked Tristan.

'It's in Warsaw. Three hours from here by car.'

'How intriguing,' said Jack. 'You certainly know how to create anticipation and make us curious.'

'You think so? I thought that was strictly the province of a successful thriller writer,' teased Serapion.

'Obviously not,' said Jack, shaking his head. 'Clerics have been doing this much better than writers for centuries.'

'Let me take you to her. The archbishop's car is waiting outside. Let's go.'

57

Capuchin Church of the Transfiguration, Warsaw: 2 February, afternoon

'Here we are,' said Serapion and pointed ahead.

'Another church?' said Jack.

'What did you expect? After all, we're investigating a holy relic here, right?'

'Beautiful building,' said Tristan. 'Baroque?'

'It is. It was commissioned by none other than Jan III Sobieski after his victories in the battles of Khotyn and Vienna,' said Serapion. 'As a votive offering. That's why part of him is buried right here.'

'I don't understand,' said Jack. 'What do you mean *part* of him is buried here? We've just seen his grave in Kraków this morning.'

'We have, but his heart is right here, and that's why we've come here to meet Magosia Kaminski, the former Carmelite nun I told you about. She'll be waiting for us in the King's Chapel. She likes to be called Sister Magosia, by the way. She's a little unusual ...'

Jack looked at Tristan. 'We've been warned, mate.'

'We have.'

'That's her,' said Serapion and pointed to a tiny woman dressed all in black – eyes closed, head bowed – kneeling on a prie-dieu facing a sarcophagus. Serapion walked ahead and helped the woman, who was struggling to get up. Leaning on Serapion's arm, the old woman turned and squinted in Tristan's direction. 'Is that the one?' she asked in English, her voice strong for someone well past ninety, and pointed a shaking finger at Tristan. Her manner displayed the impatience of the elderly who understand the value of time because it is precious, and running out.

'Yes, that's him, Sister Magosia.'

'Come closer, young man, so I can see you better.'

Tristan stepped forward.

'Abbot Serapion told me that you can hear the whisper of angels and glimpse eternity; is that true?'

'He can,' said Jack and also came closer.

'I wonder what eternity looks like. Can you describe it for us, young man?'

'Impossible to put into words,' said Tristan. 'It's more like a vision, a *feeling* that appears without warning in certain situations. Very moving.'

'Ah.' Sister Magosia looked at Jack and nodded. 'And you must be the one who found Kazanskaya Bogomater, the lost icon, and returned it to Russia?'

'Yes, that's Mr Rogan, whom I told you about,' said Serapion.

'I see. And now you've found *Golgotha*, Mr Rogan; you must be truly blessed.'

'I did. As for being blessed, I'm not so sure.'

'And that's what brings you here? *Golgotha*?'

'Yes.'

'Certain things in life are preordained, you know. Is this one of those moments, I wonder?' she prattled on. 'I think it is. I can feel it.'

Sister Magosia turned towards Tristan. 'Can you feel it too, young man?'

'I can.'

'And can you perhaps glimpse something?'

'No, but I can *feel* ...'

'And what might that be, I wonder?'

'I think this is a moment of destiny,' said Tristan softly.

Sister Magosia nodded. 'It could well turn out to be that. If somehow I were to finally find out where *Zbawiciel* originally came from, that *would* be a moment of destiny. Especially for me. I've spent most of my life trying to find the answer to that question. And if *Golgotha* can show us the way, then it would truly be *Dextera Dei*, the right hand of God guiding us.'

'We are here to find out if that is so,' said Serapion.

'Indeed. I met Pope John Paul II right here in front of this sarcophagus in 1978. He was kneeling over there, praying, just as I was when you walked in. We spoke about *Zbawiciel* and the heart of Sobieski, which is kept in that sarcophagus over there, waiting.'

'Waiting, you say? Waiting for what?' asked Tristan.

'Pope John Paul said it was waiting for an appointment with eternity.'

Sister Magosia's appearance and demeanour reminded Jack of Mother Theresa. A similarly striking, furrowed face radiating kindness and compassion, despite having seen much suffering, and bent-over frame hinting at a curved spine and advanced osteoporosis. Ravages of old age that may have restricted her movement, but hadn't defeated her spirit or agile mind.

'What can you tell us about *Zbawiciel*, the legendary relic Sobieski wore around his neck when riding into battle and never took off?' asked Serapion. 'Do you know what happened to it after he died?'

'Yes, I do.'

Sister Magosia was silent, the anticipation growing by the second.

At last, she slowly raised her arm and pointed to the sarcophagus in front of her. 'It was buried right here, next to Sobieski's heart.'

More silence as everyone digested what she had said.

'Are you suggesting it's still there?' probed Jack gently.

'No, it isn't.'

'What happened to it; do you know?'

'It answered a desperate call for help to defeat a terrible evil.'

'What evil?' asked Jack, a cold shiver tickling his neck.

'Have you heard of the Holodomor?'

'The 1932 Terror-Famine that killed millions of Ukrainians?' said Serapion.

'Yes.'

'How did an ancient relic buried in a marble sarcophagus next to a king's heart "waiting for an appointment with eternity" do that?' asked Jack.

Sister Magosia smiled. 'I'll tell you.'

Olesko, Ukraine: March 1933

So weak he was barely able to walk, Father Chernenko tried to ignore the corpses littering the streets as he staggered past them on his way back to his church. Men and women of all ages and, sadly, many children too, just collapsed and died where they fell, their contorted, emaciated bodies rotting out in the open, instead of receiving a decent burial. Victims one and all of a terrible famine that became known as the Holodomor.

Yet this was no natural famine. This Terror-Famine was strategically and intentionally created by the leaders of the Soviet Union, especially Stalin, Molotov and Kaganovich, to crush Ukrainian opposition to Soviet rule and snuff out nationalistic aspirations for an independent Ukrainian state.

In order to achieve this, the Kremlin created laws and conditions to completely deprive the Ukrainian population of food supplies. This brutal, oppressive regime had only one aim: to systematically starve Ukraine into submission, and cause death to depopulate the region. So effective was Stalin's deadly stranglehold on Ukraine, that at the height of the Holodomor in the spring of 1933, some twenty-four thousand people died of starvation every day. An estimated five million Ukrainians perished as a direct result of this genocide.

Father Chernenko staggered into church, dragged himself to the altar and fell to his knees, asking the Lord for guidance. He had just given absolution to one of his parishioners, a schoolteacher he had known for years. Just before he died, the teacher, a learned man, had whispered the words: '*Zbawiciel* is the answer.'

What did he mean by that? the priest kept asking himself. Then he remembered something. He went into the sacristy and searched for a book: *A History of Olesko Castle*, the most prominent building in the village. It didn't take long to find what he was looking for: a reference to *Zbawiciel*, a legendary relic, and Jan III Sobieski, the famous Polish king who had been born in Olesko Castle and was buried in Poland.

During the night, Chernenko had a dream. Saint Olga of Kyiv, Ukraine's patron saint of defiance and vengeance, appeared and told him what to do.

It took Chernenko several weeks to travel from Olesko to Warsaw. He walked most of the way, as almost all the horses had been eaten a long time ago and there were few farm carts left to hitch a ride on. Travel was strictly forbidden and bargaining for food severely punished. For those reasons, he had to hide in churches and deserted barns to avoid capture by the authorities, and scavenge for whatever food he could find in the deserted fields.

He crossed the border into Poland during a thunderstorm and made his way to Warsaw, where he was found by a church attendant lying unconscious in front of Sobieski's sarcophagus containing the king's heart.

Deeply moved by Chernenko's account of the horrendous famine ravaging Ukraine, and convinced of the intervention of Saint Olga, the archbishop granted Chernenko's unusual request and ordered the sarcophagus be opened.

* * *

'That happened in June 1933,' said Sister Magosia. Many years later, I spoke to someone, a priest, who actually witnessed what took place in the King's Chapel. I was doing research for my book at the time and relied on that eyewitness account to tell the story of *Zbawiciel*, and what happened to it.'

'What did happen?'

'When the sarcophagus was opened, the holy relic was found resting on a golden plate next to the vessel containing Sobieski's heart.'

'What did the relic look like; do we know?' asked Serapion, watching Sister Magosia carefully.

'Yes, we do. The priest described it to me.' Sister Magosia closed her eyes and turned her head towards the sarcophagus. 'It was a small piece of dark wood with part of an iron nail embedded in it, and a thin gold chain that had once belonged to Sobieski was threaded through a tiny hole in the wood.'

Jack looked at Serapion and nodded. Tristan reached for Jack's hand and squeezed it.

'I believe we have our answer, Sister Magosia,' said Serapion softly. 'I think this is indeed a moment of destiny.'

'Why do you say that, Abbot?'

'Because the description you just gave perfectly matches the reliable description of *Dextera Dei* we have. I have no doubt that *Zbawiciel* and *Dextera Dei* are one and the same.'

'If that is so, can you tell me how a piece of the holy cross on which the Saviour died, found its way to Warsaw, and how *Dextera Dei* became *Zbawiciel?*' asked Sister Magosia.

'I can,' said Jack. 'But before I do, can you tell us what happened after the sarcophagus was opened?'

'The archbishop presented *Zbawiciel* to Father Chernenko so he could take it back to Ukraine to fight the evil Terror-Famine, as instructed by Saint Olga in his dream.'

'And did he?'

'Yes. He returned to Ukraine and took *Zbawiciel* to the Church of the Tithes in Kyiv, where Saint Olga is buried. Sadly, by then it was too late to save the population. More than five million Ukrainians had died in the Terror-Famine. Entire villages had been wiped out and were deserted, but the Soviet government denied a famine had taken place at all, and tried to cover up the genocide. Russian settlers were brought in to repopulate the devastated countryside, and the famine subsided slowly after the 1933 harvest, but only after *Zbawiciel* had been taken from village to village to drive out evil.'

'And *Zbawiciel?* What happened to it; do you know?'

Sister Magosia shook her head sadly. 'Then, a few years later came the Germans, bringing more suffering, and *Zbawiciel* disappeared in the mists of war.'

'Is that the end of it?' asked Jack.

'I don't think so,' said Tristan. 'Saint Olga will be back to avenge the atrocities of the Holodomor, and so will *Zbawiciel*, isn't that right, Sister Magosia?'

Sister Magosia looked at Tristan in surprise. 'How do you know this? Yes, some believe this is so. After all, she is the patron saint of defiance and vengeance, and many souls are looking for the retribution they deserve.'

Sister Magosia turned towards Jack and looked at him with myopic eyes. 'Now, please tell me what you know about *Dextera Dei*.'

'It all began with Richard the Lionheart and the Battle of Jaffa in 1192, the final battle of the Third Crusade,' said Jack. He then gave a step-by-step account of what happened to *Dextera Dei* after Richard's return and incarceration in Dürnstein Castle, and how the holy relic found its way to Grotenberge after the last grand master of the Templars had been burned at the stake.

Serapion then stepped in and explained the significance of the church in van Eyck's painting *Golgotha*, and how that church had recently – thanks to Brother Frederick – shown the way to Sobieski and the Capuchin Church in Kraków.

Sister Magosia listened in silence. When she looked in Jack's direction, he noticed she was crying. Without saying a word, Jack walked over to her and put an arm around her bony shoulders. It was a spontaneous act of kindness shown towards a special human being who, nearing the end of her life, had just glimpsed eternity.

For a while the two stood in silence. Then Sister Magosia said something to Jack only he could hear: 'After all this, do you still doubt you are blessed? Now, please help me kneel. I must pray.'

Jack received a phone call from Cesaria shortly after dinner at the archbishop's residence.

'It looks like we may have a breakthrough,' said Cesaria.

'In what way?' asked Jack, trying to stay calm as he sensed excitement in her voice.

'Not on the phone. Better come back to Venice as soon as you can.'

'Do you know where she is?'

'No, not yet, but we may have found someone who does.'

'I'm on my way.'

'See you when you get here.'

'Thank you, Cesaria.'

'For you anything, my friend,' said Cesaria and hung up.

58

Looking for inspiration and hoping for a sign, Palin stood in front of Kazanskaya Bogomater, the famous icon he had brought into the Kremlin from Yekaterinburg for his own personal use. Like all men of power, surrounded by intimidated men who didn't have the courage to express their own opinions or honestly advise the president, Palin turned to spiritual sources and the occult for guidance and approval in the hope he was making the right decisions that would make history. Because the icon had guided Russian generals like Pozharsky and Kutuzov to victory before, Palin, who despite the invincible exterior he displayed in public was plagued by insecurities and doubts, needed reassurance and approval, preferably from a higher power.

Because the controversial decision he had made and was about to implement had far-reaching consequences and, in many ways, represented a point of no return, Palin was looking for some kind of sign from above to tell him that he was following the right path.

Unfortunately, Kazanskaya Bogomater, the Madonna, remained stubbornly silent.

Palin returned to his desk and looked again at the map of Russia before the humiliating disintegration brought about by Gorbachev's *glasnost* and *perestroika* in the late 1980s. Running his fingers along the old boundaries seemed to calm him because he saw in it his dream of returning Russia to its former glory and justification for his own ambitions. Palin was desperately trying to take what he considered to be his rightful place in history next to the other famous leaders like Suvorov, Lenin and Stalin, who had made Russia powerful and great.

Tired and wary of the predictable opinions of his generals and advisers, Palin picked up the phone and called the only man he believed he could trust.

'Still in your office?' asked Palin.

'Of course.'

'Could you come over to see me?'

'Sure. When?'

'Right now.'

'I'm on my way.'

When Karlov was admitted to the president's office, Palin was sitting behind his desk surrounded by a clutter of open books and papers. He looked like some possessed academic doing research. Karlov walked over to the desk, looked at the books and smiled as he recognised what Palin was doing.

The prophecies of Daniel, thought Karlov, *and Revelation 13.* Exactly what he'd suggested Palin should look at.

'Well, what do you make of it all?' asked Karlov.

Palin pointed to the clutter on his desk. 'I was hoping you would be able to help me with all this.'

'Perhaps I can.'

'Sit down and listen to this: According to Daniel here, Nebuchadnezzar II, king of Babylon, had a dream in 603 BC—'

'Sent to him by God,' said Karlov. 'In the dream, God revealed the rise and fall of certain major kingdoms.'

'Quite. In that dream, the king saw a strange statue made of different metals, each metal representing the rise of a new kingdom.'

'It begins with the rise of Babylon, a great empire, and ends with the second coming of Christ. Nebuchadnezzar destroyed the Temple of Jerusalem and was responsible for the Babylonian Captivity of the Jewish people,' said Karlov, watching Palin carefully. 'And for that he was severely punished.'

'In what way?'

'He was driven out into the wilderness for seven years, away from people and everything he knew. He lost his sanity and was forced to eat grass like a beast. He was humbled by God for boasting about his achievements.'

'A fall from grace?'

'You could say that.' Karlov pointed to the desk in front of him. 'I see you're looking at the scriptures – Daniel,' he said, changing direction.

'I am. You told me about his prophecies, remember?'

'I did, but you may not know there's a parallel prophecy in Daniel 7 to the dream you just mentioned.'

'There is? What's it about?'

'According to biblical scholars these prophecies add greater clarity to Nebuchadnezzar's famous dream.'

'In what way?'

'They help us understand what will happen after the fall of the Roman Empire. In Daniel's prophecy, instead of a statue made up of different metals, each of which represent the rise of a new kingdom, these events are represented by a beast that comes out of the sea. That brings us to the little horn, a beast with certain awesome powers.'

'How strange.'

'Perhaps, but we are given certain important clues by Daniel that help us identify this beast and what it's capable of.'

'Tell me.'

'Certain scholars believe the little horn is none other than the Roman Catholic Church. The Papacy.'

'Come on, is that what Abbot Serapion believes? You only met with him the other day in Gorky Park.'

Karlov shrugged, well aware the FSB was keeping Palin informed of his every move. Palin was keeping even his close friends close. 'He's convinced that according to the prophecies we mentioned, we're living in Earth's last days.'

'Seriously?'

'Yes. In support, he points to Revelation 13, which I see you've also been looking at.'

'I have. Just as you told me to. And this brings us to the number 666.'

'Representing the devil. And what does Revelation 13 tell us about this number?' said Karlov.

'It's the number of the beast.'

'That we have just identified as the Catholic Church.'

'That's a little far-fetched, isn't it? I would have thought the USA was a much better candidate here.'

'That country has a significant part to play in all this too, as you will see.'

'But what does all this mean?' asked Palin. 'Here, today? Prophecies are open to interpretation and speculation, and can be manipulated to fit the facts.'

'I know you're looking for a sign,' said Karlov, trying to return to the subject that really mattered. 'According to Serapion, that sign will come in the form of a holy relic, *Dextera Dei*, a piece of the holy cross on which Christ died. *Dextera Dei*, the right hand of God, will show itself when the time is right. And it will show itself to the victor who will prevail in all this,' said Karlov, well aware Palin was hanging on his every word.

'Was that the reason the Nazis were after it? Why Hitler wanted so desperately to get his hands on it?'

'Yes. Should *Dextera Dei* show itself now, it would certainly be a potent sign.'

'Is that what Serapion thinks?' asked Palin, obviously looking for reassurance.

'Yes, he does. And he believes he can find the holy relic because its time has come. He also believes the time is right for it to reveal itself, and that it will do so right here in Russia, at a significant moment in history.'

Palin gazed at Karlov, the veins throbbing at his temples the only sign of the excitement boiling within. 'And what do *you* think?' he asked.

'*Golgotha* has provided Serapion with some telling clues and is showing him the way. He's a man of destiny, and so are you.'

'I hope you're right, because we are now committed. As you know, I have given orders to prepare for the invasion of Ukraine.

Our troops are on the move already and are assembling at the border. Exercises for now, but soon ... I have even chosen a date. We can wait no longer.'

'I understand.'

'I hope you do, because once we start this, we cannot turn back,' said Palin.

'I understand that too.'

Palin pointed to the books on his desk. 'And where do we fit into all this? Is Russia part of these prophecies we've been talking about?'

Karlov took his time before giving his answer. 'We'll find out soon enough.'

'Through the right hand of God?' asked Palin.

'Yes, I believe it will show us the way. It will protect Russia, defeat the evil forces threatening to destroy it, and lead the country to victory,' said Karlov softly, well aware he was articulating a very different prophecy of his own that had nothing to do with the scriptures, but was anchored in the present.

'In that case, you better find it soon and bring it to me.'

'I will do everything in my power to make that possible.'

'I know you will, and in doing that, you too will become part of history,' said Palin.

In more ways than you can possibly imagine, thought Karlov, smiling as he remembered the deadly, secret plan involving *Dextera Dei* he had discussed with Serapion in Gorky Park.

Palin opened one of the desk drawers and took out a bottle of vodka. Then he pushed the open books aside – the gesture dismissive – placed the bottle on the top of the desk in front of him and grinned at Karlov.

'Drink?'

59

Palazzo Alberti, Venice: 3 February

Jack and Tristan took the six twenty-five flight from Warsaw to Venice. It was due to arrive at eight am.

'I told you something would turn up, didn't I?' said Tristan. 'No need to fret.'

'You can be so infuriating,' said Jack.

'I know. You've told me that many times.'

'How can you stay so calm?'

'It's the best way. Surely you can see that.'

'As I said, infuriating! What do you think Cesaria may have found?'

'I think she's closing in on the kidnapper.'

'That's what I thought. Mafia, no doubt. Could be tricky.'

'Did you expect it to be any other way?'

'I suppose not.'

Cesaria was in a meeting with Carabinieri from the police station at San Marco. She was briefing the officers in Jack's study when Jack and Tristan walked in.

'Perfect timing,' said Cesaria and made the introductions. 'Please take a seat.'

'We came as soon as we could,' said Jack.

'I can see that.' Cesaria turned to face the Carabinieri watching her intently. 'I just had a call from Chief Prosecutor Grimaldi in Florence. His reputation as a Mafia hunter speaks for itself. As you can imagine, he has access to perhaps the most extensive network of Mafia informers in Italy.'

'And this has been helpful?' asked one of the Carabinieri.

'Looks that way. I don't have to remind you that everything I'm about to tell you is strictly confidential and must not leave this room.

Lives depend on it. As you'll see in a moment, we're dealing with some of the most dangerous and desperate criminals in the country. Some of the few who are still at large and have escaped the net of the recent arrests, and the trials in Lamezia Terme in Calabria.'

Cesaria paused to let this sink in. The officers in the room nodded.

'The Squadra Mobile in Florence, and Grimaldi, in particular, have been instrumental in putting many of the prominent Mafia figures behind bars during those trials last year,' continued Cesaria. 'Some senior members of the crime families are serving time in the high-security Pagliarelli Prison in Palermo.'

'We know,' said one of the officers.

'Please keep in mind an abduction like this doesn't happen in a vacuum. This has been carefully planned and was professionally executed. It has all the hallmarks of a classic Mafia operation. Someone put a team together to carry this out. One man alone couldn't have done this. Agreed?'

The officers in the room nodded again. Then one of them asked, 'But to what purpose? As far as we know, there's been no ransom demand, no contact, nothing. This just doesn't fit. What do we make of that?'

Cesaria made eye contact with Jack. 'That brings me to the recent developments I wanted to discuss with you,' she said, ignoring the question. 'We had a breakthrough.'

'What kind of breakthrough?' asked one of the officers.

'One of Grimaldi's informers came up with a gem: a corrupt prison guard working in the Pagliarelli prison has been helping Mafia bosses make contact with the outside world. The guard was questioned yesterday by prosecutor Donizetti. Quite robustly, I understand. Donizetti was the one who put many of these high-profile Mafia players behind bars and threw away the key. You'll remember she was almost killed during an assassination attempt at Catanzaro airport last year. Mr Rogan was there and almost got shot himself; isn't that right, Jack?'

'I was right there. It happened on the tarmac as we were getting out of a helicopter. It was a close call. Prosecutor Donizetti's bodyguard was killed and Donizetti was injured and rushed to hospital. The assassin was also killed.'

'Yes, Alfonso Falcone, a particularly nasty character. The police in Calabria had been after him for years. Remember the name, because you will hear it again in a moment. The reason Donizetti was called in to interrogate the prison guard was his connection to one of the most powerful Mafia capos who Donizetti successfully prosecuted and put behind bars: Riccardo Giordano.'

'Seriously?' said Jack, surprised. '*Giordano* is involved in this?'

'He is,' said Cesaria. 'Apparently, he's been trying to rebuild his drug business by contacting his associates on the outside during his time in Pagliarelli. In many ways he's still calling the shots, especially in Florence.'

'How was he able to do that?' asked Jack.

'The prison guard gave him access to a phone and also acted as a messenger and go-between. In effect, he became a Riccardo accomplice and part of his corrupt network. Classic Mafia. Simple and effective.'

'Astonishing,' said one of the police officers, shaking his head. 'But how is this relevant to our investigation here?'

'I'm coming to that,' said Cesaria. 'I had to tell you about the background first, so you can fully appreciate what is involved here. We just spoke about Alfonso Falcone, the assassin who was killed at Catanzaro airport. Well, this is about his brother, *Fabio*, another notorious hit man and one of the most wanted fugitives in Calabria.'

Cesaria paused to let this sink in.

'I've worked closely with prosecutor Donizetti during the Lamezia Terme trials, especially the Giordano case, because Giordano was one of the key players in the drug business in Florence,' continued Cesaria. 'We'd been after him for years. So, when Donizetti was told about a certain assignment involving Giordano that the prison guard had helped to set up, she contacted me at once.'

'What kind of assignment?' asked Jack, sensing Cesaria was about to tell him something of crucial importance.

'An abduction right here in Venice.'

Looking incredulous Jack broke the stunned silence. 'Are you suggesting Giordano is behind my mother's abduction?' he asked. 'And arranged it while serving a life sentence inside a maximum-security prison in Sicily?'

'It's more complicated than that. There's another important player involved here—'

'O'Hara,' said Tristan.

Surprised, Cesaria turned and looked at Tristan. 'Correct. Somehow, O'Hara managed to get in touch with Giordano in jail, and the prison guard acted as the go-between. That's how we found out about this. Because he's fully cooperating, we now know who abducted your mother, Jack. It was Fabio Falcone. Obviously, we know a lot about him and by now the whole country is looking for him and his associates, especially here in Venice. And that's where you come in, gentlemen,' said Cesaria. 'Finding Falcone is our top priority because he will lead us to Rahima Cordoba, Mr Rogan's mother, and your local knowledge and contacts will no doubt be invaluable in that regard.'

Cesaria continued the briefing for a while and explained why O'Hara was one of the most wanted men in Europe and firmly on the ENFAST radar, but she didn't go into the connection between O'Hara and Jack. After answering a few more questions, she closed the meeting and excused herself.

As the Carabinieri began to leave, she took Jack and Tristan aside. 'Jack, we have to talk,' she said.

'There's more, isn't there?' said Tristan. 'You just didn't want them to hear it.'

'Right, as usual,' said Cesaria. 'The real reason I wanted you to come back urgently has nothing to do with what I just told these guys, but is something far more important – and dangerous.'

'What?' said Jack.

'The prison guard told Donizetti something else. Something I didn't want to share with the local police here because it's much too sensitive. And as we all know, the Mafia has eyes and ears everywhere, especially here in Venice. Keeping a secret in Italy is harder than running a brothel in a convent. That's why I'm running this operation personally. Grimaldi arranged it through his contacts in Rome, right at the top. That's how we ran the Lamezia Terme trials, and that was one of the main reasons for their success.'

'What else did the guard tell Donizetti?' asked Jack.

'If the intelligence is accurate, there could be a way for us to get to Falcone and catch him – soon.'

'How?'

'Giordano's planning something. Something big. Right now. It has to do with his wife.'

'Giuseppina? Donizetti and I met her in a safe house in Calabria. As I understand it, her evidence was the main reason Giordano and several of his close associates were convicted.'

'And that's why he wants to kill her,' said Cesaria softly.

'*What!* He's planning a hit on his own wife?'

'Yes. It's all about revenge and face. Especially face. If you can't control your own wife, how can you control a drug empire, right?'

'But she's living in some safe house under witness protection, isn't she?'

'She is, but since when has that stopped the Mafia? Eyes and ears everywhere, remember?'

'And this could somehow help us?' said Jack.

'It sure could,' said Tristan, smiling.

'You know, don't you?' said Cesaria, shaking her head.

'Giordano has engaged Falcone to kill his wife. It's obvious. This is his next assignment. And it has nothing to do with O'Hara.'

'When?' asked Jack.

'Soon, we believe. Donizetti is setting a trap at the safe house. Apparently, Giuseppina is keen to cooperate.'

'All right, but surely Tristan and I have no part in this.'

'Not directly, no. I want you here because of what will, hopefully, come *after* we capture Falcone—'

'And he tells you where Rahima's being kept,' said Tristan.

'That's the plan.'

'Why should he tell you?' asked Jack.

'Donizetti has her ways. Falcone has been involved in several murders and is facing life in prison. For him, prison could be a very dangerous place. A man like Falcone has enemies everywhere, especially in prison. Donizetti has the power to protect him in jail. Self-preservation is an excellent bargaining tool, and the power of fear can be very persuasive, especially in the hands of someone like Donizetti, who is a master of both. Should we be able to capture Falcone, he will talk. You'll see.'

'And you want me here because?'

'Once we know where Rahima's being kept, I want you right there next to me when we find her. Surely you can see why.'

'Are you afraid of what you may find?'

Cesaria shrugged. 'I'm a realist. And that's another reason I want the local police here involved. Local knowledge and contacts go a long way in cases like this.'

Jack nodded. 'I can see that. So, for now, we just sit here and wait?'

'Yes, up to a point, but there's something we can do while we wait, and it concerns O'Hara.'

'O'Hara? In what way?' said Jack.

'You've spoken to him recently, haven't you?'

'Of course. He contacted me shortly after the abduction and told me what I had to do to keep Rahima safe. He wanted to know what I was up to. I told him about *Dextera Dei*, the holy relic, and the *Golgotha* connection. Now he too wants to get his hands on the relic. For him, this is a game, a power play he has to win. That's all. And I have no choice but to go along with it, at least for the time being, to keep my mother safe.'

'Typical O'Hara,' said Tristan. 'He must be furious about ENFAST destroying his gambling empire.'

'As we've seen, that makes him even more dangerous. The abduction makes this abundantly clear,' said Jack.

'More dangerous, or desperate?' said Cesaria.

'Perhaps both. He did sound almost incoherent on the phone at times, ranting ...'

'Excellent! Desperate people make mistakes. We want you to carry on as usual. That's vital. Clara has already examined the prison guard's phone that was used to talk to O'Hara. She's found a few important clues that could help her find out where O'Hara is hiding in Belarus. Clara and the entire ENFAST organisation are working on this right now, and they want access to your phone as well. Apparently, that could help them further to pinpoint where O'Hara is hiding. You know what Clara's like. You've seen what she did with OMERTA in the Lamezia Terme trials. She's an internet and telecommunications genius.'

'She is. So, you want us to stay here and be ready; is that it?'

'Yes. I'm staying here as well, because we believe Rahima is close by.'

'I hope you're right.'

'Don't worry, Jack, we'll get her back,' said Cesaria, seeing how dejected Jack looked.

'I agree,' said Tristan and put his arm around Jack. 'These guys are doing everything they can, and have made surprising progress in record time. Surely you can see that.'

'Of course I can. It's just ...'

'I know,' said Tristan. 'Rahima will be fine. I can *feel* it.'

'Any whispers?' asked Cesaria, smiling.

'Some, but we have to be careful and ready.'

'Ready for what?' asked Jack.

'For whatever happens,' said Tristan. 'And please stop worrying about *Dextera Dei* for a while. Serapion has gone to Ukraine to investigate what Sister Magosia told us about, remember? I can think of no-one better to do this, can you?'

'No. His church contacts will achieve much more than we could hope for. And besides, he speaks Russian.'

'See? Just leave it to him for now. Nothing to worry about. We're needed here.'

'It must be boring to be right all the time, don't you think, Cesaria?'

'I wouldn't know; I don't have that problem.'

60

Somewhere in the hills in Catanzaro, Calabria: 6 February

Falcone had been watching the remote farmhouse from a distance for two days to ensure the information he had received from his 'Ndrangheta source about the safe house was reliable. Satisfied that one of the two women living inside must be Giuseppina, Giordano's wife, and that the two young men who spent most of their time outside were police officers guarding the safe house, he was ready to make his move.

Having grown up on a farm and lived in Calabria most of his life gave Falcone the edge. Not only did he know the terrain, he also knew how people who lived on the land behaved, dressed, and about their appearance. He therefore knew how to blend in.

Because he had been unable to source a high-powered rifle like the BCM Europearms F Class he had used in assassinations before, killing Giuseppina from a safe distance without having to get close to the farmhouse was not an option. And besides, Giuseppina rarely went outside. Falcone needed a different approach. He had to get close enough to the safe house to use a handgun. Most likely this meant having to get inside the house and deal with the two police guards along the way. While this presented considerable challenges, Falcone felt confident he could tackle this. What was needed was careful planning, confidence and the element of surprise.

Dressed in old, well-worn clothes like one of the many shepherds tending their flocks in the hills, Falcone glanced at the sheep he had 'borrowed' from a nearby farmer he knew. He had also borrowed a dog he intended to use in his carefully planned approach. Old 'Ndrangheta contacts always helped one another and the code of silence was sacrosanct.

Falcone checked his gun with the silencer and slipped it into his coat pocket. Then he adjusted his old felt hat and picked up his staff.

It was just after sunrise and the morning fog was beginning to lift, giving him a clear view across the valley. Because he knew how to handle sheep, Falcone had no problem driving them slowly towards the safe house with the dog's help.

Sipping mugs of hot coffee, the two young police officers guarding the safe house were sitting on a bench by the front door, watching Falcone cross the valley. It was a peaceful scene that didn't cause any alarm or concern. Shepherds drove their flocks through the valley all the time.

When Falcone was within hearing distance of the house, he picked up his dog and slit one of its paws with a piece of barbed wire. The dog cried out in pain and began to yelp and howl as it tried to lick the blood gushing from the deep wound. Falcone looked at the police officers and waved.

'The dog cut his leg on some fencing wire,' he shouted. Carrying the yelping dog in his arms and with the sheep following behind, Falcone began to walk slowly towards the house. The two plain-clothed officers stood up and watched Falcone come closer.

Giuseppina had heard the commotion outside and peered out of one of the windows facing the front of the house.

'What is it?' asked the other woman in the room who shared the safe house with her. She was a close friend who had also given evidence against her husband and brother during the Lamezia Terme trials. Both men were serving life sentences in a Sicilian jail.

'Nothing. Just a shepherd with an injured dog.'

As Falcone came closer, Giuseppina felt a shiver of fear. Having witnessed much violence in her time, Giuseppina could tell something was wrong. Something about the man carrying the dog wasn't right. She couldn't quite identify what it was, but she could sense danger as Donizetti had warned her about a possible assassination attempt.

'He's badly hurt and bleeding,' said Falcone, trying to distract the officers. 'Do you have something we could use as a bandage to stop the blood?'

The officers looked at each other and shrugged, momentarily unsure what to do. A moment of hesitation was all Falcone needed.

By now he was close enough to take a shot. He dropped the yelping dog, pulled his gun out of his pocket and before the officers could react, shot one of them between the eyes, the powerful bullet blowing away the back of the young man's head. Stunned, the other officer reached for his gun, but Falcone shot him in the forehead before he could take aim and fire. He was dead before he hit the ground.

Giuseppina had seen it all from inside. '*An assassin!*' she shouted. 'Both officers are down. Get into the other room – quickly!'

Taking deep breaths to calm herself, Giuseppina hurried across the room to the broom cupboard and took out a loaded shotgun she always kept there. Then she joined the other woman in the next room, kept the door slightly ajar, and then listened and watched.

Slowly, the front door opened. Then the barrel of a gun appeared, followed by a hand. 'I know you're in here, Giuseppina,' said Falcone, his voice chillingly calm for a man who had just killed twice. He closed the door behind him, locked it from the inside, and slipped the key into his pocket.

'Your husband sends his regards,' continued Falcone, looking around. 'You may as well come out now. There's no point in hiding. You know I'll find you.'

Giuseppina watched Falcone come closer.

'Giuseppina, you know the rules. It's time to pay your debts.'

As the clock on the mantelpiece began to chime and Falcone turned his head towards the fireplace, Giuseppina saw her chance. Taking a deep breath, she kicked the door open, took aim with the shotgun and pulled the trigger.

61

Ospedale Mater Domini, Catanzaro: 7 February

Prosecutor Donizetti was waiting in the arrivals lounge of Lamezia Terme International Airport with two police officers by her side. The afternoon flight from Venice with Cesaria, Jack and Tristan on board had just landed.

Donizetti had called Cesaria the day before and briefed her on what had happened at the safe house that morning. She had called again early the next day and suggested Cesaria and Jack should come to Catanzaro as a matter of urgency.

'How could this have happened?' asked Cesaria as she embraced Donizetti.

'I'll tell you later. We must get out of here quickly.'

'I agree,' said Jack. 'Last time I was here you almost got killed.'

Donizetti waved dismissively. 'I was lucky, but this is a dangerous place. A police helicopter is standing by and will take us to the hospital in Catanzaro. It isn't far; come.'

The short flight from the airport to the Ospedale Mater Domini took less than twenty minutes. The helicopter landed in a car park nearby, and waiting police took them straight to the hospital.

'How is he?' asked Jack as they walked towards the hospital entrance.

'Hanging on by a thread. I couldn't talk to him until after the emergency operation,' said Donizetti. 'It was well past midnight by then. He has catastrophic injuries and is unlikely to survive. Giuseppina shot him in the chest at close range with a shotgun. You can imagine ...'

'What a lady! How is she?'

'Safe.'

Jack nodded. 'But you did manage to talk to Falcone? About my mother and the abduction, I mean?'

'Yes, of course. He was quite lucid for a man on death's doorstep, but please remember I have two dead young police officers to deal with. The dreaded 'Ndrangheta is once again rearing its ugly head despite the trials. This fight is far from over.'

'I understand, it's just—'

'*And?*' prompted Cesaria. She looked at Donizetti walking alongside her.

'As I told you this morning, he refused to tell me anything. I pleaded with him and spoke about Jack and his mother. There's no point in using threats or promises with a man who's about to die.'

Donizetti stopped and looked at Jack. 'He seemed to know a lot about you, which surprised me.'

'In what way?' said Jack.

'He spoke about your books, your trip to Russia, and the story about the holy icon and the pope. He seems very religious.'

'That would explain it,' said Tristan. 'Perhaps that's the reason he asked to see Jack.'

'Could be,' said Donizetti, 'but I suspect there's more. The last thing he said before the morphine kicked in was that he would talk to Jack about his mother, but *only* to Jack. Not on the phone, but in person.'

'Why do you think he stipulated that?' asked Cesaria.

'No idea. I rang you straight away and here you are. I thought it was worth a try.'

'I agree,' said Jack. 'He may be the only one who can tell us what happened to my mother.'

'And more importantly, tell us where she is,' said Cesaria.

'I think he will,' said Tristan.

Donizetti looked at Tristan, surprised. 'What makes you say that?'

Tristan shrugged. 'Just a feeling.'

'A *feeling?*' repeated Donizetti. 'We may need a little more than that—'

'I told you about Tristan, remember?' Cesaria cut in.

'Yes, you did. Whispers of angels ... I hope he's right. We need all the help we can get.'

Jack held the hospital door open. 'We should find out soon enough,' he said and followed Donizetti to the lifts.

Donizetti hurried along the corridor on the first floor, which was teeming with police, walked up to the doctor waiting for her in front of Falcone's room and spoke to him briefly.

'He's awake,' said Donizetti, turning to Jack standing behind her, 'and waiting for you. According to the doctor here, that's what seems to be keeping him alive for now. He refused to take morphine and is in great pain. He could slip away at any moment. Better hurry. We'll wait here.'

Jack nodded, walked past the doctor and opened the door to Falcone's hospital room.

ICUs look the same wherever they are: dimmed lights, sudden silences, the flashing lights of the life-support machines, countless tubes and monitoring devices attached to the motionless body lying on the bed, a life hanging in the balance.

Falcone's head was turned towards the door. His eyes were open and he was watching Jack.

'Good. You came,' said Falcone, his voice surprisingly strong. 'Come closer so I can see you better.'

Jack walked up to the edge of the bed and just stood there, watching the man who had abducted his mother.

'Do you believe in redemption?' asked Falcone.

'I'm the wrong man to ask. I believe in destiny.'

'And forgiveness?'

'That too.'

'And keeping your word?'

'Always.'

'I thought so. We must talk. There isn't much time.'

'I'm listening.'

Fifteen minutes later, alarms went off in the hospital room and nurses and doctors came running from all directions. Moments later, Jack walked through the door, his face ashen. Cesaria went up to him and put her hand on his arm. 'Did he say anything?'

'Yes.'

'Did he tell you where your mother is?' asked Cesaria softly.

Jack nodded.

'Where is she?' said Donizetti, who had overheard the exchange.

'Hospice Santa Dymphna in Padua.'

'A *hospice*?' said Cesaria. 'That's palliative care for terminally ill patients.'

'I know,' said Jack, choking with emotion. 'I asked him about that. Do you know what he said?'

'Tell me.'

'The best place to hide a book is in the library.'

'Clever,' said Donizetti. 'There's more to this guy than I thought.'

'We better get moving,' said Cesaria. 'Excuse me.' Cesaria took Donizetti aside and spoke with her for a moment, then pulled her phone out of her pocket and made a call. Donizetti did the same.

Tristan walked over to Jack, who was staring out of the window, a dejected look on his face. 'Don't worry, Jack. She'll be all right.'

'You aren't just saying that to make me feel better?'

'No. Now that we know where she is, she'll be fine.'

'I hope so.'

'What else happened in there?' asked Tristan, changing the subject.

Jack looked at him, surprised. 'What makes you say that?'

'Come on, Jack, it's *me*.'

'Yes, there was more. I now understand why he wanted to see me. In person and alone.'

'Tell me.'

'This stays strictly between us. Clear?' whispered Jack.

'Of course. There was an exchange, wasn't there? You have to do something for him, right?'

'Why ask me if you already know?'

'A hunch isn't knowing.'

'Falcone has a disabled daughter living in a home here in Catanzaro. He pays for her upkeep. I have to empty his bank account and transfer the funds to the institution.'

'You *promised?*'

'I did.' Jack patted the coat pocket where he kept his notebook. 'He gave me all the details. Account numbers, passwords, everything.'

'Cunning to the very end.'

'Desperate, more likely.'

'All this in exchange for information about Rahima?'

'Yes, but don't tell anyone. Surely you can see why?'

'This is truly amazing, Jack. You can see the irony, though. Those funds have most likely come from O'Hara, and perhaps Giordano, financing his wife's assassination.'

'Yes. We're dealing with dirty money here that paid for my mother's abduction and an assassination. Proceeds of crime, whichever way you look at it. Several hundred thousand dollars. A moral dilemma, for sure, but I didn't hesitate. Not for a moment.'

'I understand, Jack.'

'I knew you would. Not so sure about Cesaria and Donizetti.'

'Cesaria would.'

'Better this way, trust me. I don't want to put her in a compromising position.'

Just then, a doctor came out of Falcone's room, walked over to Donizetti and spoke to her briefly. Donizetti nodded and came over to Jack.

'He's gone. You just made it,' she said, looking very tired.

'Thanks to you,' said Jack.

'Hopefully, something good comes out of this disaster.'

'Jack's a lucky guy. It will, you'll see,' said Tristan.

'What makes you say that?' asked Donizetti. 'Don't tell me. Whispering angels?'

'Something like that,' replied Tristan, smiling.

62

Hospice Santa Dymphna, Padua: 8 February

Despite the heavy rain, the drive from Venice Marco Polo airport to Padua took less than an hour. Deep in thought, Jack hardly said a word during the journey and just stared out of the window.

'That's it over there,' said the police officer who had met them at the airport earlier that morning. He pointed to a dilapidated building on the outskirts of Padua that had seen better days.

'Are you sure? That's the Hospice Santa Dymphna?' asked Cesaria. 'What a dump.'

The officer shrugged. 'My men went there last night as you asked and spoke to management. She's definitely there.'

'And?' prompted Jack.

'That's all I know. Two of my men stayed there overnight to make sure. You know, secure the place. Just in case ...'

'What do we know about this establishment?' continued Jack, sounding concerned.

Cesaria, who sat next to Jack, reached for his hand and squeezed it. 'I know how you feel. At least she's here and she's alive,' she said.

'You're right. And without Falcone, we wouldn't have found her, that's for sure.'

'True,' said Tristan. 'On occasion you have to deal with the devil and do his bidding before you can defeat him.'

Jack gave Tristan a stern look and shook his head.

'The hospice is one of several here in Padua and in Milan, owned by a corporation linked to the Mafia,' said the police officer as the car pulled up in front of the entrance. 'The Mafia has extensive business interests in aged care.'

'Ah,' said Jack. 'It's all falling into place. This looks more like the end of the road for the destitute than a place of care for the dying.'

'As I said, it's owned by the Mafia,' said the officer and got out of the car.

The manager, a tall African woman in her forties, met them in the foyer, which smelled of urine and cleaning fluid. The woman looked nervous and uncomfortable, and Jack noticed her eyes were fixed on the police officers watching her. 'I manage the staff,' she said in broken Italian. 'That's all. The office looks after the paperwork.'

'We can talk about this later,' said Cesaria. 'Please take us to her.'

The woman nodded. 'Follow me.'

On the way up the stairs they passed several more young African women, these ones carrying buckets and mops.

'Refugees,' said the police officer next to Jack. 'We checked their papers last night.'

The woman stopped in front of a door on the first floor. 'We know her as Martina. She was admitted six days ago with severe dementia.'

'Dementia?' snapped Jack.

'It's all right,' said Cesaria. 'We'll sort this out later. Let's go inside, shall we?'

The woman opened the door and stepped aside.

The tiny room looked more like a cell than a room for a patient in need of care. With barely enough space for a single bed and a chair, the room was cold, claustrophobic and musty, without curtains or embellishments of any kind.

Jack gasped as he saw the grey-haired woman sitting on a wooden chair facing the door, hands folded in her lap. Wearing a threadbare dressing gown and slippers that were several sizes too big, Rahima was staring vacantly into space.

Jack knelt down next to her and gently put his hands on hers. 'It's me; Jack,' he whispered, unable to control the tears welling from deep within.

Rahima didn't move.

Jack wiped away a few tears and then, leaning forward, kissed his mother tenderly on the forehead.

Rahima still didn't move.

Cesaria had to look away. She went outside, walked up to the manager and hissed, 'Downstairs, now! We have to talk.'

Tristan walked over to Jack and put his hand on his shoulder.

'It's no use, Jack, she's heavily sedated. We have to get her out of here fast. Come.'

'You're right. She's a prisoner of the needle. Who knows what kind of drugs they've pumped into her.' Jack stood up and stroked his mother's hair. *What have they done to you?* he thought. Then, taking a last look at the sad little person slumped in the chair, he turned and followed Tristan out of the room.

Cesaria was waiting by the front door with two police officers, the fury in her demeanour obvious.

'I've called an ambulance. It will be here shortly and take Rahima to a hospital. I've already spoken to the emergency department and arranged for her admission.'

'Thank you,' whispered Jack. 'She didn't deserve this.'

'No-one does,' said Cesaria and held up a piece of paper. 'This is a summary of the medication she's been given. It's all for dementia patients.'

'I thought this was a hospice?'

'It is, but there's also a wing for dementia patients.'

'That explains it,' said Tristan.

'Explains what?' asked Jack.

'The name. Saint Dymphna is the patron saint of dementia.'

Jack shook his head. 'The stuff you come up with is astonishing, don't you think Cesaria?'

'Obviously he gets it from whispering angels.'

'Who else?' said Jack, managing a smile for the first time in days.

Rahima was admitted to the Padova University Hospital in the Via Nicolò Giustiniani. The hospital was an excellent choice due to its outstanding research, and genetics and metabolic laboratory services in all biomedical disciplines. It was therefore the perfect facility to deal with Rahima's situation and quickly get to the bottom of what had happened to her and find a way to cure it. As a senior police officer, Cesaria had influence and could make things happen. Rahima was immediately examined by specialists and given a private room.

Jack, Tristan and Cesaria sat in the hospital corridor outside Rahima's room. It was already dark and getting late.

Looking drained and exhausted, Jack turned towards Cesaria. 'I can't tell you how grateful I am,' he said, 'for everything you've done.'

'It's a good outcome, considering the circumstances. Keep in mind it was only yesterday you spoke to Falcone on his deathbed in Catanzaro and we found out Rahima was here. I still don't quite understand how you did it. No matter; the result is all that counts.'

'Correct,' said Tristan. 'You heard what the specialist said. He's confident she'll fully recover. It's only a matter of time.'

'Fingers crossed,' said Jack.

'What are you going to do?' asked Cesaria.

'I'll stay here for as long as it takes. The specialist also said it would be helpful if someone she knew well could be around and talk to her. Well, that's going to be me. I'll take a room somewhere close by. My mother's recovery is all that matters for the moment.'

'I expected nothing less,' said Cesaria. 'I'm heading back to Venice to investigate what happened here and who's behind all this. Falcone couldn't have done this without some help.'

'Certainly not,' said Jack. 'With both Falcone brothers dead, Giordano must be running out of assassins, and O'Hara of mercenaries to do his dirty work.'

'Let's hope so. The local Carabinieri are standing by and will be a great help in this investigation. I sent Falcone's phone to Florence. Clara is examining it right now. She's quietly confident that this, in addition to the prison guard's phone records, will help her locate O'Hara. And, of course, you too will contribute here. You must try to stay in touch with O'Hara because that could well be the missing link that will ultimately lead us to him. Clara is monitoring your phone, remember?'

'Let's hope she can pull this off, because as soon as Rahima recovers, I'm going after O'Hara. He's the one who caused all this, no-one else. The only way to stop this madness is to stop him. Once and for all.'

'I expected nothing less,' said Tristan, repeating Cesaria's words. 'I'll stay here with you, if you like.'

'No. Please go back to Venice and help Cesaria. It'll do you good. Don't forget, this is the same evil network that killed Lorenza. And don't forget your birthday present.'

Tristan reached into his pocket and took out the bullet that had been left under his napkin. 'Don't worry, I have it on me all the time.'

'Good. It's an excellent reminder this is far from over. You can keep an eye on what's happening in Venice and keep me informed.'

'And you will keep in touch with Serapion and continue the search for *Dextera Dei*?'

'Of course. I'll keep in touch with everyone and use this time to review everything that's happened so far.'

Jack pulled his little notebook out of his pocket and put it on top of his iPad. 'I have everything I need right here. What I need right now, though, is a little quiet time, and some sleep.'

Cesaria stood up. 'Then let's do something about that,' she said. 'It's getting late. I've asked for a camp bed to be put in your mother's room for the night. You can sleep in there, if you like, and find a room tomorrow.'

'How on earth did you manage that?' asked Jack, surprised.

'It was Tristan's idea. Doctor's orders; simple. The doctor said it would be helpful if someone Rahima knew well could stay close to her, remember? You're it, my friend.'

'Clever. Thanks, guys. Your blood's worth bottling!'

Cesaria raised an eyebrow. 'Another curious Aussie saying, I suppose?'

'One of Jack's favourites,' said Tristan, smiling. 'Reserved for special people.'

PART IV
REVENGE OF THE SPARROW

"A state may well not survive its writers telling its people the truth."
— Kornei Chukovsky
Author of *The Monster Cockroach*, 1921

63

IK-6 Prison, Melenkhovo: 10 February

Serapion got out of the car and, ignoring the bone-chilling cold, stretched his stiff legs. Due to the heavy snow cover, the two-hundred-and-fifty-kilometre drive from Moscow had taken almost six hours.

IK-6, the infamous corrective labour colony – one of Russia's most brutal, with its fearsome reputation of abuse and torture – looked bleak and forbidding.

The guards at the gates treated Serapion with suspicion bordering on contempt, and it was only after he produced the official letter from Colonel Karlov of the FSB granting him access to the notorious prisoner that their demeanour changed. In the prison underworld, with its own rules and power structure where even the courts and the judiciary were ignored, only the FSB had any kind of authority.

Serapion was shown to a cold, bleak cell-like room without windows.

'Wait here,' said the guard and closed the heavy steel door behind him. Serapion was still not sure how Karlov had managed to pull off permission to visit Novotny, one of the most controversial prisoners in Russia. Novotny had recently been the subject of a barrage of Russian disinformation and scaremongering designed to discredit him and his sensational 'corruption-exposure videos' released by his supporters in Germany after his arrest. The overwhelming evidence presented in those videos accused Palin and his cronies of monstrous corruption and fraud that had caused outrage both in Russia and abroad.

Novotny had been on hunger strike for almost two weeks in a desperate attempt to draw attention to the brutal treatment he had received while in prison for trumped-up charges designed to silence him once and for all.

After waiting almost an hour, the door opened and two prison guards dragged Novotny, who could barely walk, into the room and dropped him unceremoniously on a chair facing Serapion.

'Please leave,' said Serapion, pointing to the door. 'I want to talk to the prisoner alone.'

The surly guards left and closed the door.

Too weak to stand or even move, Novotny just sat there with his eyes closed, seemingly oblivious of his surroundings or what was happening.

Oh my God, thought Serapion, as he looked at the emaciated shell of a man in front of him. *I hope I'm not too late.* Having seen approaching death many times before, Serapion knew all the signs: motionless, limp body; shallow breathing; closed eyes; half-open mouth. The only thing missing was an aura of defeat. Despite the sorry state he was in, Novotny radiated subtle defiance. This was by no means a man who had given up, but a man who was determined to fight to the very end.

Serapion leaned forward until his lips almost touched Novotny's ear. 'Sasha sends her love,' he whispered.

Slowly, Novotny opened his eyes and looked at Serapion. As his eyes began to focus and recognition dawned – Novotny had met Serapion before and knew him well – the expression on his face changed from indifferent resignation, to surprise.

'You, here? How can that be? Not even my lawyers are allowed to see me. In here, I don't exist.'

'But outside, you do, and that's why I'm here,' said Serapion, pleasantly surprised by Novotny's state of mind, which seemed at odds with his bruised and broken body showing signs of prolonged torture and deprivation.

'Please listen carefully, there isn't much time. How I managed to get in here to see you doesn't matter. What I'm about to tell you does. Do you understand?'

Novotny nodded.

'This is most likely the only time I, or someone like me, will be able to talk with you while you are in here. For now, the outside world is beyond your reach and there's nothing you can do in here that will make a difference, except for one thing.'

'What's that?' asked Novotny, suddenly alert. Hope can be a powerful drug.

'*Stay alive*. You must leave the rest to others. Do you understand?'

Novotny nodded.

'If you die in here – as you most certainly will if you continue with what you're doing – most of what you have achieved will have been in vain. Russia will be the loser, and your many supporters will have suffered for nothing. Not only do they deserve better, they also *need* you, and so does Russia. More than ever.'

Novotny nodded again.

'You are the sparrow who will defeat the cockroach. Against all odds. But to do that, you must be able to fly when the time comes. A dead sparrow cannot be a victor who makes history, but you can. Very soon, Russia will be at war and ironically, you will be safer here inside this horrible place than outside, fighting. Your time will come soon enough and when it does, you must be strong and ready to meet your destiny. Am I making myself clear?'

'Yes.'

'Good. Sasha lives for the day she can embrace you again. What she's doing in London to keep your movement and ideas alive and in front of the media is astonishing, and what's happening right now in the background here in Russia will one day surprise you. Don't disappoint her and those who are prepared to put their lives on the line for freedom. Now listen carefully, this is what we want you to do. Clear?'

'I'm listening.'

64

Time Machine Studios, London: 12 February

'That's quite a building,' said Sasha as the Bentley turned into the underground garage of the impressive Time Machine Studios. Unusually light London traffic meant the trip from the Ivanov mansion had taken just over an hour.

'It is,' replied Boris as he parked the car. 'But the best is on the top, as you will see in a moment. Ah, here's Lola, Isis's PA. She'll take you up.'

Isis greeted Sasha at the lift entrance to the penthouse.

'Thank you for the invitation,' said Sasha. She looked at the elegant, impeccably dressed woman she had heard so much about, finding it difficult to believe she was in fact looking at a man, albeit a megastar adored by millions.

Sasha pointed to the panoramic windows overlooking the Thames. 'This is quite something,' she said, trying to appear relaxed and nonchalant, but unable to hide the great weight of responsibility and worry pressing down on her slim shoulders.

'You should have seen this place before we started,' said Isis. 'A rundown, derelict bond store stuck in the Victorian era. Champagne?'

'Why not? I could do with a drink.'

'The news coming out of Russia has certainly been disturbing. About Anatoly, I mean. Come, let's sit by the window.'

Isis watched Sasha carefully as the maid served champagne. The enormous stress Sasha had been under since Novotny's hunger strike became public and had gone viral, was certainly showing. *No wonder Jack's worried about her,* thought Isis, recognising all the signs of tension and fatigue etched on Sasha's beautiful face. The lines under her eyes were a clear sign of lack of sleep and exhaustion.

'This was Jack's idea,' said Isis as she handed Sasha a glass of champagne. She had decided an honest, direct, meet-the-issues-head-on approach would be best under the circumstances.

'What do you mean?' said Sasha.

'Jack wanted us to meet. He's very concerned – about you, and the situation generally, I mean. I understand he spoke with you several times recently?'

'Yes, he has,' said Sasha, surprised. 'We've been in contact.'

'Because of what happened to his mother, he can't be here,' continued Isis, steering the conversation closer to the subject Jack had asked her to address. 'I'm sure you know he hasn't left his mother's bedside since her admission to hospital. So, he's asked me to stand in for him.'

'I don't understand.'

'You do know what happened to his mother?'

'Yes, he told me.'

'Then you also know who was behind it all.'

'Yes, he told me that too.'

'Good. To put all this into context, I would like to tell you something about Jack.'

Sasha looked at Isis, eyebrows raised expectantly.

'Jack is the most sincere and loyal friend I've ever known. One day I'll tell you what he did for me and my family. Once he gives you his word and makes a promise, he keeps it, come what may. I know he recently gave you his answer about finding *Dextera Dei*.'

'Yes, he did.'

'This means he's totally committed and so are the friends he relies on, and that includes me. He wants you to know that.'

'I see.'

'Friendship is one of the most precious things in life. It's a great treasure that transcends all else. If it's real, there are no barriers. It's the glue that binds us all together.'

'I agree with that,' said Sasha, wondering why Isis was telling her all this.

'I suppose what I'm saying is this: you are not alone. That's what Jack asked me to tell you.'

Sasha's cornflower-blue eyes radiated sadness tinged with some despair, but also hope.

'He's worried about Anatoly, isn't he? Just like me,' she said, her voice hoarse.

'Yes. I'm sure you know he's been in close contact with Serapion.'

'He told me.'

'Then you would know that Serapion visited Anatoly in jail two days ago.'

Sasha nodded.

'I don't know how much Serapion told you about that meeting, but Anatoly was very weak and has suffered much. His hunger strike is taking a terrible toll. It has to stop.'

'I agree, but Anatoly sees it as the only way ... I know him. This is typical Anatoly. He decided to go back to Russia against all rational advice to the contrary, to give his sensational accusations credibility. He's now using the hunger strike to keep the momentum going. He's hoping it will train the spotlight of media attention on the corruption issues.'

'It may do that, but he's made some powerful enemies along the way who are determined to silence him once and for all. And that has to be prevented, whatever it takes, or what you're trying to achieve here will all have been in vain.'

'I agree, but *how*? He's in solitary confinement in a high-security jail without any contact to the outside world.'

'That's why Serapion's visit was so important. He must have friends in high places, that's all I can say,' said Isis, taking a sip of champagne. 'As I understand it, Serapion has been able to persuade Anatoly to stop the hunger strike.'

'I hope so,' said Sasha, becoming agitated. 'But he'll never give them what they've been after since the day of his arrest.'

'What's that?'

'A retraction. Tell the world that all the accusations are part of Western propaganda without substance, designed to damage the Kremlin. Anatoly would rather die than say that.'

'I think the Kremlin realises that by now. Be assured, the last thing Palin wants right now is for Anatoly to die in jail. That would make him a martyr and give his accusations even more credibility.'

GABRIEL FARAGO

'I can see that. I only hope you're right about all this.'

'Serapion certainly seems to think so. That's why he was so adamant the hunger strike had to stop. Self-harm would achieve nothing, especially as the Kremlin is about to change tactics to muddy the waters and push this embarrassing issue into the background in the hope it will all disappear.'

'What do you mean?' asked Sasha, frowning.

'The imminent invasion of Ukraine. Serapion is convinced it's very close. A matter of days, a couple of weeks at the most. Once that starts, it will overshadow everything, except one thing.'

'What's that?'

'The only way to stop this madness and prevent Russia – and the world, for that matter – plunging into chaos, is to remove Palin.'

'That's been Anatoly's position all along, and the position of the Foundation. Nothing's changed in that regard.'

'I understand that, but how to achieve this is the issue here, right?'

'Yes, of course.'

'All we – Jack and his friends, that is – know is that the holy icon *Dextera Dei* will play a crucial role in all this, yet how this is to work is a mystery as far as we're concerned.'

Isis paused to make a point.

'Be that as it may,' she continued, 'Jack has agreed to do all he can to find the relic and deliver it to you in return for your help to bring O'Hara to justice.'

'Yes, that's the deal.'

'I'm sure you understand that in light of recent events involving Jack's mother, this has taken on a certain degree of urgency.'

'I can understand that too. And if you're concerned about whether I can deliver my part of the bargain, you needn't be; I can. As long as I'm given a location in Belarus, we can apprehend O'Hara and hand him over.'

'Outside Belarus?'

'Yes.'

'Excellent. I'm sure Jack would have told you that the whole of ENFAST is looking for O'Hara, and substantial progress has been made to locate him. O'Hara's entire darknet gambling site has imploded, and he's isolated and on his own. The experts believe it's now only a matter of time before we know exactly where he is.'

'Good. And *Dextera Dei*?'

'Ah. That's the main thing Jack wanted me to tell you. As soon as his mother recovers and is well enough to return to Venice, he will rejoin the quest.'

'You know Serapion is in Kyiv, making good progress? He believes he's getting close to finding out what happened to the holy relic,' said Sasha.

'After Father Chernenko took *Zbawiciel*, as the relic was known in Poland, back to Ukraine in 1933 to fight the Terror-Famine, as instructed by Saint Olga in his dream?'

Sasha looked at Isis, surprised. 'You're very well informed. That's correct. Father Chernenko took the holy relic to the Church of the Tithes in Kyiv where Saint Olga is buried. The trail went cold after that. Until now ...'

'Yes, Jack told me. He's in daily contact with Serapion and is eager to join him.'

'Even if Russia invades Ukraine?'

'Yes. Jack has considered this. Don't forget, he was a successful war correspondent in Afghanistan. You can rest assured he has a few tricks up his sleeve when it comes to that. He's a resourceful guy.'

'I can believe that,' said Sasha, flashing a rare smile.

'In a way, you and Jack are doing all this for the same reasons, you know.'

'We are?'

'Yes. You're both trying to protect those you love. Jack's trying to protect his family and friends, and you the man you love, as well as his ideas and dreams.'

'Very perceptive of you,' said Sasha, biting her quivering lower lip in a vain attempt to stop the tears from welling. 'I know Anatoly has been tortured. I've tried to put this out of my mind, but ...'

Sasha looked away, tears rolling down her pale cheeks.

Isis moved closer to her, put an arm around her shoulders and held her until the sobbing stopped.

'Sorry, I don't know what came over me,' said Sasha. 'I'm making a fool of myself.'

'Nonsense. You've heard about Jack's breadcrumbs of destiny, I presume?'

'Yes, Serapion told me about that.'

'Then you'll understand what Jack would say right now,' said Isis, smiling.

'What's that?'

'Not all breadcrumbs are the same. The bitter ones make you cry, but they're often the ones that show you the way.'

'And that's supposed to make me feel better?'

'No, Jack has another saying for that.'

'Oh?'

'The darkest hour is just before dawn. Do you have time to stay for lunch?' asked Isis, changing the subject.

'Yes, thank you,' said Sasha, feeling much better. 'I always wanted to have lunch with a famous rock star one day.'

Pleased by the compliment, Isis burst out laughing. The awkward moment had passed. With Isis, ego was never far away and rare compliments were eagerly soaked up like precious water by the desert sand.

65

Palazzo Alberti, Venice: 15 February

Countess Kuragin and Tristan were waiting in Jack's study on the ground floor of the palazzo, eager to hear news about the trip from the hospital in Padua after Rahima's discharge. Jack and the nurse he had engaged to look after his mother were attending to Rahima in her bedroom.

'I'm glad she's back here,' said the countess. 'I hate hospitals.'

'So does Jack,' said Tristan. 'Yet he hasn't left her side since her admission to Padova hospital. That tells you something.'

'Sure does, especially after all that's happened.'

The countess stood up as Jack walked into the room, the strain of the last two weeks etched on his drawn face.

'How is she?' she asked and walked over to Jack to embrace him.

'Surprisingly well. She enjoyed the trip. Especially the boat ride. Mentally very tough. She wants to see you. Come, let's go upstairs.'

The nurse excused herself and left the room as soon as Jack walked in, followed by the countess and Tristan. Looking calm and composed, Rahima was sitting in an armchair by the window.

The countess thought Rahima had aged and looked frail. Hardly surprising after all she'd been through.

'It's wonderful to see you,' said Rahima. 'And it's great to be back here among friends, despite what happened in this very room only a short time ago. Yet, I feel I'm a different person.'

'What do you mean?' said the countess.

'Certain events can change us in unexpected ways. What happened to me has certainly done that.'

'In what way?' asked Jack.

'To begin with, I've spent more time with you in the last few days than I've spent with you since you were born. The drugged state I was in has brought back memories and emotions with a clarity that's difficult to explain. Do you know I heard every word that was said while you were with me in hospital? Yet I was unable to speak or communicate in any way. I was a prisoner of my drugged, almost paralysed body, but with my mind unaffected and roaming free. Strange, don't you think?'

'Not really,' said Tristan. 'That's exactly what happened to me. As you all know, I was in a coma for several years, confined to bed and on life support after a terrible accident that almost killed me. I was only a teenager at the time, yet I can clearly remember everything that happened. Every visit. Every word spoken. Everything.'

'Ah, then you know exactly what I mean. It felt like I was outside my body, hovering and looking down on what was happening around me. Detached, yet fully aware of what was taking place. If there's such a thing as a near-death experience, then surely that must have been it.'

'You describe it well,' said Tristan. 'I believe that was when I began to hear the whisper of angels. Those whispers made my condition bearable at the time. Like a soothing balm on a burnt limb. It was a gift that's stayed with me ever since.'

Jack was surprised. He had never heard Tristan speak of these things before.

'I want to thank you all for what you've done for me during this difficult time, and that includes Cesaria with her tireless pursuit of the culprits involved. Without that, I wouldn't be sitting here, that's for sure. I heard that the man in the Medico della Peste mask who abducted me died in dramatic circumstances, and Jack told me how my whereabouts were discovered just before he passed away. Surely, all that tells us something, don't you think?'

'What do you mean?' asked the countess.

Rahima looked at Tristan. 'You know, don't you?'

'Yes. *Destiny.*'

'Exactly. If I look back on my life, it's been full of moments of destiny just like this, especially during my time in Colombia when I was surrounded by violence and sudden death. You can therefore see I'm no stranger to such things.'

Jack looked at his mother, worried and afraid she might be slipping back into some form of confused, comatose state brought on by exhaustion.

'You must rest,' said Jack. 'You must be exhausted. We should go.'

'Far from it. I haven't felt this well since Medico della Peste woke me in the middle of the night, right here in this room, and took me away at gunpoint. I would like to tell you something about destiny while we are all together. Especially you, Jack, because you often talk about your breadcrumbs ...'

'What would you like to tell us?' said Jack, feeling the little hairs on the back of his neck begin to tingle.

'When we face a moment of destiny, we have choices. We can follow the right path, which often isn't easy and is paved with nails; or we can decide to take the safer option and stay behind; or we can ignore it altogether.'

Rahima turned towards Jack, the love for her long-lost son almost filling the room. 'You are facing such a moment right now. Don't forget, I've overheard every word of what you told me, and all your telephone conversations. I therefore know all about *Golgotha*, Serapion, the search for *Dextera Dei*, and the threat O'Hara poses to us all.'

Amazed, Jack shook his head, wondering where his mother was going with this, but impressed by the clarity of her observations.

'So far, you have followed the path of duty. That was all about your concern for me and my safety. I'm back home now, safe and among friends. Nothing more has to be done in that regard. What *you* must do now, is follow the path of destiny. I'm sure you know exactly what I mean, and what you have to do, my son. Please follow your breadcrumbs. Your work here is done. I'm sure your friends will understand that too. You must go and find *Dextera Dei*. I've seen things I cannot talk about right now. Soon, a dark cloud rising in the east will be descending on us all. It is evil, and must be stopped. I'm sure Tristan knows ...'

Tristan nodded.

Looking exhausted, Rahima closed her eyes. 'Now, please leave me. I have to rest. Go and do what has to be done, Jack. It's your destiny,' she whispered, 'and mine too. Behold the memory trees ...'

66

National Museum of the Holodomor-Genocide, Kyiv: 24 February

In the distance, Jack could see the imposing monument: a 30-metre-high candle known as the Candle of Memory, with its potent symbolism. He left the Arsenalna metro station near the Pechersk Hills on the right bank of the Dnieper River and, head down against the ice-cold wind, walked towards the memorial to meet Serapion. Ukraine's spectacular national museum dedicated to the horrendous 1932–1933 Holodomor-genocide was a reminder of a heinous crime: a devastating, catastrophic famine created by Stalin to crush a nation, etched deep into the Ukrainian psyche, never to be forgotten.

As Jack approached the entrance, he waved at Serapion standing next to one of the Angels of Sorrow, the two large stone statues guarding the alley leading up to the memorial complex.

'We seem to meet in the most unexpected places,' said Jack, shaking hands with the abbot. 'Last time it was the Wawel Cathedral in Kraków, and now this. And to think we were there only three weeks ago. Difficult to believe. I've been to hell and back since then.'

'I know.'

'Have you really found it?' asked Jack.

'The trail of *Dextera Dei* is full of surprises and well hidden.'

'But not from you, it seems.'

Serapion shrugged, deflecting the question. 'How's your mother?'

'Recovering. She's a strong woman.'

'A fortuitous outcome. Considering the circumstances.'

'You can say that again.'

'Look around you. What do you see?' said Serapion.

'Two stone angels.'

'They are the guardians of the souls. The souls of those who starved to death during the Holodomor. All five million of them.'

'Almost inconceivable!'

'Genocide always is. This place is full of symbolism. Look over there.'

Serapion pointed to a set of large stones arranged in a circle. 'These are twenty-four millstones representing a twenty-four-hour clock. This is a reminder that twenty-four thousand people starved to death *every day* during the Holodomor because there was no corn to grind. But the most moving reminder of what happened is over there. Come, follow me.'

Serapion began to walk along the alley towards a statue of a wide-eyed, frightfully thin young girl clutching a bundle of wheat strands with her bony fingers. 'That's the famous statue *Bitter Memory of Childhood*, which is also the title of a famous poem by a lady you're about to meet. That's her standing over there next to the statue.'

Serapion walked over to a tall woman in her forties wearing jeans, riding boots, and a military-style parker with a fur-lined hood, and shook hands with her. 'Jack, I'd like you to meet Ivanna Vasylenko, a famous poet who helped set up this place.'

Jack looked at the woman with interest. *What a striking face*, he thought, *but sad eyes. This woman knows suffering.*

'I've heard a lot about you, Mr Rogan. Not just from Abbot Serapion, but from many others. You're well known here in Ukraine,' said Vasylenko in perfect English, extending her hand.

'I'm always a little worried when I hear something like that,' replied Jack, smiling and a little taken aback.

'No need to be. I've read some of your books.'

'Ah. That's a relief.'

'But it's not your writing you're known for around here ...'

'Oh? What then?'

'Kazanskaya Bogomater. The return of the holy icon to Yekaterinburg. It was all on national television. Very moving and symbolic. And for someone like me, very significant. That's the main reason I agreed to this meeting.'

'I see. Please forgive me, but I know very little about this meeting. In fact, I've no idea what this is all about. Abbot Serapion called me yesterday and asked me to come to Kyiv urgently, and meet him here. That's all he told me and here I am.'

'Is that right?'

Serapion nodded. 'I thought it best if Jack could hear everything we talked about directly from you.'

'Do you always follow instructions blindly, Mr Rogan?' said Vasylenko, raising an eyebrow. 'You came all the way from Venice because Abbot Serapion asked you to?'

'Yes. He's very difficult to resist.'

'That I can understand. He has friends in high places.' Vasylenko pointed towards heaven.

'He sure has. A man of destiny, full of surprises.'

'And so are you, I believe, Mr Rogan. Let's go inside,' said Vasylenko. 'It's a lot warmer and I have a lot to show you.'

Vasylenko turned and walked towards the entrance to the underground Hall of Memory. 'In November 2006, a law "On the Holodomor of 1932–1933 in Ukraine" was passed, officially recognising for the first time the Holodomor as genocide of the Ukrainian people. While there are many exhibits of great interest in here, the one that's particularly relevant to what we'll be talking about are the Blackboards of Memory over there.'

'What are they?'

'Symbolic boards engraved with the names of 14,000 villages and towns that suffered unspeakable hardship, which give us some idea of the scale of the horror. Many of those villages had no survivors and were left empty. Difficult to imagine, I know.'

Vasylenko stood in front of the boards, head bowed in silence. Then she pointed to one of the names on the board in front of her. 'That's the village of my grandparents. Our family was almost entirely wiped out. I cannot come here without being deeply affected by this,' said Vasylenko quietly. 'Our nation has suffered much, and I'm afraid is about to suffer much more. And that's what brings us here to this place.'

Vasylenko turned towards Jack. 'As I understand it, you and Abbot Serapion want to find out what happened to *Zbawiciel*, the holy relic, after it was brought to Ukraine from Warsaw by Father Chernenko in 1933.'

'Yes,' said Jack. 'We know it as *Dextera Dei*, the right hand of God.'

'Ah, van Eyck and the *Golgotha* painting. Abbot Serapion told me all about that.'

'When Abbot Serapion called me the other day and asked me to come here urgently, he told me one more thing,' said Jack.

'Yes?'

'He told me that he had found *Zbawiciel*. Can you shed some light on that?'

'Before I answer your question, let me tell you something about these villages here.' Vasylenko pointed to the board in front of her.

'By the time Father Chernenko returned with *Zbawiciel* from Warsaw in 1933, more than five million Ukrainians had already died as a result of the Terror-Famine. *Zbawiciel* was taken to the Church of the Tithes here in Kyiv where Saint Olga was buried, and it was decided to take the holy relic on a journey.'

'What kind of journey?'

'A journey of hope, and faith. *Zbawiciel* was taken from one ravaged village to another, to banish evil in the hope the famine would pass, and the horror subside.'

'And did it?' asked Jack.

'Yes. The famine retreated slowly after the next harvest in late 1933.'

'And *Zbawiciel*? What happened to it?'

'It was taken back to the Church of the Tithes and placed in an urn next to the altar.'

'And is it still there?' asked Jack, sounding hoarse.

Vasylenko held up her hand. 'No. Towards the end of the Second World War, *Zbawiciel* was sent on another journey around Ukraine. As you no doubt know, Nazi occupation of Ukraine was devastating. More than four million Ukrainians perished after German troops invaded Ukraine as part of Operation Barbarossa in 1941.'

'I remember reading about Babi Yar, a ravine right here in Kyiv. More than thirty-three thousand were killed by the Germans in two days in September 1941 alone,' said Jack.

'Correct. The atrocities committed here are almost too difficult to imagine. Sadly, our country is soaked in blood.'

'Tell Jack what happened to *Zbawiciel* after the war,' said Serapion.

'Once again, evil was gradually defeated and Ukraine began the long road of rebuilding the hundreds of villages and towns destroyed during the war.'

'And *Zbawiciel*?'

'Was again returned to the Church of the Tithes, where it remained until 2008, when this place here was opened.'

'And then? Where is it today?' asked Jack, unable to hide the impatience in his voice.

Vasylenko took her time before replying. 'You're standing on top of it.'

'What do you mean?'

'*Zbawiciel* and a number of other precious artefacts that played a significant role in the Holodomor are kept in a secure underground chamber directly below us.'

Jack shot Serapion a meaningful look. '*Really*?' he said.

'Yes, *Dextera Dei* is right here,' said Serapion. 'It's a Ukrainian national treasure and an important part of this memorial. Ivanna was instrumental in bringing it here and wrote a famous poem about it, which is part of the school curriculum in Ukraine. Every schoolkid knows it by heart. It's like a national anthem. Isn't that right?'

'Yes, something like that. If you want to keep a memory alive, you have to start with the young. That was all part of creating this memorial. All part of our healing.'

'Clever. Is *Zbawiciel* ever taken out of the chamber?' asked Jack.

'No. It's in here, watching over Ukraine. We believe it will show itself again in times of need and defeat evil, just as it has done before.'

'A lovely thought,' said Jack, 'but—'

Jack was interrupted by what sounded like a loud explosion coming from somewhere outside. Moments later, it was followed by another.

'What was that?' asked Serapion, looking worried.

'Let's have a look and find out,' said Vasylenko and hurried to the exit.

Outside, the area in front of the entrance was crowded with visitors of all ages looking down towards the city below. Many were pointing to columns of smoke rising in the distance like accusing fingers pointing to heaven.

Vasylenko looked at Serapion and paled. 'Could this be it?'

'Yes, it has begun.'

'What has begun?' asked Jack.

'The invasion of Ukraine. These are Russian missiles fired from Belarus. Russian troops would have crossed the borders by now, and tanks are on their way here.'

'Jesus!'

'I must go,' said Vasylenko, barely able to speak. She turned towards Jack. 'Where are you staying?'

'Hyatt Regency.'

'What are you going to do now?'

'Not sure yet. I was a war correspondent in Afghanistan ...'

'Looks like you've found another war.'

'Looks like it.'

Vasylenko jotted down her phone number on a piece of paper and handed it to Jack. 'You can reach me on this number any time.'

'Thanks.'

'Should you decide to stay, you can come with me.'

'Come where?'

'Later. The whole of Ukraine will fight, and you can tell the world about it. This is a moment of history in the making.'

As Vasylenko hurried past Serapion, she stopped. 'I didn't want to believe you but you were right, as usual. Looks like *Zbawiciel* will have a lot of work to do.'

'Certainly looks that way. God be with you,' said Serapion and made the sign of the cross as Vasylenko pushed through the excited crowd and disappeared down the alley.

67

Kyiv: 25 February

Jack sat in the corner of the crowded lobby of the Hyatt Regency full of anxious tourists lining up at the counter, eager to pay their bills and check out. It was just after eight am. The staff were doing their best to make the hotel function as normal, but the turmoil and chaos gripping the city were impossible to ignore. Massive explosions, sirens and fires during the night had kept everybody awake, confused, and desperate for answers and news of what was happening.

After breakfast with Serapion early that morning, Jack had called Vasylenko as the abbot had suggested. Jack had almost given up, when Vasylenko finally answered the phone and agreed to meet him. Jack was on his third espresso when she walked in.

'You look like you need some coffee,' said Jack.

'I do. Thank you.' Vasylenko took off her parker, threw it on an empty chair and sat down next to Jack. 'Where's Abbot Serapion?'

'He was here earlier, but had to leave. He's returning to Russia.'

'He told me.'

'He stayed at St Michael's Golden-Domed Monastery not far from here,' said Jack.

'As I said, he's well connected. That's the headquarters of the Orthodox Church of Ukraine. Only church dignitaries stay there as guests of the Metropolitan of Kyiv and All Ukraine.'

'Serapion mentioned that. Apparently, he knows the Metropolitan well. He asked me to call you and arrange a meeting.'

Vasylenko nodded. 'I see. You said it was urgent. Here I am.'

'What did you mean when you said I could come with you, should I decide to stay?'

'Have you?'

'Thinking about it.'

'The world changed yesterday. I just didn't have any idea exactly by how much or how quickly. Today, I know.'

'We both know. Things appear to be moving very fast.'

'Yes, too fast for my liking. I just hope we're ready for this,' added Vasylenko, frowning.

'You haven't answered my question.'

'As of yesterday, Ukraine is at war with Russia. You may not have heard but martial law has been declared, with full mobilisation of all able-bodied males between eighteen and sixty.'

'My contacts at the *New York Times* told me.'

Vasylenko looked at Jack, surprised. 'They knew already?'

'Yes. And apparently, thousands are crossing the border into Poland as we speak. Leaving Ukraine. Hundreds of thousands are expected to follow.'

'You're well informed. One could be forgiven for thinking you're a war correspondent on assignment,' teased Vasylenko.

'Who knows? Perhaps I am ...'

'Are you going to stay?'

'Serapion strongly suggested I do. Apparently, the Metropolitan suggested the same. He said this was another moment of destiny, and I was in the right place at the right time.'

'And you still haven't made up your mind?'

'He also suggested I should talk to you first.'

'I see.'

'I also spoke to my contact in New York about this earlier. The *New York Times* is very keen for me to stay here as an observer and report back. Freelance.'

'Just as you did from Afghanistan? "Voices from the Front Line"?'

'I'm not the only one who's well informed. Abbot Serapion was right about you.'

'In what way?'

Jack waved dismissively. 'Another time, perhaps.'

Vasylenko shrugged.

'So, what did you mean: I could come with you?' Jack asked again.

'We cannot fight this war alone. We need the support of the whole world, especially Europe, to fight Russia in a meaningful way.'

'I can see that, but it still doesn't answer my question.'

'There's someone who can do that much better than me.'

'Oh? Who?'

'Vira Zubenska, the president's wife. We did our military training together. I spent most of the night with her.'

'You were in the army?'

'No. We trained as military reservists. She would like to meet you.'

'When?'

'Now, if possible. She lives not far from here.'

'Then what are we waiting for? Let's go.'

'Exactly what I would have expected to hear from a war correspondent on assignment,' Vasylenko said, grinning, and put on her parker.

As Jack followed her to the exit, the sense of excitement and anticipation churning in his stomach made him smile.

'Here we are,' said Vasylenko as the taxi pulled up in front of a modest house on the outskirts of Kyiv. The house was surrounded by armed guards, and Vasylenko had to identify herself before one of the guards made a phone call, escorted Vasylenko and Jack to the front door, and pressed the doorbell.

The first thing Jack noticed about the woman who answered the door was a close resemblance to Vasylenko: same bearing, impossible-to-ignore presence and striking face, only a little younger.

'This is Vira Zubenska ... my sister,' said Vasylenko casually. 'Our president's wife.'

Jack was surprised, but concealed it.

'Delighted to meet you, Mr Rogan,' said Zubenska. 'The Metropolitan told me a lot about you this morning. Would you like some breakfast?'

'No, thank you. I already had some.'

'Some tea, perhaps?'

'That would be nice.'

'The reason I asked my sister to bring you here is as simple as it is obvious.'

'Oh?'

'We want to persuade you to stay in Ukraine and report what is happening to our country in your famous "Voices from the Front Line". Here, right now, as it's happening.'

'Do you think that could make a difference?'

'Oh yes,' said Zubenska. 'Ukraine will need all the help and support it can muster to win this war. This is a fight for survival. And for that help to materialise quickly, we need people like you.'

'What do you mean?'

'Come on. The voice of a well-connected, high-profile ex-journalist with an international reputation like yours, could not only influence public opinion, but the entire European Parliament as well.'

'You think so?'

'Yes. We all know the pen is more powerful than the sword, don't we?' said Vasylenko, stepping into the argument.

'You sound just like Abbot Serapion. Is that what he told you?'

'Perhaps ... but I don't come empty-handed.'

'I don't understand.'

'You made it clear yesterday you're very interested in *Zbawiciel*.'

'I am.'

'I'm offering you an opportunity to find out more about the holy relic and what it means to Ukraine. And most importantly, what it can *do*.'

'How?'

'By coming with me.'

'To do what exactly?'

'Fight evil.'

'I don't understand.'

'I think you do,' said Vasylenko, becoming quite animated. 'This war will be fought, won, or lost, not through the use of sophisticated weapons, but through morale and courage. Through the will and determination to fight and do whatever it takes to succeed, regardless of the sacrifices involved. That's what will eventually bring us victory. The only thing that's unclear at the moment is at what cost. It depends on many things, and someone like you can make a huge difference here. Many will listen to you. The *West* will listen to you,' said Vasylenko with passion in her voice.

Jack saw Zubenska watching him intently. 'Is that what you believe too?'

'Yes, and that's what my husband, the president, also believes.'

'You spoke to him about this?'

'Yes. Last night.'

'I asked your sister a question earlier, but she chose not to answer it because according to her, you could answer it much better,' said Jack.

'What question?'

'I told Mr Rogan that if he decided to stay, he could come with me,' said Vasylenko, stepping in.

'Ah. As you know, my sister is a well-known poet here in Ukraine. She's also an expert on the Terror-Famine, the Holodomor, inflicted on this country by Stalin and the Soviet Regime. She's a great patriot and passionate about these things. Shortly, my husband will send her on an important mission to boost morale during these difficult times.'

'And how will she do that? By reciting patriotic poetry?' Jack immediately regretted what he'd said, because it sounded cynical and harsh. 'Sorry, I didn't mean that …'

Zubenska held up her hand. 'A bit of that, sure, but she will have help.'

'What kind of help?'

'The same help that finally stopped the Holodomor in 1933, a few years later defeated the Nazis, and helped rebuild the country after the war. You cannot defeat evil of that magnitude alone. You need help.'

Jack looked at Zubenska, surprised, because he could see where this was heading. *'Zbawiciel?'* he asked quietly.

'Yes. My sister will take the holy relic on a journey around the country in the name of St Olga, our patron saint, and you could go with her and see firsthand what this can do for morale, not only among our troops, but also the population at large. Interested?'

'"Postcards from the Battlefield"?' asked Jack.

'A potent title, don't you think, Vira?' said Vasylenko, smiling.

'Sure is,' replied Zubenska, sensing persuasion victory.

'When do we start?' said Jack.

'We already have,' said Zubenska. 'But now, we should definitely have some tea.'

68

Palin's office, Kremlin, Moscow: 2 March

Palin looked at the subdued generals assembled in his office, his clenched fists and stern expression the only signs of what was to come. 'You told me three days, gentlemen,' he said. 'Ukraine would welcome us with open arms, and we would enter Kyiv as liberators, remember? And have a victory parade.'

Palin hesitated, trying to compose himself. 'But that's not what happened, is it?'

Silence.

'I tell you what happened instead. *Armed resistance* of a most ferocious kind. Burning Russian tanks, hundreds of dead soldiers, whole columns of armoured vehicles wiped out. Supply chains destroyed. The invasion has stalled. Despite your assurances, Kyiv has not been captured. No-one has surrendered. Grandmothers are hurling grenades at our soldiers instead of flowers. Can someone please explain to me how that could have happened?'

'We misread the mood of the population and underestimated their capabilities,' said one brave general. 'And resolve.'

Palin nodded.

'Our troops were ill prepared for such resistance, and our tactics were wrong,' said another general. 'We had not expected this.'

'I see. And whose fault was that?' asked Palin.

More silence.

Palin slammed his right fist down on the desktop. 'This is a humiliation! The whole world is watching, no doubt surprised by the fiasco and our failure. We've become the laughing-stock of Europe. I will tell you what will happen now.'

Palin stood up, walked over to a large map of Ukraine hanging on the wall, and then outlined a detailed battle plan, attacking Ukraine from several directions. 'May I remind you, this is war! The spirit of the civilian population has to be broken. Use whatever means you deem necessary, but *break the resistance.* Quickly. Am I making myself clear?'

The generals nodded, relieved to be getting off so lightly.

'Now go!' said Palin as he strutted back to his desk. 'I want results!'

Karlov, who had been carefully watching the spectacle from the back, was about to follow the generals out of the room when Palin made eye contact. 'Not you,' said Palin.

Karlov waited until the generals had left and then joined Palin at his desk.

'You heard what they said. What do you make of all this?' said Palin.

'They're right. We underestimated the mood of the population. We failed to have a close look at history.'

'What do you mean?'

'Know your enemy. One of the basic rules of war. And the best way to know your enemy, is by having a close look at history. Why? Because all the answers are right there.'

'Can you elaborate?'

'Sure. Stalin and the Holodomor – 1933. It explains everything.'

'You think so?'

'Absolutely. Stalin's Terror-Famine is etched into Ukrainian national consciousness. They hate Russia and the Russians. It's obvious. This resistance should come as no surprise. This is a fight for national survival.'

Palin nodded.

'And there's another thing that's been underestimated here. Gravely.'

'What?'

'Zubenskyy, the president. He's far more capable than expected. We thought he was just an ineffective little upstart with no political experience. We were wrong. Just look at how he's manipulating the international media. He's already addressed the European Parliament and asked for help.'

'You're right. I thought that too, but none of the generals mentioned this.'

'Too embarrassing. Getting your ass kicked by a novice during an invasion that should have been a walk in the park isn't something a general wants to face.'

'True.'

'And then there's one more thing.'

'What's that?'

'The resolve of the West to support Ukraine. The European Union will do everything it can to help Ukraine fight this. And so will their allies. Why? Because Ukraine desperately wants to join the European Union and become part of NATO, and to have Ukraine a part of NATO would be quite a prize, don't you think? And we, of course, want to prevent that. At all costs. Right?'

'Correct,' said Palin, looking pensively at the map of Ukraine on the wall. *Ukraine as part of NATO would be a disaster,* he thought.

'Last time we spoke about this you were looking for a sign. A sign that would tell you that you've made the right decision,' said Karlov, steering the conversation back to where he wanted it to go.

'To invade Ukraine?'

'Yes.'

'That was all about that relic, the right hand of God, and what Serapion said about it.'

'That's right, *Dextera Dei.* Serapion said that should the holy relic with its spiritual powers show itself now, that would certainly be a potent sign.'

'I remember.'

Karlov smiled at Palin. 'Well, it has done just that, but perhaps not quite in the way we expected.'

'*Seriously?* How?'

'Serapion thinks he's found it.'

'Where?'

'In Kyiv. There it's known as *Zbawiciel,* the Saviour, and is kept at the National Museum of the Holodomor-Genocide. It's a revered national treasure.'

'Are you sure about this?'

'Absolutely. It's revered because it has saved Ukraine before. And right now, it's touring the country, just as it had done during the Holodomor and the Nazi occupation.'

Palin looked at Karlov, impressed. 'How do you know all this?'

'It's my job.'

'I wish my generals would do their job as well as you do. Why is this *Zbawiciel* touring the country?'

'To boost morale. Ivanna Vasylenko, a famous, patriotic poet, is taking it to the front line, showing it to the troops and the civilian defenders. They *believe,* you see. They know their history.'

Karlov pointed to Kazanskaya Bogomater hanging on the wall. 'The power of such things must not be underestimated.'

'Are you suggesting this unexpected resistance, and its success, have something to do with all this?'

Karlov shrugged. 'One way to find out.'

'What do you mean?'

'Remove the right hand of God from Ukraine, and make it change sides.'

'And how are you planning to do that?'

'As you know, I'm in close contact with Serapion. He has his ways,' said Karlov instead of answering the question directly. Often what is left unsaid is more important than the words actually spoken.

Because Palin heard what he wanted to hear, he didn't probe any further, satisfied that Karlov would, as usual, do what was necessary and expected of him. He was certain Karlov would secure the holy relic and bring it to him, just as he had done with Kazanskaya Bogomater.

69

Palazzo Alberti, 10 March

Countess Kuragin dropped in to see Rahima, as she did most days. Tristan had already arrived and was sitting next to Rahima, at her favourite place by the window overlooking the Grand Canal. The main topic of conversation was always the same: Jack, and what he was doing in Ukraine.

'Have you seen the latest?' asked the countess. She held up a copy of *La Nuova Venezia*, the local paper. 'It was all over TV last night.'

'Astonishing. Tristan told me.'

'President Zubenskyy addressed the European Parliament again, virtually, and quoted from Jack's eyewitness report about atrocities being committed by the retreating Russian forces in Bucha. Everyone was shocked. You could see it on their faces.'

'Terrible. And to think Jack was actually there and witnessed it all.'

'That's what he does best,' said Tristan. 'He's a man of the moment. Right place, right time. His forte. He did the same in Afghanistan.'

'Without fear for his own safety,' said the countess. 'His "Postcards from the Battlefield" are having a huge impact.'

'Just like his "Voices from the Front Line" used to—'

'Until he was injured,' interjected the countess.

'Ah. Yes, he told me about that,' said Rahima.

'The impact of his reports can be felt not just here in Europe, but around the world too,' said Tristan. 'His friend Celia Crawford at the *New York Times* made sure of that. She arranged his press credentials for Ukraine.'

'Bucha,' said Rahima, shaking her head. 'It's difficult to imagine this is actually happening right now, not that far from here.'

'Bodies lying in the street. Mainly women and children and the elderly. Shot at point blank. Civilians, dozens of them, slaughtered by soldiers. Shocking. All the Ukrainian men are in the army, fighting the war,' said the countess. 'Quite successfully, so it would seem. The Russians are in retreat.'

'That makes them even more dangerous and desperate. These atrocities are supposed to intimidate the local population and crush morale, yet they're doing the opposite,' said Tristan. 'Another Russian miscalculation.'

Rahima shrugged and stared out of the window as her mind began to wander. Again.

The countess looked at Tristan, shook her head and stood up. 'I have to get back. New guests are due to arrive shortly.'

Tristan stood up too. 'I'll walk you back,' he said. Then he kissed Rahima on the cheek. 'I'll come back later,' he whispered, well aware it was unlikely Rahima could hear him. She had become a different person since her abduction and hospitalisation. The drugs had infiltrated her mind, causing frequent disorientation and confusion. Lucid moments were rare and could disappear without warning, plunging Rahima into her own world of memories, suspended between a nebulous present and a distant past. Tristan understood this better than most. Years in a coma had taught him that reality was but a perception the mind could alter and distort without notice.

'Do you think she'll get better?' asked the countess as they were walking across the Rialto Bridge.

'Who knows?' replied Tristan. 'The mind is a strange place. I'm just glad Jack isn't here to see this. He would take it badly.'

'You're right.'

'He calls me often, you know,' said Tristan.

The countess stopped and looked at Tristan, surprised. 'He does?'

'Yes.'

'So, you know a lot more about what's going on in Ukraine? With Jack, I mean.'

'I suppose I do.'

'You always had a special bond.'

'Yes.'

'Can you tell me more? We're all terribly worried about him. You know that. He's in the middle of a war!'

'No need to be. He's exactly where he's supposed to be. Following his breadcrumbs.'

'Can be infuriating at times.'

'Tell me about it. But that's Jack. He has found *Dextera Dei*,' said Tristan softly.

'You didn't mention that before!'

'I only found out the other day myself. Jack and Abbot Serapion are working on something big.'

'To do with the relic?'

'Looks that way.'

'Did he say what it was?'

'Not as such. He mentioned destiny, that's all, but he hinted it could change the course of history. Typical Jack. Always chasing that big story. With him, you never know where fact and fiction intersect, do you?'

'That's his genius. That's what makes his books so interesting,' said the countess. 'And his stories so realistic and relevant.'

'At least he got out of Bucha in one piece,' said Tristan. 'A miracle by itself.'

'He did?'

'I spoke to him this morning.'

'Did he say what he was doing next?'

'Yes. He was on a train to Mariupol with the president's sister-in-law and her bodyguards. He sounded very excited.'

'To do what?'

'Boost the morale of the people trapped there.'

'Sounds dangerous.'

'What do you think? Adventure junkie stuff!'

The countess shook her head. 'I don't know how he does it.'

Tristan put his hand on the countess's arm. 'You should be used to this by now. It's *Jack* we are talking about here.'

'You're right. It's just …'

'I know,' said Tristan and linked arms with the countess. 'He'll let us know when he needs help. And when he does, we'll be right there. Yes?'

'When destiny calls?'

'Something like that.'

'You two are very similar, you know.'

'In what way?'

'You don't question fate.'

'No. To do that would be pointless.'

'My point exactly.'

70

Donetsk Academic Regional Drama Theatre,
Mariupol: 16 March

Since the meeting with Vira Zubenska, the president's wife, in Kyiv on 25 February, events had unfolded very quickly. Within hours, columns of Russian tanks had crossed the Ukrainian border and were advancing towards Kyiv, only to be met with unexpectedly fierce resistance and coming under attack.

Jack was given official press credentials, handed a flak jacket and a helmet, and armed with his satellite phone, camera and trusty notebook, he joined Vasylenko and her two bodyguards on their way to the front to meet the invaders. Instead of encircling Kyiv and taking the capital, the invasion had stalled and the Russian forces sustained heavy losses.

Over the next two weeks, Jack and Vasylenko met with Ukrainian troops, witnessed the bravery of civilians throwing Molotov cocktails at tanks and armoured convoys, and even accompanied President Zubenskyy on his secret train during one of his visits to the front. Jack managed to interview Zubenskyy and get to know the man who was fighting a war on a scale no-one had expected. Not surprisingly, the two of them got on very well, and Jack was particularly impressed by Zubenskyy's ability to use social media and the press as major tools to marshal support from the West to fight the war. Jack sent his freelance articles to his friend Celia Crawford at the *New York Times*, who then passed them on to various networks for maximum exposure.

While Jack's interview with Zubenskyy introduced the president, a gifted public speaker, to a wider audience, it was Jack's reports about the Battle of Bucha and the atrocities committed there that once again propelled him overnight into the international spotlight. His balanced and incisive reports of what he saw without sensationalising or over-dramatising events gave his articles a raw and quite confronting eyewitness quality that showed war as it really was: brutal, unforgiving and often totally senseless. As the battle intensified, Jack and Vasylenko left Bucha and travelled to the south, as word spread that Mariupol was under heavy attack and in a desperate situation.

By the time they reached Mariupol, there was very little left of the city. Almost every building, including apartment blocks, had been bombed and reduced to smouldering rubble by relentless, indiscriminate shelling and missile attacks that had killed thousands. Burnt-out shells of cars littered the streets pockmarked with deep craters, all part of a monstrous, systematic destruction not seen since the Second World War. Stray dogs and cats foraged for food in the rubble, and the few people huddling in the ruins next to obscene, contorted bodies, or walking aimlessly about, looked frightened and lost, with nowhere to go.

'Good God!' said Vasylenko, 'I had no idea it would be this bad.' She reached for *Zbawiciel*, the holy relic she wore around her neck, and held it tight as their car drove slowly down the deserted street towards the theatre, their destination.

Ambulance crews they had met on the outskirts of the city had told them about the theatre in the centre of town – one of the few buildings still standing – that had become a refuge for civilians, mainly women, children and the elderly, seeking shelter from the unrelenting bombardment.

Erected in 1960 on the site of the former Church of Mary Magdalene, the Donetsk Academic Regional Drama Theatre was a large, impressive building.

The first thing Jack noticed as they approached the theatre was something painted in Russian on the ground in front of the building, the large letters unmissable, even from a distance. 'What does it say?' he asked.

'Children,' replied Vasylenko. 'To tell attackers that women and children are sheltering inside.'

'In the hope of keeping the building safe to avert a missile strike?'

'What else?' said Vasylenko. 'Let's hope it works. Come, let's go inside and have a look,' she continued and began to walk towards the entrance, followed by her two heavily armed bodyguards wearing blue-and-yellow arm bands to identify them as Ukrainians.

'Can you believe this?' said Jack as they walked into the building, 'There must be hundreds in here.' Inside, the theatre resembled a crowded refugee camp: noisy, claustrophobic, chaotic, the pungent smell of unwashed bodies and fear hanging in the fetid air. Sitting in small groups on the ground, mainly mothers and their children – some of them asleep, wrapped in blankets and clinging to one another – families tried to stay together. Jack looked at an old woman holding a little dog and smiled at her. The old woman smiled back. A little girl sitting next to her held up her pet rabbit as Jack walked past, her eyes radiating intelligence and curiosity. Jack stopped, bent down and tickled the rabbit behind the ears. The girl beamed.

Vasylenko walked up to a woman handing out bottled water and spoke to her briefly. Shaking her head, Vasylenko turned around. 'There are about eight hundred people in here and in the basement,' she said. 'Can you imagine what this means?'

'No, I can't,' said Jack. 'Obviously, they have nowhere else to go.'

'No. Their homes have been destroyed and there is virtually no support here to look after them.'

'No food?'

'Only what they brought with them, which couldn't be much. This is a desperate situation.'

And a death trap, thought Jack, looking around. 'What are we going to do?' he asked.

'Try to cheer them up.'

'How?'

'I have an idea. Come.'

At the far end of the main hall packed with people was a small stage with part of an old podium in the middle. One of the few places that wasn't occupied because it was too narrow and unstable. Vasylenko climbed onto the stage and found a spot on the rickety podium she could stand on. Then she clapped her hands together until people began to look at her.

'May I have your attention, please,' she said. 'I am Ivanna Vasylenko. I bring greetings from President Zubenskyy. He sends you a message …'

'That's Vasylenko, the poet!' shouted someone in the crowd.

'Yes, that's her!' shouted someone else. Soon, all eyes in the crowded hall were on the tall woman holding up her hands, the gesture obvious. Slowly, the hall fell silent. Vasylenko cleared her throat and began to recite her famous poem about *Zbawiciel*, the holy relic that saved Ukraine from the Holodomor.

It was a long poem that told a story of unimaginable hardship, suffering and death, imposed on the Ukrainian people by forces of evil set on destroying the nation, but most important of all, it was a story about hope and faith, and how *Zbawiciel* and the people had been able to defeat evil and triumph in the end.

Because the poem was taught in school and was therefore well known, soon many joined in, young and old, until the entire hall recited the poem with one voice, rising to a crescendo in the last stanza, and moving many to tears.

After finishing the poem, Vasylenko stood in silence like a messenger of hope, letting the potent verses find their mark. Then she raised her hands again and looked at the crowd in front of her.

'*Zbawiciel* has saved Ukraine before, and it will do so again,' she said. 'St Olga is watching over you and so is the president. To show you have not been abandoned or forgotten, he has sent you something.'

Vasylenko reached under her shirt, pulled out the golden chain with the holy relic dangling at the end and held it up.

'This is *Zbawiciel*,' she said, her voice quivering with emotion, 'also known as *Dextera Dei*, the right hand of God, because part of the nail embedded in the sliver of wood here once pierced the right hand of Jesus nailed to the cross …'

Stunned silence.

Then someone began to sing the national anthem. Within moments everyone in the hall stood up and joined in, the mood in the theatre electric. Standing below the podium, Jack pulled his notebook out of his backpack. *She's amazing*, he thought, and began to jot down ideas for his next article. He always tried to do this while impressions were fresh. This was one of the main reasons his reports were so gripping and authentic, because they captured the moment and transported the reader to the scene in a way that was both realistic and plausible.

Once the last words of the anthem had ebbed away and a hush descended on the crowded hall, Vasylenko held up the relic once more for all to see.

'Anyone who would like to touch *Zbawiciel* and draw strength from something sacred, can do so now,' she said and stepped down from the podium. 'Please come forward and form a queue. Bring your children and help the elderly. I will stay here for as long as it takes.'

A few women stepped forward and began to organise the excited crowd until one long, orderly queue had been formed and people began to slowly file past Vasylenko standing between her two bodyguards like the stone angels, the guardians of souls, at the entrance to the Holodomor Museum in Kyiv.

Most of the women kissed the relic and held up their children to do the same. Some of the older women curtsied, or briefly knelt down, heads bowed and mumbling prayers. It was an intensely moving demonstration of hope and faith that Jack would never forget.

As Jack looked up, trying to find the right words to put down on paper, he could see the little girl with the rabbit standing next to her mother in front of Vasylenko. The mother was holding a baby in her arms and bent down to kiss the relic, but was obviously unable to lift up the little girl to do the same. Jack put down his notebook, walked over to the girl and held out his arms. The little girl smiled as Jack lifted her up so she could brush her pursed lips against the relic. As he gently put her down again and walked back to his place, he could hear the roar of jet engines. Distant at first, but getting louder by the second.

As the Russian fighter jet came in low at great speed, the pilot could see the target approaching below. He could also see the word 'CHILDREN' painted in Russian on the ground and once again confirmed his orders. As the jet screamed past the theatre, the pilot released two five-hundred-kilogram bombs. It was a direct hit, causing maximum destruction as the lethal bombs exploded simultaneously. Within seconds, the large building was reduced to rubble, a raging fireball rising angrily towards heaven the only evidence of the hundreds of souls buried below.

Jack opened his eyes. Darkness. He could barely breathe as something heavy was pressing down on his chest. He closed his eyes and concentrated on his breathing. Then he tried to move his legs. Nothing. Only numbness from the waist down.

Then suddenly, Jack could feel someone shaking him by the shoulder. Slowly, he opened his eyes.

'Good, he's conscious,' said one of the bodyguards.

'Let's dig him out,' said the other, and began to lift chunks of plaster and debris off Jack's trapped legs. Feeling a little better, Jack looked around. The stage and podium had all but disappeared under two massive steel girders and lumps of concrete connected to each other by twisted steel rods.

'Ivanna?' asked Jack. One of the bodyguards pointed with his chin towards the crushed stage. 'Over there,' he said. 'We just dug her out.'

'Is she—?' asked Jack.

'Barely.'

'Can you stand up?' asked the other bodyguard as the last piece of concrete was lifted off Jack's legs.

'I think so,' said Jack and tried to get up, but his legs wouldn't obey.

'All right. Let's do this another way,' said the bodyguard. He lifted Jack, carried him over to the stage and put him down next to Vasylenko.

Jack looked at Vasylenko, her blood-covered face only inches from his. Vasylenko slowly opened her eyes and looked at Jack. 'You look a mess,' she said.

'You don't look much better,' said Jack, relieved to see Vasylenko was alive.

'Listen, Jack. There isn't much time,' said Vasylenko, her eyes glazing over. 'I'm not going to make it.'

'What are you talking about?'

'My whole stomach is an open wound. I'm bleeding ...'

'Nonsense!'

Vasylenko shook her head. 'I won't make it, but you will; trust me.'

Vasylenko shakily lifted her right hand, slipped the golden chain with the relic over her head and handed it to Jack.

'Take it, Jack. You know what this is. It's up to you now. *Zbawiciel* will tell you what to do and show you the way. It's all about destiny.'

Exhausted, Vasylenko turned her head away, her laboured breathing the only sound as her body began to convulse.

'I've instructed my bodyguards to do everything they can to get you out of Ukraine,' she continued. 'They're two of our country's finest soldiers. The president made sure of that. You must tell the world what happened here. The Russians will try to cover it up. I know they will because this is a monstrous war crime. You must make sure the hundreds who just perished here didn't die in vain ...'

Vasylenko's voice became faint and almost faded away. Mustering all her remaining strength, she looked at Jack for the last time. 'Can you promise me that?' she whispered, blood seeping from her mouth as her life ebbed away.

'I promise,' said Jack, choking with emotion. Then he slipped the gold chain over his head, reached across to Vasylenko and closed her eyes.

'There's a way out,' said one of the bodyguards. 'Over there. I can see it.'

'Many survivors?' asked Jack.

'A few.'

'I'll carry him. You show us the way,' said the second bodyguard.

Jack could feel two strong arms lifting him off the ground. 'What about her?' he said and pointed to Vasylenko.

'She doesn't need us anymore. You do. We must get out of here, quickly! Look at the fire!'

Jack could see his notebook lying on the floor. 'I must have that,' he said. The bodyguard leading the way nodded, picked up the notebook and slipped it into his backpack.

As he was being carried past the broken podium, Jack could see the body of the little girl with the rabbit, her face unrecognisable, lying next to her dead mother still holding what was left of her baby in her arms. They had all been crushed by the same steel beam that had fatally injured Vasylenko moments after Jack had lifted the little girl to kiss *Dextera Dei*.

71

Time Machine Studios, London: 24 March

Isis had just finished eating breakfast in her study with Lola after their morning exercise routine, when her phone rang.

'It's Jack,' said Isis, excited, as she looked at the screen before answering the call.

'At last!' said Lola. They hadn't heard from Jack since the Mariupol Theatre disaster. Jack had filed a report the day after the theatre bombing that had killed six hundred, mainly women and children. The report went viral and was featured on countless news channels around the world. It was the only credible eyewitness account of a war crime that had made the Western world hold its breath in disbelief.

'Where are you?' Isis almost shouted. 'Odessa? *In hospital?*'

After a few minutes Isis put down the phone, a worried look on her face.

'Well?' prompted Lola.

'He's been badly injured during the attack in Mariupol. It's a miracle he made it out alive. He's in a hospital in Odessa. Hiding.'

'What do you mean, *hiding?*'

'Apparently, there's a price on his head since he filed that theatre piece that made all those headlines calling the attack a war crime. Palin must be furious. The Russians are looking for him.'

'Jesus! That could explain why he didn't call earlier. He must be lying low.'

'Most likely. He said if he doesn't get out of Ukraine soon ...'

'He needs our help, right?'

'Yes. Desperately. He wanted to know if the *Caritas* has made it to the Black Sea.'

'He requested that after the Bucha massacre, didn't he?' said Lola.

'Yes. I told him the ship arrived a few days ago from Malta, and is now in Moldova, in Giurgiulesti, an international free port. That's as close as she could get to Ukraine with the Russian blockade in place. The ship is now ready to help injured refugees. He seemed very relieved to hear that because thousands of Ukrainians are crossing the border into Moldova every day, many of them injured.'

The *Caritas* was a hospital ship, a mercy ship, supported by the Isis Foundation and Jack's mother. It operated mainly in Africa, but was based in Malta.

'Did he say how bad his injuries are?'

'No, he didn't, but he obviously needs hospital care.'

'Typical Jack. So, what's the plan?'

'We go to Giurgiulesti as soon as possible. That's what Jack asked for.'

'What kind of place is that?'

'It's a significant port situated at the confluence of two great rivers, the Danube and the Prut, which gives Moldova, a landlocked country, access to the Black Sea.'

'Along the river?'

'Yes. At one point you can actually see the borders of Ukraine and Romania. Quite unique.'

'And then what?'

'He'll let us know. But he wants us to bring Tristan with us. We both know what he can do ...'

'Makes sense.'

'Isn't it exciting?' said Isis, who had been desperately waiting for an opportunity to become involved in the search for *Dextera Dei* that had taken Jack to Ukraine in the first place.

'Did he mention the relic?'

'No. This was all about getting out of Ukraine.'

'All right. I'll get the plane ready,' said Lola. 'This looks like an emergency to me.'

'Sure does.'

'I'll tell Sasha,' said Isis. 'She may want to come with us. After all, we have common interests.'

'*Golgotha* and the holy relic?'

'Of course. You know how much that relic means to her.'

'When do you want to leave?'

'Right away. I'll tell Tristan to meet us at Venice airport.'

Three hours later, *Pegasus* left London Luton Airport, where Isis's private jet was based. Sasha had gratefully accepted the invitation and met Isis and Lola at the airport. Lola was at the controls, enjoying the take-off.

She looks exhausted, thought Isis, sitting next to Sasha in the main cabin as the plane ascended. Not surprising, considering what had been going on in Russia and Ukraine.

'Any news from Anatoly?' asked Isis as the plane reached cruising altitude and levelled out.

Sasha shook her head. 'The silence is the worst, but he seems to have abandoned the hunger strike. Russian papers reported that.'

'At least that's something.'

'I had a call from Serapion last night.'

'Oh? What about?'

'Jack.'

'He's been in touch with him?' asked Isis, surprised.

'Frequently, it would seem. Serapion knows President Zubenskyy and his wife very well, and the Metropolitan of Kyiv is a good friend. Apparently, both are keen to get Jack out of Ukraine after the Mariupol Theatre disaster and are doing everything they can to make this possible.'

'Encouraging. Because of Jack's high profile and influence with the press, I suppose? His latest report was a sensation.'

'Of course that's part of it, but there's more.'

'What do you mean?'

Sasha looked at Isis and smiled sanguinely. 'According to Serapion, Jack has something precious with him that must under no circumstances be lost or fall into Russian hands ...'

'*Dextera Dei?*' ventured Isis softly.

Sasha nodded.

'Those breadcrumbs again.' Isis shook her head. 'After all, that was the main reason he went to Ukraine. I don't know how he does it. Somehow, he always seems to come up with the goods. In most unexpected ways.'

'Certainly looks that way. Serapion was very excited. Apparently, two elite bodyguards provided by the president are with Jack and helped him get out of Mariupol and reach Odessa. They're protecting him.'

'And we have to somehow get him out of there, right?'

'Yes. I got the impression his injuries are quite serious ...'

'Well, we have an entire hospital ship with a helicopter on board standing by not that far from the Ukrainian border.'

'That should help. Serapion indicated *Dextera Dei* could change the outcome of the entire war and have a direct bearing on Anatoly's future, and the future of Russia.'

'Did he explain how?'

'No.'

'We thought you knew,' said Isis, watching Sasha carefully.

'No. Not the details. Serapion kept all that to himself. He said it was too dangerous for others to know more. All I know is he needs the relic to make it all work.'

'A bit strange, don't you think?'

'It is, but if you're as desperate as I am, you cling to everything you can, even miracles.'

Isis put her hand on Sasha's arm. 'I understand, but don't forget we'll have some serious help in this rescue mission.'

'What help?'

'Tristan, of course. He has certain gifts ...'

'And that could help?'

'I've seen him do things that are difficult to explain. Rationally, I mean. His instincts and insights are extraordinary. He's saved Jack from peril before. In Somalia and Colombia, and then not that long ago in Bavaria. The O'Hara affair ... the two have a special bond. We'll pick up Tristan in Venice on our way.'

442

Feeling better, Sasha looked at Isis. 'Do you think this is destiny in action?'

'After all that's happened so far, how can you have any doubts about that?'

'If you look at it that way, you're right. Anatoly would certainly agree with you. He's a firm believer in destiny, and he also believes that removing Palin and his corrupt regime and returning Russia to the right path is his destiny. That's what keeps him going.'

'Now, relax and enjoy the flight. I suspect we'll need all our faculties functioning perfectly once we get to Moldova. Whichever way you look at it, this won't be easy.'

'You're enjoying this,' said Sasha.

'Is it that obvious?'

'It is.'

Because Isis was well known in Venice and very popular, the authorities again waived most of the Italian red tape and *Pegasus* was allowed to continue its journey shortly after Tristan had come on board. This saved precious time.

Isis poured Tristan a glass of orange juice shortly after take-off and handed it to him. 'You don't seem surprised to see us,' she said.

'No. I've been expecting something like this.'

'How come?'

Tristan shrugged. 'I knew Jack was in trouble days ago. I couldn't sleep. I saw things; I could even feel his pain.'

Isis made eye contact with Sasha and nodded. 'Somalia all over again.'

'And Yekaterinburg. The stabbing. That was really bad,' said Tristan. 'And not just because of the injuries. Anielka ...'

Sasha shook her head. 'How many lives does this man have?'

'I've often asked myself the same question,' replied Tristan. 'I think only one, but it's a charmed life.'

'Because of friends like you?' said Sasha.

'That certainly has something to do with it,' said Isis, smiling. 'But friendships don't happen in a vacuum.'

'It's karma, actually,' said Tristan.

Sasha looked at Tristan, surprised. 'What do you mean?'

'Tristan's absolutely right,' said Isis. 'Jack does amazing, selfless things for other people. Instinctively and without hesitation, especially for friends and people he knows, but often also for total strangers. It comes naturally to him. And when he's in trouble and needs help, they reciprocate. Good karma, see?'

'Is it really that simple?'

'Perhaps not, but just look at the *Caritas*, the hospital ship that just arrived in Giurgiulesti. The man in charge of that ship is Dr Agabe, a gifted surgeon from Africa. He and Jack know each other well and have shared some astonishing adventures—'

'The Stolzfus matter,' interjected Lola, who had handed controls to the co-pilot after leaving Venice and now sat in the cabin next to Isis. 'The revolutionary head transplant.'

'Exactly. You remember Dr Agabe, Tristan, don't you?'

'Of course. He saved Rahima's life in Colombia a few years ago, and the ship itself has a long history; quite a tragic one, actually, until you purchased it and are now running it as a refurbished mercy ship financed by the Isis Foundation.'

'And Countess Kuragin helped Dr Agabe, a refugee, obtain French citizenship. She used her influence and money to make that possible,' said Isis. 'Wheels within wheels and more good karma.'

'And now the ship is right here on the Ukrainian border in case Jack needs some urgent medical assistance, which, I suspect, he certainly will,' said Tristan. 'Administered by his friend Dr Agabe. Coincidence? What do you think?'

Sasha sighed. 'You're all very fortunate. You have a rare friendship that binds you together in a special way,' said Sasha. 'I've never known anything quite like it. You function as a unit of goodwill, looking after one another. Unfortunately, I'm alone. And that's very hard ...'

'What are you talking about?' said Isis. 'Just look around. Do you seriously think you're alone? No, you're among friends. Surely you can see that? *Dextera Dei* has brought us together.'

GABRIEL FARAGO

'You really mean that?' whispered Sasha, tears glistening in her cornflower-blue eyes.

'Absolutely!'

'I have some good news,' said Tristan, changing the subject to give Sasha some space.

'Oh? What about?' asked Lola.

'I spoke to Cesaria last night. Apparently, Samartini had an unexpected breakthrough in locating O'Hara in Belarus.'

'*Really?* Tell us,' said Isis.

'It's quite a story, as you will see in a moment.'

'You sound just like Jack,' said Lola.

'Samartini and her colleagues at ENFAST set a trap for O'Hara,' continued Tristan, undeterred.

'What kind of trap?' asked Lola.

'By offering the disgraced prison guard at the Pagliarelli Prison in Palermo a deal, they managed to make contact with O'Hara by using the illegal phone Giordano had been given by the guard. The guard pretended to be calling on behalf of Giordano with a proposal, and it all went from there.'

'And O'Hara fell for this?' said Isis.

'He did. Of course, he didn't know the guard had been arrested, and the whole Giordano connection exposed and shut down. Desperate people do desperate things, and O'Hara seems to be very desperate at the moment. Frustrated by his isolation and the loss of his gambling empire, I'd say. A difficult situation for someone used to being in control and pulling all the strings. That's when mistakes happen.'

'So, what happened?' Sasha asked.

'To cut a long story short, by setting up and monitoring several carefully planned calls, Samartini managed to pinpoint O'Hara's location through some clever cellphone triangulation. We know exactly where he is, and he's unlikely to go anywhere soon. He's in a small village just outside Minsk.'

'It's all falling into place,' said Isis. 'All we need now is *Dextera Dei* to pull it all together, right?'

445

Sasha nodded. 'And a bit of luck and good karma.'

Isis turned to Lola sitting next to her. 'So, what's the plan when we arrive?'

'I've arranged a car to take us to Giurgiulesti. Should take about three hours. We're staying on the ship. Agabe insisted. From there we can deal with Jack's situation, whatever happens. It's the best place. Don't forget there's a chopper on board. That gives us many options.'

'Provided he can get close,' said Tristan.

Isis nodded. 'You're right, but we all know Jack. He'll come up with something. He knows the ship is at Giurgiulesti and he asked us to get there as soon as possible. That's going to be his destination. I'm sure he has a plan.'

As the plane began its descent, the loudspeakers crackled into life.

'All right, guys. Time to buckle up,' said the pilot. 'What you can see down there is Chisinau, the capital of Moldova, the poorest country in Europe. Chisinau International Airport awaits. Here we go.'

72

Palin had hardly left his office in three days, nor had he slept much, which made him irritable and aggressive. The setbacks in Ukraine were taking their toll. Despite assurances from his generals, the ruthless attacks on civilian targets he had authorised to crush Ukrainian morale were not having the desired effect. The invasion was going badly. Russian casualties were massive and the Ukrainians were fighting the invaders with more courage and resolve than ever before. President Zubenskyy's leadership had also surprised many, and his speeches televised around the world were hugely successful in marshalling support from the West.

After another frustrating briefing session with his generals, Palin walked over to Kazanskaya Bogomater and looked pensively at the icon.

'Why isn't it working?' he asked himself aloud. Then he returned to his desk, fuming, and called the only man he thought he could trust and rely on to tell him how things were really going. Despite the late hour – it was just past eleven – Karlov was admitted to Palin's office thirty minutes later.

'I know what you're going to say,' said Palin, holding up his hand. 'The Mariupol Theatre strike was a mistake.'

'It was,' said Karlov. 'And so was Bucha. Brutal, clumsy attacks on unarmed civilians like this only galvanise resistance and resolve, and strengthen the enemy. Not to forget the condemnation around the world, and the accusations of war crimes.'

'That's what I told the generals. They don't seem to understand! Ignorant fools, one and all. I sacked two of them just a short while ago.'

'You did tell them to crush morale and do whatever it takes to achieve that,' Karlov reminded Palin.

'True.' Palin pointed to Kazanskaya Bogomater behind Karlov. 'Do you think she disapproves? Is that why?'

Karlov shrugged.

'What's the mood like out there?' asked Palin.

'Difficult to say. All seems quiet at the moment.'

'Good. Media reports are, of course, strictly controlled, right? The people know very little about what's happening in Ukraine. This is a military operation, not a war. They hear only what we tell them.'

'But they know about the body bags coming home. That's difficult to hide,' said Karlov.

Palin waved dismissively. Casualties didn't bother him. 'At least we seem to have silenced the annoying opposition. Isolating Novotny in jail was certainly the way to go. No more rousing speeches, no more embarrassing videos.'

He can't see it, thought Karlov. This was the quiet before the storm. Palin was completely out of touch with reality. His generals knew it, but were too afraid to tell him.

'And no more hunger strikes, thanks to Serapion,' said Karlov, steering the conversation towards the subject he wanted to talk about, because he knew it was Palin's vulnerable side, full of doubts and desperately seeking reassurance.

'Sending him to see Novotny was clever,' said Palin. 'Novotny obviously listened to him. I wonder what Serapion said to him?'

'Serapion is a mystic. He has his ways ...'

'And are his ways getting us any closer to *Dextera Dei*?' asked Palin, watching Karlov carefully.

'Yes, in fact they are. I just spoke to Serapion. He believes *Dextera Dei* is about to change sides.'

'*Really?* And why do you think it would do that?' said Palin, becoming excited.

Karlov took his time before answering the question because he sensed danger. He knew he was dealing with an unstable megalomaniac out of touch with reality and drunk on power, who was prepared to do anything to satisfy his dark desires.

'A mystic like Serapion can see things.'

'What kind of things?'

'Things that are often hidden and difficult to understand.'

'You speak in riddles.'

'Not that long ago we discussed the prophecies of Daniel and Revelation 13 right here in this office, remember?'

'Of course.'

'Well, Serapion knows a lot about these things, especially Revelation 13.'

'You told me.'

'He believes that *Dextera Dei*, the right hand of God, is the sign that will show itself to the victor when the time is right. It's the sign you've been waiting for.'

'Seriously? And is that what you believe too?'

'Yes, I do.'

'And could that change the war and reverse our setbacks, do you think?'

'Yes, it could certainly do that, but only if the holy relic reaches you personally. That would be the telling sign. Only then will Russia prevail and triumph,' said Karlov, preparing the way for what he was hoping would soon come to pass.

Palin nodded as he remembered the prophecies and Revelation 13. Because he so desperately wanted to believe, he did.

Karlov knew he was playing a dangerous game full of uncertainties and the slippery traps of the unexpected. Yet he smiled because he was certain all he had to do was leave the bait dangling in front of Palin, convinced he would be unable to resist and swallow it eagerly when the time came.

However, when he looked at the expression on Palin's face, a cold shudder rippled through him as he glimpsed something profoundly frightening. Strangely, it had nothing to do with Palin. What Karlov had glimpsed at that moment, was his own mortality.

'When you speak to Serapion next, please tell him to hurry.' Mollified, Palin reached into one of the desk drawers and took out a bottle of vodka and two glasses. 'It's getting late. Drink?'

73

On the way to Moldova: 26 March

Bohdan, one of the bodyguards who had been watching over Jack, hadn't left the crowded hospital ward all night. He walked over to Jack's bed and shook Jack by the shoulder. 'Wake up,' he said. It was just after sunrise.

Jack opened his eyes and winced as the veil of sleep lifted and the pain returned. 'Something wrong?' he asked.

'Petro was here a moment ago. Two men have been asking about an injured foreigner downstairs.'

'FSB?'

'Most likely. We know they're looking for you, but there are Russian sympathisers and saboteurs everywhere. Even in here. We can't be too careful.'

'Where's Petro now?'

'Getting the van ready.'

'We're leaving?'

'No choice.'

'But the doctor said two more days at least?'

Bohdan shrugged. 'It's no longer safe here. And besides, can you hear the explosions? The city is under attack right now. Who knows how this will end. Look what they did to Mariupol.'

Getting out of the bombed theatre in Mariupol alive had taken its toll. Jack's injuries had made him immobile, and he had to be carried all the way by Bohdan and Petro, his new bodyguards. It had taken them hours to make it to the relative safety of the Azovstal Iron and Steel Works, where most of the Ukrainian troops left in Mariupol were holding out in bunkers, fighting the Russians.

Because of specific orders from the president, doors opened for Jack. He was evacuated to a small village near Berdyansk on the Sea of Azov on one of the helicopters flying out injured soldiers. From there, the long, five-hundred-kilometre journey to Odessa had taken more than a week because travelling on main roads during the day had been far too dangerous. For that reason, they had to hide in villages, sometimes for many hours, to avoid Russian patrols.

The medical attention Jack had received at the steel works had only been basic. It wasn't until they reached Odessa and Jack was taken to a hospital that a closer examination of his injuries had been possible. His right leg was a mess, with deep flesh wounds that had to be operated on, and his ankle was broken in two places. Apart from that and extensive bruising, he had several cracked ribs that caused a lot of pain, and a deep cut on his forehead that had required stitches.

'All right,' said Jack and sat up. 'You'll have to carry me down. There's no way I can walk. Please hand me my trousers.'

'No problem. Ah, here comes Petro,' said Bohdan as he helped Jack get dressed.

'FSB, no doubt about it,' said Petro. 'We must hurry!'

'You saw them?'

'Yes. They're going through the wards right now, looking for Jack. They even have a photo!' Petro gathered up Jack's clothes and backpack. 'We'll take the back stairs. Let's go! You can finished getting dressed later.'

Lying on a mattress in the back of an old baker's van Bohdan had commandeered in Berdyansk, Jack was relatively comfortable as the strong painkillers kicked in and helped him cope with the pain. His main problem was mobility. The broken ankle made walking impossible, and because of the cracked ribs, he couldn't use crutches. This made Jack totally reliant on his bodyguards.

'Moldova?' asked Jack.

'Yes,' said Bohdan, who was driving.

'At least the border isn't far. Fifty kilometres, would you say?'

'We're not going to Palanca. Too dangerous. That's the main entry point for refugees into Moldova from here. I'm sure they'll be watching that.'

'And you'd be quite easy to spot, my friend,' said Petro, 'don't you think?' He reached into his pocket, pulled out a packet of cigarettes and lit up. 'We're staying in Ukraine and going to Giurgiulesti using back roads in the south east, hugging the coast, just as we've done before. We'll cross the border there.'

'But that's three hundred kilometres from here,' said Jack.

'It is. It's our best option, trust me.'

'You're right. I understand.' Jack reached for his backpack and took out his satellite phone. 'Could we stop for a moment, please? I want to make a phone call.'

Tristan was talking with Dr Agabe on the bridge of the *Caritas* when Isis burst in.

'I just had a call from Jack,' said Isis, excited. 'He isn't that far away.'

'That's great,' said Tristan. 'He's already in Moldova?'

'No. Still in Ukraine. He's coming in from the coast. Safer that way, he said. He asked us to meet him at the border. He'll call and let us know when.'

Agabe pointed to the east. 'That's just over there,' he said. 'Very close. We're right on the border here.'

'Did he say how he was travelling?' asked Tristan.

'By car. With his bodyguards,' said Isis.

Tristan shook his head. 'That's Jack. He may be injured, but he has his own bodyguards!'

Exhausted, Jack was desperately trying to get some sleep in the back of the lurching van that made him very uncomfortable and caused a lot of pain even the strong painkillers couldn't mask. The long, arduous journey along rutted backroads towards Giurgiulesti on the Danube just over the border was taking its toll.

'How much longer?' asked Jack.

Petro pointed to the map on his lap. 'We're about here. Quite close to the border. Not far now.'

Bohdan, who was driving, had been watching a black SUV in the rear vision mirror for some time. When he turned into a narrow, deserted side road to bypass a village and the SUV did the same, he was certain.

'I think we're being followed, guys,' said Bohdan.

'Are you sure?' said Petro. He put down the map and reached for the machine gun next to him on the seat. When he turned to have a look, he noticed the SUV was accelerating. 'Shit! He's coming up behind us, *fast!*'

'I can't outrun him. Not here!' shouted Bohdan. He pulled a handgun out of his belt and kept watching the SUV in the mirror. That's when he noticed a man leaning out of one of the car windows. He was holding what looked like a rocket launcher. 'Jesus! I think he's got an NLAW!' An NLAW was a single-soldier missile system that could knock out a tank with just one shot. 'If this hits us, we're gone!'

When Bohdan saw a flash he instinctively turned the steering wheel sharply to the left, narrowly missing a small truck coming towards them. The van mounted the kerb, rolled several times and came to rest against a tree. Having missed its target, the missile smashed into the ongoing truck, blowing it apart and setting it on fire. Travelling at high speed, the SUV crashed into the burning truck and exploded.

Wedged against the mangled back of the van, Jack looked around, disorientated. The mattress he had been lying on had somehow protected him from the worst of the impact. The back door of the van was missing and Jack could see the twisted wreck of the SUV and the burning truck.

'Bohdan's dead,' said Petro, gasping. 'How are you?'

'Okay, I think. You?'

'Fine. I've been lucky. We must get out of here – fast! Drag yourself out the back. I'll try to open my door here and get out from this side.'

Ignoring the excruciating pain in his chest, Jack pulled himself slowly towards the back of the van. He had the presence of mind to grab his backpack and throw it out onto the road before crawling after it. All he could think of was his satellite phone. *I hope it still works*, he thought and almost passed out as he finally dragged himself out of the van and collapsed on the muddy ground, exhausted.

After several attempts, Petro managed to prise open the passenger door and crawl outside. When he looked towards the burning truck on the road, he saw a man standing next to the wreck of the SUV. His face was covered in blood and he was holding a machine gun.

That's all I need, thought Petro and turned around, searching for his AK-74. He found it under the twisted front seat and managed to pull it out. When he turned back, he could see the man limping towards him, trying to aim the gun. Before Petro could lift his gun, the man fired but missed because he could barely lift the gun or see properly. He then turned and staggered back to the wreck of the SUV and disappeared behind it just as Petro was about to fire.

'What's going on?' shouted Jack from the back of the van.

'Man with a machine gun. Over there, behind the wreck. I think he's the only survivor from the SUV.'

'*Great!* I'll call the ship. Do you know where we are?'

'Very close to the border. Giurgiulesti is just over there. You can see it from here. We almost made it. You stay exactly where you are. I'll keep us covered. He's injured and very unsteady on his feet.'

Lola ran towards the helicopter at the back of the ship and got in. As an experienced pilot, she knew exactly what to do.

'Just like Mogadishu,' said Tristan and got in next to her.

'I'll come too,' said Dr Agabe, holding a machine gun. Having grown up in Somalia, he knew how to handle a gun. Jack had called a few minutes earlier and told them about his predicament and where he was. Moments later, the chopper took off and headed towards the Ukrainian border.

'He said he was very close. A truck's on fire. We should see the smoke,' said Lola, flying quite low.

'There!' shouted Tristan, pointing ahead. 'Smoke.'

Jack could hear the loud engine noise of the approaching chopper and smiled. 'The cavalry is coming,' he shouted.

'Not a moment too soon,' replied Petro and fired another round towards the SUV.

'There they are,' said Tristan as the chopper flew over the burning wreck of the truck.

Lola turned the chopper around and hovered above it for a better look. 'Can you see anything?' she said.

The man behind the crushed SUV looked up and fired at the helicopter.

'Gun, eleven o'clock!' shouted Tristan.

Agabe leaned out of the open window and fired as Lola prepared to land on the road behind the wreck.

Finding himself under fire from two sides, the man behind the SUV tried to find better cover. Firing his gun at the chopper hovering above, he stood up and began to run towards a farmhouse by the side of the road. For an instant, Petro had him in his sights. Just before the man reached the farmhouse, Petro fired. It was a clean shot hitting the man in the back of the head. He was dead before he hit the ground.

'There's Jack!' shouted Tristan, pointing down. Moments later, the chopper landed and Tristan came running towards Jack. 'How are you, mate?' he said.

'Still kicking, sort of.'

'Agabe's here, he'll look after you.' Tristan knelt down beside Jack. 'You look a wreck.'

'Hardly surprising. It's a bit of a miracle I'm here at all.' Jack reached under his shirt, pulled out the golden chain with the relic and held it up. 'I think it's all thanks to this,' he said, grinning.

'*Dextera Dei?* The right hand of God?' asked Tristan.

'Yes. The price was high, but here it is.'

74

Time Machine Studios: 29 March

Sasha and Serapion arrived together. Serapion had flown in from Moscow the day before, and had spent the night at the Ivanov mansion.

'He seems to have pulled it off. Against all odds,' he said in the lift taking them up to Isis's study on the top floor.

'The helicopter rescue in Moldova was something else,' said Sasha. 'Lola is an amazing pilot. I was outside on the deck of the *Caritas* when they came back. Jack was covered in blood and looked barely alive. Are you ready for this?'

'What do you mean?'

'You've been looking for *Dextera Dei*, the right hand of God, for a long time, haven't you?'

'I have, but I never doubted this moment would come.'

Sasha shook her head. 'You're a fortunate man.'

'In what way?'

'You're a man of faith; I'm merely a woman of hope, and that can be very challenging at times. Especially in the current climate with Anatoly in a dreadful jail in Russia, and his supporters silenced and living in fear.'

'We're about to change that, aren't we?'

'I hope so, but I still don't know how. You've told me very little ...'

'With the help of *Dextera Dei*, of course,' said Serapion, deflecting the implied question he wasn't ready, or able, to answer. 'Anatoly is the sparrow who will defeat the cockroach – soon,' he said instead. 'You'll see.'

'You mean fairy tales can come true?'

'Yes, but only if you believe in them.'

Isis and Tristan met them at the lift and greeted them warmly.

'How is he?' asked Serapion.

'Getting better. He's been through a lot and has seen things no-one should have to,' said Isis.

'And he almost got killed during that attack at the border,' said Tristan. 'We just got there in the nick of time. You should have seen him when we brought him back in the chopper.'

'I did,' said Sasha.

'Two days in care on the hospital ship have done wonders for him,' said Isis. 'Dr Agabe is a magician when it comes to surgery. He patched him up and prepared him for the flight home. Difficult to believe, but it was only yesterday we came back.'

'I've read his "Postcards from the Battlefield",' said Serapion. 'The ones from Bucha and Mariupol put the horrors of this war into perspective.'

Isis nodded. 'He hasn't said much about that. I think he's trying to digest it all and come to terms with what's happened there. Now the adrenaline rush of the moment has worn off, the haunting memories are taking their toll.'

'I know exactly what you mean,' said Serapion. 'It's a dark place. I've been there,' he added softly.

'Jack wanted us to meet up here in my study. He loves this room. He finds it relaxing. He calls it a "journey room" because of all the memorabilia I've collected along the way. Reminders of life's special moments we treasure. I think it appeals to the storyteller in him.'

'No doubt,' said Serapion, looking around. 'I can see what he means.'

Isis pointed to a comfortable lounge and chairs facing the panoramic windows overlooking the Thames. 'Please take a seat.'

Moments later, the lift door opened and Lola pushed Jack's wheelchair into the room. 'Here's the patient,' said Lola. 'He's hard work, I can tell you.'

Jack waved dismissively. 'Don't listen to her. She enjoys being in charge.'

Serapion was shocked by Jack's appearance, but encouraged by his irrepressible humour and spirit. The old Jack was definitely there, but he appeared to have lost a lot of weight, and his pallid complexion and the bandage around his forehead made him look like a wounded soldier who had just returned from war.

Sasha walked over to him, bent down and gave him a peck on the cheek. 'How are you?'

'Improving.'

Jack noticed Serapion watching him. 'In case you're wondering ... if you go into the lion's den, you must be prepared to get mauled.' Jack pointed to his bandaged head and foot. 'I got mauled,' he said, laughing. 'Nothing serious, just a bloody nuisance. My main problem's the ankle; it's a bugger. Anyway, it's wonderful to see you. Are we going to have a drink? I hope so, because we have something to celebrate!'

'In that case, champagne?' said Isis.

'Perfect.' Jack turned to Tristan. 'Could you please bring *Golgotha* over here?'

Tristan nodded, walked over to the piano and brought the easel with the little painting over to the window for all to see.

'I'm not used to this,' said Jack, squirming in his seat as he tried to turn his wheelchair around.

'Better get used to it, buster,' said Lola. 'You can't put any weight on that foot for at least a couple of weeks. You heard what Agabe said.'

Jack shrugged. 'It's difficult to believe it was just over two months ago we found *Golgotha* in Doha; perhaps the most unlikely place if we consider what *Golgotha* is, and where it came from. But all this is now part of its remarkable history. And, of course, it didn't stop there. In many ways, finding *Golgotha* was just the beginning. There are so many threads to this story that it's easy to get lost in the complex tapestry.'

Isis walked over to Jack and handed him a glass of champagne. Jack took a sip and looked pensively at *Golgotha*. 'Who would have believed this painting could hold the key to something so precious that an artist like van Eyck decided to incorporate it into his divine masterpiece, which has astonished and inspired countless generations to this very day.'

Jack turned his wheelchair around and looked at Sasha. 'Not that long ago, we shared what you called a moment of destiny. You told me that I had a decision to make. I could either join you and Abbot Serapion in the search for *Dextera Dei* – and become an instrument of destiny that could shape the future not only of Russia, but also of mankind – or I could walk away and forget all about it. Heady words. I'm sure you remember what happened next.'

'You rang me the next day after your meeting with Abbot Serapion in Ghent and gave me your answer,' said Sasha.

'And we all know what that answer was. Fateful as it turned out, because so much has happened since then. Sadly, death and destruction on an almost unimaginable scale were part of it—'

'And you almost got killed,' interjected Tristan.

'But I didn't. I'm here, and I firmly believe I owe it all to this.'

Jack reached under his shirt, pulled out the gold chain with the holy relic and held it up. A long moment of silence followed as everyone in the room stared at the small piece of wood with the iron nail embedded in it.

'I believe we're witnessing a historic moment,' said Jack. Slowly, he wheeled himself over to the easel and draped the golden chain with the relic over the frame of the small painting. The relic came to rest against the church in the background and for a brief moment became part of it.

Sasha walked over to Jack and put her hand on his shoulder. 'You've kept your side of the bargain. I'm ready to keep mine.'

'O'Hara?'

'Yes. All you have to do is tell me where to find him.'

'As you know, I can help here,' said Tristan, stepping in. 'Samartini and her colleagues have located O'Hara in Belarus. He's in a small village just outside Minsk. They know exactly where he is.'

Serapion joined Sasha at the wheelchair and put his hand on Jack's other shoulder.

'You have just given the sparrow the power to defeat the cockroach,' he said. 'And for that, Russia will be forever in your debt, my friend. This is a true moment of destiny.'

'And what a story for his next book,' said Lola, a sparkle in her eyes.

Jack was beaming. For the first time in days he felt relaxed and at ease. 'You know me too well, guys.' Enjoying himself, Jack looked around the room and held up his glass.

'A toast. To *Golgotha* and *Dextera Dei*. May the right hand of God protect Ukraine and continue to defeat evil. Cheers!'

'And may it liberate Russia from the yoke of tyranny and corruption,' added Serapion gravely.

Jack nodded. 'And let's not forget David Herzl, master forger and Postmaster of Treblinka, in all this. Without him, none of this would have been possible. In the true sense, this is his legacy.'

'To David Herzl,' said Isis and raised her glass.

'To David Herzl,' said the others and did the same.

75

Gorky Park, Moscow: 1 April

Serapion approached the meeting with Karlov with trepidation. So much had happened since their last meeting two months earlier. In a way, the world had changed. The invasion of Ukraine had seen to that. Palin's grip on power had become more dictatorial. Opposing voices had been brutally silenced and freedom of speech had all but disappeared. Russia had become a pariah on the world stage, with drastic sanctions that threatened to cripple the economy.

Like all dictators who find themselves with their backs to the wall and under pressure, any kind of defeat or retreat wasn't an option. A catastrophic miscalculation was rapidly turning into a national disaster that had to be covered up and turned around at all costs, and Palin was prepared to do whatever was necessary to make this possible, even if it meant turning to the supernatural and the occult for answers.

Karlov had carefully nurtured and encouraged this predilection that had recently almost turned into an obsession of a desperate man looking for reassurance. Karlov's entire strategy was based on that, and *Dextera Dei* was the centrepiece of a daring plan to remove Palin and liberate Russia from the greedy, corrupt grip of a megalomaniac who threatened to destroy the country and take Russia back to a Soviet-like era that had failed.

This time it had been Serapion who had called for an urgent meeting. Instead of telling Karlov that he had secured the precious relic, he decided to hold back that vital information and ask Karlov to explain how an ancient relic could remove a dictator like Palin and pull Russia, and the world, back from the brink. Only after that, would he hand over *Dextera Dei*.

Serapion could see Karlov standing under the colonnade near the main entrance. It was a lonely figure and Serapion asked himself how one man, however well-connected and close to the president, could possibly change history – because that was precisely the question he intended to put to Karlov. Serapion realised this was his only chance to find answers to this vital question because once he handed over *Dextera Dei*, events would have a momentum of their own that most likely wouldn't include him.

While Serapion and Karlov had, of course, communicated since their last meeting, they hadn't met face to face. For obvious reasons, a face-to-face meeting in a secure place like Gorky Park, where they couldn't be overheard, was the only occasion when they could speak frankly and discuss sensitive matters.

Karlov realised Serapion wouldn't have called for the meeting without good reason and had made the necessary arrangements accordingly, regardless of the obvious risks involved.

'Good to see you, my friend,' said Karlov and extended his hand.

'Events have overtaken us since our last meeting and not for the better, I'm afraid,' said Serapion. 'Bucha and the Mariupol Theatre massacre. How could these atrocities have happened? I'm struggling to understand.'

'You're not alone, but the explanation is in fact simple. Once a deranged megalomaniac like Palin starts a war, anything goes. History is full of examples. I'm sure you can think of a few and so can I.'

'True. Last time we met, you told me that we were involved in a race against one man's insanity and burning ambition.'

'Correct. Recent events have made that abundantly clear.'

'They have. You also said there was only one way to stop a man with so much power. Do you remember what I asked you then?'

'Yes, of course. You asked if that meant stopping, or removing …'

'And you said?'

'That the two mean the same thing.'

'If I understand you correctly,' continued Serapion. '*Dextera Dei* will play a pivotal role in removing Palin from office. Am I right?'

'Yes.'

'And you've carefully prepared the way to make this possible?'

'I have.'

For a while, the two men walked along in silence. Then Karlov stopped and looked at his friend. 'Rogan has found *Dextera Dei*. Correct?'

Put on the spot with nowhere to go, Serapion nodded.

Karlov took a deep breath. 'Thank God! I was desperately hoping this meeting would be about that, because time's running out. Have you got it with you?'

'Before I answer that, I'd like to ask you a question. I've asked it before, but your answer has always been the same.'

'Evasive, you mean?'

'Yes.'

'With good reason, as you will see in a moment.'

'Perhaps so, but the time has come.'

'For me to tell you how this will work? How a two-thousand-year-old relic can defeat an evil man and change history?'

'Yes, I need to know.'

'All right. Come, let's walk and I'll tell you.'

For the next half-hour Serapion and Karlov strolled through Gorky Park. Stunned by what Karlov told him, Serapion stopped several times and questioned his friend about various aspects of a plan so daring it left him almost speechless.

'I'm sure you can see now why I couldn't tell you any of this earlier. If a single word of this got out ...'

'I can. And you sincerely believe you can pull this off?'

'I do. Why? Because this is too important to fail.'

'You're putting your life on the line for this?'

'Without hesitation.'

'When?'

'The sooner the better. Every hour counts here.'

'In that case, let's start the clock right now.' Serapion reached under his shirt and pulled out the golden chain with the relic, just as Jack had done a few days earlier.

Karlov looked at it and held his breath, his eyes wide with wonder. '*Is that it?*' he stammered, momentarily overcome by emotion.

'It is. This is *Dextera Dei*, the right hand of God that has the power to defeat evil,' said Serapion softly.

'Thank you, my friend,' said Karlov and embraced Serapion. Slowly, Serapion lifted the golden chain over Karlov's head and placed it gently around his neck. Then he disengaged from the embrace and stood back.

'It's yours now.'

'Thanks to you. This is most likely the last time we will see each other. You know why.'

'I do. God be with you, my friend, and may his right hand guide you and give you strength.'

'A little divine intervention could go a long way here.'

'With a little secular help?' said Serapion, raising an eyebrow.

'Oh, yes. That will certainly be needed.'

'I can see why,' said Serapion and made the sign of the cross as Karlov turned and, as he always did after their Gorky Park meetings, walked to the waiting black Aurus Senat parked nearby.

76

O'Hara's control centre, Minsk: 5 April

Irina Zarubina was in her element. She hadn't been on a raid for years and enjoyed the sense of anticipation and danger. But most important of all, she enjoyed the sense of power that being in charge gave her. Dressed in casual military-style fatigues, she was sitting in the back of a black van parked across the road from O'Hara's house. It was just after two in the morning, and one of her Chechen agents was delivering his report.

'We've had the house under surveillance for two days, and made some enquiries in the village,' he said. 'During this time, he only left the house once to go to a grocery store down the road.'

'Is that it?' asked Irina, surprised.

'Yes. According to the man who runs the store, a woman from the village comes to the house every morning to do housework and some cooking.'

'He lives in the house alone?'

'Yes.'

'He's in there now?'

'He is.'

Irina nodded. 'We go in five minutes. Understood?'

The two other agents sitting in the back of the van nodded.

'We'll use the back door.'

O'Hara rarely left the basement of the old farmhouse. He even slept down there and only came up to the kitchen for meals. From the outside, the modest building in the small village just outside Minsk looked ordinary and neglected. The only distinguishing feature was a large satellite dish on the roof that few would have noticed. For O'Hara, this was the perfect hiding place and cover for his clandestine operations.

O'Hara sat in front of his computer screens as usual. He had his earphones on and was talking to an old contact in Serbia when he noticed some movement out of the corner of his eye. When he turned to investigate, he saw Irina and two men standing motionless at the bottom of the stairs like wax figures in Madame Tussauds, frozen in time. One of the men was pointing a gun at him.

His mind racing, O'Hara took off his earphones and stared at the intruders, well aware of the seriousness of his predicament. His cover had obviously been blown and armed strangers – clearly professionals – had broken into his house unnoticed. That's when he recognised Irina, whom he had met before, but only virtually during Skype meetings.

'To what do I owe this unexpected pleasure, Colonel Zarubina?' said O'Hara, evaluating the situation.

This guy's good, thought Irina, admiring O'Hara's presence of mind and self-control in what had to have been a shock and very intimidating situation for a man on the run.

'I wanted to see what you look like, Mr O'Hara,' replied Irina. 'You never showed your face during our meetings. Understandable, when you consider you're wanted by just about every major European law enforcement agency.'

'Disappointed?'

'Not really. A little surprised, perhaps, but not disappointed. You're much older than I imagined.'

'Experience comes at a price. You came to inspect my little operation here, is that it? How did you find me?'

'I didn't. Jack Rogan and his friends did,' said Irina, watching O'Hara carefully. She knew this would be infuriating news, but O'Hara showed no reaction.

'Ah. I can show you around if you like,' he said instead.

'That won't be necessary. Orlov here will remove all the hard drives from your computers and anything else he deems necessary.'

'Necessary for what?'

'The prosecution for your cybercrimes, of course; what else?' said Irina casually. She reached into her pocket and pulled out a packet of Camel cigarettes, her favourite.

'You like them too?' said O'Hara. 'Best blend of Turkish and Virginia tobacco. At least we have that in common.'

Irina looked at O'Hara, surprised. 'Would you like one?'

'No, thank you. I gave up years ago. I'm older than I look.'

Irina lit up and blew some smoke in O'Hara's direction. 'In that case, I suppose you won't mind too much.'

'Mind what?'

'The end of the road.'

'Is that what you think this is?'

'It's the beginning of the end.'

'I see,' said O'Hara as he watched Orlov go to work on his computers. 'I couldn't persuade you and Orlov here to leave things as they are and just go away in return for more money than you could hope to make in several lifetimes? As you no doubt know, I could make that happen with the click of that mouse over there.'

'No, I don't think so,' said Irina, enjoying the nicotine rush as she inhaled deeply. 'I made a promise, you see. And I always keep my promises.'

'What kind of promise?'

'To hand you over.'

'Sounds a bit melodramatic, don't you think? Hand me over? To whom?'

'To someone who's been looking for you for a long time with a big, bloody debt to settle.'

'Can you tell me who that might be? There are so many, you see. I lost count over the years.'

'You had two of his men killed.'

'Ah. So, no deal?'

'I'm afraid not.'

'Do you want to think about it, or at least discuss it with your friends here first? Who knows, they may be interested?'

Irina knew exactly what O'Hara was up to: divide and conquer.

'No. Firstly, these are not my friends, but seasoned professionals used to dealing with scum like you.'

'That's a little harsh coming from a despicable has-been mercenary well past her prime, don't you think? I'll have that cigarette now, if you don't mind.'

'I thought you didn't smoke?'

'I don't, but a condemned man should be allowed to indulge a little while he can.'

Irina threw the packet of cigarettes and a lighter to O'Hara. 'I suppose so. As soon as Orlov's ready, we are leaving.'

'We are going somewhere?'

'Yes. To the border.'

'In that case, do you mind if I put on a jumper and get my coat?' said O'Hara cheerfully. 'It's really cold outside.'

The guy's got balls, thought Irina. 'Not at all.' Irina turned to the agent with the gun standing next to her. 'Watch him,' she said softly. 'This man is more dangerous than a cobra hiding in your bedroom. Don't take your eyes off him!'

Kuźnica, on the Belarus–Poland border: sunrise

As soon as Sasha told Jack about the planned raid on O'Hara's bolthole in Belarus, he contacted Dupree and Lapointe and asked them to make arrangements for a possible handover. Isis offered to fly Jack to Lodz, the closest airport, and arrange suitable transport from there, as he was still incapacitated and not supposed to walk. Jack invited Bartolli to join them as he thought she deserved to be present at what Jack hoped would be the final showdown with O'Hara.

Dense fog hovered above the border crossing like a shroud and a cold, bone-chilling wind was blowing in from the east. Jack turned to Bartolli sitting between him and Tristan in the car. 'Not long now. Irina said just after sunrise, remember?'

'How do you feel?' asked Bartolli.

'Mixed feelings. It's all a little surreal, don't you think? Here we are on the border between Poland and Belarus, where only a year ago refugees risked all by cutting through the border fence with wire cutters and axes for a shot at freedom.'

'With tools provided by Belarus to cause a politically motivated refugee crisis in the EU and muddy the waters about President Lukashenko's rigged re-election,' said Lola, who was behind the wheel.

'Correct. Yet here we are, hoping to finally capture one of Europe's most wanted criminals and put him behind bars. Ironic, don't you think?'

'I see what you mean,' said Bartolli.

'There, *look*!' said Isis, who sat next to Lola in the front, and pointed to the border crossing. Lapointe and Dupree were talking to a group of Polish border guards who had just waved a black van through. One of the guards pointed to a parking bay on the Polish side. The van drove through the crossing and stopped behind another van with French number plates. The back door opened almost immediately and several heavily armed men – members of the National Gendarmerie Intervention Group, the elite police tactical unit of the National Gendarmerie of France – jumped out and surrounded the vehicle.

'This is it, Jack!' said Tristan. 'Let's go over. We've been waiting a long time for this.'

'Let's, but I'm not taking the wheelchair, that's for bloody sure.'

'You can lean on me, Jack,' said Bartolli, smiling.

'As I've done so many times before, you mean? In more ways than one.'

'You do very well standing on your own two feet, but perhaps not today. Come.'

'What do you think he looks like?' asked Jack as he got awkwardly out of the car.

'We all have a picture in our minds about this man, but I'm sure he'll look quite different from what we imagine,' said Tristan. 'He's quite old, don't forget.'

'Evil has no age limit,' said Jack.

Supported by Bartolli and Isis, Jack hobbled over to Dupree who stood at the back of the black van. 'Where is he?' said Jack.

'Still in the van. Lapointe has just arrested him. Look, they're coming out now,' said Dupree.

Handcuffed and wearing a long black double-breasted leather coat and Russian ushanka hat made of rabbit fur, O'Hara climbed out of the van and looked around. Jack held his breath as he locked eyes with the little man with round glasses standing in front of him, finding it difficult to believe this was the monster he had been pursuing for so long. O'Hara reminded him of a photograph he once saw of Himmler standing next to Hitler on the Obersalzberg. Same arrogance, confidence and aura of evil; a dangerous man capable of the unthinkable, lurking behind an ordinary appearance.

'See? I told you so,' said Tristan. 'Not what you thought he would look like, right?'

'Certainly not!'

'Ah, Mr Rogan,' said O'Hara, a crooked smile creasing the corners of his mouth. 'We meet at last. And Professor Bartolli too, and Tristan. What a welcome on this cold and miserable morning.'

'It's over, O'Hara, you've lost. Checkmate,' was all Jack could think of saying. 'You'll spend the rest of your miserable life in a French prison, where you belong.'

O'Hara began to laugh. An eerie laugh that was at odds with his grave situation. 'Don't be so sure.'

Lapointe, who had followed O'Hara out of the van, turned to one of the armed men. 'Take him away,' he said. 'You know what to do. Lodz airport.'

'Just one moment,' said O'Hara. He looked at Bartolli. 'What do you think happens now, Professor?' he asked. 'After all, you're the expert here. Tell us!'

Taken aback by the unexpected question, Bartolli stared at O'Hara without saying anything, a strange feeling of dread clawing at her stomach.

'You don't know, do you? *Watch!*'

O'Hara lifted his handcuffed hands, reached under his collar and pulled out something he quickly slipped into his mouth. It was a cyanide suicide pill he had concealed in a flap under the collar. The whole thing took only seconds, but Lapointe had seen it all and realised at once what was happening. He also realised it was already too late to do anything about it.

O'Hara crushed the pill with his teeth and swallowed the cyanide.

'See you all in hell!' he said, beginning to choke. Within moments he suffocated and collapsed. Death was almost instantaneous, all over in less than a minute.

Irina looked at the contorted body lying on the ground, her face expressionless, and then calmly turned towards Jack. 'Sasha has kept her side of the bargain,' she said and reached into one of the deep pockets of her baggy cargo pants. 'She also sends you this.' Irina pulled something out of the pocket and handed it to Jack, who recognised it at once.

'Thank you. This means a lot,' said Jack.

'What is it?' asked Tristan, who had overheard the exchange.

'David Herzl's original diary, stolen by O'Hara from Rabbi Stein's study.'

'Jack. You and your breadcrumbs,' said Tristan, shaking his head.

77

Palin's office, Kremlin, Moscow: 6 April

Karlov approached the security checkpoint, with all its sophisticated scanning devices in front of Palin's office, with dread. Palin, like Stalin before him, was obsessed with security and had not only his food, but even his bottled water checked before drinking it.

Karlov realised the next few minutes were the most crucial and dangerous. So far everything had gone according to plan, but an incident at the FSB laboratory earlier that morning involving one of the technicians made him feel uneasy. While the technician didn't openly question Karlov because of his rank and close relationship with the president, Karlov gained the impression he didn't quite believe the explanation he had provided for the unusual request. He suspected the technician would report the matter to his superior, just to cover himself. Karlov was hoping this would take some time and move at the usual snail's pace up the chain of command.

Karlov's palms began to sweat as the queue in front of him became shorter and the generals filed into Palin's office at the end of the corridor.

Taking a deep breath, Karlov put his briefcase into the tray to be scanned and watched the tray move slowly along the conveyor belt towards the machine. *This is it*, he thought as he reached the point of no return and walked slowly through the body scanner.

'What's this, do you think?' asked the officer looking at the monitor. He pointed to a strange-looking object in a box inside the briefcase. His colleague sitting next to him shrugged. 'Ask him.'

'Could be tricky. It's Karlov.'

'Matter for you, but I wouldn't bother. You know what he's like.'

The officer nodded and watched Karlov collect his briefcase, and then walk towards the president's office.

Relieved but with his heart in his throat, Karlov took up his usual position at the back of the room. He placed his briefcase carefully on the desk in front of him and listened to Palin's tirade about the failures and disasters of the Ukrainian 'military operation' as he still called it.

Used to being chastised, the generals gave their reports and blamed their shortcomings – and the mounting number of body bags coming home – on the unexpected level of support provided to Ukraine by the West. For a while, Palin listened in silence. Then he got up and walked over to the map of Ukraine on the wall and looked at it for a while. He turned and faced his generals. 'So, what is it we need?' he demanded.

'We need more men,' said one of the generals. 'In Ukraine, every able-bodied man is fighting with conviction. Morale is high, despite the casualties. The dead seem to pass on their resolve to the living, who then seem to fight even harder. We're not fighting an army here; we're fighting a nation that's equipped with sophisticated weapons provided by the West.'

'We're fighting them with inexperienced and poorly trained troops who don't understand why they're fighting in the first place,' admitted another general, taking a considerable risk in expressing such an opinion. Everyone in the room knew the army had been neglected for years and was ill prepared to fight what had turned out to be a conventional war on the ground.

'How many do you need?' asked Palin, the impatience in his voice obvious. Surprised, the generals looked at one another. 'Three hundred thousand new conscripts should do it,' said one of the generals. 'For now.'

'We must be aware this will be very unpopular,' interjected another general. 'There will be protests.'

'Don't you worry about that,' snapped Palin. 'I'll deal with that. You focus on the battlefield and leave the rest to me. Clear?'

'Absolutely,' chorused the generals, relieved.

'That will be all,' said Palin. As the generals left the room, Palin returned to his desk and looked pensively at the map on his desk showing Russia as the mighty empire it once was.

Taking deep breaths to calm himself, Karlov waited until the last of the generals had left the room and closed the door behind him.

'May I have a word?' said Karlov, his voice hoarse because his throat was dry.

Palin looked up, surprised. 'You're still here? What is it?'

'I may have the answer.'

'What are you talking about?'

'You remember the prophecies? The sign?'

'Yes, of course.' Palin gasped. 'You *haven't*,' he said, the excitement in his voice building. 'Have you?'

Karlov opened his briefcase, took out a small sealed box with a glass lid and carefully carried it over to Palin's desk. 'Here it is. The sign you've been waiting for,' said Karlov. He put the box on the desk and stepped back.

'You found it!' Palin stared at the box, his eyes wide with astonishment and wonder. Then he sat down and pulled the box towards him. '*Dextera Dei*? The right hand of God?'

'It is,' said Karlov. 'Open the box, put the chain around your neck and take possession. Only then will the holy relic transfer its power to you.'

Palin opened the lid.

Karlov held his breath, aware the next few seconds would decide the future of Russia.

Instead of taking the golden chain with the relic out of the box, Palin looked at Karlov. 'Come on, you do it,' he said. 'You earned it.'

Stunned, Karlov looked at Palin, his mind racing as the implications of what had just been said began to sink in. Realising he had reached a point of no return a long time ago, Karlov began to walk slowly around the desk, well aware he was walking towards his nemesis.

The chief of security answered his phone, listened, and then swore. The call had come from the secret lab of the FSB. He slipped the phone into his pocket and ran over to the scanning machine. 'Did you see anything unusual in Karlov's briefcase?' he shouted.

The man sitting at the monitor looked surprised at first, then worried. 'I suppose there was something,' he said.

'What?' demanded the chief.

'A box with something in it. A chain with some kind of pendant.'

'*My God!*' said the chief and ran towards the president's door.

Slowly, Karlov opened the glass lid and took out the golden chain, his fingers trembling. 'Unbutton your collar,' he said.

Palin loosened his tie and unbuttoned his shirt.

Smiling, Karlov put the chain around Palin's neck, slipped the relic under the president's shirt, and pressed it gently against his chest near his heart.

The office door flew open and the chief of security burst into the room.

'Don't touch it!' he shouted and drew his gun.

'How dare you! What's this all about?' thundered Palin, furious at the intrusion.

'*Novichok!* The chain and the pendant are covered in novichok! Step back, Colonel Karlov!'

Ignoring the order, Karlov kept pressing the relic against Palin's bare chest.

'He's right, you know,' said Karlov, bending down to whisper in Palin's left ear. '*Dextera Dei* has just transferred its power to you.'

Palin looked up, confused. However, the expression on Karlov's face told him all he had to know. He grabbed the chain and tried in vain to yank it out of Karlov's hands.

'*Shoot!*' shouted Palin and tried to get up.

'Your death will be much more painful than mine,' said Karlov, smiling.

'For the last time. Step away! *Now!*'

As Karlov shook his head, the chief of security pulled the trigger. The bullet went straight through Karlov's forehead and blew away the back of his head.

Four weeks later
Capuchin Church of the Transfiguration, Warsaw

After the assassination attempt, Palin was rushed to a military hospital in Moscow in a critical condition. It seemed unlikely he would survive the deadly novichok attack. News about the attempt on the president's life spread like wildfire through the corridors of the Kremlin and changed the dynamics of power almost instantly. Palin supporters considered their position, while his opponents saw an unexpected opportunity and seized it.

As far as the outside world was concerned, it was announced that Palin had had a heart attack in his office and was recovering in hospital. Rumours about his health – cancer – had circulated for months, and only compounded an already critical situation dominated by speculation.

Within days, relieved generals were putting out feelers for a ceasefire in Ukraine and placed the mobilisation of three hundred thousand new Russian recruits on hold. The war in Ukraine was stalling and a jubilant Ukraine was sensing victory.

As soon as Sasha heard the news in London, she instructed Novotny's lawyers to lodge an urgent appeal against his fabricated conviction, and announced this on social media. Huge crowds gathered outside Novotny's prison and demanded his immediate release. To appease the angry crowd, Novotny was transferred to a low-security prison in Moscow and given access to his lawyers. He was even allowed to release a statement to the press that instantly mobilised his supporters, sensing that Palin's tyranny was coming to an end.

Almost overnight, the grip of oppression began to lift and a nation yearning for freedom could see that the sparrow who had languished in a prison-cage was finally gaining the upper hand and defeating the cockroach. A number of poignant videos released by Novotny's Foundation reminded his supporters of the horrendous corruption in the Kremlin. This further fuelled outrage, and thousands took to the streets demanding change. Talk about elections and a new, freely elected government were on everyone's lips, and even state-controlled TV channels were no longer afraid to explore this forbidden subject because they could sense the rule of the cockroach was rapidly coming to an end. The freedom genie had escaped the bottle of oppression and had, almost overnight, become unstoppable.

Serapion was waiting for Jack and Tristan in front of the church. While they had spoken several times on the phone, it was their first meeting since the attempt on Palin's life, which the Kremlin had, despite persistent corridor whispers leaked to the press, continued to insist was a heart attack.

Jack thought Serapion looked drained and exhausted, his haunted expression a clear reflection of the turbulent events of the past four weeks.

'It's so good to see you both,' said Serapion as he embraced Jack. 'Thank you for coming.'

'We wouldn't have missed this for the world,' said Jack. 'Isn't that right, Tristan?'

Tristan nodded.

'Let's go inside,' continued Serapion. 'The archbishop and Sister Magosia are waiting. Everything's ready.'

Jack and Tristan followed Serapion into the church, just as they had done on their first visit. Because it was still quite early, the church was almost deserted.

Jack looked at Sister Magosia – eyes closed and kneeling on the prie-dieu in front of Sobieski's sarcophagus – and smiled as a feeling of déjà vu washed over him.

Standing at the back of the chapel, the archbishop was talking to two workmen who had just removed the heavy lid of Jan III Sobieski's sarcophagus. He came over to Jack and Tristan and greeted them warmly.

'A historic occasion,' said the archbishop. 'Abbot Serapion has told me all about your ordeal in Ukraine.'

Jack waved dismissively. 'I was lucky.'

'Perhaps he was protected,' said Tristan, 'by the right hand of God.'

Sister Magosia opened her eyes and looked at Tristan. 'The right hand of God? Ah, the young man who can glimpse eternity,' she said, 'and his friend who found Kazanskaya Bogomater and returned it to Russia.'

'Yes, Sister, and he seems to have done it again,' said the archbishop.

'What do you mean, Excellency?'

'You will see in a moment.'

Abbot Serapion walked over to Sister Magosia. 'We are about to witness something remarkable, Sister. A true moment of destiny that you will understand better than all of us here.'

'Really? His Excellency didn't tell me about that. All he said was I should come here this morning to witness something I couldn't afford to miss,' said Sister Magosia and tried awkwardly to get up.

Serapion put his hand on her shoulder, his touch gentle. 'Please stay where you are.' Serapion reached under his shirt and pulled out the golden chain with the holy relic. 'Jack, could you please help me?'

Jack walked over to Serapion, lifted the chain with the relic over his head and coat and was about to hand it to him, when Serapion held up his hand. 'No, you do it,' he said. 'You earned it. You put it back where it belongs. Right there next to the heart of the king. Its work is done. For now,' said Serapion softly.

Jack nodded and looked at Sister Magosia watching him intently, her watery, myopic eyes wide with wonder. Then he walked over to her and considered the diminutive woman kneeling in front of him as an idea took shape in his mind. Bending down, he draped the golden chain over her hands folded in prayer and pressed the relic into the palm of her right hand.

'Behold *Zbawiciel*, Sister, the right hand of God,' he said, his eyes moist with emotion. 'Would you do us the honour of returning it to where it belongs?' continued Jack, and then looked at the archbishop.

The archbishop nodded.

Sister Magosia kept staring at her shaking hands. 'Is this really ...?' she whispered.

'It is,' replied the archbishop. '*Zbawiciel* has returned home.'

Sister Magosia nodded and looked at Tristan watching her. 'Could you please help me stand up?'

Tristan walked over to the prie-dieu and, with Jack helping him, lifted Sister Magosia to her feet. Then, supported by Jack and Tristan, she walked slowly towards the sarcophagus, one small step at a time.

Serapion and the archbishop came closer. The archbishop pointed to the ornate golden plate next to the urn inside the sarcophagus. 'There, that's where it belongs.'

Leaning against the cool marble to support herself, Sister Magosia lifted the holy relic to her lips, her fingers trembling. Then she looked first at Tristan, and then at Jack standing next to her.

'We should do this together,' she said. 'What do you think, Excellency? The young man who can glimpse eternity, and his blessed friend who found Kazanskaya Bogomater.'

'That would be the right way,' said the archbishop. 'I'm sure Saint Olga would agree.'

Jack and Tristan put their hands on Sister Magosia's bony fingers, and together they placed the holy relic on the golden plate next to the urn.

'Please help me kneel. I must pray,' said Sister Magosia as she turned away from the sarcophagus. 'Now that I have glimpsed eternity, I am content,' she said, tears rolling down her hollow cheeks.

Before leaving the church, Jack stopped in front of one of the altars and turned to Serapion walking along beside him. 'How did you manage it?'

'To get the relic out of Russia?'

'Yes.'

Serapion shrugged. 'The Church has friends everywhere, even in the Kremlin and the FSB laboratories where the novichok was removed after the attempt on Palin's life, to hide the truth. You'll be pleased to hear I also managed to get Kazanskaya Bogomater returned to the Alexander Nevsky Cathedral.'

Jack looked impressed. 'No doubt about you, Abbot.'

'I understand Kazanskaya Bogomater wasn't the only precious painting returned to where it belongs?'

'No. We returned *Golgotha* to Ghent last week. Even Leonardo da Baggio was there. To the great delight of Bishop Peeters and Brother Frederick, *Golgotha* was finally reunited with the *Ghent Altarpiece*, as promised. As you can imagine, it was all very emotional.'

'Bishop Peeters told me. Another historic moment: van Eyck's masterpiece is complete again. No doubt about you, Jack,' said Serapion. 'You pulled it off; all of it. How, I wonder?'

'By following his breadcrumbs, of course,' said Tristan, who had overheard the question. 'But I suspect this time, he had a little help.'

'Help? What kind of help?' asked Serapion.

'The right hand of God; what else?'

Nine months later
Gūr-e Amīr, Samarkand: 17 February 2023

Jack pointed to Gūr-e Amīr, the stunning Mausoleum of Timur, its azure tiles covering the huge, fluted dome glistening in the morning sun like little reminders of glory days long gone, but not forgotten.

'This is it, guys,' he said, following the procession of dignitaries into the mausoleum.

'What a great idea to do this on the anniversary of Timur's death,' said Tristan. 'This will have quite an impact. Clever.'

Isis, Lola, Tristan and Jack had flown in from London the day before.

'Six hundred and eighteen years later, we honour and remember a remarkable man,' said Isis, enjoying the spectacle. Dressed in a fabulous embroidered African abaya kaftan with matching hijab – similar to the one she had worn in Muscat – Isis certainly looked the part.

Sheikh Khalid greeted them at the entrance. 'A momentous day,' he said, making a bow. 'My father and I are honoured by your presence.'

'Thank you for your invitation and allowing us to be part of this historic occasion,' said Jack.

'It would not have been possible without you, and *Golgotha*.'

'Certain things are meant to be, and are beyond our control,' said Tristan.

'How right you are,' said Sheik Khalid. 'Dr Abdalla would certainly agree with you on that. My father's only regret is that his dear friend Haji Abdalla can't be here to witness this.'

'I'm sure he's right here in spirit,' said Tristan.

'Without doubt. Like you, he can see things … Please come inside. Follow me.'

Aware all eyes were on her, Isis followed Sheik Khalid into the mausoleum, desperately trying to look demure and resisting the urge to wave, much to the amusement of Lola who was walking alongside her.

The spacious inner chamber of the mausoleum with its ornate headstones marking the tombs located in a crypt below, was the work of an architectural genius called Muhammad ibn Mahmud from Isfahan.

The tombs of Timur, his sons Miran Shah and Shah Rukh, and grandsons Muhammad Sultan and the famous Ulugh Beg, all formed part of the impressive family crypt of the Timurid dynasty. Meticulously restored to its former glory during the 1970s, the spectacular mausoleum had been saved from total ruin to become a major tourist attraction and part of the Samarkand UNESCO World Heritage site.

Even at eighty, Sheikh Mohammed looked impressive in his modest white dishdasha and embroidered Kuma, the traditional, rounded Omani cap, his striking face and white beard setting him apart from the Muslim clerics and European dignitaries attending the occasion. Sitting on a simple wooden stool facing Timur's headstone, it was clear to everyone this was Sheikh Mohammed's day.

Shrouded in mystery, the story of the unexpected discovery of the legendary Amulet of Timur had circulated through the Muslim world for months, and had created a lot of interest and attention. Clerics and scholars alike had been looking forward to the occasion with great anticipation, albeit with some justified scepticism.

Once the last of the invited guests had been admitted, Sheikh Mohammed stood up and turned towards the life-size bronze bust of Timur standing on a marble plinth next to him, as a sudden hush descended on the crowded chamber.

Deliberately taking his time to let the anticipation grow, Sheikh Mohammed kept looking at Timur, the legendary warrior who, as the sword of Islam, had conquered nations and killed hundreds of thousands standing in his way.

'We all face certain moments of destiny throughout our lives,' began Sheikh Mohammed, sounding solemn. 'I certainly have. But what I hadn't expected was that the most important of those moments should reach me towards the end of my days. Yet, that is precisely what is happening here, right now.' Sheikh Mohammed raised his hands in a gesture of prayer and closed his eyes.

'As you are obviously all aware, the lost Amulet of Timur has recently been found,' he continued. 'How that came about is a long, fascinating story for another day. For now it is, I believe, sufficient to state the amulet has been authenticated by none other than Dr Haji Abdalla, the undisputed authority on the subject. Dr Abdalla will soon publish a paper that will explain all the reasoning behind his findings.'

Sheikh Mohammed turned towards his son standing next to him and held out his hand. Sheikh Khalid stepped forward and handed him a small golden box. Taking a deep breath, Sheikh Mohammed opened the box, took out the jewel-encrusted miniature Quran dangling on a gold chain – and held it up for all to see. 'Behold, the Amulet of Timur,' he said, his voice quivering with emotion.

A ripple of excitement ran through the mesmerised crowd as Sheikh Mohammed walked slowly over to the bust of Timur he had commissioned, and placed the golden chain around the fabled conqueror's neck.

'A moment of destiny,' whispered Sheikh Mohammed, 'which shall be repeated every year on the anniversary of Timur's death. The amulet will remain here until the end of Ramadan. After that, it shall return to the Islamic Museum in Muscat, where it will be on display throughout the year for all to see.'

Sheikh Mohammed stepped away from the bust and turned to face the crowd. 'Please feel free to come closer and have a look. After all, you are witnessing history.'

Momentarily overcome by emotion, Sheikh Mohammed began to teeter. Noticing his father's distress, Sheikh Khalid walked over to him to make sure he didn't fall. Jack, who was close by, did the same. Supported by his son and Jack, Sheikh Mohammed walked slowly out of the mausoleum. As Jack walked past, Isis began to clap. Soon, everyone in the chamber joined in, expressing praise and admiration for a remarkable old man who had just made history.

Feeling refreshed after a glass of water, Sheikh Mohammed sat down on a stone bench under a shady acacia, and noticed Jack and Tristan watching him with concern on their faces.

'Don't worry, I'm fine,' he said and waved dismissively. 'I have something to show you.'

'Oh? What?' asked Jack.

'During his recent amulet authentication research, Dr Abdalla made a surprising discovery you will find interesting.'

'What kind of discovery?' said Jack.

'Persuasive proof that the critical part the da Baggio family has played in this remarkable saga is based on fact, and is at the very heart of the amulet's extraordinary story.'

Sheikh Mohammed turned towards Tristan and locked eyes with him.

'You know what it is, don't you?'

Tristan nodded.

'I thought so. My son will show you. It isn't far. I will stay here in the shade and rest.'

Accompanied by one of his bodyguards, Sheikh Khalid led the way to a modest mausoleum close by.

'This is the final resting place of a prominent, seventeenth-century Astrakanid family, the last of the Genghisids,' he said. 'Over there under the dome is the headstone of one of the family's famous patriarchs, a direct descendant of Ulugh Beg, one of Timur's grandsons. He was blind and almost ninety when he died. An exceptionally high age at the time.'

Jack nodded and walked over to the headstone for a closer look.

'I remember exactly what Dr Abdalla said about all this,' said Isis.

'So do I,' said Tristan. 'Fatma Hatun was at the very centre of that remarkable story. You'll remember she was sold to a prominent family here in Samarkand, obviously this one.'

'And according to the historical texts Abdalla referred to, it was all recorded, especially the extraordinary payment for a slave and the reasons for it,' said Jack.

'The Amulet of Timur exchanged for a slave?' said Isis, shaking her head.

'Not just any slave, but a very special one. A slave who became a much-loved companion of the ailing patriarch and an honoured member of the family,' said Tristan.

'Who survived the patriarch she had cared for and entertained with her famous stories by many years,' said Jack. 'And was eventually buried next to him. This was a great honour only bestowed on someone held in high esteem.'

'Very good,' said Sheikh Khalid, impressed. 'And what I'm about to show you is the very proof Dr Abdalla discovered that tells us this remarkable story is true.'

'What kind of proof?' asked Jack.

'Ah. That's where the letter you found recently in Venice comes into play.'

'It does? How?'

'It was the missing link that led us to this place here,' said Sheikh Khalid. 'Proof the amulet that found its way to the da Baggio family in Venice is in fact the Amulet of Timur, given as payment to a Tajik trader.'

'Who had bought Fatma Hatun in the slave market of Khiva in 1606 from the sultan's janissaries,' said Jack, 'and then sold her to this illustrious family here?'

Sheikh Khalid nodded, walked around the headstone and pointed to a smaller one behind it. 'This is what Dr Abdalla discovered. There's an inscription here, see? Let me tell you what it says:

"'Here rests the soul of Fatma Hatun, who lifted the spirits of all who knew her with her wit, sparkling stories, and her smile.'"

For a while no-one spoke as Jack reached for Tristan's hand and held it.

'If only Lorenza could see this,' he said softly.

'Perhaps she can,' replied Tristan and let go of Jack's hand. Then slowly, he bent down and placed his right hand on the headstone, his touch gentle, like a caress.

'Why do you think that?' asked Jack, well aware Lorenza's death was a deep wound on Tristan's heart that often still bled.

'Because she's joined the whispering angels ...'

'Is that what took away your grief when you stood in front of the altar in St Peter's in Rome the day Pope Pius died?'

Smiling through tears, Tristan looked at Jack and nodded.

'It did. But I'm sure you knew that all along.'

A PARTING NOTE FROM THE AUTHOR

Because the multi-layered storylines woven into the fabric of this book often explore remote and hidden corners of history, a few observations are warranted here that will add further insight into how I approach the many diverse and often quite sensitive subjects explored in my work.

The amount of research involved in meshing the various story-strands featured in *The Stolen Altarpiece* seamlessly together has been particularly complex and demanding. For me as a writer, authenticity and accuracy are paramount. Without that, it isn't possible to create believable characters and stories where the boundaries between fact and fiction are blurred, so the reader is never quite sure where one ends and the other begins.

This is, of course, quite deliberate and one of the hallmarks of my books that my readers have come to expect and look forward to. Why? Because it creates the illusion of reality in a work that is pure fiction. In my view, a successful work of fiction is a balancing act: reality must rub shoulders with imagination in a way that is both entertaining and plausible, and this can only be achieved through meticulous research and painstaking attention to detail.

In addition to all this, I often draw on events and current affairs that define our times, to give the story and the characters contemporary meaning and relevance. In this book, I turned to the devastating, bloody conflict between Russia and Ukraine, to give the book a raw authenticity that I hope will resonate with readers and create awareness of what is happening right now, and the reasons behind it.

While all the characters in the book are, of course, fictitious, the historical aspects and issues dealt with are not. For example, the atrocities in Bucha and Mariupol have, to the best of my knowledge, been described accurately, based on the most reliable eyewitness reports I could find.

The same applies to the horrendous Holodomor, the devastating Ukrainian Terror-Famine of 1932–33, which explains Ukraine and its people's loathing of Russia that is as relevant today as it was then. However, to my surprise, little is known about these events outside Ukraine. It is my sincere hope this book will, at least in some small way, change that and create awareness of the historical facts that drive this dreadful conflict.

With awareness comes understanding, and once that happens real change is possible. This dreadful war has to be stopped before it spirals out of control and destroys not only a nation, but also draws the rest of the world into its orbit – with consequences too horrible to contemplate.

Two of the driving forces behind my writing are curiosity and the joy of learning. Without these, the huge amount of research required to explore the often esoteric and complex subjects featured in my work in a realistic and plausible way, just wouldn't be possible.

I'm often asked how the ideas for the characters originate and where the various storylines featured in my books come from. The answer may surprise you. These ideas are often inspired by historical facts and events I discover during my research, which can be very rewarding in unexpected ways.

Many of the surprising twists and turns in the storylines are actually based on historical facts I have woven into the scenes and characters featured in my books. This was definitely the case with *The Stolen Altarpiece*. While it isn't possible to mention them all, a few definitely stand out and provide instructive insights into the creative process.

Richard the Lionheart and *'Ja nus hons pris'*

On his return from the Third Crusade in 1192, Richard was shipwrecked near Aquileia in northern Italy and forced to embark on a dangerous overland journey to reach the territory of his brother-in-law, Henry the Lion, Duke of Saxony and Bavaria. Disguised as a Templar knight, Richard was captured near Vienna just before Christmas and imprisoned by Leopold of Austria in Dürnstein Castle high above the Danube, where he languished for over a year in harsh conditions unfit for someone of his station.

During this period, Richard, who was also an accomplished singer and composer of ballads, wrote a song to express his feelings of abandonment, loneliness and despair. This is how the famous song, *'Ja nus hons pris'* – 'No man who is imprisoned' – was created.

This little historical gem provided the perfect setting for the introduction of *Dextera Dei* and the creation of a dramatic scene to show how the holy relic entered Europe and began its extraordinary journey through history.

Another intriguing morsel about Richard's famous song is far more recent. In 2002, Bryan Ferry recorded Richard's ballad on his album *Frantic*, making it one of the few songs composed by a medieval English king that has been recorded by a modern-day international star.

The Curse of Timur

Timur, or Tamerlane, was one of the most ruthless and successful conquerors of all time, responsible for more than seventeen million deaths. He features prominently in the book and the Amulet of Timur is a centrepiece of the storyline. Timur's tomb – Gūr-e Amīr – is located in Samarkand and is the stuff of legends.

The curse of Timur has its origin in two inscriptions engraved on his tomb: one on the tombstone, the other inside the tomb itself.

The inscription on the tombstone tells the world, *'When I Rise from the Dead, the World Shall Tremble'*, and the inscription inside the tomb warns, *'Whoever Disturbs My Tomb Will Unleash an Invader More Terrible than I.'*

It is said the curse of Timur changed the course of WWII on two separate occasions.

On Stalin's orders, the tomb was opened on 20 June 1942 by renowned Russian anthropologist Mikhail Gerasimov. Muslim clerics told Gerasimov about Timur's curse and urged him not to disturb the tomb. The warning was ignored and the tomb was opened. Two days later, Hitler invaded Russia: 'Operation Barbarossa', which would cost the lives of millions, had begun.

Stalin, who had heard about the curse, began to have second thoughts about Timur's remains, which Gerasimov had brought to Moscow to study and to reconstruct a sculptural portrait of Timur from his skull. Because the war was going badly, with catastrophic losses, legend has it that Stalin ordered that Timur's remains be flown over the front line for a month to inspire Muslim soldiers in the Red Army, before being returned to Samarkand for reburial.

On 20 December 1942, Timur was reburied with full Islamic honours at the height of the Battle of Stalingrad – one of the bloodiest battles of all time – which the Germans lost in early February 1942. It is said that Timur's reburial was the turning point in the war.

The curse of Timur was the inspiration behind *Dextera Dei* and the inclusion of a fascinating subject in the book: the sacralisation of secular objects that gives those objects a divine aura with the power to change history.

Gerasimov's forensic reconstruction of Timur's face

After opening the tomb of Timur in 1941 and taking the remains back to Moscow for study, the famous anthropologist Gerasimov went to work. Best known for his stunning sculptural portraits, Gerasimov reconstructed a likeness of Timur just from studying his skull. The classic South Siberian Mongol features are clearly visible, with the dominant cheekbones and other facial characteristics found in Central Asia. Gerasimov's work relating to the Timurid dynasty is exhibited in the museums of Uzbekistan.

In 1991, Gerasimov's methods were used by Russian investigators to identify the remains of the murdered family of Tsar Nicholas II.

Gerasimov's famous bust of Timur became the inspiration for the moving scene in Timur's mausoleum in Samarkand where Sheikh Mohammed places the Amulet of Timur around Timur's neck, symbolically reuniting the two after centuries of separation.

This is another pertinent illustration of how fact and fiction can be 'fused' to create a realistic scenario partially anchored in real life, which adds excitement and mystery to a work of fiction, specifically designed to entertain the reader and tease the intellect.

I suppose that's why one dedicated reader, Paul Bennington from Yorkshire, England, paid me a delightful compliment I'm particularly proud of. He even coined a new phrase. He called me his favourite 'faction author'!

Favourite *faction author*? I can live with that!

You can find Paul's book review video on my website www.gabrielfarago.com.au

Gabriel Farago M.A., LL.B.
Leura, Blue Mountains, Australia
April 2023

MORE BOOKS BY THE AUTHOR

In 2013, I released my first adventure thriller –
The Empress Holds the Key.

THE EMPRESS HOLDS THE KEY

A disturbing, edge-of-your-seat historical mystery thriller

Jack Rogan Mysteries Book 1

Dark secrets. A holy relic. An ancient quest reignited.
Jack Rogan's discovery of a disturbing old photograph in the ashes of
a rural Australian cottage draws the journalist into a dangerous hunt
with the ultimate stakes.

The tangled web of clues – including hoards of Nazi gold, hidden
Swiss bank accounts, and a long-forgotten mass grave – implicate
wealthy banker Sir Eric Newman and lead to a trial with shocking
revelations.

A holy relic mysteriously erased from the pages of history is
suddenly up for grabs to those willing to sacrifice everything to find
it. Rogan and his companions must follow historical leads through
ancient Egypt, to the Crusades and the Knights Templar, to uncover
a secret that could destroy the foundations of the Catholic Church
and challenge the history of Christianity itself.

Will Rogan succeed in bringing the dark mystery into the light, or will the powers desperately working against him ensure the ancient truths remain buried forever?

The Empress Holds the Key
is now available in ebook and paperback

Encouraged by the reception of *The Empress Holds the Key*, I released my next thriller –*The Disappearance of Anna Popov* – in 2014.

THE DISAPPEARANCE OF ANNA POPOV

A dark, page-turning psychological thriller

Jack Rogan Mysteries Book 2

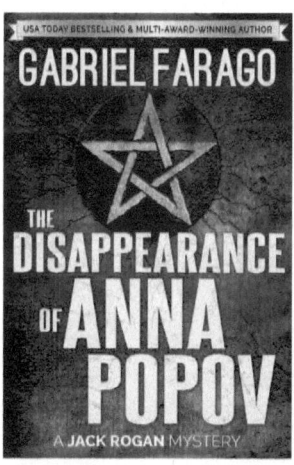

A mysterious disappearance. An outlaw bikie gang. One dangerous investigation.

Journalist Jack Rogan cannot resist a good mystery. When he stumbles across a hidden clue about the tragic disappearance of two girls from Alice Springs years earlier, he's determined to investigate.

Joining forces with his New York literary agent; a retired Aboriginal police officer; and Cassandra, an enigmatic psychic, Rogan enters the dark and dangerous world of an outlaw bikie gang ruled by an evil master.

Entangled in a web of violence, superstition and fear, Rogan and his friends follow the trail of the missing girls into the remote Dreamtime-wilderness of outback Australia, where they face their greatest challenge yet.

Cassandra has a secret agenda of her own and uses her occult powers to conjure up an epic showdown where the stakes are high, and the loser faces death and oblivion.

Will Rogan succeed in finding the truth, or will the forces of evil prevail, causing untold misery and destroying even more lives?

The Disappearance of Anna Popov
is now available in ebook and paperback

My next book, *The Hidden Genes of Professor K*, was released in 2016.

THE HIDDEN GENES OF PROFESSOR K

A dark, disturbing and nail-biting medical thriller

Jack Rogan Mysteries Book 3

A medical breakthrough. A greedy pharmaceutical magnate. A brutal double-murder. One tangled web of lies.

World-renowned scientist Professor K is close to a groundbreaking discovery. He's also dying. With his last breath, he anoints Dr Alexandra Delacroix as his successor and pleads with her to carry on his work.

But powerful forces will stop at nothing to possess the research, unwittingly plunging Delacroix into a treacherous world of unbridled ambition and greed.

Desperate and alone, she turns to celebrated author and journalist Jack Rogan.

Rogan must help Delacroix, while also assisting famous rock star Isis in the seemingly unrelated investigation into the brutal murder of her parents.

With the support of Isis's resourceful PA, Lola; a former police officer; a tireless campaigner for the destitute and forgotten; and a gifted boy with psychic powers, Rogan exposes a complex web of fiercely guarded secrets and heinous crimes of the past that can ruin them all and change history.

Will the dreams of a visionary scientist with the power to change the future of medicine fall into the wrong hands, or will his genius benefit mankind and prevent untold misery and suffering for generations to come?

Outstanding Thriller of 2017
Thriller Category Winner
Independent Author Network Book of the Year Awards

The Hidden Genes of Professor K
is now available in ebook and paperback

My next book, *Professor K: The Final Quest*,
was released in October 2018.

PROFESSOR K: THE FINAL QUEST

An action-packed historical medical mystery

Jack Rogan Mysteries Book 4

A desperate plea from the Vatican. A kidnapped chef. An ambitious mob boss. One perilous game.

When Professor Alexandra Delacroix is called in to find a cure for the dying pope, she follows clues left by her mentor and friend, the late Professor K, which lead her on a breathtaking search through historical secrets, some of them deadly.

Her old friend Jack Rogan must step in to assist while also searching for kidnapped Top Chef Europe winner Lorenza da Baggio.

He joins forces with his young friend and gifted psychic, Tristan; a dedicated Mafia-hunting prosecutor; a fearless young police officer; and an enigmatic Egyptian detective who is on a perilous hunt for a notorious IS terrorist.

Together, they stand off with the head of a powerful Mafia family in Florence and uncover a network of corruption and heinous crimes reaching to the very top.

Will Rogan and his friends succeed in finding Lorenza and curing the pope, or will the dark forces swirling around them prevail in their sinister plots?

Gold Medal Winner in the Fiction
Thriller - Medical Category
Readers' Favorite 2019 International Book Awards Contest

Professor K: The Final Quest
is now available in ebook and paperback

My next book, *The Curious Case of the Missing Head*,
was released in November 2019.

THE CURIOUS CASE OF THE MISSING HEAD

A gripping medical thriller

Jack Rogan Mysteries Book 5

A headless body on a boat. An international conspiracy. Can a kidnapped genius survive a controversial scientific discovery?
Esteemed Australian journalist Jack Rogan is on a mission to solve the disappearance of his mother in the 70s. But when a friend needs help rescuing a kidnapped world-renowned astrophysicist, he doesn't hesitate. Struggling with more questions than answers, his investigation leads them aboard a hellish hospital ship, where instead of finding the kidnap victim, he's confronted with a decapitated corpse.

As the search intensifies, Jack bumps up against diabolical cartels with hidden agendas. And when his research reveals dubious experiments, a criminal on death row, and a shocking revelation about his mother's fate, he must uncover how it's all linked.

Can Jack unravel the twisted connections and catch the scientist's killer, or will the next obituary published be his own?

Gold Medal Winner in the Fiction
Thriller – Conspiracy Category
Readers' Favorite 2020 International Book Awards Contest

Outstanding Thriller/Suspense of 2020
Thriller/Suspense Category Winner
Independent Author Network Book of the Year Awards

The Curious Case of the Missing Head
is now available in ebook and paperback

My latest book, *The Lost Symphony*, was released in November 2020.

THE LOST SYMPHONY

A historical mystery thriller

Jack Rogan Mysteries Book 6

A murdered tsarina. A lost musical masterpiece. A stolen Russian icon. Can Jack honour a promise made a long time ago, and solve an age-old mystery?
When acclaimed Australian journalist and author Jack Rogan inherits an old music box with a curious letter hidden inside, he decides to investigate. As he delves deeper into a murky past of secrets and violence, he soon discovers he's not the only one interested in solving the puzzle.

Frieda Malenkova, a ruthless art dealer; and Victor Sokolov, a Russian billionaire with a dark past, will stop at nothing to achieve their dark desires and foil Jack's valiant struggle to uncover the truth.

Joining forces with Mademoiselle Darrieux, a flamboyant Paris socialite; and Claude Dupree, a retired French police officer, Jack enters a dangerous world of unbridled ambition, murder and greed that threatens to destroy him.

On a perilous journey that takes him deep into Russia, Jack follows a tortuous path of discovery, disappointment and betrayal that brings him face to face with his destiny.

Will Jack unravel the hidden clues left behind by a desperate empress? Can he save the precious legacy of a genius before it's too late, and return a holy icon revered by generations to where it belongs?

Gold Medal Winner in the
Fiction – Mystery – Historical Category
Readers' Favorite 2021 International Book Awards Contest

Award-Winning Finalist in the Fiction:
Thriller/Adventure category
The 2021 International Book Awards

The Lost Symphony
is now available in ebook and paperback

My next book, *The Death Mask Murders*,
was released in December 2021.

THE DEATH MASK MURDERS

A historical mystery crime thriller

Jack Rogan Mysteries Book 7

**Seven brutal murders. A cursed Inca burial mask. A lost
treasure. One deadly game.**
When convicted killer Maurice Landru reaches out from a Paris
prison and asks for help to prove his innocence, celebrated author
Jack Rogan cannot resist. Drawn into a web of hidden clues pointing
to an ancient mystery, Jack decides to investigate.

Joining forces with Francesca Bartolli, a glamorous criminal
profiler; Mademoiselle Darrieux, an eccentric Paris socialite; and
Claude Dupree, a retired French police officer, Jack enters a
dangerous world of depraved cyber-gambling, where the stakes are
high and the players will stop at nothing to satisfy their dark desires.

Following his 'breadcrumbs of destiny', Jack soon comes up
against an evil genius who terminates his enemies without mercy and
is prepared to risk all to win.

On a perilous journey littered with violence and death, Jack uncovers dark secrets of a murky past of ruthless conquistadors, bloodthirsty pirates and shipwrecked priests, all pointing to a fabulous treasure, waiting to be discovered.

Can Jack expose the mastermind behind the horrific murders and retrieve the legendary treasure before it falls into the wrong hands, or will the forces of darkness overwhelm him and destroy everything he believes in?

The Death Mask Murders is now available
on Amazon and major retailers.

The Death Mask Murders
is now available in ebook and paperback

ABOUT THE AUTHOR

Gabriel Farago is the *USA Today* bestsel-
ling and multi-award-winning Australian
author of the *Jack Rogan Mysteries Series*
for the thinking reader.

As a lawyer with a passion for history
and archaeology, Gabriel Farago had to
wait for many years before being able to
pursue another passion – writing – in
earnest. However, his love of books and
storytelling started long before that.

'I remember as a young boy, reading
biographies and history books with a torch under the bed covers,' he
recalls, 'and then writing stories about archaeologists and explorers
the next day, instead of doing homework. While I regularly got into
trouble for this, I believe we can only do well in our endeavours if we
are passionate about the things we love. For me, writing has become
a passion.'

Born in Budapest, Gabriel grew up in post-war Europe and, after
fleeing Hungary with his parents during the Revolution in 1956, he
went to school in Austria before arriving in Australia as a teenager.
This allowed him to become multilingual and feel 'at home' in
different countries and diverse cultures.

Shaped by a long legal career and experiences spanning several
decades and continents, his is a mature voice. Gabriel holds degrees
in literature and law, speaks several languages and takes research and
authenticity very seriously. Inquisitive by nature, he studied
Egyptology and learned to read the hieroglyphs. He travels
extensively and visits all the locations mentioned in his books.

'I try to weave fact and fiction into a seamless storyline,' he
explains. 'By blurring the boundaries between the two, the reader is
never quite sure where one ends, and the other begins. This is, of

course, quite deliberate as it creates the illusion of authenticity and reality in a work that is pure fiction. A successful work of fiction is a balancing act: reality must rub shoulders with imagination in a way that is both entertaining and plausible.'

Gabriel lives just outside Sydney, Australia, in the Blue Mountains, surrounded by a World Heritage National Park. 'The beauty and solitude of this unique environment,' he points out, 'gives me the inspiration and energy to weave my thoughts and ideas into stories that in turn, I sincerely hope, will entertain and inspire my readers.'

Gabriel Farago

AUTHOR'S NOTE

I hope you enjoyed reading this book as much as I enjoyed writing it. I'd be very grateful if you'd post a short review on Amazon. Your support really does make a difference.

CONNECT WITH THE AUTHOR

Website
https://gabrielfarago.com.au/

Amazon
http://www.amazon.com/Gabriel-Farago/e/B00GUVY2UW/

Goodreads
https://www.goodreads.com/author/show/7435911.Gabriel_Farago

Facebook
https://www.facebook.com/GabrielFaragoAuthor

BookBub
https://www.bookbub.com/profile/gabriel-farago

Signup for the author's New Releases mailing list and get a free copy of *The Forgotten Painting** Novella and find out where it all began ...

https://gabrielfarago.com.au/free-download-forgotten-painting/

* I'm delighted to tell you that *The Forgotten Painting* has received two major literary awards in the US. It was awarded the Gold Medal by Readers' Favorite in the Short Stories and Novellas category and was named the 'Outstanding Novella' of 2018 by the IAN Book of the Year Awards.

www.ingramcontent.com/pod-product-compliance
Lightning Source LLC
Chambersburg PA
CBHW030844030726
47495CB00005B/1364